I'm almost halfway across the room when I see it.

Sitting on the table, where I threw it as I went to grab the house phone, is the thing that Priscilla tried to give me earlier.

The book that ended up on the floor and I scooped up on the way to get help.

The diary.

The book of everyone's secrets.

Also by

DOROTHY KOOMSON

DOROTHY
KOOMSON

I know what you've done

REVIEW

First published in 2021 by Headline Review
An imprint of HEADLINE PUBLISHING GROUP

First published in paperback in 2021 by Headline Review
An imprint of HEADLINE PUBLISHING GROUP

1

Cataloguing in Publication Data is available from the British Library

ISBN 978 1 4722 7737 4

Typeset in Times LT Std 10.25/15pt by Jouve (UK), Milton Keynes

Printed and bound in Great Britain by Clays Ltd, Elcograf S.p.A.

Headline's policy is to use papers that are natural, renewable and recyclable
products and made from wood grown in well-managed forests and other
controlled sources. The logging and manufacturing processes are expected
to conform to the environmental regulations of the country of origin.

HEADLINE PUBLISHING GROUP
An Hachette UK Company
Carmelite House
50 Victoria Embankment
London EC4Y 0DZ

www.headline.co.uk
www.hachette.co.uk

For all of us,
however we made it through.

Prologue

Priscilla

21 Acacia Villas

May 2021, Brighton

I know who is going to do it.

That is, I know the person most likely to kill me.

I'm not sure how, but I do know *why*, and I do know it's going to be soon.

Should I tell someone? Probably. But who will believe me? Until it happens, no one will care. And therein lies my problem: until I'm dead, or as close to dead as I can be, no one will believe my life is in danger. They'll think it's all petty jealousies, problems best talked out over tea and biscuits.

They will not see the bigger picture until it is splattered with my blood and stained with the crocodile tears of those who mean me harm . . . *then* there'll be investigations, *then* there'll be the pulling out all the stops to uncover the truth.

Until then, I know that someone is coming to kill me.

I know who.

I know why.

I know soon.

I just don't know how or exactly when.

This is what happens when you know what people have done: danger stalks your every breath.

Would I do it again? Probably. It's not like I can change who I am.

So this is it. My declaration: I know who is going to kill me.

I hope I am wrong. I hope it doesn't happen or I hope that I find a way to outwit them.

That is all I have: hope.

Plain old hope.

Will it be enough?

Part 1

Rae

11 Acacia Villas

1 June 2021, Brighton

KnockKnockKnockKnockKnockKnockKnockKnockKnock!

Loud and unexpected, the banging at my front door makes me jump.

KnockKnockKnockKnockKnockKnockKnockKnockKnock! Comes again, louder this time. That should, technically, be impossible since the brass door knocker, something unique and beautiful when we got it six years ago, has pretty much rusted into place and hasn't been properly lifted in at least a couple of years.

KnockKnockKnockKnockKnockKnockKnockKnockKnock!

All right, all right, all right, I mumble, more irritated at the noise than the fact they are taking me away from the deadline I've been fighting the past week.

KnockKnockKnockKnockKnockKnockKnockKnockKnock!

It genuinely sounds like whoever is on the other side of my door is properly trying to enter my house via the door knocker.

KnockKnockKnockKnockKnockKnockKnockKnockKnock!

'*There is NO NEED for all of that*,' is teetering murderously on the tip of my tongue when I yank the door open, but it evaporates when I see who is on the other side.

Priscilla.

I draw back.

Priscilla is my neighbour who lives at number 21 to our 11 Acacia Villas. And I could not be more surprised to see her standing there.

I've spoken to her a couple of dozen times – mainly, when I'm delivering her stuff that has been sent to our house by mistake, and a couple of times at our Neighbour–2–Neighbour Watch meetings.

We live in a well-to-do area of Brighton and a lot of the people are 'well-spoken', but even among them Priscilla is in a different league: her clothes are always bespoke or casually designer; her black, grey and white hair is cut into the sharpest bob; her make-up is always perfectly applied – smoky eyes, glossy coloured lips, flawless foundation; and she is always – *always* – scented to perfection. From the moment I met her, I knew she held herself above us. Not just from looking at her, but also from the way she would respond to anyone saying hello to her in the street. She would look at you, ever so slightly lift her chin – so slightly, you'd barely notice – and then offer a short, curt nod, before moving on.

Even at the Neighbour–2–Neighbour Watch meetings where I got the chance to speak to her for more than two seconds, it was highly controlled – she swept in, spoke to each person in turn, asking a few perfunctory questions, often making pointed and unsettling comments, then moving on to someone else. By the time the person who had called the meeting had stood up to talk, Priscilla would have spoken to everyone, settled with no one and made sure she left before the end, so, I guessed, she wouldn't be forced to walk home with anyone.

That is why I'm confused about her being on my doorstep. What could she possibly want with me?

'Hello?' I ask cautiously.

Priscilla lives by herself in one of the biggest houses on Acacia Villas. She's older than me, maybe mid-fifties, but with what I'm sure is a lifetime of expensive products and a commitment to skincare, her pale-cream complexion makes her look younger than my forty-eight.

Although, as my eyes sweep over her, I have to admit I've never seen her looking like this before – her usually pristine clothes are dishevelled, her hallmark bobbed hair is a bird's nest halo of messiness, her eye make-up is like a Rorschach pattern smudged under her eyes, while her trademark glossy lipstick (today's colour is pink) is smeared from her mouth to her right cheek. Her usually dewy skin is a blotchy mass of sweat.

'Are you all right?' I ask, worried and a little scared. *Why is she here*? bolts through my head again.

'I know what you've done,' she gasps, her voice laboured, as if speaking is difficult, arduous, painful.

'What did you say?' I ask her.

Instead of replying, she sways dramatically on her pink, heeled shoes and I realise all of a sudden that all it'll take is for her weight to be off balance for a moment too long and she'll topple backwards down the stone steps leading up to our front door, possibly breaking something on the way.

Priscilla pants and gasps a while longer before saying again, 'I know what you've done . . . I know what all of you have done.' She suddenly thrusts what she's holding in her arms at me, and it takes me a moment to work out what it is: a book. A large blue hardback notebook, the type Clark uses to write his notes in. But this one is thick, the cover battered and worn, pieces of paper stuffed into its pages bulking it out even more.

'It's . . . it's all in here . . . I know what you've all been up to.'

'What are you talking about?' I ask her, not taking the book she is holding out to me. 'What's going on?'

She doubles over so suddenly, so violently, almost guillotining herself in half on the book in her hands.

I reach for her, but she brushes me away before slowly uncurling herself to shove the book at me again. 'Take this,' she orders. 'It's all in there . . . Who's done this . . . Why . . . It's all in there . . . Take it . . . Take it and find out who tried to kill me.'

I don't take the book – why would I? – instead I say, 'You're not making any sense, Priscilla. Look, come in. Have a cup of tea. Is there anyone you want me to call for you? Anyone who can come and be—'

'No,' she wails with such a strangled voice, it's as though someone has their hand around her throat and is squeezing tight. 'No . . . time . . . attacked . . . attacked.'

She sways again and this time the force throws her weight completely off balance, and she starts to fall. Without thinking, my hand snaps out to grab her and my fingers close around her bicep. In the beat that follows, the revulsion of having to touch her – *anyone* – shudders through me. *I can't do this*, I decide, and my fingers are desperate to let her go, to just let her fall, while I dash to the bathroom to scrub my hands. *This is a nightmare, I can't just touch someone like this.*

Before I can snatch my hand away in disgust, Priscilla lifts her gaze to meet mine. Her usually aloof blue eyes are tainted with terror, full of fear. She is scared. That is it: she is scared. Something bad has happened to her, something bad is still happening to her, and she is scared. I can't release her. I have issues that spark my anxiety, but I can't just let her fall and live with myself, especially not when I know that type of acute fright in her eyes, and so instead, I pull Priscilla towards me over the doorstep.

Once in my corridor, she lets out a silent scream and folds in half, dropping the book, which spins halfway across our golden, oak-floored hallway.

It is horrible to see what is happening to her; dreadful to watch and be so powerless to help.

'Are you saying someone attacked you?' I ask gently, not sure whether to cuddle her, ease her onto the ground or leave her be.

'Trust no one,' she manages between gasps, answering an entirely different question. 'Not even *him*.'

Him? Does she mean Clark? My husband?

I don't understand any of this – why has she come here in this state when she could have called an ambulance or the police? And why me of all people? I'm sure there are other people who live on this stretch of Acacia Villas that she's known longer and she can trust more.

'Trust—' Her breathing is so heavy now, forced, strained, awkward, that a new terror shoots through my heart. She's going to die. In my hallway. *In my hallway. Not only will that be horrific for her and those who love her, I will not be able to live here any more.* I can't let that happen.

'I'll call an ambulance!' I cry, before I rush down the corridor and partially trip on her book. I stop to scoop it up and then continue into the kitchen. Dumping the book on the table in front of the unit nearest the door, I snatch the house phone from its cradle by the stereo. It doesn't bleep, which means . . . I check the display . . . yup, it's dead. Momentarily furious, I notice someone has unplugged the phone to plug in the stereo but didn't bother to put the phone back on charge when they'd finished. Just yesterday, when the phone had bleeped a warning that it was running low on battery, I ignored it. It wasn't important. I have my mobile. No one calls me on the landline except 'Your computer has been hacked' creeps and very occasionally, my mother. So no, I didn't need to worry about the house phone being charged. *And now look. Now look!*

My heart is racing and my body is trembling. This is bad. This is very, very bad. A terrible situation has landed – *literally* – on my doorstep and rather than being able to sort it efficiently, I have to run upstairs to grab my mobile, causing more delay.

I practically throw the handset down and rush back to go upstairs for my mobile, completely forgetting about the handset in the living room. I'm almost halfway down the corridor before it registers that my hallway is empty. Completely empty.

The front door is wide open, but there is no Priscilla, there is no sign that she was ever there.

I stop and stare, shock mingling with the adrenalin whizzing around my body. 'Where is she?' I ask myself out loud. 'Where did she go?'

How long was I in the kitchen? I think. *Because you don't go from being pretty much at death's door to completely disappearing ... unless ...*

Unless it never happened. Unless I imagined the whole thing.

No, surely I can't have? Surely not.

I stand very still in the middle of my wide hallway, staring at the open front door, and trying to work out what is going on. And what I should do next.

The thing is, if I shut the door and go back to what I was doing, it could be a sign that I am admitting there is something wrong with me. I mean, there must be for me to have conjured up something so detailed and terrifying and realistic about Priscilla.

But on the other hand, if I go outside to see if I can spot Priscilla, then I could be either taking a step towards actively seeking out the trouble she brought to my door ... or immersing myself even deeper into the delusion I have conjured up.

What do I do? What's the best thing to do?

Right, the grown up part of me decides. *What I need to do is shut this door and pretend none of this ever happened. I won't think about it and I certainly won't talk about it. I am going to put Priscilla out of my mind until I hear something else about her.*

I'm about to shut the door, when my eyes snag on a smudge of something against the magnolia-painted wall of our hallway near where Priscilla initially stood. The faintest hint of red. *Blood? Is that blood?*

I go to step closer to have a proper look, when a flash of pink catches my eye from outside. I peer at the pink at the bottom of my grey stone steps: a shoe. The type Priscilla was wearing.

Maybe I'm not going crazy after all, maybe she was here.

From somewhere to the right of the house, a shout cuts through the Tuesday afternoon quiet. Right now, most people are out shopping, or working, or exercising. Lots of us who worked from home before it was forced on us, now deliberately go out to sit in cafés and libraries and shared office spaces rather than be trapped at home after more than a year of doing it. I don't mind being at home – I know it's safe, I know it's clean, I know I very rarely have to interact with people and have my anxieties triggered.

I pause, strain my ears, wondering if I did hear a shout or not?

'Help!' comes again. A man's voice, again shouting: 'Help!'

Cautiously, I leave my hallway and go down the stone steps. At the bottom the pink shoe is lying on its side waiting to be rescued, and just to the right of my gate is its twin, lying on its opposite side but waiting just as patiently to be picked up.

Now on the pavement, I can see clearly where the shout is coming from: one of my male neighbours is leaning over someone. Without my glasses, it takes me a moment to properly realise that it's Priscilla on the ground.

'It's Priscilla!' Dunstan, my neighbour, yells when he spots me, standing there frozen and, basically, useless. 'She's hurt! Get an ambulance!'

Get an ambulance. Get an ambulance. Get an ambulance. It's like I know the words but I can't get them to connect in my head. I can't get myself to understand what to do.

'Rae!' Dunstan shouts, his voice loud and stern. 'Wake up! Get an ambulance! I think she's dying!'

That startles me out of my stupor, puts words into my brain in a place where they connect and I understand what actions I need to take.

Spinning on my sock-covered feet, I run back up the stone steps, into my house and then dash up to my office to get my mobile and dial 999.

Rae

11 Acacia Villas

1 June 2021, Brighton

Dunstan and I stand at the bottom of my steps, both of us awkward, acting as though we've been on a date that hasn't gone very well, *but* we both fancied each other so we slept together and now we're both desperate to get away so we can properly blame the other person for how bad the non-sex part had been.

Dunstan lives in a flat around the corner at number 36. I'm pretty sure Dunstan is his surname, but I haven't heard anyone call him anything else; I think he even introduces himself as Dunstan.

There isn't much to say to each other. The air is only just calming down, the molecules seeming to settle like soft-falling snow after the violence of the ambulance people trying to revive and then save an unconscious Priscilla, and I think we're both trying to formulate what to say, or even what to think. There wasn't much time to talk before and now we're not sure what to say. I keep wanting to say out loud that I wished I smoked or didn't mind drinking in front of my children, because I could do with a drink and/or a ciggie right now.

After I'd called the ambulance, I had returned – with shoes and gloves on – to wait with them. Dunstan had continually taken her pulse as though he knew what he was doing, and I'd had nothing to do but hold her hand saying soothing things – at least, I hoped they were comforting and not just generic and dull. Then when the ambulance pulled up and the paramedics took over, we lurked in the background, answering the questions we could and generally feeling utterly useless.

I am a freelance magazine and newsletter editor and Dunstan is a policeman – not sure of the grade or anything – so neither of us had anything to offer. But we exchanged looks several times when the paramedics kept repeating that her injuries – mainly on the back of her head from where she'd been hit quite hard, apparently – didn't match the wildly fluctuating vital signs.

The ambulance people stayed for a long time trying to stabilise Priscilla, and nothing had really worked. In the end they carefully loaded her into their vehicle and took her away.

Clark, my husband, approaches at a near run because our two dogs – Yam and Okra – are dragging him along as they bound home. The funny part of that is they are Yorkshire Terriers who are actually quite small for their breed. But from day one they have had the ability and stubbornness of much bigger dogs, and even someone as big and strong as Clark sometimes struggles to not be swept along by them. 'Dunstan,' Clark says with a nod, coming to a halt near us. 'What's up?'

I shoot my husband of twelve years a 'where do I even start' look and he instantly understands that something huge has happened and tries to pull the dogs back on their leads so they don't get involved. Yam, who has been a good girl since she arrived with her human dad, slinking around Clark's ankles like a snake, suddenly decides that she doesn't actually like Dunstan. She's looked at him, assessed his smell and his physique – all of which are more than acceptable to most humans – and has decided she's not impressed. In fact, she is completely unimpressed and she needs to express that displeasure – loudly.

She plants her back legs wide, sits back, lowers her tail and starts to remonstrate at him, telling him what she thinks of him in no uncertain barking terms. Okra, on the other hand, has made a similar assessment of the man standing with me and has been taken in completely by him, so much so, she wants to get as close as possible to him and starts to strain on her lead, her front paws in the air as she tries to get to him.

'Stop it, girls,' Clark says.

The reactions of our dogs seems to wake up Dunstan from the silent stupor he has been standing with me in, and he bends to chuckle Okra under her chin, blows a wry kiss to a still-complaining Yam and then nods a goodbye to Clark and me. His gaze lingers on me, asking, I think, if I'm all right because he certainly isn't. I nod in reply, while trying to express that I am not OK either.

'Yam, stop it,' Clark says again, this time sounding more absent and disengaged because he knows the barking will soon stop now the source is walking away.

My husband is wearing his usual work fug; it sits on his broad shoulders like a heavy, velvet cloak that he has to drag home with him every night. I can't imagine who he's spoken to today, what stories he's heard and how he's tried to resolve those issues that are, technically, nothing to do with him. Being a property solicitor you'd think that it would be very straightforward and emotionless, but the buying and selling of people's homes, no matter how small or seemingly insignificant, has so much emotion, sentiment and feelings of identity wrapped up in it, that he often acts like an unpaid therapist to his clients as he gets the necessary paperwork in order.

Clark used to travel to London three days a week after we moved to Brighton six years ago, but after the period when we were all forced to work at home for months on end, Clark had needed office space outside the house. We were fortunate to have a house big enough that while we were all at home, it wasn't as difficult for us to work under the same roof as it was for some. He still has an office upstairs but when we were all allowed out again after the first lockdown, Clark declared, more than once, that he really needed a way to physically separate work from family life. He needed that commute, even if – like now – it was a fifteen-minute stroll along the seafront to a building that had been converted to accommodate lots of small offices with a communal café-type area downstairs.

He needed the decompression time, he told me. I understood completely. And, because he was getting a nice space to himself in a building full of other people who'd also had to reassess their working environment, it'd been agreed he take our two Yorkies with him every day. ('Agreed' makes it sound like I gave him a choice. If he wanted out of the house during working hours, then he took the dogs with him, that was the deal.)

'What's gone on?' Clark asks as we climb the steps together, his gaze constantly going to Dunstan's retreating form.

We enter the house and 'Oh, it's—' I begin, but my sharing of my despair is cut short by Yam, the bigger of the two dogs, making a dash for the stairs the second Clark drops her lead.

'Oh, what!' he says, letting go of Okra's lead, causing her to make a similar dash for freedom. Our one-year-old puppies are not allowed upstairs, which is precisely why they rush up there whenever they get the chance. I'm always telling Clark as well as our daughters, Bria and Mella, to hold on to the leads until they're in the kitchen to stop them darting upstairs like it is the gateway to doggie wonderland.

Clark looks at me, the expression on his handsome face appealing for me to do my usual dash up after our dogs. Out of everyone, I am the one who hates dog hair all over the house the most, so I am the one who is always running to catch them and bring them back. Today, my other half is out of luck. Even with the expert way his beautiful liquid-brown eyes gaze at me, and his full, delicious lips are twisted to make him seem vulnerable, I ain't playing.

I will not be running up after dogs today.

In the second or two after he realises that his 'puppy dog' expression is not going to work on me, Clark dashes up the stairs, calling after the dogs as he goes.

As I turn away, the smudge of blood confronts me. And it immediately turns my stomach. It reminds me of the stillness of Priscilla's features as they fitted an oxygen mask over her face, the way the paramedics kept changing places as they worked on her. She might be dead now, for all I know. And I might be the last person to have held her hand before she died.

That reminder catapults me into the toilet under the stairs, where I rip off my burgundy gloves and dump them into the small washing basket under the sink. I pump copious amounts of organic peppermint handwash over my fingers and palms, before foaming them up and scrubbing and scrubbing until my hands have got some semblance of cleanliness back.

Once my hands are as clean as they can be without being dunked in bleach, I head for the kitchen and as I move, I realise a cold, burning-hot sensation has taken over my body – I am cold and burning hot at the same time, my muscles quivering out the disparity as I move. I think I'm in slight shock. All of this with Priscilla, being confronted by her mortality, has shaken me. It's one of the worst things that has ever happened.

I am almost halfway across the room when I see it.

Sitting on the table, where I threw it as I went to grab the house phone, is the thing that Priscilla tried to give me earlier.

The item that ended up on the floor and I scooped up on the way to get help.

The diary.

The book of everyone's secrets.

Nora

Attending Paramedic, Acacia Villas Incident

1 June 2021, Brighton

'I don't get it – we've stabilised the head wound. Why is she still so tachycardic?'

Nora Helling has been a paramedic for fifteen years and she still finds ways to be surprised. She often feels that she's seen every type of injury the human body can experience, but then she'll be called to another emergency and there will be something she hasn't seen before.

Like this woman. Fifty-something, white female. From one of the posh roads in Brighton. Assault victim, not sexual, an easy-to-treat wound, not much blood loss. And yet, she keeps crashing. Her vitals erratic, her heart promising to either race its way out of her chest or stop beating altogether. Nothing they do is working for any length of time. 'Her heart rate is all over the place,' Nora calls to her partner. 'She seemed stable then her vitals just went haywire again. There's something else going on. What is it, though?'

'Poison?' replies Fenn, the paramedic driving the ambulance.

Nora shakes her head. 'If it was a poison, she'd most likely be dead by now. And she doesn't have anything to indicate it is – no discolouring of her lips or nails or skin.'

'Maybe it's a slow-acting poison? One we're not familiar with? Either way, we're going to have to call the police.'

'Surprised those two didn't while they were waiting for us to arrive,' Nora replies. 'But wait, are you saying someone tried to poison her and then caved her head in just to be sure?'

Nora looks over the patient on the stretcher in front of her. The rush of an emergency rarely allows her to do this: to look at a person, see them in serenity. Even with her face obscured by an oxygen mask and her top ripped open to put the pads on to monitor her heart, she is still beautiful.

This is one of those surprises for Nora. This woman – Priscilla Calvert, the others called her – didn't look like the sort of woman any-one would hate enough to try to murder – *twice*. Assault, that's the sort of thing that happens all the time. But possibly poison? That is inten-tional. That is planned. That is executed. And this Priscilla *really* doesn't look like the sort of person you would try to murder once, let alone twice.

'Why would someone try to murder her twice?' Nora says out loud, not really expecting an answer.

'Why do people do anything? You've been doing this long enough to know that people will do anything for any reason.'

'True,' Nora says. But that doesn't seem enough. There has to be more to this than that. There has to be a proper explanation. Yes, she's constantly surprised – by the human body, by what happens to it, by the things that humans do – but at times like this, she isn't just sur-prised. She is also baffled. Appalled. And ever so sad.

Rae

11 Acacia Villas

1 June 2021, Brighton

I've been standing here staring at this book my neighbour gave me for a long time. More than anything, I can't believe I just tossed it onto the table without wiping it down with bleach first. If Clark had done that I would have had a breakdown! The thought of all those germs and bacteria and viruses crawling over the table where we sit to eat would have fired up my anxiety – and my nerves and fears would have twisted themselves so tightly inside I would have had to clean the entire house.

I was distracted at the time, though. I'd been trying to help a woman who I thought was going to die in my corridor. But now this whole matter has moved on and away from me, I'm confronted with this.

What should I do with it?

I can't touch it, obviously. What if the fingerprints of the person who attacked her are on it? What if I pick it up and get rid of the other person's fingerprints and the police don't believe me when I say I didn't attack her because mine are the only ones on there?

I can't touch it, but it can't stay here. Not on the table, not in this house.

I hear Clark chasing one of the dogs around Bria and Mella's bedroom, which is above the kitchen, the dog's little legs beating out a comedic drumbeat as it darts from place to place, no doubt seeking socks, her favourite thing in the world after chewing on my long cardigans. I'm guessing, because I can only hear one dog's pawsteps, that Clark has got one already and any minute now he's going to capture the other, descend the stairs like a triumphant returning soldier and find me standing here, staring at this thing.

And he's going to ask me what it is.

And I'll say . . . I'll say . . .

I'll say, it's at times like this I wished I smoked or didn't have a problem drinking in front of my children because I need one of those things right now.

Slowly, because it feels like a violation simply looking at it, let alone touching it, I set aside my fingerprint worries and pick up the book. It's heavy, although probably a fraction of the weight of the secrets it holds, if Priscilla meant what she said and she honestly does know what everyone has done. I weigh it in my hands like I'm getting ready to pitch it across the room and need to check its form first.

I should look, shouldn't I? See if they are just the mad ramblings of a person who spends far too much time on her own or if there is substance to her claims; a hook to hang many, many revelations on.

But then . . . if someone read my 'diary', meaning a few private thoughts I jotted down, or even the letter I once wrote Clark because I thought he was getting ready to dump me . . . if someone read either of those, or simply put eyes on them in a meaningful way, I would be horrified. Just the thought of it sends spikes of horror shuddering through me.

Priscilla *did* give it to me, though. She *did* tell me to read it. It's not like I came across this by accident or went hunting for it. She *wanted* me to know what was in there. She said it would help to disclose who had done this to her. And because of that, this is probably something I should pass straight on to the police.

BUT . . . I am nosy as hell.

I am nosy as hell and I'm sure a peek, a little flick through, won't hurt.

Before I delay things any longer by spinning off into another round of pros and cons, my hands pull open the book at a random page. I should probably start at the beginning, but I'll end up getting drawn in if I do, and I *don't* want Clark to catch me doing this because this feels like something that needs to be kept secret for now.

My eyes scan the page in front of me: in her small, scratchy but neat handwriting, Priscilla has scrawled a conversation. I can't work out who it's between without flicking back, but it's something to do with the bins. One person going on at another person for encroaching on the space outside the front of their house, for moving their bin far too close to the other's boundary. And because this thing kept happening, there was now bad blood between the two households.

This is it? This is what she came to my door clinging on to after she'd been attacked? Literally: 'Your bin is too close to my house?' And page after page of it, too?

Well, at least that's cured my shaking. Priscilla is clearly a fantasist and I was sucked in. For a few moments, I was as ridiculous as her. I flick on a few more pages, and it's more of the same. More about bins, about dogs encroaching on property, parties that were too loud and too long. I was wrong about Priscilla. She wasn't the local sophisticate, she was the local nosy parker. She used the position of her house, on the corner plot of the bend of Acacia Villas and its unique view of pretty much all of the street and the houses on it (even the ones around the bend), to watch people. To write down the things they did and said. To create this 'dossier' that suckered me in for a few seconds. How sad am I?

I flick on a bit more, my eyes casually scanning each page to see if there's anything of real interest, anything that might be a devastating secret. Nothing. I toss the book on the table. Imagine if I'd gone to the police, clutching this in my hot little hands, telling them that Priscilla's attacker was in those pages. Just imagine their faces, the side-eyeing, the gentle suggestion that I might need to get—*Hang on*, I think. *HANG ON.*

I immediately snatch up the book again, furiously flicking through to get back to where I was. *Did I just see . . .? Did I just— Yes, yes, I* did *see that.*

Clark Whickman is written there bold as day, clear as spring water. *Clark Whickman from number 11 Acacia Villas.*

And there, on the same page as my husband's name, is *her* name.

Bryony

24 Acacia Villas

1 June 2021, Brighton

'And so, I rather calmly told him that this wasn't the first time it had happened and if the subscribers list was that inaccurate again, I would have to escalate the matter.'

I sit across from my husband at our immaculately laid dining table in our immaculately tidy dining room and wonder, as I do every day, if he knows how irritating his voice is.

Most things about Grayson Hinter – head of a prestigious charity trust, father of two, husband of one – are exasperating. From the super cilious smirk he'll have had on his face as he told off his staff member to the flaccid handkerchief tucked into his jacket pocket, hiding his solitary cigarette; from the neatly cut hair on his balding head to his constant attempt to appear militarily trained when he's never had any armed services experience, there is a lot that could rub you the wrong way about Grayson. But it's his voice that gets to most people. He speaks a whole two seconds slower than anyone I have ever met, and when you have to listen to every single thing that has happened to him in detail every day, a slow voice and a superior attitude are just the ultimate nuisance.

And I think I might actually hate him for it.

Every day Trent, our fifteen year old, Tilly, our fourteen year old, and I sit and listen to the detailed breakdown of his day. Whether it is instructing a member of staff how they'd made an error on one of the spreadsheets or telling someone they didn't quite qualify for assistance from their charity, we are treated to a detailed dissection and replay of it – all . . . in . . . that . . . slow . . . patronising . . . voice.

I used to love his voice. I used to adore him and everything about him; the way he spoke was calming and authoritative and I admired that about him. After the chaos of my upbringing and the instability of my family life, the calm certainty of someone who spoke slowly, spoke well, spoke often was exactly what I craved.

I stab the dark green broccoli that sits in the middle of my plate, and for a moment, just a moment, the image of snatching up my fork, pushing off the broccoli and ramming it straight through Grayson's left eyeball flashes in my head. The thought of how I would then sit back down, wipe off the blood, pick up my knife and do my level best to finish the lasagne I'd made, causes me to giggle.

I'm not known for giggling, especially not during Grayson's daily debrief, so naturally everyone around the table stops eating to look at me. Tilly and Trent are both wide-eyed, scared. No one interrupts their father like this, no one.

'You're in a rather jovial mood, darling,' Grayson says.

Tilly and Trent will have noticed, just as I have, the twitch of irritation around his mouth and eyes. He'd been on a roll with today's tale of how he had very gently and expertly knocked order into Westlann Charitable Trust (Independent Charity of the Year five years in a row) and he is not happy at being even slightly interrupted. 'What is it that is amusing you, Bryony?'

'Oh, nothing,' I reply as I try to settle my face into its usual expression of interest, instead of one that wants to keep laughing at the thought of Grayson having a fork sticking out of his eye. Instead of Harold with an arrow in the eye, it's Grayson with a fork in his eye. 'It was just a silly thing.'

'Well, if it was a silly thing and not "nothing" as you originally stated, then do share. I'm sure all of us around the table would be delighted to hear something amusing.' My husband looks first at Trent, his younger and taller doppelganger, who, seeing his father is looking at him and expects backup, nods as though he is interested too, and then Grayson looks to Tilly, who hasn't raised her gaze from her almost full dinner plate all evening, which is par for the course.

I want to glare at Grayson across the table. I would like to whip away the napkin on my lap and drop it onto my plate of unfinished food while screaming: 'I am not a member of your staff, nor am I a person who has come to you for help that you can lord it over, so I'll thank you not to speak to me as though I am! I am your wife! Your equal! I'll thank you again to remember that!' I would then push out my chair and stomp my way up to my sewing room where I could calm down by sitting in front of my sewing machine and starting on a few orders.

In front of the sewing machine I know my physical transformation would be almost instant: my shoulders would fall, my furious heart would slow, the burning blood would cool in my veins.

I would love to do all those things but I cannot. I simply cannot.

'I'm sorry, Grayson,' I say, quietly. 'I was just—'

BRRIINNNGGGG . . . The loud, intrusive chime of the doorbell interrupts my scrabbling for an explanation, and that upsets Grayson. He doesn't have time for interruptions and me being erratic. He is on a schedule to unload his day on to us and he does not like being disturbed while doing it.

'I'll just see who that is,' I say, and dash for the door. Grayson obviously has a desire to know what is going on and reaches the door a moment after me.

It is he, though, who tugs open the heavy front door. I don't think either of us could be any more surprised to find two police officers on his doorstep. On the street behind them, several police cars are parked. Along this tree-lined, leafy road, police officers are approaching different doors.

They have come for me! I realise, and the feeling engulfs my whole body almost straight away. *They've found out and they've come for me.*

'Good evening, sir,' the first officer begins. 'Sorry to disturb you. We're investigating a serious assault – possible attempted murder – that occurred along this road this afternoon.'

Grayson doesn't know what to say and neither do I.

'Do you mind if we come in and ask you a few questions?' the officer persists.

Grayson turns his head slightly to look at me – he seems to have genuinely blanked out and is not sure which way is up.

'Sir?' the policeman prompts.

'Oh, of course, of course,' he says, recovering.

He steps aside to let the police officers in and I know that this is the beginning of the end.

Lilly

47 Acacia Villas

1 June 2021, Brighton

The cork comes out of the bottle of fizz at such speed and with such force that I can tell it's been waiting to do that since it was originally stuffed in there.

I understand how it feels. That's how I've felt today. Like all the tension, the unrelenting pressure of the last few years have finally been unleashed . . . And everything has exploded.

The bubbles catch the light and they glint as I glug the cold liquid into a large wine glass. No, I shouldn't use alcohol as a crutch. Yes, I should find a way to work through all these feelings and express them in a constructive, positive way. And, yeah, F that for a game of soldiers.

I need this liquid to rampage through my body, erasing everything that has happened in the last twenty-four hours – failing that, I need it to sparkle through my veins, effervescing away anything resembling a feeling.

I shouldn't have left.

This is the conclusion I am coming to about where my life is now. Eighteen years ago, I should not have left Brighton to go and live in Italy. But at the time, when I lived in England, I vividly remember thinking: *what am I doing here? I'm just sitting around waiting to get fat while obsessing about parking permits, what days the bins (recycling and general) go out and who doesn't pick up their dog's poo. Really? This is what my life is going to be?*

It's hard for me to believe, sometimes, that I was so sneery about everything. That I looked down on what was a perfectly good existence – *life* – and thought I deserved more. *Better.*

Turns out, Italy was gorgeous and fun and different. But not better. Nowhere near better, just different.

I can see that now, nearly eighteen years later, when I practically inhale a bottle of fizz at the end of every day and I spend way too much time staring at the photo of my college friends that sits on my mantelpiece – things are very rarely better, just different. I spent all that time running from the me I thought I was becoming; only to find myself here anyway and not hating it as much as I thought I would.

The fact I am now stuck and scared; terrified and trapped is because I went away. If I'd stayed, I don't think it would have come to this.

If I had stayed, I'd still be with him. And he would have rescued me from all of this before it even began.

1991, Leeds

In our halls, he was the coolest. One of those guys who was always on the periphery of our group and lots of other groups, but was intriguing enough to catch my eye. I had noticed him. When he walked into the canteen at breakfast, when he sat in the common room at lunch, when he walked into the on-campus student bar, I would notice him. I would smile at him. He would smile back. And I'd wonder what it would be like to kiss him – the big guy with the cool name and sweet smile.

It was never going to happen, though, I'd kind of accepted that. He was the guy I was destined to crush on from afar. Until that night I ran out of money and couldn't go into town with my friends. I'd hoped that one of them would lend me the cash, or even cover me, but every one of them just kept avoiding my eye, and ignoring the sad-girl sighs as they got ready and gambolled off to get the bus, leaving me alone. Despite the strong feelings of poor me – literally and emotionally – I was not going to sit up in my room on my own, no way. I was *not* that sad person who spent Friday night alone, so I went to the student bar, found some people I vaguely knew who didn't mind buying me the odd pint, then I moved on to the students' union, where someone paid the two pounds for me to get in and another someone bought me a few drinks. I felt bad getting people to buy me stuff when I couldn't immediately pay them back, but I would pay them back. I wasn't someone who wouldn't – eventually – stand her round.

I had just been considering my options – find someone else to get me another drink or go home to bed since I was more than a little drunk – when he walked in. I was standing right by the door, so when I grinned at him, he saw me and smiled back in recognition and didn't flinch when I leapt at him for a hug.

'That was unexpected,' he said, a little confused as he let me go.

The music thumped loudly, and the perfect mix of snakebite (cider and lager) and the drags of cigarettes I'd had were working nicely to make me bold. 'You're gorgeous,' I slurred, my arms slung like a stole around his neck. 'Has anyone ever told you that?'

'No one as drunk as you,' he teased.

'Do you have a girlfriend?' I asked, having to get closer to him because the music seemed to have gone up a notch and I couldn't hear him from that far away. I mean, it was a real chore, pushing my body closer to him and my face nearer to his.

'No,' he replied.

'Do you want one?' I persisted. Shouldn't he have kissed me by now? *Do you have a girlfriend*? was *literally* code for 'kiss me'.

'Are you offering yourself up for the position?' he joked.

Oh my goodness! Was he really that slow on the uptake? Because that was going to irritate me in a couple of hours, let alone in the year or so I'd been planning on us being together.

'Because if you are, then you've got the position,' he said, and covered my lips with his in a movie-style kiss.

1 June 2021, Brighton

Most of these mouthfuls of Prosecco – well-priced, delicious and on repeat order from the local wine dealer – don't even register as they go down.

If I hadn't gone to Italy in search of something 'better' eighteen years ago, how would my life have panned out? Because all that stuff I ran away from – it's still here, and I didn't realise that just because I didn't care about things like parking permits and the days the bins went out back then, didn't mean I would never care about them. Those sort of things might have seemed boring and unimportant to someone who was young and didn't have to care about anything other than her career, but that all changes. As you become part of a community, part of the society around you, caring about people not parking recklessly, avoiding littering, picking up after their dog, and putting the bins out on the right day is essential to making your own living environment pleasant.

Like it or not, those are the small acts of community service we all carry out to make our world better. I really wish I had the chance to explain that to past Lilly; to show her how important those things she once sneered at actually are and how, if she'd just given them a chance, she'd still be with the love of her life.

Past Lilly, I think, assumed that the pause button would be hit on life in England while she was away; that nothing would change and she would be able to slot back into the life she had left behind when she was ready. Everyone and everything would stay exactly the same, would wait where they were in their lives for me to return and we could carry on where we left off.

None of it happened like that, of course. The world kept on turning, the people continued to live and learn and love and hate and succeed and fail.

It wasn't even an issue, at first, that he didn't want to come with me. That he wanted to stay here and carry on living the same old life I hated so much. I initially assumed that since his position at work had stalled, and since he hardly saw his family who lived in London, and since we hadn't had even one conversation about moving to a bigger place nor starting a family and/or getting married, that he would very quickly decide to come with me.

I was a little arrogant, too, I suppose.

I stare at the picture on the mantelpiece, drinking in his smile and the way he is looking at me as I take a photo of the group.

We were meant to make long distance work, but in all honesty, I thought he would come with me – that a month or two without me would have him packing his bags and heading over. Because he always said he couldn't live without me. But the months became years, and long distance was what we worked on, and long-distance difficulties were what we put it down to when things started to drift. When you love each other, you don't think that what will wear you both out is the constant having to get to know someone again – how to be with them, live with them, relax with them – every ten days when you get to spend time together.

We tried to keep our relationship going but once the 'drifting apart' process started (not speaking as regularly, things coming up that stop visits, long, uncomfortable silences on the phone, several calls where you forget to say, 'I love you'), I realised it meant the rot had set in. There was no way to stop it – it was like a virulent fungus and it needed to be excised. What I didn't want was our previous years together to be washed away on tides of resentment and bitterness, on forgetting how much we meant to each other as our relationship broke down, so I said it was over and we should finish it.

And suddenly, he started talking about moving to be with me, he begged me to come home, he suggested we find a country in the middle where we could both base ourselves and travel from . . . But all of this came *after I ended it* . . . nothing was too much trouble or impossible for him after that, as long as we stayed together.

By that point, though, I knew that splitting up was the best thing for both of us so I stuck to my guns: we were split, we should stay split. And we would both be able to move on.

I was wrong. This thought flitters across the surface of my mind before it skitters down to settle in the pit of my stomach. That happens every time I think about him.

I was wrong. I should have stuck it out. I shouldn't have given him the chance to marry someone else.

I take three big gulps of Prosecco, wait for the familiar sensation of fuzzy warmth to effervesce in my stomach. I stretch out my neck by moving it side to side, pull air into my lungs, force my body to relax, to be calm. Slowly I release. Let go. Let the booze swirl itself into my veins and unhook me from stress and tension.

At times like this, I miss him. Properly miss him and who I was with him. I've never had someone treat me as well as he did, I've never been with someone who makes me feel as real as he did. Yes, it's been a good fifteen years since we split, but I know all this stuff would not be happening now if I was still with him. I would be safe. I would be secure. I would not walk around with an anvil of fear where my heart should be.

Everything is spiralling out of control. And because it's a slow spin, the revolutions gradual, I've been lulled into thinking that the crash, when it happens, will be fine. That I'll walk away without a scratch; in fact that the crash may not happen at all.

But it's coming. The tension of its approach, the vibes thrown out there before the collision, have been hanging in the air for a while now. I've been ignoring them, but it's coming, it's definitely coming.

The thought of *that* has me lifting the glass to my lips to take the biggest gulp yet.

KNOCK! KNOCK! KNOCK! on the front door stops the wine glass just before it hits my lips.

That is not the knock of a delivery driver or someone who knows me; there is nothing efficient or pleasant about it, it is something officious and slightly threatening.

The anvil in my chest expands then drops. What if it's the police? What if they've finally come for me? What if this is the start of the crash?

My glass makes a small clinking sound as I place it on the table to go to the door. Is that noise, a tiny insignificant sound, what I'm going to remember after I answer the door? Is that the last sound I'm going to hear as a free woman?

There are two of them: one male, one female.

Both seem inexplicably tall. Both have the same razor-cut black hair, muddy brown eyes and sallow skin.

'We'd like to talk to you about an incident that took place on this street earlier today,' one of them says.

I'm not sure which one of them speaks because my mind is racing, I am desperately trying to get my story together, get all the stuff straight in my head.

I need to get my story straight.

I need to get my story straight but all I can hear is the clink of my glass on the table, and how I knew it was going to be the last sound I remember hearing as a free woman.

'Do you have a few minutes to answer our questions?' one of the police officers asks.

I nod and stand aside, the sound of glass on wood tinkling loudly in my ears.

Rae

11 Acacia Villas

1 June 2021, Brighton

'Why can't the sun go to university?' Mella asks at the dinner table.

'I don't know,' Clark replies, 'why can't the sun go to university?'

'Because it already has too many degrees!' Bria cuts in, stealing her sister's punchline glory. Mella narrows her eyes at her sister while simultaneously furiously trying to think of an alternative punchline so that she can reclaim her joke by telling Bria that she is wrong.

Bria is always doing this to her younger sister, but if Mella dares to retaliate by doing the same to her, Bria loses the plot beyond all proportion. We've actually told our eldest off before because she gets so disproportionally angry about being joke gazumped but has no problem doing it to her sister.

Clark laughs at the joke, pausing to chide Bria with a 'Don't do that to your sister' before laughing again.

This is the calm after the storm. The police turned up within half an hour of the ambulance leaving – I'm guessing they stepped to it because one of their own (Dunstan) was involved. The forensic team dusted down our corridor, took a sample of the smudge of blood and then left almost as quickly as they arrived. They seemed to believe me when I said she hadn't gone anywhere beyond the front door mat. The uniformed

officers who arrived with them spoke to me briefly, and because I'd interacted with Priscilla before she collapsed in the street, they said detectives
would come back tomorrow to speak to me properly.

I didn't mention the diary to them because I wasn't sure what I was
going to do with it yet. And if more officers were coming back tomorrow, then there was no need to hand it over just yet.

Not until I'd had a chance to have a proper look at it, anyway.

I needed time to have a proper look. Have a proper check.

In this serenity after the earlier incident, I constantly look at my
husband and think: *I have no idea who you are and what you're capable of.*

I keep thinking this as we finish dinner, as the girls finish off homework, as they go through their bedtime routines. I have no idea who he
is and what he is capable of. If the Year Of Our Lord 2020 taught me
anything, though, it is just this: that you have no idea who anyone is
and what they're capable of.

Moments after I read his name along with her name, I heard his
heavy tread on the stairs so I had stuffed the book – unsanitised – into
the kitchen drawer nearest to where I was standing, shoving it under
the neatly folded stack of tea towels – I was going to have to wash all
of them and clean out that drawer later. The second Clark went to collect the girls and the police forensic people and officers had gone, I'd
moved it to my office. I did not want anyone finding it before I got a
chance to check *why* my husband's name was in there with *hers*.

And now with the book burning such a big hole where it is hidden,
I am going through the motions of getting everyone ready for bed, with
the thought that I have no idea what Clark is capable of thumping
through my mind.

The thing of it is, Clark is trustworthy and open. I have utter faith that he would tell me if there were anything going on. I truly believe that. Like me, he can't abide lying. It's the very worst thing. We've drummed it into the children, we've lived by it ourselves. We do everything we can to uphold honesty in this house.

We are honest and we are true.

So if we're so honest and true and anti-lying, why is his name in that book? And not just on its own, but with *her* name.

Lilly

47 Acacia Villas

1 June 2021, Brighton

This is the worst time in the world to be alone.

I had no idea what the police were going to say to me and I'd been trembling when I showed them into the living room. I sort of braced myself, running through the things I could say, how I'd explain things, who I would call if they took me in.

As we all sat down, my heart was pounding so hard it hurt, and the blood was rushing so forcefully in my head I couldn't hear properly. I had to strain to listen as they asked me where I was just after two p.m. My voice was stuttery and quiet as I explained that I'd probably been on my way home from work in London to go to a meeting in Brighton. And then they explained why they were asking: Priscilla Calvert who lives at number 21 had been attacked in or outside her house and she was pretty much at death's door.

That had been a body blow of shock and I'd stared at them, not knowing what to say. My mind was racing as the creeping fear of knowing I was more involved in this than I could tell the two officers in front of me climbed like wild ivy all over me. I kept wanting to ask: what did she say? Did she tell people her secrets before she was taken into hospital?

I told the officers I was shocked. I told them I didn't know anything more. I told them I would contact them if I thought of anything else relating to this case. I told them I hoped they found who did this thing to a woman I barely knew. And then I showed them out, noticing for the first time other officers going door to door on my street, being let in to various houses.

Since they left, I've downed two more large glasses of fizz to steady my nerves. Are my nerves steadied? No. Are they just that little bit less shaky? No. Has drinking ever made me feel steady? Also no. But I'm not going to stop now.

I pick up my mobile, call up his number.

> Can you come over? I'm scared about being here on my own.
> Please come over. Please? x

I don't usually message at this time, not when it's likely his wife will be around. And this text isn't like the ones I usually send, which are careful and modulated, innocuous to everyone who doesn't know. But I have to establish a timeline, a pattern of behaviour that makes everyone think that I really don't know what happened to Priscilla. *Why* it happened to her. What she knew that would bring all of this about. Playing the innocent via text is a good start, even if it could get him into trouble.

I notice it's eight p.m., so I hit send on the message without rereading it and go to the kitchen to grab my iPad.

As I log on, the 'video call' box is already flashing up and I click the green 'accept' button. Her beautiful face fills the screen almost straight away. I can't help but grin when I see her. Her brown, black and gold ringlets are gathered up into a high, messy ponytail, her huge brown eyes are dancing with laughter, while her full lips are pursed as they suck on a lollipop. *Bad for your teeth, bad for your blood sugar levels, bad for having a conversation.* Three things that immediately come to mind. *And don't get me started with the mascara, eyeliner and tinted lipgloss.*

'Hi, Baby Girl,' I say to her as she settles back on her bed. The latest Beyoncé album is pumping out somewhere in her room and she doesn't bother to turn it down.

She removes the red lollipop from her mouth momentarily. '*Non sono un bambino,*' she replies, and starts to suck on her sweet again.

'In English, please, sweetheart, you know my Italian is shaky.'

'OK. Mum, I'm not a baby. Stop calling me "Baby Girl". I'm fifteen.'

'I know you are, sweetheart. But you'll always be a baby to me. And you're nearly fifteen.'

She rolls her eyes and the music in the background gets louder, if that's possible.

'Tell me about your day, baby—' I say. 'Sorry, sorry, sorry. Tell me about your day, "Big Girl".'

She sticks her tongue out and rolls her eyes before she starts to chat. And I settle back with my refilled glass of fizz.

As I listen to my daughter talk, my eyes keep straying to the business card the police officers left for me to contact them if I thought of anything else *and* to my mobile phone sitting silently on the table, telling me loud and clear that he's ignoring me.

Bryony

24 Acacia Villas

1 June 2021, Brighton

How dare she! I know that's what Grayson is thinking right now. *How dare she!*

That chat with the police officers didn't quite go to plan and Grayson is furious. So furious that he doesn't even speak – he just jerks his head in the direction of the stairs, telling me he needs to speak to me in our bedroom. Urgently.

He follows me closely up the carpeted stairs to make sure I don't try to go back down to clear away the dinner things, which would be me trying to escape the consequences of my actions.

Earlier . . .

'Did you see anything, Mrs Hinter?' the lead police officer asked once they were installed on the slightly less comfy leather sofa in the living room.

'No,' I replied. 'I have been in most of the day, but I have been in the greenhouse a lot of the time, preparing for sowing various plants and vegetables. When I was in the house, I was in my sewing room with headphones on. The first time I noticed anything was when I went to meet my daughter from school so we could go shopping together. I saw the ambulance leaving and a couple of my neighbours standing out on the street. But I was a little late so I didn't stop. An attack, you say? How awful.'

I could almost hear Grayson grinding his teeth and straining not to apologise to them because he thought I was babbling on, adding irrelevant detail, embarrassing him by being myself.

'And you, Mr Hinter? Did you see or hear anything that might be able to help us with our enquiries?'

'Unfortunately not,' he replied. 'As you may be aware, I am in charge of Westlann Charitable Trust? We have won Independent Charity of the Year five years in a row?' Neither of the officers responded to that, because I'm sure they didn't know and didn't care. They literally wanted an answer to their question. 'My duties as Chief Executive Officer keep me very busy,' he stated. 'I was at the office all morning and afternoon.'

'No, you weren't,' I interjected. The three other people in the room looked at me with varying levels of surprise. Grayson was obviously the most taken aback – because he had no clue how I knew and why on *Earth* I was telling the police officers.

I sat straight-backed in my seat and looked at the others. 'I called the Trust around midday because I wanted to check something with you, and your secretary told me that you had left for the day. I thought, understandably, that you were headed home so I went back to working in the greenhouse. When a couple of hours had passed and you didn't materialise, I called again. I mean, I didn't bother trying your mobile, we all know it's never on, so I called the Trust again to double-check that you had indeed left for the day. And they confirmed that you had left, saying you were going to work at home. Imagine my surprise when you didn't return home until your usual time of six thirty. I mean, by that point I had tried your mobile a few times, but as always, it was either off or you didn't answer.'

Saying all that, it sounded a little like I wanted to incriminate Grayson. And I knew what would happen the second the officers left.

At the top of the stairs, Grayson clears his throat so I know not to even think about heading for the solitude – *privacy* – of my sewing room until he is done with me. I'm sure my shoulders visibly droop as I turn towards the now foreboding antique oak wood rectangle of our bedroom door.

'Where *were* you this afternoon?' the police officer who recovered first from my revelation asked. They were both now completely focused on Grayson, and their eyes were reassessing him, questioning his honesty and integrity. All thanks to me.

'This is a bit of a misunderstanding,' he began. I could see he was thinking fast, trying to work out what he could say without revealing all. 'I had a meeting that wasn't strictly Westlann Trust business, but would undoubtedly benefit the charity's dependents. I am always looking for ways to improve the lives of those the charity helps. They deserve the best, after all. The meeting overran a fraction and I had to find somewhere quiet to complete my work that I had set aside for the afternoon. Time and CEO work wait for no man, after all.' He added a smile and a small, inoffensive chuckle at the end to show them he was telling the truth.

'Where were you exactly, sir? We'd like to check. Just to be as thorough as we possibly can. I'm sure you can understand that.'

He'd had to tell them; he'd had to give the Club's name, the address and the names of people to talk to. He gave up this information goodnaturedly, but I could see he was furious. Absolutely raging.

It did not help that both police officers then looked at me as though asking if he was telling the truth and if I would offer up any more helpful nuggets. *No, no, I've done enough*, I thought with a smile. *More than enough.*

Grayson uses the flat of his hand to completely shut the bedroom door, making sure it seals me in and won't accidentally pop open.

I am halfway across our bedroom. It is comfortable in here, cosy, with the hospital corners on our neatly made king-size bed, and marble fireplace with twin wardrobes on either side of it. The matching bedside lights have grand, brass-cast stands with white shades that I keep immaculately dust-free. The carpet doesn't quite have sink-in-toes depth but it is luxurious underfoot.

I turn to face him and Grayson is mid swing before I realise what he is doing. When the back of his hand connects with my cheek, he looks almost as shocked as I am. I can feel my eyes are saucer-wide with surprise, both hands flying up to where he has made contact. He's never done that before; he's never hit me! Never even threatened to.

Tears spring into my eyes from the shock of it and the pain of it. How could he? Just like that. He doesn't even look that angry. If anything, he looks . . . pleased with himself.

I take a wary step back but there is nowhere else I can go in here. The only way out of this room is behind him. I'm trapped. The air becomes thick with fast-approaching violence and he has a look in his eye that I have not seen before. I am suddenly scared. Very, very scared.

Grayson reaches for his belt buckle.

And I am not scared any more, *I am terrified.*

Rae

11 Acacia Villas

1 June 2021, Brighton

'Mum, I'm not sure I feel safe,' Mella says to me during the suddenly very long goodnight.

Since officially going to bed forty minutes ago and this moment, we have had five toilet visits, eight requests for a drink of water, nine cuddles and now, one conversation starter that is pretty full-on.

I indicate to my ten-year-old, wrapped up in a grey blanket, to avoid the boxes of samples that need to be sent out or written about littering my office floor, and to come closer, around to my side of the desk. When she arrives, I immediately envelop her in a hug and pull her towards my body so she can partially sit on my lap. Her sister is well asleep – Bria has a habit of falling fast asleep the moment the light is out.

Mella has Welly, her pink, super-soft bunny, under her blanket with her and her small hands are clinging tightly on to it. The two have always been inseparable since Mella was two.

'Why don't you feel safe?' I ask. I snuggle my face into the crook of her neck, holding her as close as I can. I want her to feel safe, that's what all of this has always been about, our family feeling safe.

'The police were outside when we came home earlier. There's that police tape outside the house up the road. Something bad happened, didn't it? Do we have to move again?'

'Yes, something bad happened, but it's nothing to do with us, not really. And no, we don't have to move again.' I am saying that with my fingers crossed in my head and my toes crossed in my shoes. I am making statements designed to allow my daughter to sleep but which might not be true. We may need to move again, we may not. I suspect I'll find out in the coming days, especially if I dare to dive into the diary's pages.

'Good, because I do not want to move again.'

'Neither do I.' *But that doesn't mean we won't*, I complete in my head. 'Although, my babiest of babies, I need you to go to bed. I have work to do and you have sleep to sleep.'

Mella's five neat rows of canerows going from the front of her forehead to the nape of her neck are secured under her pink Kente-design bonnet. She is my pink child, she loves everything pink and sparkly and has a whole host of dolls she spends time dressing and styling. Bria is my wonder child, she loves everything, full stop. She can find the positive in almost any situation and will go out of her way to make you feel better if you're feeling down.

Mella accepts that she has come to the end of the bedtime stall, and dramatically throws her blanket across her body, before she sweeps off to her shared bedroom. My office door has only just shut when it opens again. *You are really pushing it tonight, little girl*, I think as I focus on the door again, but Clark enters instead, ready for bed with his chest bare and wearing his grey joggers.

'Don't work tonight,' he says quietly. 'You've had a huge shock and it must have reminded you of what happened in London. Don't sit here on your own working tonight, come to bed and let me cuddle you up.'

I would love it. I would absolutely love it, but what have you been up to with her? Have you been cuddling her up? I can't even contemplate that without feeling sick, without wanting to actually, physically throw up. 'I've got too much to do. I missed so much earlier because of what happened. I need to catch up now.'

My husband moves into the room and because of his size and height, he seems to take up quite a bit of the available space. I love that about him. I'm not exactly thin – not like her – and I like being with someone who makes me feel normal sized. He too navigates the boxes and papers I've dumped on the floor until he has reached the safe harbour of my desk. 'Please,' he says. 'I don't want you to get yourself into a state like last time. Come to bed. I'll put something on the TV that I don't want to get sucked into but I will, and then we can fall asleep to it.'

'No, I—'

'You can get up in the middle of the night and go back to work, but come now. Please. *Please.*'

He needs cuddling up, too, I realise. Just like Mella had drawn out bedtime and then goodnight time until she could ask if things were going to be all right, Clark has been 'up' and normal all evening and now he needs to let go a little, soften and allow his worries to surface.

I look at the document in front of me, hit the save button then shut my laptop and put the big desktop computer on sleep. Then I get up and go to join my husband in getting ready for bed – even though it feels like I have a dozen reasons not to want him anywhere near me.

Bryony

24 Acacia Villas

He's never done that before. He's been a bit rough, and he's gone a little further than agreed sometimes, but he's always restrained himself, he's always stopped before it gets to . . .

I can't really move right now.

He's asleep, snoring beside me like nothing untoward has occurred, like he didn't do *that*, even though the initial smack was horrific enough

Historically, he's never been physically vicious – not even to the children. He has never really laid a hand on them in anger or in discipline. And whenever it looks like his temper is tipping over, I employ my distraction techniques: I apologise to him, talk to him, take him to bed and do whatever it is that he wants, even if it turns my stomach. I have rarely just stood by while he verbally brutalised them, while he has physically roughed them up, I have always done what I can to protect them.

Sometimes it hasn't been possible to stop him from grabbing them or shaking them, and I have to comfort them afterwards, but he is – overall – a good father, a good provider. He never *beat* the children exactly and he has never laid a hand on me until tonight. And because it has only been tonight, I have been able to look back and say that him being a good father and good provider outweighs him being a rotten husband. Especially since his cruelty and moods could be managed, which means there hasn't been enough to justify disrupting the children's lives by leaving.

I never thought he'd do something like this, though. That he would *deliberately* hurt me. That he *would*— My mind comes away from that thought, from the flashback that the thought ignites.

Grayson had obviously lied to the police again. After he was forced to say something about where he really was, he must have carried on lying, because his anger and rage wouldn't have been so explosive if not driven by the fear of getting caught out. He had obviously been up to something.

And that is why I spoke up. *Why does he have the capacity and privilege of doing whatever he wants, whenever he wants and I don't?* I can usually keep such thoughts under wraps, but tonight I couldn't, I simply couldn't.

The children must have heard what he did. I tried to be quiet, to not let what was happening come screaming out of my mouth, but I couldn't all the time. That they possibly bore aural witness to the activities in our bedroom turns my stomach. I do not want that for them. That is just a miserable, frightening experience. This is the sort of thing I worry about. And it is only me who worries. Obviously Grayson doesn't. The way he is now peacefully asleep turns my stomach even more.

Swallowing the whimper of agony that wants to escape my lips because every part of me feels bruised and tenderised, I roll over in bed. Try to curl up into a ball, try to comfort myself.

I want to cry. I want this to be different. My life was not meant to be like this. Nothing was meant to be like this.

I have to get out.

Part 2

Priscilla

21 Acacia Villas
Diary Excerpt

12 March 2021

Every day, *every* day right in the middle of the path outside my gate, I am confronted with a dark-brown swirl that reminds me why I have never fancied eating a Walnut Whip.

If I don't go out one day, the following day I will be confronted with two of them. So whoever it is has their dog stop and empty its bowels right next to the original item, and their owner does nothing but allow the dog to walk away and do it again the next day.

It makes me sad, them treating their dog like that. Picking up after your dog is part of taking care of them. If you don't pick up after them, you don't care about your pet or your neighbourhood, it's as simple as that. Dog poo is disgusting. Right outside my door is even more disgusting.

After thinking it through, I've decided to set up a camera from an upstairs window, trained on that particular area so I can hopefully record the person who allows their dog to do this thing. And I am compiling this dossier, too, as evidence that I can present to the council's animal protection arm. They will have no problem, then, when it comes to removing that animal from the culprit's care. As I stated: if you don't pick up after your dog, you don't care about them and you shouldn't have them.

I need this diary to be full of facts – not conjecture and fancy; it needs to be clinical and impartial, so when whoever needs to see it to solve the dog problem reads it, they'll know it is nothing personal against the perpetrator. It is simply a presentation of facts of neglect.

Despite how it might seem, I do actually like most of the people who live on Acacia Villas. I don't speak to any of them very often but there are so many who are decent people; kind-hearted and honest. The other day, Liesha McNamara from number 42 brought me a box of fairy cakes – she does that because sometimes a person comes into her mind so she makes them cakes. And over the last few months, Natalie Evans from number 53 has been leaving pot plants on everyone's doorstep to cheer them up. And Rae Whickman from number 11 *never* complains when the flowers from my secret admirer – so secret even I don't know who it is – are sent to her address and she has to bring them over.

Oh dear, this is getting personal. I suppose I wanted it noted that Acacia Villas is mostly filled with nice people. But there are others who are not so nice. Any one of them could be behind this, or they may not. I am going to find out either way.

All things going well, I should get to the bottom of this by the end of this month at the very, very latest.

Rae

11 Acacia Villas

2006, London

Clark and I stood outside Chancery Lane tube station, the bustle of a London evening whirling around us as we got ready to say goodbye. We'd known each other from being in the same group of friends at the college and we'd all kind of kept in touch afterwards.

I'd moved to London, he'd moved to London, and the kind of keeping in touch continued until he moved to Brighton. After that, things got busy and seemed to drift and we never really caught up.

Chancery Lane sounded like it should be a quiet area, but it wasn't. It was a constant fizz of people passing through, entering the station and being whisked away to other places. Very few people did what Clark and I were doing – standing just to the right of the entrance, chatting and trying to eke out as many minutes and seconds as we could from our time together.

We'd bumped into each other at lunchtime on Oxford Street and we'd made arrangements to meet for a quick drink after work near where he was based. That had segued easily and pleasantly into dinner with more drinks. We'd shared all the news about our mutual friends and had talked about . . . I couldn't think what we'd talked about. But we had talked. And the things we'd discussed had chimed with me, making me feel like I wasn't the only person who saw the world in the way I did.

I'd never thought of Clark like this – as someone who was dancing on the same wavelength as me. I'd never really felt the need to dissect or ponder the things he said; nor to notice how close he stood to me or how he looked at me. Mainly because he'd been going out with a mutual friend for all of the time we were in college and all of the time after college, including now.

'Well, I guess this is where I leave you,' he eventually said when we couldn't string out the night any longer. 'I'm going to jump on the bus to Victoria to catch my train back to Brighton.'

'Wouldn't it be quicker to get the Tube to Oxford Circus from here and then change for Victoria on the, you know, Victoria line?' I replied.

His smile was close-mouthed but definitely sheepish. 'I can't,' he said with a shake of his head. He had a nicely shaped head. He'd taken to cutting his once wild Afro to a smooth and slick grade one all over that showed off the wonderful contours of his head. Why I thought of that, I didn't know. It wasn't like I was given to thinking about people's heads – or even noticing them beyond the fact that most people I interacted with had one.

'Why can't you?' I asked, confused. 'Are you banned from the Underground system or something?'

He moved closer, making me painfully aware of how my body had started to want him to be close enough for it to be inappropriate. Well, here was a thing I hadn't expected. His partner was one of the nicest people, and look what was going through my mind.

Obviously, he was thinking the same because he moved closer still, until we had definitely pushed the boundaries of whatever level of friendship we allegedly had.

'If I get on the Tube with you, I'll spend the whole journey wondering . . .' Without warning, he reached out and stroked his thumb across my cheek. He moved even closer, his body pressed deliciously, *dangerously* against mine. I couldn't tear my gaze away from his, even if I wanted to. And I did not want to. *Ever.* 'I want to go home with you. I want to spend the night talking to you and doing a lot of other *tings* with you . . . and well, we can't do this . . . *I* can't . . . So I need to walk away right now and go reassess my relationship.'

I did an unsubtle double-take. 'Reassess your relationship because you've had a nice night out with someone you haven't seen in years?'

'You know it's not just that.'

'Do I?' I responded.

'All right . . . I haven't spoken to her in a month,' he confessed.

'What? Why?' How come this was just coming out now? We'd spent the last few hours catching each other up on our lives and our friends' lives and this hadn't come up when he'd told me that she had a job in Turin and he had reordered his working life so he worked from home Monday and Friday, meaning he could fly to Turin on Thursday night and get the flight home Monday morning. 'I thought you were—'

'I haven't been in a month. First I had a meeting I couldn't move, then she had a meeting that took her out of town and then . . . I don't know . . . It's just become not speaking.'

'Why didn't you mention any of this before? We've spent the whole night talking and you didn't bring it up.'

'Not exactly something I like to talk or even think about.'

'So what do you think is going on?'

'The end, I guess,' he said miserably. 'The beginning of the end or the middle or just the end. Who knows? But I need to sort that out, stop avoiding it.'

He pressed his lips against my cheek. 'Until I talk to her, I'm going to be stuck in this limbo of wanting to kiss you very, very much but not wanting to be a cheat.'

I hoped he didn't feel the way my heart pretty much leapt in my chest when his lips grazed across my skin; I did not want him to know that this conversation was making me unbearably sick and pleasantly shaky at the same time. 'How do you know I don't have a boyfriend?' I asked.

'I don't. And I didn't ask because I didn't want to know. I can only deal with one thing at a time when it comes to things like this. If I hang on to how I feel about you, I can sort out my relationship. And then I can deal with whether or not you're interested in me, and whether or not you're single.'

'So you're basically using me,' I was trying to lighten things up because a beautiful evening had suddenly become heavy and burdened.

Instead of making him laugh, it made him slip his arm around me and tug me right up against his body. 'Don't say things like that,' he murmured against my ear. 'That only makes it harder to walk away.'

A thrill went through me. It wouldn't be the worst thing in the world if we stayed like this a bit longer; it wouldn't be anything approaching terrible if I just turned my head and his lips found mine . . .

I felt like I was drunk, that alcohol was pumping these reckless thoughts through my brain, but I wasn't. It was a work night and I had a long journey home ahead of me – those two things meant I'd had one drink and several cranberry and sodas . . . I should not be feeling anything at all like I was.

Clark's words resonated properly for the first time: *We can't do this.* Cheating wasn't something either of us were about. Especially when she was such a nice person. She did not deserve this type of betrayal.

Even thinking about it was bad enough, doing this was terrible, so anything else would be unforgiveable. And we would always have started from doing something shady.

We can't do this.

Even though he smelt so good, and felt so delicious pressed up against my body . . . I could literally . . .

We can't do this.

I stepped back out of his hold and forced a smile on my face. 'All right, then. So, we agree to never see each other again,' I laughed, as the lights of London continued to pulsate around us, an ever-moving backdrop to this story we'd found ourselves in.

This was a form of torture – I'd been single forever because I could not stir up any type of interest in anyone, and now I was interested in someone who wasn't available. Or maybe that was it. Maybe I was doing this because I couldn't have him. Ultimately, though, it didn't matter – because we couldn't do this.

'No, we probably shouldn't see each other again until I've—' He stopped talking, smiled that sweet smile of his.

'Let's talk whenever, yeah?' I said.

He nodded and we both took a step away from each other to say goodbye. No embellishments, just the word 'goodbye' before we parted ways. Anything else, *anything* else would lead somewhere we couldn't go.

1 June 2021, Brighton

We can't do this.

I remember so vividly how it felt to accept that I had to walk away and allow Clark to walk away so we wouldn't cheat.

We can't do this.

I wonder how many times Clark said that to Lilly before he kissed her, held her, took her to bed.

We can't do this.

Oh the irony: I wouldn't cheat with him when he was dating Lilly, only for him, fifteen years later, to cheat on me with her now that we live around the corner from her.

We can't do this.

Yeah, I should've just screwed him and had done with it.

Rae

11 Acacia Villas

2 June 2021, Brighton

I have spent most of the night flat on my back obsessing about Clark and Lilly.

I haven't been near my office to try to catch up on work I missed yesterday or to go through Priscilla's diary. Mainly because it could be as bad as or even worse than I fear it might be. What if this is confirmation of what I've always thought: do I not even come close to measuring up when he compares his life with Lilly to his life with me?

What if I am simply not 'up there' with Lilly for him?

Because, deep down, deep, deep down, that's how it's always felt. After that night in London, I didn't hear from him for six months. Obviously, once the touchpaper of him and me had been lit, once the thought was in my mind, I couldn't stop thinking about him. It was like an obsession that bloomed from nowhere. I had literally only thought of him briefly and occasionally in the three or four years before we bumped into each other, and then after that night all I could do was think about him, obsess about him, try to fathom out the ending of our particular story.

I cringe now when I think about it. How I regressed to my teenage behaviour – but instead of obsessing about television stars, I was consumed by thoughts of a real-life man. Suddenly, the world had no other men, no other potential boyfriends or partners or husbands than Clark Whickman. I wince even more when I think of my work colleagues' faces – fixed with rictus smiles – as I regaled them with yet *another* Clark and me story from way back when. I had taken a huge dose of the Clark Whickman drug and nothing could control me until the phone rang and his voice on the other end asked if I fancied a drink.

When I heard his voice, I'd paused because I was wondering if he was really speaking to me or if my fantasies had finally completely taken over. Clark misinterpreted it as me still being mired in the middle of 'We Can't Do This' avenue.

'It's over with Lilly and me. For real. She came and got her stuff. We're still legally sorting out dividing assets, but even that is nearly over.'

For some reason, what he said reminded me of the time I'd slept with a lawyer who was, on the one hand, overly positive about life and what people could achieve, but then on the other, was properly bitter about people, and relationships in particular. The sex had been all right, I suppose, but having an insight into the way his competing world views lived in his mind and played out in his life meant I did not want to see him again. In any shape or form.

'You're not interested any more, are you?' Clark said quietly. 'I left it too long.'

'It's not that,' I replied. 'I'm just thinking about lawyers and what an odd job they do when dividing up other people's assets.'

Clark had been silent for a moment or two. 'Have you always been this random?' he asked.

'Yes. What of it?'

'Nothing, nothing. I quite like it. So, meeting up?'

'You were with Lilly a long time . . .' I began.

'Yes, I know.'

'Are you sure you should be jumping into something else so soon?'

'No. But I can't stop thinking about you. I want to talk to you all the time, I want to be with you all the time . . . I . . . I can't stop thinking about you.'

Looking back, I probably should have been more cautious. Should not have let him dismiss over fifteen years with someone as 'yes, I know', should not have jumped in with both feet because he said he couldn't stop thinking about me, twice. I should have interrogated him and myself a bit more.

Because who knows how much he still felt for her? It wasn't him who ended it – she did. She'd stopped contacting him and answering calls and texts to him for that month to see if she could survive without him. And she could. So it had limped on for a few weeks after that dinner with me. Which meant, while I was doing my sad teenager act and mooning over him, he was . . . well, he was still in a relationship and hadn't even come close to finishing it.

And that's always been there at the back of my mind – if she'd wanted to try again, he maybe, just maybe, would have gone for it because breaking up wasn't something he *chose* to do.

Yes, we eventually got married and had our children, bought our house and got on with our lives, and if she featured, she was a sliver of an atom right at the back of my mind. Then London got too dangerous and we had to move quickly. Clark suggested Brighton and I thought nothing of it. Literally nothing. It was, like, the coolest place on Earth, as far as I was concerned. I loved visiting him there before he moved to London to be with me, so no worries. No stress. Not even when the house in our budget and for our 'as soon as is humanly possible' timescale was around the corner from where he'd lived before with Lilly, and *on the same street* as Lilly. It didn't matter, honestly. Why would it? I had bigger things on my mind so I didn't care. We moved. And I could finally breathe. The claustrophobia of my last few months in London relaxed its chokehold, and I could unclench. I could stop the fretting and fearing and just enjoy life again.

All good. All fine.

Until I saw in a neighbour's diary that my husband has been visiting his ex-girlfriend at her house. She wasn't just any girlfriend, either. She was *THE GIRLFRIEND*; his first love.

You can never compete with someone's first love.

I'm not sure what to do.

If I ask him and he lies to me, that's pretty much game over. If I read the diary and it says he's been having an affair with her, then that's pretty much game over, too.

And if I pretend I don't know anything, it's pretty much game over because I can't talk to my husband. This is why I don't know what to do with the diary. It seems like 'game over' whatever I do.

So, which type of 'game over' do I want?

Which type of 'game over' do I choose?

Actually, what do I do?

Bryony

24 Acacia Villas

2 June 2021, Brighton

He was smug.

He hurt me, he scared the children from the look on their faces as they studiously avoided either of our gazes and concentrated on cereal and toast and juice, and Grayson was smug. Almost triumphant and revelling in what he had got away with.

My mobile phone, sitting on the table in front of me, bleeps with an incoming message.

> Morning, darling. How are you? Did you speak to the rozzers last night? So sad about Priscilla. Hope she makes it. You coming over to work later? What time can I expect you? A x

Alana, who lives around the corner on Acacia Villas, speaks exactly how she texts – like her posh side is at war with her cockney side. Over the last few months we have created something great together, really special. She has helped respark life for me. And I can't let her see me like this. The bruising from where he struck me is coming out, a mottling of dark green and blue that sits along my jawline and cheek, and my neck is a garland of red from where he choked so hard at some

67

points I thought I was going to die. No one outside of this house, least of all a friend like Alana, can see me like this. My cover-up has been good, make-up and a scarf hiding the evidence, but I'm sure you can see it in my eyes, in the way I shape words: I am hurt.

I have made excuses for the excesses in Grayson's behaviour over the years and now I am hurt.

Morning! Can't today, sorry. Hopefully tomorrow, or the day after. Sorry not to see you, really looking forward to a proper catch up. B X

I always try to be upbeat with Alana because she's that kind of friend who is naturally positive and happy. It's never forced, always natural and almost always exactly what I need. But not today. Today I need to regroup, stare into space and possibly start to process what happened.

Oh, boo, miss you. See you soon. Kisses.

I place my phone back on the table and check the time: 8:05 a.m.

My husband will be installed behind his big charity worker desk by now. Ready for the day, that smug smile he wore this morning as I served breakfast will still be on his lips. He'll be jolly and upbeat because he hurt me beyond anything approaching normal and he got away with it. He thought he was the big man last night. Forcing himself on me, choking me, hurting me. And he got away with it.

Or so he thinks. In another ten minutes or so, he'll discover how much he *hasn't* got away with it when the massive amount of laxative I put in the extra-strong coffee I made him this morning hits.

68

He is going to spend a lot of the next few hours sitting on the toilet. Maybe, just maybe, when he is sitting there with his stomach painfully cramping, he'll have the time to think, really think, about how what he did to me last night was wrong.

Lilly

47 Acacia Villas

January 1992, Leeds

'What would you do to show how much you love me?' I asked him.

Times like these were so rare. Our halls were virtually silent, only a radio throwing out thin, tinny sounds filtered down to us. The night outside was that comforting black where you felt you could reach out and wrap its velvety form around you and luxuriate in the darkness.

He was easing himself in and out of me, his face contorting in pleasure with every stroke.

'I don't know,' he said breathlessly. 'Anything. Anything.'

'Would you lie for me?'

He hesitated. For some people, I realised, lying was a big thing. Maybe I shouldn't have gone for such a huge thing. Maybe I should have started with would you miss church for me, because he went every week. Every week and didn't care who knew it. But that would be a big thing, too, I suppose. What would be a little thing that would have him immediately saying yes? I didn't know. I preferred big gestures – they were open and they were clear. Someone doing little things for you was all well and good, but you always knew where you stood with someone when they were willing to do the big stuff.

'I would do anything to make you happy,' he said, pushing deep into my body.

I gasped loudly and threw my head back, momentarily silenced by a wave of pleasure. When those seconds passed, I asked again: 'Then would you lie for me?'

Clark kissed me deeply to avoid answering and sped up his rhythm a little to distract me. And it worked for a few seconds because I'd never had sex like this before. Nothing so *complete*. Sex is sex is sex. You can get sex and you can have sex and it's usually as good as you want it to be. But sex when you feel something for a person, when you *love* a person, is different. It's whole. Complete.

And I was craving more. That was what I was like. I wanted more of a good thing. Always. Show me someone who said they didn't want that when things were going well, and I will show you a card-carrying liar. And people lied all the time. So why wouldn't he say he would do it for me when he knew it would make me happy?

I took his head and stared into his eyes. I could see the sweat glistening on his skin, I could feel his hot breath on my cheeks, but I held him far enough away to hear him speak.

'Would you lie for me?' I asked again. I had to know if his love was big enough to do that. He'd said 'I love you' for the first time after six weeks. I'd felt it, he'd said it, and we were so going to be together for ever. Of course we were. So why wouldn't he say it?

'I love you,' he murmured and tried to start moving again. But I stopped him. Why wouldn't he say it? He could always say no, but I had to have an answer either way – I had to know what he would do for me. Was lying such a big deal, especially when the person who was asking you to do it was someone you professed to love? How could I be sure he loved me when he wouldn't do this one thing for me? It wasn't as if I had asked him to actually do it, just say if he *would* do it.

'Lilly,' he breathed, closing his eyes as if in pain. '*Lilly.*'

'If you can't answer . . .' I said, starting to shift away because what were we doing if he wasn't all in? What was the point?

'Yes,' Clark whispered so quietly it was almost as though he didn't want to hear himself say it.

I took his head in my hands again, looked deep into his eyes. I had to see into him while he answered this question. 'Would you lie for me?'

'Yes,' he whispered again, even quieter this time.

But that didn't matter. He'd said it, he'd admitted it – he would lie for me. That was all I wanted – *needed* – to hear.

As if to take away the taste of what he'd said, he kissed me – long and deep, even as his desire wilted.

We kissed and kissed and kissed. I didn't even care that the love-making was over. He'd said he would lie for me and that was all I needed right then.

I'd leave it for a bit before I found out if he would kill for me.

2 June 2021, Brighton

I technically shouldn't be on this part of the road. My journey to the station is quicker the other way out of Acacia Villas, but I had to come this way to see for myself. To see where she ended up.

On the spot where Priscilla was found, there is a police appeal board. They are asking for witnesses to a very serious incident (assault) that took place at this spot yesterday.

I read the words over and over, not feeling them register in any real way. Since I spoke to the police last night, and I didn't get a reply to my text, I haven't been able to stop thinking about making Clark say he would lie for me.

I just wanted someone – him – to prove to me that he loved me so much he would do anything for me. I needed, back then, to know that he would move the world, if he had to, to be with me.

It was a terrible thing to do, but at the time, I didn't know any better. I had no real concept of what forcing someone to go against their personal code would do to a person or yourself.

What about the world is honest and real if you can browbeat a good person into saying they'd do something terrible? Because lying is terrible, I know that. I've always known that, but I understand it now, too.

I'm sure that's Priscilla's blood I can see staining the pavement – a Jackson Pollock-type splatter stain reminder that we all bleed the same.

I remember Rae saying how trite that sounded when I'd said that one time in college. I think we were all in the common room but I have no idea why I'd said it. But this was the response it inspired.

'What sort of "I wanna deny racism" bollocks is that?' she'd continued with a laugh. ' "We all bleed the same." Like people don't know that. Like saying that is going to change what's in their hearts and minds.' I'd gone bright red at what she was saying, especially when the idea was correct and the sentiment was also correct, but when they are conclusively dismissed by someone who should know what they are talking about, it smarted and it humiliated. Even though I'd never repeated that in front of anyone like Rae ever again, I *still* thought it sounded cool, and look . . . *look* . . . there on the pavement – wasn't it true? Priscilla's blood and my blood were the same colour. We could not be more different if you tried. And I also knew Rae's blood was the same as mine.

I told the police I hadn't seen Priscilla at around two o'clock because I hadn't. I'd been so blinded by rage that I didn't really see her. The shape of her was there, but her detail was lost in the angry words we were flinging around. And that wasn't around two o'clock, either. It was earlier.

I'm coming round to the idea that maybe I should go to the police first. Tell them about the row and the way Priscilla had pushed herself into my life, because that should steer them away from the other stuff. That was the risk I wasn't really sure I should take, though. Telling them that might not throw them off the scent of the bigger fish I have hidden, it might inspire them to investigate me completely.

My feet should be moving, walking me to the station to jump on a train to whisk me away to London. Instead, I stand here, frozen and fixated on the forbidden part of my road.

Lilly

47 Acacia Villas

March 1992, Leeds

'No, Lilly, I won't,' he said, his anger a blowtorch on every word.

I'd asked him. It'd taken several more weeks, many, many more moments in bed treating him to the best sex either of us had ever had (he told me this more than once), before I had whispered it in the dark. And he'd stopped. Just like that, like he hadn't been enjoying making love to me. He stopped, he withdrew from me and then lay back on the bed. And he said to me: 'No.' Without even the slightest hesitation, without the tiniest hint of doubt.

'You already made me say I'd lie for you,' the blowtorch continued to char his words. 'But I am not going to kill for you. Not even theoretically. I won't kill for you, Lilly. I won't kill for anyone.'

He ran his hands over his head, and even in the dark I could see and feel his frustration.

'I don't know what this is, Lilly, but you need to stop. It's not normal to ask people questions like that. It's not normal to want people to lie for you or to kill for you. Just stop this. I am telling you this now, without a single shred of doubt: I will not kill for you.'

You sound so sure, I wanted to say but didn't because he was already so angry. *You sound so sure but how do you* know?

How can any of us know what we may do, who we may kill, until we might actually have to do it?

2 *June 2021, Brighton*

There she is. Rae.

My dithering has meant I've been here for so long that she is rounding the corner, all dressed up in workout clothes, probably returning from the school run. She does most of the morning ones, Clark does the afternoon. I probably shouldn't know that, but I do.

I notice the exact moment she clocks me and I can see her misstep as she slows down. It's totally obvious, even from a distance, that she's ready to turn around and walk very fast in the opposite direction. But seeing as she lives on this part of the road and I do not, she's decided to carry on. I should move on, but now she's seen me I can't – it'd be impolite.

I sometimes wish either of us had it in us to go the full Alexis and Krystle Carrington from classic *Dynasty* and start scrapping in the street like two well-dressed, well-groomed grown women who should know better. I even wish we'd just completely blank each other by refusing to acknowledge the other one exists on those rare occasions we do see each other.

But no, neither of us are ever going to do either of those things because we are polite. We have both been well brought up and wouldn't dream of any impropriety. And also, we have a history. We have a history of proper, genuine friendship that goes well beyond this. It's a shame, a real shame that she married the man I love. And that I want him back so desperately, I'm willing to do almost anything – hurt almost anyone – to make it happen.

August 1998, Brighton

'I don't get it, Rae, I really don't,' I cooed. 'You're, like, so nice, why can't you get a boyfriend?'

'Who knows?' she replied and knocked back a large glass of Tia Maria and Coke. Awful stuff as far as I was concerned – far too sweet and sickly for me – but Rae was always downing it like it was expensive champagne or something. 'And, to be fair, who cares?'

'Well, you do, otherwise you wouldn't keep going on ridiculous dates.'

'That's the thing, Lilly, I'm not actually sure why I do it. I'll go out clubbing and I'll think, oh, is this the night I'm going to meet "The One"? And sometimes I pull and he's nice and it's all good and then I won't sleep with them so he doesn't want to know. Or I do sleep with them and they don't want to know. And I feel sad, proper gutted sometimes, but then it kind of goes away really quickly. It's almost like my mind expects me to want to meet someone and then when it doesn't happen I kind of realise that I didn't want to meet anyone.' She paused, thought for a few moments as her honesty settled over us. 'That could very well be cognitive dissonance, though – my mind telling me I didn't want to meet anyone so I can make sense of not meeting anyone. Who knows?'

Rae was pretty, not conventionally, but still pretty. And I knew there were men out there who liked dark girls, it was just rotten luck on her part that she hadn't met any of them yet.

'It'll happen for you one day,' I said to her firmly. I nudged Clark, who was watching football on the screen in the corner of the pub and could not care less what we were talking about. 'Don't you think?'

He tore his eyes away from the television screen to focus on me and then Rae, who was watching him also. 'Yes, absolutely,' he said.

Useless. He wasn't even listening and Rae and I both knew it.

Gina, one of the other people in our college group, had once said that I should be careful of Rae and Clark. *'Two dark people who are around each other all the time can't help themselves,'* she said as a word to the wise. *'Be careful or they'll be at it behind your back and then at it in front of your face. Just watch out for him showing any type of interest in her or showing no interest in her. That's when it's happening.'*

I told Gina to play back what she'd said: if he acts not interested then he fancies her and if he acts interested he fancies her. What sort of stupid logic was that? And besides, Clark had been nothing but attentive and focused on me since the night I threw myself at him in the students' union back in 1992. He didn't look at other women, comment on other women's bodies – nicely or disparagingly – whether in real life or on-screen. In fact, he chatted away to women like he chatted to men. My man was loyal and I think that bothered some people like Gina. Sometimes she would say things and I would wonder why she was trying to poke holes in a rock-solid relationship like mine. Because she couldn't get a man? Because she didn't believe in true love? Because there was a 'y' in the name of the day? Who knows, but I had to work hard not to let what she said niggle at me because I did not want to believe that Clark and Rae were anything other than friends.

2 June 2021, Brighton

If I'm not imagining it, Rae is slowing down as she approaches the crime scene area. Maybe hoping I'll head off to the station before she reaches the spot.

Rae is still pretty. Now that I have a biracial daughter and I've heard some of the things people say to her, I cringe at how I used to negate

Rae's beauty. 'Not conventionally pretty', 'some men like dark girls', as though she should be grateful for that. I wasn't being malicious when I thought those things – or even sometimes when I said those things – but it was still appalling. I often cringe at how casually racist I was. In my head there was only one type of beauty, and anyone who wasn't that kind of 'beautiful' wasn't 'beautiful' at all, as far as I was unconsciously concerned – they were pretty with caveats; in other words, they were 'attractive for a non-white female archetype'. Just cringe.

If I hadn't been so patronising in my head about Rae's looks or, rather, limitations to them, I probably would have been a bit more aware of something going on when Clark told me he'd bumped into her in the street. But I'd thought nothing of it. I didn't even think to ask if she was finally seeing someone or was still perpetually, painfully single.

If I had acknowledged Rae was pretty, hell, *beautiful*, and could rival me in the looks stakes, and also had the advantage of being right there with him instead of a plane ride away, I might have paid attention to what was happening right in front of my face.

Because, even now, I constantly wonder *when* they actually got together; even now it eats me up inside a little that my life could have been so different if I'd known early on that he was falling for Rae.

Priscilla

21 Acacia Villas
Diary Excerpt

18 March 2021

I missed it <u>again</u>.

The camera missed it. So frustrating!

Or maybe I missed it in the playback. Because I forgot that when you set up a camera, you have to watch the whole thing back unless you have a vague idea of when the thing happened so you can skip to it.

Watching out for who has been allowing their dog to violate my doorstep has thrown up some unexpected benefits, though. I say benefits, but what I mean is I'm learning some really interesting things about my neighbourhood.

I've moved the furniture around upstairs so I can sit in the bay window that runs the full length of the front of the house and look both ways down Acacia Villas. Having the house on the corner plot means I can see very far down both directions of the street, as well as diagonally opposite if I go to the other side of my desk. I can't believe this is the first time I've utilised this view. And got to hear what happens on this side of my street.

Like the drama that unfolded earlier on. I didn't see how it started, but I heard it because of the raised voices. And my goodness were those voices loud!

'You are always putting your bins in front of my house,' Bette from number 14 informed Bert from number 16.

'Only if your house is where my house is,' Bert shot back.

'I think you'll find that the boundary line is this, right here.' And she's gesticulating wildly while kicking at his green wheelie bin. And then he's kicking it back.

'You're mad. You're a mad cat woman!' he shouted at her.

'If I was Catwoman I would have trussed your stupid ass up somewhere Batman would never find you ages ago!' she shouted back.

'Oh, very funny.'

'I thought so.'

'Well you would, wouldn't you?'

On and on they went like that, scoring points off each other. It was strangely comforting, how wonderfully banal it was. After the high anxiety the world has been living under for the last fifteen months or so, it feels like this is the normal I've been craving. Arguing about bins? Calling someone a mad cat woman? Bringing Batman into it? It was strangely beautiful. The kind of pettiness that isn't often played out in the real world any more.

Lilly

47 Acacia Villas

2007, Turin

'What's the problem, Clark? I thought we were friends? Why won't you come and visit me? Why do you keep making excuses? I need to see you.'

We'd been apart for nearly a year and I'd realised that I'd made a mistake. I couldn't do it on my own and I wanted him back. I *needed* him back. I'd been asking him to visit me in various ways from the subtle to the blatant and he always had a reason why it wouldn't be possible. I'd come to the end of my tether and was just asking him outright.

'It wouldn't be right . . . I'm with Rae,' he confessed.

'Rae?' I replied, even though my tongue had suddenly gone numb and I couldn't feel most of my face. I was shocked that he was seeing someone else, but completely knocked sideways that it was: 'Raelynn, our friend?'

'Yes,' he said.

'When did that happen?' I replied.

'Erm . . . three months ago.'

Three months ago was well after he and I were over, but really? Was I really meant to believe he'd been avoiding coming to see me after we were together fifteen years for a three-month-old relationship? He wouldn't, unless . . . 'Is it serious?'

'Yes,' he replied without hesitation.

'How can it be? Has it really only been three months?' I didn't believe it.

'I had feelings for her before that.'

'You were cheating on me,' I said, the words like twice-burnt ash in my mouth.

'No. No, I wouldn't do that. When I came to see you the time before our final time together, I told you that I'd bumped into her, remember? I went for a drink with her and I realised how I felt so I walked away. We didn't do anything. It was the catalyst I needed to see if you and I had anything left to salvage. And you didn't think so. I wanted to do anything I could to keep us together but you said no. Even after we finished I left it months before I got in touch with her.'

'I don't believe you,' I told him.

'I'm not like you,' he said quietly. 'I wouldn't do what you did.'

'What?' I asked, suddenly scared because what he was saying sounded like he knew.

'I know that guy – the Swedish economist – was your boyfriend from not long after you got to Italy. Even though you were doing it to me, I didn't do it to you.'

I froze. How could he know that? How could he know that and not say anything? 'What are you talking about?'

'I know you think I'm this big dumb lump and have no clue. But it was so obvious you were sleeping with someone else. I thought it wouldn't last, but I was wrong.'

I moistened my lips, ready to explain the inexplicable, when he

said, 'It doesn't matter, does it? You're with someone, I'm with someone, we can just move on.'

Move on? Did he really say that? Move on, just like that? Like our
years and years and years together meant nothing? 'Clark . . . I—'

'I love her,' he interrupted, because he knew what I was going to
say, what I'd confess. 'It hasn't been long, but I love her and my future
is with her.'

What about me? I asked inside as tears flooded up to my eyes.

'You're happy with your guy, aren't you?' he pressed on.

'Erm . . . erm . . . yeah.'

'That's good. We're both happy, we've both moved on.'

'Yes, yes, I guess we have,' I said. And that was it.

2 *June 2021, Brighton*

After that conversation, we all kept vaguely in touch. I sent a gift when
they got married but (thankfully) work kept me away. I made the appropriate noises and sent cards when they had their children, and everything
was all so civilised.

I'd been outraged, though, properly raging when he messaged to say
they were moving into the same road as me. He hadn't even asked if I
was all right with it, just said they'd be there within a few weeks and that
was that. I didn't want to see them. Yes, they'd been together more than
ten years, but my feelings for him hadn't changed. How could they?
When I compared every man I met to Clark? When no man ever treated
me with the love, respect, kindness, caring and adulation that Clark had,
obviously I wasn't going to get over him; my feelings would be stuck on
the Clark part of the cycle indefinitely. So why were they rushing to push
their relationship in my face?

I felt, too, that he was trying to recreate his life with me with her; as if he wanted that life again, just with someone new because he thought I was not available to him in that way.

The way Acacia Villas is set out – a three-sided oblong with a through road about three quarters of the way down – you can go for years without seeing anyone. And we have, in the main, gone years without seeing each other. I certainly haven't seen Rae very much. But when I do see her or when Clark mentions her, I get that familiar niggle in the middle of my chest. Did she take him before he was free? Did she make a move on him while he was mine?

'Hi,' I say as she arrives in front of me.

'Hi,' she replies.

Awkwardness.

'So this is a thing, huh?' I say to her.

'Yes. Still feels very surreal. One minute she was standing there, the next she was being rushed off to hospital.'

I have that exact same feeling as I had when Clark told me about dating Rae – my tongue is numb and I can't feel my face. 'You were with her before it happened?'

'Yes. And I held her hand until the ambulance arrived.' Rae's expression is . . . I can't read it, not properly. Does she know something?

'How was she?' I ask, meaning: *did Priscilla say something to you? Did she tell you about Clark and me like she was threatening to?*

'I was a bit nervous when I saw you standing there, Lilly,' she says, not answering my question. 'But now I'm glad I've run into you because there's something I've wanted to say to you for a long time.'

I take a step back, ready to run. No one says that in a positive way, do they? I've said it a few times and it's almost always preceded me firing someone/encouraging them to resign or letting someone know I'll be taking them to court for something they've done.

'What's that then?' I ask cautiously.

'He didn't cheat on you with me. Clark, that is.'

What? Can she read my mind or something? Or do my eyes always shoot narrowed daggers of suspicion at her? 'What makes you say that?'

'Because it's awkward. It's been awkward for years. We used to be mates and the three of us used to get on really well. And it's a shame we haven't really got that back when you're literally around the corner. I think that's because you think that we cheated on you. I've wanted to say that so many times.

'We bumped into each other on the street, went for a drink and he wouldn't get on the same train as me because he was tempted. And I didn't hear from him again until six months after you finished with him and even then we didn't get together until a couple of months after that. We didn't do anything while you were together.'

'OK,' I say. 'Thank you for telling me that. I suppose I'd better get on to work.'

She nods and fishes her keys out of her pocket. 'Have a good day,' she says, and walks towards her house.

'You, too,' I reply.

There's only one reason why Rae would say that to me at this moment in time: that bitch Priscilla told her something.

Rae

11 Acacia Villas

2 June 2021, Brighton

While I was taking the girls to school, Clark has showered, made himself an espresso and got the dogs food. He's also tidied away the breakfast things, washed up and got a lasagne out of the freezer for dinner tonight.

All normal. Everything normal. I don't feel bad that I didn't twig something was going on with him and Lilly . . . how could I when he is – and has been – this normal? Some women might be able to say that 'he started taking an interest in family life, which is why – looking back – I should have known that he was cheating', or 'he stopped being interested in us, which is why I should have known', but nothing from Clark. He's always been engaged with family life, he's always done sixty per cent in some areas and forty per cent in others. We've always had a balance that makes our relationship work.

I listen to him moving around upstairs, probably tidying away my clothes that he'd taken out of the dryer and which I haven't managed to put away because they always seem perfectly fine on the bedroom armchair. I know that sort of thing irritates him, but he deals with it by simply putting stuff away. Or maybe he deals with it by going up the road to screw his ex. I don't even know any more.

My attention keeps straying to where I stashed the diary. I want to read it so much, but then, I don't. What good is it going to do me? I mean, I've read at most five complete pages and it's already got me doubting the fabric of the universe. Well, my universe, where Clark, one of the nicest people ever, can have a whole life based on deception without me having a clue.

I'm standing by the kitchen table, not even contemplating work. I've usually got the kettle on by now while I go through my daily ritual of should I work in my office or should I work at the kitchen table. The kitchen table is in the room with the snacks and the good telly box with all the stuff I've taped on. In my office is the good office chair – excellent for my back – but my telly up there is old and the telly box doesn't have even half as many shows recorded on it.

Upstairs is where I'm most productive, downstairs is where I'm most comfortable. Obviously upstairs wins most of the time but today I don't even care enough to start that conversation with myself. Today I care about very little.

That makes me feel bad, and I automatically glance over at Okra and Yam, snuggled up in my favourite pashmina – claimed as their own a while ago – on their dog sofa. 'I care about you two, obviously,' I say to my sleeping dogs.

'Upstairs or downstairs?' Clark asks as he enters the kitchen.

I nearly jump out of my skin, even though I listened to every one of his steps as they descended and walked along the corridor.

'Whoa, what's that all about?' Clark asks, alarmed at my reaction.

I shake my head, rub my fingers into my cheeks. 'Stressed. On edge. I keep replaying yesterday over and over.'

'Oh, yeah, sorry, I forgot. How are you?'

'Who knows?' I ask. I lean on the table to keep myself upright.

Clark and I work because we are different; we balance each

other – messy and neat; serious and silly; calm and passionate. We both have these traits and others in different concentrations, they come out at the right time and we just work without too much effort. But do we?

Have I been fooling myself?

'Shall I stay home today?' he says. 'The dogs don't look ready to go anywhere. I'll stay home, we can write off today and—'

'No,' I interrupt. I can think of nothing worse than holding in this secret with him around. I need the house to myself so I can go through that book, find out what Priscilla knew, see how bad the damage is. And find out who might have bludgeoned her, of course. 'No, I just want to chill out before I do some work.'

'If you're sure?'

I nod.

'All right,' he says.

'I saw Lilly earlier,' I say.

'Oh, right.' He moves over to where the leads and harnesses are kept and starts to gather things together. This causes the girls to lift their heads, the sound of the lead promising them their escape from the house. 'How is she?' He sounds nonchalant, casual. And I want to scream at him that I know.

'She seemed all right, I don't know. I told her that we didn't cheat on her.'

He stops reaching for Okra and straightens up to face me. 'You did what?'

'I needed her to know that we didn't cheat on her. I'm not sure if you've ever told her that, but now I have. It felt like the right thing to do.'

'You felt it was the right thing to do to put her on notice? Why?'

When he says that, he means, I've put her on notice of intention to cause her distress at some point in the future. Probably the near future.

'Who said I've put her on notice?'

'You and every single person you've ever said something vaguely similar to.'

I suppose he does know me. 'I just needed her to know in case she's been wondering all these years. It's the sort of thing that eats away at a person. Makes them do unwise things.'

'What sort of unwise things?' he asks. He is staring directly at me and it feels like he is challenging me. He wants me to declare what I mean so we can talk about it. Argue about it, probably. Split up over it, maybe.

I shake my head, shrug my shoulders. 'I don't know. It's one of those things that depends on who you are and what your backstory is, isn't it?'

'I suppose so,' my husband replies. He returns to looking at our dogs, who are yapping and barking and dancing around his feet, desperate to get their leads on and get going.

There it is.

That is the moment I will be able to point to in the future and say: 'There, that's when I should have known he was cheating'. Because Clark always challenges me on things, always wants me to be open about whatever it is that is bothering me. And for me to have said that to Lilly, something must have been bothering me. He doesn't seem to care to get to the bottom of it as usual, though.

In the early days of us, I was so paranoid about him and Lilly. They had been the shiny, golden couple at college. Everything about them clicked. They didn't disgust you by how they were together, and they weren't the type, either, who would go out of their way to downplay their relationship so us single types weren't intimidated. They were the gold standard in how to be together without pissing off or patronising everyone around you.

I thought Clark and I had that: a relationship that worked. Not perfect, not without arguments and petty resentments, but one that worked. And he, instead, has been looking backwards, *going* backwards to her. What the hell have I been doing all this time?

'It's not going to be like London, you know?' Clark says as he clips the D ring on Yam's lead into place on her harness. 'We're not going to have to do a moonlight flit again. We're safe here.'

'Yeah, sure,' I reply.

'I mean it, Rae – we're safe here. We're going to continue being safe here.'

He is trying to speak it into existence. If he says it often enough, firmly enough, maybe the universe will listen and we'll be all right.

'I'll see you later,' I reply and leave the room before I ask him if he really believes that, or if he's just saying it so he won't have to stop fucking his ex around the corner?

Priscilla

21 Acacia Villas
Diary Excerpt

24 March 2021

Every weekday morning, the Whickman girls from number 11 walk past my house on the way to school with either their mother or their father. Usually their mother because their father goes to collect them after he's dropped the dogs home in the afternoon.

And every weekday morning, the youngest Whickman girl, Mella, tells a joke. I'm not sure if it's one joke, or several, but it usually begins and ends in the cone of sound by my house. Today's is:

Why did the hedgehog cross the road?
To go and see his flatmate!

For some reason it made me laugh way too long and way too loud. That's why I had to write it down – just so I can remember something silly that made me laugh.

Bryony

24 Acacia Villas

2 June 2021, Brighton

When she was younger, Tilly used to love to draw. She was a talented thing, I thought. No, the pictures weren't perfect or even mostly accurate depictions of what she was trying to display on the page, but there was always something warm about them. They used to make you smile for the way they captured the essence of what she was trying to draw. It was almost as if she could see the object or person's heart, and that was what she was so beautifully presenting. She drew Grayson as grey. I wasn't ever quite convinced it was because of his name, but more to do with the fact she could see what was inside him. There were the occasional flashes of red, probably a child's reference to the flares of temper he had, but in the main, Grayson was grey inside. Stagnant, uninteresting, lifeless.

She would draw Trent and me as full-colour people – obviously how she saw us. And we would all be smiling, happy together or apart, but Grayson – always grey. Always.

Eventually, he noticed. Initially, he must have just brushed it off as something of a quirk, but finally he decided Tilly needed to stop any artistic endeavours. One of the unnecessary fripperies of academic life, he called it; something that took time and effort away from her homework so had to be ceased.

When she defiantly continued to draw after finishing her homework to the best of her ability, he began a campaign of destruction. He would criticise everything she produced. No matter how abstract or realistic, no matter how sketched or detailed, he would find something to pick apart about it. 'That line is completely out of perspective and is at odds with the rest of the "picture".' 'That composition is far inferior to the one you could have created had you centred the dog.' 'I've never seen a heart shaped like that, have you?'

When she stopped drawing in his presence, he would go through her room, hunt it down, present her with it at the dinner table: 'I'm not surprised you tried to hide these, they really are, at best, mediocre.' To drive the message home, quite literally, he would bring printout artwork from schoolchildren displayed online as an example for Tilly to fail to live up to. 'This, *this* is the type of standard I would have expected you to have reached by now, Tilly. I must say I find it disappointing that you are nowhere near that level.' 'How I would have enjoyed finding something of this calibre among your efforts, Tilly, so I could proudly display it in my office for all to see. As the situation stands, I don't think I could allow my important visitors to see anything you have "created".'

Of course, he eventually achieved his desired outcome: Tilly stopped drawing. She was ten and he had killed her dream.

I can hear his voice now, and every word is a brand of shame on my skin. I let him do that. I kept thinking that it would be all right. He would stop. He wouldn't keep on and on; if I just gently prodded him away from saying such things, nothing bad would come of it. He wasn't hitting her – not beyond the odd shake – so he wasn't really hurting her. I kept telling myself that I loved this man once, so he can't be all bad, not all monster. All we had to do was ride it out and he would find something else to focus on and Tilly could go back to drawing as she loved to do.

I am a terrible mother.

I throw Grayson's cup that I had been returning to the cupboard from the dishwasher – washing away any evidence of what I did – down into the sink. It bumps but doesn't break. I snatch it up and this time when I slam it down into the sink, it cracks, enough to cleave apart the words 'WORLD'S COOLEST BOSS', leaving them in two huge pieces.

I am a terrible mother.

That's what Priscilla said to me.

And she was right.

Rae

11 Acacia Villas

November 2019, Brighton

'It's Rae, isn't it?' the woman someone told me was called Priscilla asked.

She lived in the big house on the corner and she never really interacted with you if you said hello to her in the street. Most people were friendly around here, and I was on nodding terms with so many neighbours I passed on the way to and from taking the girls to school. But this woman, Priscilla, was stand-offish, and wouldn't engage. Fair play to her – I was a Londoner and I knew people mostly didn't speak to each other so I wasn't offended. I was surprised, though, that she knew my name and was speaking to me now.

'Yes, and you're Priscilla?'

'That's right.' She smiled. She was so classy and well turned out, I'd taken to calling her Poshie in my head. 'This is a thing, isn't it?'

She was talking about the Neighbour–2–Neighbour Watch meeting that we were both attending at 24 Acacia Villas. Hollie Stoltz, who lived at number 29, had been broken into the week before and we were all hugely unsettled. She'd been asleep in bed and they had got in through the patio doors, stolen her laptop and iPad, and any money they could find. They'd also taken her spare keys so they could – presumably – come back at a later date.

Hollie was on her way to standing for Parliament so almost everyone knew her around here.

'Yeah, we're all kind of freaked out in our house,' I said. 'Not at all what you want.'

'Really? You're freaked out? Didn't you move here from South East London? Isn't that like the crime capital of the Capital?'

What? I stopped moving the biscuit I had in my hand to my mouth. 'What did you just say?' I asked her.

'I'd imagine coming from where you do, you're no stranger to crime?'

'I'm sorry, what are you saying to me?'

She moved nearer and lowered her voice. 'It happens to the best of us, experiencing or witnessing a crime. The mother of the Sibfords from number 32 once saw a hit and run accident down near Five Ways.' She moved even closer and lowered her voice even more. 'She couldn't stop to help because she'd had one too many glasses of wine with her lunch.'

'What?' I said, squeezing up my face.

'Oh, I'm not gossiping as such. It all came out because the police spotted her number plate at the scene and tracked her down. Quite tight on her since they never caught the hit-and-run driver but she was done for drink driving.'

'That's horrible,' I said to her. And I didn't just mean what happened to the Sibford mother. What Priscilla was doing was horrible.

'Yeah, I know,' she replied. 'Crimes like that happen all the time. Like I said, you must know that coming from South London.'

'I guess,' I replied.

Priscilla smiled at me and then moved on to talk to someone else. To gossip about someone else, probably. Priscilla didn't come across as a nasty person, someone who viciously set about spreading rumours – it was more like she just couldn't help herself. She had so much information and whenever she spoke to you, she couldn't help dropping those nuggets into the conversation.

I didn't have time to worry about it right then, though, because the meeting was about to start and I had to concentrate on listening to how to better protect my home.

2 June 2021, Brighton

I make tea for the police officers who have come to see me about yesterday's 'incident' because I want to get them on side.

Not on side in the sense of being my new pals, but more that since they've arrived before I can have a proper look at the diary, I won't feel too bad about not giving it to them straight away if I'm nice to them. I'm pretty sure that, technically, I should tell them about it and hand it over, so being almost welcoming is the way forward right now.

Priscilla seemed to think that something in the diary was the reason why she'd been attacked, so it may be helpful for their enquiries. However, if I let them have it before I read it thoroughly, I may never find out exactly what my husband has been up to, who he is sleeping with. ('Sleeping with' sounds sedate, innocuous – not at all like what it is: an active choice to betray someone. But 'fucking' and 'screwing' sound so coarse, and not what I suspect Clark and Lilly are doing. I need a way to describe it without diminishing the intention part or cheapening its significance.)

But if I don't hand it over to the police so they can get a true overview of Priscilla's life and connections, then the attacker may well go unpunished.

'Thank you for taking the time to speak to us, Mrs Whickman,' the police officer with shiny black hair and dark-blue eyes says. He has a look about him, actually it's a way of looking at you that suggests he knows you're lying – or, in my case, that I'm hiding something. It's quite a skill to make people feel guilt without trying – probably something he's cultivated over a long period of time because his face looks pleasant enough even though he knows how to unsettle you.

The other police officer is rather unassuming with light-brown hair and the pale complexion of a person who has spent a lot of time indoors. She's probably the one who'll watch my reactions to what the other says. I've worked out that this is how they work: one destabilizes, the other watches.

Or maybe I'm reading too much into this and I'm not that important in the grand scheme of things. Maybe I'm painting myself a bigger role in this drama than necessary.

'As my colleagues explained yesterday, Mrs Priscilla Calvert was attacked yesterday; it looks like the attack happened in her home.'

I nod. 'OK.'

'This doesn't surprise you?' he asks.

'Well, no. She turned up at my house, as I told the officers yesterday, and said she'd been attacked. She didn't have a coat or bag or anything so I assumed it happened at home.'

'Right. And you didn't think to call the ambulance for . . .' he flicks through his notes '. . . eleven minutes. Can you tell us why?'

That rankles and causes a spike of worry. If I tell them about the book now, they'll wonder if I was busy attacking her and hiding the book before I decided to call the ambulance. Actually, they probably won't think that, but they *might*. And that's the thing that scares me: they might.

'As I tried to explain yesterday to the other copp— I mean, the other officers before they said someone would come back and speak to me today, it all happened so quickly. I was working upstairs, she turned up and it was a few minutes before I realised she'd been hit over the head . . . and I knew that because she said she'd been attacked and kind of pointed to her head,' I add speedily before they start down that road of questioning and where that might lead. 'It did take a few minutes to work out what she was saying and then she— but before that, she was swaying at the top of the stairs outside and I thought she was going to fall, so I kind of grabbed her here . . .' I show them by clamping my hand around my own bicep '. . . and pulled her in. So if you find hand prints around her arm, that was from me trying to stop her pitching backwards down the steps outside my house.'

'You knew how bad she was and you still didn't call an ambulance straight away. Why is that?'

'It wasn't like that at all. She kind of stood in the corridor burbling at me and I couldn't really understand her. So I said I'd make her a cup of tea and she collapsed against the wall. I said I was going to call an ambulance and went to the kitchen to get my phone. But then I found the kitchen phone was flat so I went to go upstairs to get my mobile and she was gone.'

'Gone?'

'Yes, gone. The door was wide open and she was gone. And I thought for a minute or two that I'd imagined it.'

Wrong thing to say. Totally wrong thing. Both their eyebrows arch upwards. 'Do you often imagine things like this?' one officer asks.

'Or have such detailed delusions?'

I lick my lips and check my breathing. Too fast. Just that bit too fast to sound plausible. 'No,' I say. *Sometimes*, I think. 'But it wasn't a delusion in the end, was it? She really did turn up at my door.'

'Yes, we've been wondering about that. Why your door in particular? Were you especially close to the victim?'

'No,' I reply with all the conviction of a woman hiding something. 'Not at all. I barely knew the woman.'

'That is odd,' the male officer says. 'Before she slipped into what doctors believe is a terminal coma, Ms Calvert was talking about you. She repeatedly said your name and said you knew her secr—'

Every single word dances icily down my spine. 'Did you say terminal coma? You think she's going to die?' I interrupt. 'From being hit over the head?'

The thought of that causes the ice to spread out from my spine and freeze every part of my body.

'There are other factors we're investigating right now that we believe have contributed to her condition.'

'Other factors such as what? Me not calling an ambulance straight away? That's what you're saying, isn't it? Because of me, Priscilla might die?'

'That's not what we're saying at all,' the police officer who hasn't said much so far chimes in. 'We are simply pursuing several lines of enquiry.'

One of them clearly being me and what my role is in all of this. I must be a suspect. Me, a suspect. The last twenty-four hours have been a real trip into how your life can change in an instant – and how all the other instants after that will keep the change going.

'Poor Priscilla,' I say quietly.

'Can you explain why she said you had her secrets?' the female police officer asks.

Can you just give me a minute to think? I want to say. I need to tell them, don't I? About the diary. Now that it's moved from assault to possible murder, I have to tell them about the diary. But if there's more stuff in there about Clark, won't that make him a suspect as someone who might want to attack her? And what about me? If I'm in there and I'm already a suspect, won't this throw even more shade on me?

Also, if the police go digging too deeply into our lives, what will they find? I mean, *really* find. There's the story of our lives that everyone knows and there's the one that had us packing up and leaving, and me not really caring I was moving into Lilly's territory.

'Mrs Whickman? Can you explain what she meant?'

'Not really.' I feel sick at the lie, the way it sounds coming out of my mouth. 'When she was rambling on, she said she knew what we'd all done.' Truth. 'I couldn't work out what she meant by that.' Another spike of nausea as I push the rotten words out of my mouth. 'But maybe that's what she meant when she said I had her secrets – that she'd told me that she knew what we'd all done?' Lie. Again. It's not as easy as it should be this lying thing. The girls know that lying about something you've done wrong is generally as bad as the actual thing you did wrong. But when you're sitting in your living room confronted with the police, and with finding out the veracity of your life, the truth as told to other people becomes fluid in a way that didn't seem conceivable before.

'Possibly,' the male police officer says. He doesn't believe me. But I don't think that's anything special to me – I get the impression he doesn't believe anyone . . . ever.

'Do you have any idea what secret she thought she knew about you? What you had done?'

I shake my head rather than speaking because I need to stop talking. Always the best way. Just stop talking. The less I talk, the less I can get myself into trouble. Even from here I can hear the siren's call of the diary from my office. Calling to me, telling me to reveal its existence. It's so loud, so compelling, I can't believe people up and down the street can't hear it, let alone the people who would be relying on the things in its pages to do their job.

'Is there anything else you can tell us, Mrs Whickman?' I'm always a little surprised when people call me that. It's been five years and yet I still have to remind myself that they're talking about and to me. I hadn't changed my surname until I had to. Until the girls had to drop the double-barrel (Manadacko-Whickman) bit and we all became Whickmans because it was simpler to erase my surname than to erase all trace of ourselves by, say, leaving the country. Because that was an option that none of us would have been happy exploring. Although after yesterday and today, it's an option that is gathering more appeal in my mind.

'Sorry?' I reply.

'Is there anything else you can tell us that might help us to find out what happened to Priscilla Calvert?'

Is there? I mean, really, is there? Do I honestly have that option of telling them about having the diary instead of finding out what my neighbours have been up to?

And aren't I more likely to understand what she's written than they are? They don't live around here, they won't understand the meanings and nuances of the things she might have observed and noted.

I'd be doing them a favour by going through it first, wouldn't I?

I can steer them in the right direction if I find anything.

This is actually for the best, keeping quiet for now. And it is for now. If there's anything there, I will tell the police.

Yes, this is for the best. This is the best way to help everyone.

'Is there anything else you can tell us about the attack on Ms Calvert? Anything at all?'

I look him right in the eye.

I shake my head.

I open my mouth.

I say: 'No.'

Because I am definitely going to find out what everyone has done.

Priscilla

21 Acacia Villas
Diary Excerpt

26 March 2021

I wonder what Bryony and Alana are up to? I can't find out. It's weird, they sell children's clothes on their website and that's it. Bryony makes them, Alana knits them and they sell them.

Nothing strange or hokey, but there is something going on. I know there is!! Alana's husband was a drug trafficker. I suspect things haven't changed that much now he's not here.

But there is literally no evidence of it. Usually there's something suss in bank accounts or tax returns, but nope. All of it is above board and straight down the line. My gut as a human being and private investigator tells me, though, that they are up to something and I have no clue what it might be.

That is frustrating. And . . . quite impressive that they've managed to keep it so hidden. I'll find out, honestly, I will. I just need a little bit more time.

Mella Whickman's joke today:

Why are bananas never lonely?

Because they hang around in bunches.

29 March

Lilly Masson from number 47. There's an enigma. Single woman. Like me. Lives in a big house on her own. Like me. Lived and worked abroad for a long time. A bit like me.

But she has a whole life abroad, still.

Watched her talking to Hollie Stoltz from number 29. Those two used to be thick as thieves. They'd have these really intense conversations and I'd sometimes wonder what they were about. Hollie Stoltz is not an enigma. From way back I always thought her one ambition in life was to become a corrupt politician. When she used to sit on the planning committee, I used to say a little prayer for all the decent people who were submitting planning applications because there was no rhyme or reason to what she and her colleagues rejected and put through.

Now she does something with Lilly and that gremlin Ralph Bieler from 28 and Dodgy as Hell Milburn from number 7. And let's not forget the great Grayson Hinter. For the most part, Hollie and Lilly stay away from each other nowadays and that makes me suspicious. You only do that if you don't want evidence of meet-ups and associations to be recorded and passed on to the police.

I wonder what they are really up to?

I think I'll have a quick look into it. Won't take long.

Mella Whickman's joke today:

Knock, knock
Who's there?
Boo!
Boo who?
Don't cry, it's only a joke.

31 March

High drama on Acacia Villas today!

Car tyres came screeching to a halt further round the road at number 43. It was an ultra-souped-up Mini. Out hops a woman with one shoe on, jogging bottoms and what looked like a kimono on top of a silky camisole top. I didn't need to be any closer to see that her red hair was wild. She'd barely slammed the Mini door shut behind her before she was running at the front door of number 39 and hammering away. Unfortunately, I was too far away to hear much, even though I immediately opened the window. As soon as a woman who looked pretty similar to the one braying on the door came out, she started screaming: 'How could you!' And, 'YOU . . . KNEW . . . MARRIED!' I wished she would keep her volume up! So frustrating for the rest of us who weren't near enough to hear properly.

I remember the man, Dennis Fisher, moved into the ground-floor flat about a year ago? Maybe less time? He has his children, Ritchie and Hannah, over every other weekend and one night during the week. I've always wondered if those sorts of arrangements are good for the children? Going from pillar to post several times a week. But what would I know? I don't have children, I don't know how they work.

Mella Whickman's joke today:

What do you call a fake Bolognese?
An impasta!

6 April

It's raining this morning and yet at ten o'clock the door to number 9 opened and out came Fennie, all dressed up for a run. I've seen her out running in full-on gales before so this shouldn't shock me.

She's one of those women that I could have been if I'd met a nice man and had children with him. Her two children – Rocco and Rohan – are really polite, and I've never seen them have a public meltdown. I do wonder what I would be like if I had someone like her Pete in my life? If I'd had my own Rocco and Rohan?

Would I go out running in the rain because I was training for a marathon? (She's done Brighton and, her social media suggests, she's thinking about doing London so she can meet up with a friend who lives down here who runs marathons, too.) Would I cheerily wave to other neighbours even though the rain was starting to come down a bit harder?

Before the last lockdown, I would have said no way. But I've started to get a bit claustrophobic if I don't leave the house every day. So, maybe I would.

One thing I've noticed? Writing this and paying much more real-world attention – as opposed to virtual attention – to those who live round here is starting to trigger some existential introspection. I wonder how my life would have played out if I'd done a little more of that?

Probably wouldn't have married husband number three, if I had.

Fennie came back after forty minutes and both of the kids were waiting there with towels for her. I imagined Pete was running a shower and putting on the kettle.

Since writing this diary, I seem to mention it a lot – not having children. Is part of me regretting it now? Most of me isn't. Most of me is perfectly happy with the choices I've made. But I do get a bit envious of the nice families. But that envy is only as far as wanting that life, not actually creating it for myself. That ship sailed a long time ago.

12 April

Have to come clean. I have a new interlude. And, oh my goodness. Oh my goodness!!

Mr Afternoon Delight.

It started a few weeks ago and I haven't written about it because I wasn't sure if anything was going to come of it. I wasn't sure if anything should come of it. He spends a bit of time here, helping me to decorate, doing odd jobs, and then doing me like I've never been done before.

That is so crude, but sometimes, what we do is nothing short of crude. Sometimes it's beautiful and tender and I want to cry afterwards. Other times I think he's going to ruin me for any other man with how he fucks me.

I can't even describe how he makes me feel. Even when he's not here I can't get enough of him. I am constantly playing with myself and thinking about him.

Not sure at all where it's going but I'm going to have to start thinking about giving him a key so he can come and go as he pleases . . . Oh, terrible pun.

I can't believe how much I'm enjoying this thing with Mr Afternoon Delight.

Didn't think I would experience this again after three failed marriages. But here I am, getting loved up in all the right ways. Will not be marrying this one, though. Oh no. Have honestly learnt <u>that</u> lesson.

Bryony

24 Acacia Villas

2 June 2021, Brighton

When Grayson walks into the dining room where the three of us are eating dinner, he is pale – as grey as Tilly used to draw him.

He hasn't put down his briefcase or taken off his coat or washed his hands, but he has taken off his shoes. That is something, I suppose.

He looks utterly drained – a day on the toilet will do that to you – but still has enough about him to look completely outraged at the fact we didn't wait for him to return before we sat down to dinner.

'Oh, hello there,' I say with a smile brighter than the Sun and a voice cheerier than a rainbow. 'How was your day?'

Grayson blinks a couple of times in disbelief. Probably at my tone as much as the fact we didn't wait for him to be there for us to continue our lives. Both children had come down with alarmed frowns on their faces when I called them for dinner, but they hadn't questioned it. They probably thought Grayson was working late and had issued an order to allow us to eat before he arrived home. Usually we wait. No matter how late he is – sometimes he doesn't appear until nine o' clock – we wait for him before we really do anything including having dinner.

'Are you OK?' I ask him. 'You look a bit . . . peaky.'

He's confused. My tone, my actions, they are not what he expects after he so resoundingly put me in my place last night, especially after I was reserved and obviously in physical and emotional pain this morning.

'Well, don't just stand there, go and get washed up, and come and join us. I wasn't sure what time you would be back, so I started dinner. It's your favourite – gammon stew with the haricot beans you love so much. It's keeping warm in the oven. Grab yourself a bowlful on your way back. Oh, and cut yourself a few slices of bread, too, we've demolished this basket.'

Without looking at them, I can tell the children are open-mouthed and wide-eyed. This is the sort of conversation that would never normally happen in our house, this is the type of interaction that would more likely end like last night did.

Grayson is stumped, too. He hasn't had to do anything like serve his own food or cut his own bread in many, many years, and he just stands there looking at me. Shocked. Confused. He hasn't got to outrage yet, but I'm sure it's coming. With someone like Grayson, outrage and anger are always there, always coming.

Yesterday was the moment when everything changed. I'm not only talking about Grayson brutalising me. I'm talking about what happened to Priscilla.

My life, and my children's lives, were on a very specific trajectory before. I had no way out, but this has shown me the way. There are several possibilities as to what I can do next that I didn't dare to contemplate before. Now I know I can not only think about them, I can explore them, too.

Part 3

Priscilla

21 Acacia Villas
Diary Excerpt

16 April 2021

Something odd and quite upsetting happened today.

I saw Clark Whickman (from number 11) going into Lilly Masson's place at number 47. It was eight o'clock at night and he looked very uncomfortable. Suspicious.

It's upsetting because I wouldn't have had him down as a cheater.

He seems dedicated to Rae and his girls. And those dogs. It's not them who do their business outside my house. I've seen him stop and pick up their mess in dark-green poo bags. Eco-friendly. Everything about their lives seems to be eco-friendly, wholesome.

I remember when they first moved in, Rae was so friendly to everyone and I used to be in awe of it. She didn't impose, she just had a way of approaching people and getting them to engage with her. I can't talk to people – I decided to keep myself to myself a long time ago because it was easier that way. I know people often dislike me for it, think I'm rude, superior and stand-offish. But I am who I am.

I am surprised at Clark, though.

After what happened with them in London, I'd have thought he'd be more careful. And I certainly would not expect him to cheat with a woman on his street.

I know Lilly would cheat in a heartbeat. That is the tenet at the core of who she is – she thinks the world owes her the life she wants. Oh, she's more than willing to work for it, and work quite hard, too. But when it comes to things you cannot influence – like whether someone loves you – she will do anything she can to get what she wants.

She clearly wants Clark Whickman. I can't help wondering what he's playing at, though? Someone like her takes any interest – good or bad – as a signal that you want them. It is virtually impossible to extract yourself from someone like that.

I need to look into Clark's past again. Find out if he's done this before.

I feel sorry for Rae if he is a cheater. Once a cheater, always a cheater. I didn't believe that until husband number three cheated on me with the woman husband number two had left me for. (That is what you get when you try to be grown-up and civilised about relationships.)

I hate that my life is like a soap opera. That's another one of the reasons why I have trouble speaking to people. Humiliation and heart-ache will do that to a person. I became that way to cope, and I stayed that way because it was easier.

I'll be so disappointed if Clark is cheating. So disappointed.

19 April

Had the briefest of chats with Katy Markey today. She lives at number 10 with her partner, Jack, her daughter, Evie, her best friend, Max, and her mother, Carol. Katy used to put on shows before the world shut down theatres, and I was asking her if she might go back to putting on adult shows.

I quite fancy being in a show. When I was much younger I used to be a dancer. I was also good at acting. I remember being heartbroken when I was turned down for a performing arts scholarship at a school not too dissimilar to the one Grayson Hinter used to teach at before he began working at the charity. Last laugh was on them, though, when one of the parents in the audience for the school's show spotted me and asked me to sign on with her agency. She got me some really good work – television ads and some modelling work. The school were gutted because they couldn't claim to have done anything to help my career because I didn't have a scholarship. Still smile when I think of that.

Katy is hoping to put a show on early next year and says she'll keep me in mind. Can't wait.

Always nice to see Katy and her brood out, they make such a nice family, I think we're very lucky to have so many nice families in our community.

Writing this diary is, I think, bringing me out of my shell. So much for clinical and impartial! I like being like this, though.

21 April

Clark Whickman was at Lilly's house again today. Not for very long, and he had the dogs with him, but he was still there. I can't find evidence of him cheating before, but he did have a relationship with Lilly in the past so that breaks down a lot of the barriers about going with someone you don't know. I mean, really, why though? Rae seems a perfectly nice woman, so why would he destroy his life like this? Why?

23 April

One of the things I liked from when we were all at home was seeing families together. They would come out of their houses together, most of the time only half ready, one person driving the need to get out before everyone else clogged up the streets and the seafront.

I used to love to watch Lauren Sparks and her family come out of their house, the little one, Raffael, rocking and stumbling along in his Minions T-shirt, determined to walk, even though his little legs couldn't carry him that far. Nico, who was around eight, dressed as Darth Vader, would be bringing up the rear with his dad, Paolo. I would watch them and smile because they were like a family I could be a part of as well.

I'm sitting here watching them now: Raffael is so much bigger, around three now so he can wander much further, and Nico is still working the Darth Vader look. They are heading off on a walk together and it brings a lump to my throat, how happy they are. How complete they seem.

Maybe it's wanting children that are nice and that other people have done all the hard bits with that I'm craving here. Because I think I'm getting broody. Now there's a thing. Me, broody. Ha. It's definitely watching families like the Sparks-Sadnys having a calm moment and basking in the glow of those tranquil waves. That's what it is.

26 April

I'm on the horns of a dilemma.

What if you know something about someone? Something terrible. I mean, truly awful, and this person is married with children and this involves the children. It involves a lot of things, but the main thing is the children.

Do you tell the wife?

Do I tell the wife her husband is involved with the scum of the universe because he is pretty much scum of the universe too, or do I go straight to the police?

Part of me wants to rush in, snatch up the children and move them in with me. I would care for them. I would keep them safe. There is space here, there is love here.

I think what I need to do is gather up my evidence – everything that I have found – and put it all together. Then I can get her over, sit her down and show her what I have. Once she sees everything, once she realises that there is evidence to back up any worries she might have, we should be able to go to the police. She's bound to have heard or seen something that wasn't quite right, but because she doesn't know what I know, she won't have been able to make proper sense of it. When I show her what I have, she'll understand. And, like I say, I will go to the police with her. I'll even tell them how I came about the information if it helps. But I wouldn't make her do it on her own. She could even take another friend if she wanted. It doesn't really matter, does it? As long as she knows there's support for her.

Clark was with Lilly today. It's making me increasingly agitated. Especially when Rae brings over the flowers delivered to her address by mistake with such grace. (We've worked out that someone has probably accidentally hit the '1' on the keyboard instead of the '2' so the flowers for me go to her house.) I have to be stand-offish so I don't get sucked into her orbit and end up telling her to get rid of her cheating husband. Because I am so close to doing that. So close.

28 April

Bin day. And OH MY Gs!

It was like *Battle Royale* out there. Bert (number 16) kicked Bette's (number 14) bin because now the tables have turned and her bin was encroaching on his space. He gave it a full-on ninja kick, like he was taking down a league of assassins. Bette must have been sitting at her window watching because the second the bin skidded across the pavement she came flying out of the house, screaming, rolling pin in hand ready to brain him. I certainly wasn't expecting it and I sat at my desk, hands paused mid-air over my keyboard, watching. He just stood there staring at her as she came at him. I think he thought she would slow down then stop, but no, she kept running and when she got close enough, she swung at him.

Then he realised she wasn't messing about so he turned and ran. He's shouting at her to stop and could they talk about this. She's chasing him down the road swinging her rolling pin, going, 'Oh, *now* he wants to talk. *Now* he wants to talk. Go on Bert Boy, talk!' in between screaming obscenities.

Think I can safely say I have never seen anything like that in my life.

Not sure how we're all supposed to act on bin day from now on. Because . . . wow!

Mella Whickman's joke today:

What do you call a guitar-playing cow?
A Moo-sician!

Part 4

Bryony

24 Acacia Villas

4 May 2021, Brighton

'Hello, Priscilla,' I said as I approached her house on my way home from a brisk walk. I hadn't quite got back the urge to run like I used to in the first lockdown when it was the only thing we were allowed to do outdoors; when I had to get out of the house at least once a day in case I snapped.

She was examining the large lavender bush that she grow in large stone troughs on the perimeter of her house. She had a huge house but a very small front garden because of the stone steps that led up to her grand front door.

'Bryony,' she said with a smile. 'I was just this minute thinking about you.'

'Were you?' I asked, surprised that I would come into her head at all, let alone rest there long enough for her to consider me.

'Yes. Would you like a cup of tea? I've just put the kettle on.'

'That would be lovely,' I replied. I couldn't believe my luck. I was always keen to have a look inside other people's houses, but to be invited into Priscilla's, the biggest on this road? Heavenly.

She was a very private person so I wasn't sure how many people had actually been offered the chance to move beyond the front door. She wasn't one for wild parties, but if she had friends down for the weekend, I don't suppose I would see them because our house is just that bit turned away from hers as the road curves. She can see our house, but it's a bit of a struggle to see hers.

In her grand kitchen, as discreetly as possible, I whipped my head around, trying to take in the sheer opulence of the space. Breath-taking. It's the size of half of my entire ground floor, for one thing. And our house is massive if you think about the three-up, two-down South London place that I grew up in.

I kept looking around trying to take it all in, while trying to decide on my favourite thing. The expensive copper pan set, hooked with S hooks onto the overhead black iron pan rack suspended from the ceiling? The white bevelled tiles with red grout? The large chrome fridge with its touchscreen front and water dispenser? The iconic stand mixer? The pasta-drying rack that stood on the side, with its acrylic arms extended as it dried the red and green ribbons she had clearly recently made? The huge, black range cooker with eight burners, two ovens, matching hood and stainless-steel splashback? The expensive coffee machine? The double Belfast sink, each with a bowl that I could easily fit into? The chunky wood dining table with six chairs around it that marked where the cooking area ended and the relaxing area began? The sumptuous souk-type area with low, plump red sofas topped with a brightly coloured rainbow of blankets, throws and cushions that led you to the back doors, which could be opened up to let the outside in?

No, none of those things. I loved them, but they weren't my favourite. My favourite was the island that dominated the part of the kitchen closest to the front door. It was all my island dreams come true – it had space for cookbooks, a chopping board, cupboards, sunken cubbyholes for electrical plugs. Growing up and then going to friends' houses in university, I had come to see islands as the height of sophistication and style. You were a proper grown-up when you owned a kitchen island, I had decided.

I thought when Grayson and I bought our forever home (that phrase has come to mean something quite morbid and moribund to me now) that I would finally have the space and the resources for an island. Grayson disagreed. He preferred a table where we could all sit and eat. *What about the dining room*? I'd asked. *We could eat in there*? He'd been insistent – we weren't getting an island, a table would be better. And, like most things with Grayson, I went with his will. He had a way, a certainty about the things he said that, especially back then when I was younger and adored him more than life itself, meant I deferred to him about everything. I really did believe he knew best. My biggest regret has always been the lack of an island in my large kitchen.

'Have a seat,' Priscilla said. 'Tea or coffee?'

I was still a little in awe at how expansive her kitchen was and stood by the door taking everything in, thinking about how ours could look like this on a smaller scale if I had her style and money and freedom to do whatever I wanted.

'Do you live here alone?' I asked her as I took my place at the table, which was uneven and weathered, knotted and whorled. I was sure there would be an excellent story attached to the wood and how it became a table. I moved my fingers over the ridge that ran like a river through the grain in front of me. So beautiful.

'Yes, yes, I do,' Priscilla stated. 'I have people to stay at various points, although last year that didn't happen for obvious 2020 reasons, but in the main, I live alone. I like it that way.'

She said it in such a way that – and I was obviously extrapolating – made it clear she liked to live alone because she didn't like people that much. Or at all.

I was dying to ask her how she made her money, how she could afford to live in such luxury without relying on another's wages to top things up.

'This isn't an easy subject to approach with you, Bryony, since we're not especially close. But broach this I must.'

My spine stiffened and I paused as I reached to pick up the hot cup of tea that she had just placed in front of me. What could Priscilla, who I did not know and who did not know me, have to tell me that needed such a dramatic introduction? 'I don't understand,' I said in a neutral voice, not sure how I was meant to respond.

'I have . . . come across some information that is not going to be easy to share,' she said gently. 'I'm sure it's going to come as a bit of a shock to you, and I don't want you to blame yourself in any way . . .' Her voice got gentler and gentler, and with each softening of her tone, the more I stiffened. What was she going to say?

By the time she had finished pre-comforting me and started talking, I couldn't move from how frozen I was. By the time she had finished what she had to say, I was no longer looking at her, I was staring out at her garden. It wasn't as large as you'd expect for a house as big as hers, but it was a good size and it was immaculately kept. She didn't have a greenhouse, like I had. I only had a greenhouse because I had learnt over the years to do the things I wanted, and deal with Grayson's displeasure afterwards. If I tried to talk to him about making any sort of change, it ended up exactly like the island – he had a better alternative that didn't suit my wants or needs and just ended up with me feeling resentful.

What Priscilla had said made me feel sick; truly nauseous to my stomach. And how she knew made me feel even sicker. When she stopped talking, I kept looking at the notebook on the table in front of her. She'd noted down dates and times. She had it all there in writing and I couldn't dispute it. Why would I try to dispute it? She wasn't telling me anything that I hadn't suspected.

We sat in silence for long seconds, me looking at the notebook and the garden and then back to the notebook. Nothing I could say could explain it.

'I see this is not a surprise to you,' Priscilla eventually stated. All the comfort and concern that had led her to make the proclamation was now gone.

'Why do you say that?'

'You're not exactly reacting to this in the way most people would,' she said quietly, staring at me in the manner of someone who was disgusted and appalled in equal measure.

It was disgusting and appalling, if it was true.

'It's not that simple,' I said quietly. 'You might have seen Grayson with a couple of these people, but I don't believe he would do what you said.'

I carried on talking and talking, trying to explain to Priscilla why she had got the wrong end of the stick.

Eventually, 'You're a terrible mother,' Priscilla damned me with those four words. She got to her feet. 'I'd like you to leave my house. Immediately.'

I was on my feet too. 'How dare you say such a thing to me,' I said.

Priscilla moved closer, put her smooth-skinned, barely lined face right in mine. Her plump, glossy lips were pulled right back like an animal baring its teeth before an attack, her eyes were narrowed but focused on my face. She was usually so pretty but her anger had transmuted her into this creature. '*You're a terrible mother*,' she snarled. 'Now get out of my house.'

Where was the concern she'd shown earlier? Why was she suddenly being like this? Why was she so determined not to show me even a modicum of understanding? And why would she call me that when she didn't even know me?

It wasn't how she was saying it, either. It couldn't be. You can suspect something, but it doesn't mean it is exactly as it seems. There can still be a margin of error and misunderstanding that explains everything.

I thought for a moment that Priscilla was going to hit me, to shove me or strike me to reiterate her disgust. Instead, she stood back, looking down her nose at me in that imperious way she was so good at and that Grayson had mastered, too.

I almost said that having a bigger house, more money and being more attractive didn't make her any better than me. It didn't mean she wouldn't have been forced to make the choices that I've been forced into.

But it did. Of course it did.

Because Priscilla would never have to make the choices that I had out of need and fear. She was captain of her own ship in this world where the rollicking sea could change at any moment to be hostile or peaceful or somewhere in between.

I left her house in disgrace.

I came home in despair and I greeted my husband that night in anger. In the complete realisation that I hated him.

I hadn't admitted it to myself before now, but I hated him sometimes more than I needed to breathe.

And, thanks to him, I now hated myself just as much. Because

Priscilla was right. In the following days when she was crossing the road to avoid walking anywhere near me, when she was looking right through me as she tended to her lavender bush, when she was looking down on me from the top of her stone steps, I knew she was right: I was a terrible mother.

Rae

11 Acacia Villas

3 June 2021, Brighton

Any knock at the door is going to make me jump from now on, I've almost resigned myself to that.

It was years after we left (fled) London that I stopped jumping every time a knock came, stopped panicking that it was the police or – worse – the reason why we left London tracking us down. Eventually, I'd started to feel safe here. Our house was a stone's throw from the sea – ten minutes and you were on the beach, facing out to sea, pebbles under your feet, sharp, salty air skipping abrasively over your skin and moving into your lungs.

Relocating to Brighton had never been on my list of things to do with our lives. After Clark and I got married and had the girls, we'd kind of fallen into the rut most people do – work, school, dinner, homework, dozing off in front of the telly, sleep, wake up, start again – and there had been nothing wrong with it.

When we were having those hurried, harried discussions about moving, Brighton had come up because Clark had lived here before. We weren't exactly beggars who couldn't be choosers, but our choices were severely truncated because we wanted to escape as soon as possible. We saw the house in Brighton and we loved it – I hadn't even freaked out too much when I spotted Lilly on the street.

In the move and after making a life down here that was once again all about the work and the school and the dinner and the falling asleep in front of the telly, I'd managed to forget to be scared every time someone knocked on the front door.

Priscilla's antics have put paid to that.

Today, when there's a knock on the door, I am immediately scared.

Most people know what it's like to be startled, to jump out of their skin, to be nervous. But few people have been scared. Properly, *properly* scared.

And that momentary heart-stopping to heart-thundering feeling is prolonged in my chest as I head towards the door. I would consider not opening it if I didn't prefer to know what was coming rather than have it sneak up on me.

'Remember me?' Dunstan says with a smile that shouldn't be allowed. He is obscenely good-looking. You can't help but notice how attractive he is. Tall and rugged, but with kind eyes and a ready smile. It's not often that I have my head 'turned' by other men in real life, but Dunstan is one of them.

'How could I forget?' I reply.

'Do you have a moment?' he asks. 'For a chat?'

'About?'

'I'm a bit freaked out about what happened the other day.' A bold opener – bold enough for me to take a step back and open the door to him.

This has got to stop happening – people need to stop turning up on my doorstep and saying things that make me let them in. I lead the way into the kitchen but don't stop and go straight outside to the garden. That's why I let him keep his shoes on when he crossed the threshold, and didn't ask him to wash his hands.

For a house that is as large as ours, the garden is impressively compact. It doesn't provide much space for the children to run around and if there's one thing I could change about our home it would be the size of its outside space. Once you step out of the double doors from the kitchen, there is a patio area paved with large white quarry tiles. Less than six metres opposite is a step-up wooden patio/platform with three high, dark-cherry wood sides that I had installed so we could eat outside or, in my more hippy moments, put down a load of rugs and cushions and sit staring up at the stars. As it turned out, the neighbours' tree found it the perfect place to drop its sap and sticky red fruit, much favoured by squirrels, seagulls and other birds. If I don't go out and clean up every few days, it resembles a buffet where no one has any manners and the restaurant staff have decided to ignore the mess. To the right of the wooden patio we have a bit of green lawn that gets waterlogged in winter and autumn, then dry and scrabbly the moment the sun comes out. We've tried reseeding, but nothing works. Absolutely nothing. In the far back right corner is the girls' climbing frame that is shaped like a flip-topped rocket ship. I'd had fantasies of starting a wild flower garden inside it, but I never seemed to get round to it.

Dunstan stands at the edge of the stone patio. I see him double-take when I step out with my burgundy leather gloves on. He raises an eyebrow at me but doesn't say anything.

'One of my biggest underlying conditions is extreme health anxiety with a sprinkling of OCD,' I say, raising my hands to properly show off the gloves. 'Wearing these stops me losing the plot. I'm very partial to bleaching everything down every time someone comes into the house, or trying to burn everything they touch. These help to focus my attention on something I can control. As does being outside like we are now and you keeping that distance.'

Dunstan walks to the other end of the patio and grabs one of the stacked-up hardwood chairs and drags it to the back door area. I sit on the floor of the kitchen, half in and half out.

'You weren't wearing those the other day,' he says, nodding at my gloves.

'Not originally, but when I came back from calling the ambulance I was. You obviously didn't notice,' I respond. 'I felt bad having the gloves on while I was holding her hand, but it looked like she was dying so she probably didn't mind or even notice to be honest.'

Dunstan nods. He is contemplative all of a sudden, his dark eyes staring away into the world beyond. He is the kind of guy I think I would be with if I hadn't got together with Clark. Dunstan is bad-boy vibes even though I've never had cause to think that apart from his devastating good looks. Everyone knows he's a policeman and everyone knows he's an affable person who will stop and talk to you in the street if you're after a natter or he'll nod and move on if you're the type to want to be left alone. When a break-in happened a while back, a bit further around at the Titus's house at number 18, Dunstan sort of became an unofficial liaison between them and the police. I think it was his gentle pressing that got the police to do anything at all, although ultimately they never found the culprits and Hollie Stoltz was broken into a bit after that. But on the flip side, whenever we have Neighbour–2–Neighbour Watch meetings, Dunstan always blends in, being a resident who is just as concerned as the rest of us. (Although, obviously *my* brain has him down as being there to watch everyone to see if they give themselves away as being involved in the crime.)

When Dunstan stares off into space now, he reminds me a bit of a '*MAN*' in an advert – just too good to be anywhere near true.

'It must have been hell for you,' he says. 'Assuming you had these worries before it all kicked off in 2020.'

Describing it as hell seems fitting. I was often burning up with anxiety and unable to settle – the worry and fear that lined the bottom of my stomach never really went away. I was worried about someone I knew getting it, about me getting it, about taking my eye off the ball for one second and doing something that would be disastrous for everyone.

'You're a frontline worker, it must have been a real hell for you,' I reply.

'It was not fun, I can confirm that.'

'So, why has what happened to Priscilla freaked you out so much? You must have seen so much worse.'

'Yes, yes, I have. But when you know the person . . . Usually I just compartmentalise stuff. It's not like I don't care . . . I do. It's . . . More than once I've had to break into a house where someone has passed alone and it's awful. There's so much to deal with but you don't let it get to you. You cope with it by reminding yourself it's work, there's nothing you could have done. That what you can do is make it as all right as possible for the people who knew them. But when you know the person, when you're one of those who needs it to be made all right . . . not easy to insulate yourself from that. Not easy at all.'

'Did you know Priscilla well?' I ask, because he's talking as if she was a member of his family.

'Not in the way that you mean,' he replies. 'When things happen on your doorstep, it makes it real in a way that you can't step back from.'

'I *am* a bit freaked out about it to be honest,' I confess. 'I still don't quite understand why she turned up at my place first. Maybe it's because I delivered her some flowers earlier that day. They'd accidentally been sent here – that's always happening. I wonder if because I was one of the last people she had a positive interaction with, she came to me when she was hurt?'

'What do you mean, last people she had a positive interaction with?'

'I mean the last person to see her was the person who attacked her?' I frown at him. Is he really here because he's freaked out or because he's a copper and he thinks I'm dodgy as hell? I mean, in many ways, I am *acting* dodgy as hell, all the while thinking I'm glacial and cool on the outside. 'What did you think I meant?'

'No idea, which is why I asked. Did you tell the police that you'd seen her earlier in the day?'

I shake my head. 'No, I didn't. I've only really remembered just now. Mainly because another vase of flowers came for her earlier. But I assume you'll be reporting back so I've no need to worry about telling them.'

Dunstan gives me a quick lift of his right eyebrow as if to say 'touché', without admitting that he is here for the police. 'How are you feeling about it all?' he says instead.

'I don't know, to be honest. It wasn't like I knew Priscilla – delivering misaddressed flowers aside. But she was someone I had dealings with. The thought that she's dying in a hospital bed because of such violence . . . well, it doesn't do much for my underlying health condition. I keep wondering who would attack her like that and whether they've finished their rampage.'

'Yeah, same,' Dunstan says.

He's totally here for the police, but is that a bad thing? Doors open two ways – he might be here for information or quiet interrogation; that gives me just as much chance to find out what the police know.

Combine what I have in the diary (I haven't got too far into her book, yet, but from what I have read, a few people would be very upset with her if they found out what she knew about them) with anything I can eke out of Dunstan and I can work out who attacked her in no time. I just have to check out one thing.

'Am I a suspect?' I ask. 'I know you're freaked out and everything, but have the police sent you here because I'm a suspect?'

'Nobody sent me. I found her and I know her so I can't work on the case. And, no, you're not a suspect . . . but you are a "person of interest". She came from your house and had been attacked. No one saw what happened before I found her in the street, so of course my colleagues are "interested" in you. If you were a suspect they would have searched your house by now.'

'No one saw what happened before you "found" her in the street, either. You could have been hunting her after you attacked her for all I know. Well, for all the police know.'

Dunstan looks embarrassed, probably because what I've said is true. 'No, I'm not a suspect or person of interest. Not in the way you mean. I've told them what I know.'

'And they sent you here to find out if I was keeping things from them or if I'd drop my nefarious motive for wanting Priscilla dead during a convo over a cuppa and biscuits?'

'Not exactly. No one asked me to come because I'm not allowed to work on the case. I came because I was concerned about you and I wanted to say out loud that I was freaked out. Can't say that to the people I work with. I live on my own. My parents aren't the type you open up to about this. My siblings worry enough. The only person I could say those words to who might understand is you.'

I'm not sure what to say right now. Even if I'm not a full-on suspect like he says, getting info out of him might not be that easy. And having him around might not go well for me. Will I get done for not handing over the 'evidence' I have burning a hole in my office right now?

'Despite this and the more recent spate of break-ins in the local area, it is safe around here, you know?' Dunstan remarks. 'This is a safe area.'

'I'm sure,' I state, frost coating my words. He clearly knows about London and has been sent in to find out more. Why can't people just leave well enough alone? Why can't they let what happened in London stay in the past?

'No, I mean it. If you've got a type of anxiety that centres around people's safety as well as their health, this sort of thing can really throw you for a loop, as well as bringing all your worries to the fore. I want you to know and believe that it's safe here.'

'OK.' I conjure up a smile. 'Thanks, Dunstan.' I get up with purpose, indicating that I would like him to leave.

He catches on quickly, lifts himself out of his seat and comes to his full height. He really is handsome, this man. *This is a police officer, don't forget that, Rae,* I warn myself. *Don't forget how he could make your troubles a million times worse, no matter how nice he is being to you now.*

'Do you want to take the flowers with you?' I say to him.

'Erm . . .'

'I mean, they're for Priscilla, they were just delivered here. Like I said, that's been happening for a while. I asked them to just take the flowers to her house as they have her name on, but they always say no – they can only deliver to the address on the order. They're in the corridor, you can take them as evidence or whatever.'

'OK.' He shrugs. 'I'll make sure they get to the right person.'

'Is it OK to come and talk to you sometime?' Dunstan asks at the front door. He has on those blue gloves police officers use, which he produced from his pocket, and he is holding the vase of today's delivered flowers.

'If you want,' I reply. 'But after you tell them about the flowers and hand over these ones to your mates, you and the police will hopefully have no more need for me.'

'I wouldn't be coming for the police, I'd be coming to see how a woman who had a nasty shock is doing, while sharing my troubles with her.'

'All right then, if that's really why you're coming, then yes, you can absolutely come and talk to me sometime.'

'Great.'

As he starts down my stone steps, I begin to shut the door. Just as he moves on to the pavement, he glances back over his shoulder and the look he shoots me causes almost every cell in my body to catch fire – half with fear that he somehow knows about the diary and half with a very strong urge to run down and ask Dunstan to kiss me.

Priscilla

21 Acacia Villas
Diary Excerpt

30 April 2021

Had a nice palate cleanser today from all the Clark and Lilly stuff when I saw Foluke Akinlose and her partner, Andy Cantona, from number 5. They were out knocking on people's doors because their indoor cat, Jacko, had somehow managed to escape. Andy kept singing 'Who Let The Cat Out' under his breath and Foluke good-naturedly rolled her eyes and shook her head. Jacko wasn't here, but it was good to be around a couple who were so nice. I'm sure there's a better word, but nice is the one that comes to mind because it made me happy to see them together and that's a nice feeling.

2 May

I'm impressed and disgusted in equal measure. Lilly Masson's business is doing really well. Really well. Too well, considering how small a county this is and how little new development space there actually is. But everyone they consult for does seem to get their planning straight through.

Impressive. But a little bit more digging and I found some really odd stuff.

<u>Really</u> odd.

Thinking that this business has more to it than meets the eye, and even what does meet the eye is dodgy as hell.

She's still screwing Clark Whickman at least twice a week and his wife has no idea. They make me sick, they really do.

Bryony

24 Acacia Villas

4 June 2021, Brighton

My phone beeps for the sixth time and I know who the message will be from. She's been texting me all morning.

> You honestly need to get yourself over here today. I have orders mounting up. Everyone wants that cute dungarees and headscarf set. Get over here and working   now! X

Alana has been messaging me since eight o'clock and I don't know what to tell her. I am behind in my sewing and it's always a pleasure to see her, but I'm not feeling up to it. Two days of making Grayson dish up his own food while being upbeat and seemingly unbothered by his seething rage has taken its toll. I need to sit here and fortify myself for tonight. I know, however, that Alana won't stop until I go over there, because I know all she wants is the best for me – and working, making money, is the best for me. Because that's why I'm in this situation, isn't it? Money. Or the lack thereof.

August 2020, Brighton

What I hate most about my life is feeling like a victim. I kept thinking this, over and over as I stood in the supermarket staring unseeingly at the shelves in front of me.

This thought invaded every moment of my existence. I was a victim; I was powerless because I had no money of my own. I had no money of my own so I was trapped in my marriage, my family set-up, my current life. And that made me a victim.

I wanted out; I wanted, desperately wanted, rid of Grayson, but I couldn't get out because I had no money. I had no way of making money. Long ago I had an education that I worked hard for – I clawed my way to the top of every class I took. I never lost focus and I excelled at everything I did. I was meant to do great things with the education I earned, despite my less-than-salubrious background. I was meant to take on the world on my own terms.

I wasn't meant to become a woman who wore wellies and wax jackets and who was never far from a pair of pruning shears. I wouldn't mind becoming that woman if that was what I had *chosen*, but it wasn't. I am that woman because I have nothing else in my life that is mine. It wasn't the wax jacket and wellies that were the problem. It was the having nothing else that was the problem. *What happened to me? Where did I go?*

Down the aisle with a con artist, that's where. I often thought that they should make one of those dreadful advertisements about me: 'Have you been missold a marriage? Did you think you'd be getting a bountiful and interesting life with a man who loved you and who you adored? Did you instead end up resentful and lonely, with no life of your own? Then you may be entitled to some compensation.'

What I am, I thought as I trailed around the supermarket, *is a walking cliché. I married the wealthy, handsome prince only to realise that his wealth was his alone – although he expected me to do everything to facilitate him accumulating more – and his handsomeness was really vain arrogance that I was meant to service on every level at my own expense, too. Handsome prince? Trolls and ogres had never looked so good.*

'Oh, Bryony, are you all right?' Alana asked, stopping her trolley in front of mine. She lived at number 19 and she, like Priscilla, was doing her fifties so much better than me. She had grown-up children who visited alternate weekends so she wouldn't get lonely, and then they'd get together at Christmas and other holidays, and she volunteered at the library and one of the charity shops down in Hove. Six years ago, her husband had run off to Spain with his secretary, leaving Alana in dire straits. She only managed to keep the house, so the local gossip went, by turning tricks in her spare bedroom (also known as being a prostitute). When I asked her about it, she'd told me that the house, the mortgage of which had been paid off, had formed her divorce settlement. *'He hadn't wanted to give me Jack shit but I made him a counter offer,'* she told me. *'He's lucky I just wanted the house.'*

'What was in the counter offer that made him change his mind?' I asked.

'I reminded him that I know where the bodies are buried. Could have meant literally, could have meant figuratively. He couldn't do enough for me after that.'

That wouldn't work with Grayson, I'd thought, hopelessness spiralling up inside again. Nothing would work on Grayson. He was so darn respectable; and being in charge of such a successful charity gave him extra gravitas and standing in the community. I did sometimes wonder what he would have to do for people to see the real him.

'You look very upset, is there anything I can do?' Alana asked in the supermarket.

I shook my head, touched that someone had noticed my distress and a little unsettled that my upset was so plain, so public.

'Come back to my place, have a cup of tea and tell me all about it.'

I doubted I could tell her all about it. Everyone loved Grayson around here – indeed one of Alana's children had once done work experience at the charity and Grayson had given him a glowing reference, which Alana had been so grateful for. Even the situation with the huge building development near our houses, where Grayson had loudly and publicly endorsed something that would have long-term detrimental effects on the community, hadn't done him too much damage. People were annoyed, upset and felt betrayed for a while; he was publicly and privately criticised for a bit, but only one voice on the council called for his resignation as the charity head. No one else did. That all fuelled the idea that as a community leader, as a human being, Grayson Hinter was untouchable. And that I was stuck.

August 2020, Brighton

Alana did not have an island. She had rustic antique oak units that lined every wall of the kitchen except where the window sat next to the glazed back door. Her style was a little old-fashioned and frumpy but still appealing to modern sensibilities. It was cosy and I felt immediately at home.

'What's the matter, Bryony? I don't like to see you so upset.'

'It's nothing. I was being silly, that's all.'

'It didn't seem like nothing,' she gently probed. 'It seemed very much like something.'

'What I hate most is feeling like a victim,' I said to her. The surroundings, the tea in large antique Victorian teacups and the feeling of being about to explode loosened my tongue. 'I hate not having my own money. I hate being forced to fit into what Grayson thinks a wife should be. He has more aspirations for the people he helps out of poverty at the charity than the adult he shares his life with. I feel like a victim, even though I know it's actually me who put myself here.'

'I'm sorry to hear that,' Alana said. 'So you can't get a job or anything like that?'

'Every time I try, even just volunteering, he puts pressure on me until I resign. He nags me and says I'm not doing the best by the children, he tells me they need me home, he says if they do badly in their exams or go on to do badly in life, it will be down to me putting myself first and working outside of the home. But if I try to do anything from home, he claims I'm focusing on the wrong things and I need to think about how my family have become afterthoughts to me. I just don't have the money to make leaving a possibility. Or the opportunity to make any.'

'I know a way you can make money,' Alana said simply, fixing me with her piercing eyes.

'You do?'

'Yes, but let me tell you now, it's not for the faint-hearted.'

Oh no! I thought. *She's going to try to recruit me into her prostitution ring.*

'And I'm not a madam who's going to ask you to turn tricks in my spare bedroom, before you start to wonder.'

'What is it then?'

'I can only tell you if you tell me something that would be devastating if it were found out.'

Where would I start? I thought. 'I once "serviced" Grayson as he sat behind his desk at the charity.'

Alana's eyes nearly popped out of her head and her jaw dropped open. 'I'm sure he would be sacked if they were to ever find out, but it was his fantasy. It was right in the middle of the working day. He implied that if I didn't get down on my knees under his desk and do it, he would find someone else who would. I'd almost told him to be my guest, but having no income of my own means I have to be careful about what I will and won't do.'

'I don't think I could be more shocked if I tried,' Alana replied.

'Is that good enough?'

'Yes, yes, that will do.'

'So what is it then?'

Alana grinned at me. Her smile was so wide, so enigmatic, that my heartbeat skipped up a pace. And then she talked. She talked and talked and by the time she had finished, my jaw was on the floor, my eyes were like saucers.

And I was so in.

September 2020, Brighton

'Do you knit?' Alana asked me as we sat at my kitchen table.

'No,' I said. 'I do sew, though.'

'Excellent. I really hope you've got more than one sewing machine because it will be so much better if you could bring one over to my place. When we're working together, it's so much easier than dragging your creations back and forth, especially as we send the items from my place.'

'Oh, OK,' I said, confused. That wasn't what she sold her business to me as.

'Children's clothes are the most popular,' she'd explained, 'so get yourself some really nice patterns and material. I send some orders via courier and some in the post. Sometimes we get returns, which we have to fill in forms for. It's not too complicated but you'll get used to it.'

I was still confused. Had I completely imagined what we discussed the other day at her house? Now that she was in my house, she was talking about making children's clothes? Selling them on the Internet?

'That's great,' I mumbled. 'I'll look through what I have upstairs.'

Grayson, who was home early from work, came wandering into the kitchen. He had taken off his jacket and loosened his tie, so he looked casual. His eyes lit up when he saw Alana, just like they did whenever he saw Priscilla. His attraction to other women had always been a double-edged sword for me. On the one edge, I should be grateful that he only had eyes for women around my age. On the other edge, he'd once told me that he admired me because I wasn't like a female: 'In all the years I have known you, you have kept your emotions in check and have refrained from any natural tendency for the melodrama that I have seen my friends suffer from at the hands of their wives. I don't think of you as a woman.' He actually said that. And he was baffled, genuinely, head-scratchingly perplexed that I didn't take it as a compliment. He was puzzled for days about why I wouldn't speak to him because he essentially told me he didn't think of me as a woman until he needed sex.

'Hello, Alana!' Grayson said in a tone not too dissimilar to a radio host introducing their first entrant for an on-air competition. 'How delightful to see you here.'

'You too, Grayson,' Alana replied, matching his tone.

'From the sounds of it, you and my charming wife are planning something?'

'Well, I need more pin money, Bryony here is an excellent seamstress, so with my website, which is already getting good traffic, and her skills, I think I can take my business to the next level.'

'Sounds delightful, like your good self.'

'And don't worry, Grayson, I am not going to allow this to interfere with family life in any way. If I think she's taking on too much work, I will ask her to step back. Does that sound acceptable to you?'

'More than acceptable. And thank you, Alana, for being so thoughtful and considering the needs of my family when offering Bryony this position.'

'No problem. Now, if it's OK with you, I would like to ask Bryony to bring her sewing machine over to my place so that we can start first thing tomorrow?'

'Yes, yes, that's more than acceptable.'

With each passing second, as Alana talked to my husband like he was my owner and my husband talked to my neighbour as though she was my boss, I became more and more furious. *How dare they! How could she and how dare he!*

Every step to Alana's house, carrying my very heavy white Singer sewing machine in my arms, fuelled my fury. *She basically sided with Grayson.* Maybe his attention had turned her head, made her more sympathetic to him than me, but I couldn't believe the gall of her.

I almost threw down my sewing machine when Alana shut her front door behind us. My mouth twisted itself into a facsimile of the rage-filled ball that was burning through my sensibilities.

'He was so easy!' Alana said. 'We have your alibi nicely set up now.

If anyone questions why we spend so much time together, that is what Grayson will tell them.'

'So that was why you were saying all that?'

'Of course! Bryony, we are all about operating in plain sight. So that plain sight has to be talked about and legitimate. Grayson needs to feel like he's in control and that this is only being done with his blessing. That is the type of person he is. You play him by making him think you are playing by his rules. All the while, you do whatever it takes to set yourself free.'

The relief was immense! She wasn't a back-stabber, she was genuinely helping me. Alana and I set up my sewing machine in one of the upstairs rooms. Like her kitchen, it was cosy, with a radio, a big table with space for the machine, a chair for me, a large comfy seat where she could sit and knit, and a coffee machine. It was my perfect work set-up, created by someone who I was starting to like very much.

4 June 2021, Brighton

'Has he hit you?' Alana asks the second I cross her threshold.

'Why do you ask that?' I reply, avoiding her eyes. It's been three days and I am wearing enough make-up to cover the bruising along my jawline and cheek, which is slowly making its way through a spectrum of colours.

'Because I know what cover-up make-up looks like. Because I know what cover-up eyes look like.'

'It was my own fault – I told the police he wasn't at work when Priscilla was attacked. He retaliated.'

'It's not your fault,' she replies. 'It's absolutely not your fault.'

'I know I should do what you say and play dead, don't antagonise him, but I get so frustrated. He gets to do whatever he wants whenever he wants and I have to appease him. I'm fed up of it.'

'I know, sweets, I know. But be careful – the most dangerous time for a woman is when she tries to leave a man like Grayson. Men like him will do anything to keep you in the place and situation they've worked so hard to get you into.'

'So should I stop making him dish up his own dinner and not waiting for him to come back before we eat?'

'If you've started, then only do it once a week, twice a week at most. And be apologetic with it, say it's because of me or something. I want you to be safe.'

'I know you do.' I think this is the first time in my life someone has cared for me this much. I thought Grayson did, when I first met him, I thought he adored me and that all he wanted was to look after me. But looking back, it was all done to suck me in, get me to fall for him. He never put himself out for me. He just told me he cared for me – he never actually showed it. For example, when I was pregnant with Trent and had cravings, he would sympathise and advise me to note them down so I could add them to my weekly shopping list – not even the slightest thought of maybe going to the shop to get me what I wanted. By the end of my pregnancy, he was sighing so much whenever I mentioned any discomfort or symptom that I almost didn't tell him when I went into labour because of the inconvenience it might have caused him.

I used to make all sorts of excuses for Grayson because I loved him so much. I felt he had rescued me from a backstory that I didn't like to think about, that he saw me as I wanted to be seen – not a girl from the wrong side of the tracks but someone who had the potential to be something, and more. And yet, did he really? Was I ever anything except someone to mould into the wife he wanted, to give him the family and respectability he craved? Did he love me once? I hope so. Did he love me once because of what I could do for him as he navigated his way through the world? I know so.

This is why Alana's friendship has been so invaluable. She is helping me in so many ways, ways I didn't even know I needed assistance with. I feel bad, not telling her about Priscilla and what happened there. But I can't have Alana looking at me like Priscilla did, I can't have her calling me a terrible mother, too. Terrible mother I may be, but I am trying to solve that problem.

I don't want Alana to hate me while I sort it out, I don't want her to take away her support, because without her and the money we make I won't be able to escape.

'Sweets, we're going to have to up our production,' Alana says. 'We have got to get you enough money to leave that bastard.'

I can't help but smile. I haven't even told Alana half of what has happened in my marriage and she is rooting for me to get out.

One day soon, I think I'll be able to tell her what happened with Priscilla and see if she can help me get my hands on the book I saw she had written everything down in. Because without that, my dream of leaving Grayson may never come true.

Part 5

Lilly

47 Acacia Villas

4 June 2021, Brighton

'Why didn't you answer my text?'

I sound like his wife. Not his actual wife, but a woman who he is married to that has legitimate claim on his time and his life. I sound like a nag as well, someone who gives him a hard time for the slightest misdemeanour. That so isn't me, but he does bring it out in me. Especially since he has been coming to see me at my house. I try to be welcoming, fun, the epitome of everything a man who is even vaguely unhappy in his marriage would want to spend time around. But it irks me that he didn't respond. I told him I was scared of being alone, I told him that I needed him and I got nothing. Absolutely nothing.

His response to what I've just said is nothing, too. Clark is good at not engaging in anything he doesn't want to. He just goes silent. Well, that's how he is with me. I've never really known him as part of a couple with Rae. Or a couple with anyone else, for that matter.

That's a thought that always freaks me out – he went from a relationship with me to her so that's nearly thirty years of only having sex with two women. How can he stand it? How can he not have a wandering eye? I often wonder, when we're sitting together on the sofa, if he minds not being that experienced. If he wishes that after me, he'd spent more time sowing his wild oats.

My ex hangs around by the front door like any visitor would, waiting to be explicitly invited in and then led into the living room. No matter how many times I try to get him to act like this is his home, he keeps himself removed – he acts like a stranger.

'Clark,' I say quietly, calmly, ditching the shrewish tone I've just used.

'Yup?' he replies. His shoes come off easily, revealing the type of bright pink socks I know, as a person does, his daughter bought for him. He used to go through socks at a rate of knots when we were together. I could never understand it – after a couple of months he'd hold up his foot to show the threadbare bottom or newly minted hole in a pair of brand-new socks. I wonder how long these ones will have before they go the same way. He often joked about one of us taking up darning to cut down on the number of socks he had to buy, but let's be honest, that was never going to be me, was it?

'Nice socks,' I comment.

That makes him smile. 'Yes, birthday present. Surprisingly comfy. Reinforced soles. Will be interesting to see if they work or if they go the same way as every other pair of socks I've owned.'

'I have never known a person to go through as many socks as you do!'

'Feet of steel,' he says.

That's what I used to call him, I realise. My heart leaps that he's remembered, that a part of our time together – of me – is still in there inside him. I knew it. I knew he didn't just discard everything, that I remain a part of him.

February 2019, London

The train pulled into London Victoria extra slowly. Everything felt like it was moving slowly today, under a low-hanging sky.

I could tell it was going to be one of *those* days. One where you just had to keep pushing through, pushing on, and find that you haven't made very much progress at all.

I was moving through the carriages, trying to get nearer to the front so that when the train stopped, I wouldn't have to walk the length of the platform to get out. I was saving myself a few minutes of time – three or four at the most, but sometimes every little did help.

'Excuse me,' I said to the big, solid form that stood in the aisle.

'Oh, sorry.' The man moved without tutting or sighing or being generally unpleasant. I edged past, laptop first and glanced over my shoulder to have a look at this man who did not mind being moved. 'Clark.' I couldn't help smiling. Everything good about being with him came rushing to the surface, and I was sure that I was now flushed with the joy of those memories. My face felt hot and I was probably glowing. 'Clark.'

'Lilly,' he said. He frowned, as though surprised that he recognised me and wasn't sure how he felt about this chance meeting.

'You often get this train?' I asked, the train still inching its way into place.

'Three times a week. You?'

'Same. Can't believe I've never seen you.'

'Well, not never, you're seeing me now.'

Yes, I am, I thought lustily. *Yes, I am.*

'Rae works from home. I still think I've got the better part of the deal – she has to do the school run and make dinner all by herself three times a week.'

Impressive. He managed to crowbar his wife into the conversation within two minutes.

'Don't worry, Clark, I'm not going to jump you,' I joked quietly. 'I know you're married, etc.'

He looked embarrassed, as well he should. That was such an amateur move. I was not going to jump on him – *yet*. And it was so *yet* when he looked so damn gorgeous. And it was going to happen because it was him that changed the terms of our break-up by moving into my area. By putting us together. From what I remembered of the story he told me about him and Rae, it was bumping into each other that brought them back together. And you didn't get any more bumping into each other-y than this.

Train to work three times a week for the foreseeable . . . It was almost like Fate wanted us to be together.

4 June 2021, Brighton

At the kitchen table, with the iPad in front of us and our chairs pressed close together so we can both be in the frame, I try again. 'Why didn't you reply to my text last night, Clark?' The tip of my finger circles the rim of my wine glass. I noticed Clark's disapproving look when he saw me glugging fizz into a glass earlier. He may have had issues with me using a wide balloon wine glass for Prosecco, but I suspect it was the fact I was drinking at all that he was less enamoured with. He could be so puritanical sometimes.

'I'm not the person you should be texting in those situations,' he said plainly.

'Who am I supposed to text? Mr Bieler at number 28?'

'Yes, if it comes down to it. You're in business with him so maybe he should be the one you contact.'

'You said it – business – you don't blur those lines. I know it's just a part-time business but I can't be texting him to say I'm scared.'

'You can't do that with me, either.'

'Why? Because your wife might find out?'

'No. Because that's not who I am to you.'

'I thought we were friends.'

He's been avoiding looking at me since we sat down. He's stared at the large window over the sink, the bi-fold doors that lead to my garden, the black marble countertops, my designer fridge, the wall cupboards, the chopping board, the butcher's block, the appliances – everywhere but at me. Until now.

Slowly he spins in his seat and stares directly at me. 'We are not friends,' he states.

'Cla—'

'We are *not* friends. I am here for one reason and one reason only.'

As if on cue, the iPad lights up, its precursor to a call coming through, before

Opal calling . . .

starts to flash on the screen and Clark rips his eviscerating glare away from me to focus on the call. He takes a few seconds to reset his face, to put on the persona that he usually presents to the world.

My cheeks are burning up. Shame, humiliation, a little fear. I thought he was going to verbally hit me then. I thought he was going to name all the awful things I am to him, I thought he was going to say

159

that when he said all those years ago that he would lie for me, he wishes he'd said no.

I thought he was going to say he wished he'd never met me, which would be the one thing he could say that would hurt me more than any slap to the face could.

June 2019, London

My neat, little gym-sculpted bottom fit right in the middle of the train seat of the 19:52 out of London. It was the aisle seat and at this time the train was pretty empty. I was usually on an earlier train (regularly the 18:22), vacuum-packed with the other passengers until we got to East Croydon, then sardined until beyond Haywards Heath. If I had known this train was so much emptier, I would have contemplated getting it more often. Especially since it contained the being known as Clark Whickman. I could have been a Whickman. Lilly Whickman sounded *great*.

'Fancy getting on a million trains over the past six months and finally bumping into you on here!' I joked.

Clark froze, his body quite literally petrified in his well-cut, posh grey suit. He'd sexily loosened his red tie, had probably flicked open the top button, let a couple of those muscles unclench for a second or two as he was leaving work; now he was all wound up again.

'So, I wasn't imagining it? You have been avoiding me on the train?' I asked.

Uncomfortable, looking a little trapped, he glanced at his hands, which had been flying over his laptop keyboard. 'Not exactly.'

'Did your wife say you can't play with me?' I teased. A little teasing, a little probing – did Rae feel threatened by me? That would be a good sign.

'I didn't tell her I'd seen you. I completely forgot.'

'And yet, you changed your travelling habits to avoid me. Somebody's telling porkies, I think.'

He rubbed his hands over his eyes, then his face, a clear sign that he was tired of this conversation. Rae must really have put her foot down. For someone to go out of their way to keep their partner away from a third party . . .

'All right, look, I honestly didn't tell Rae . . . it was me. I didn't want to . . .' He paused as though trying to find the right words. He obviously didn't want to admit to himself that he still had feelings for me and he was scared that spending too much time with me would make him want to act on those feelings. 'I like peace and quiet on the train. If I get a seat I do some work. If I can't get a seat, I read or collect my thoughts. I don't want a train buddy or even anybody to sit in silence with. I just want to prepare myself for the day.'

Sounded reasonable, *plausible*, even. But I knew him and I knew he loved company. He loved talking to people and was gregarious and gracious with his companions. This didn't ring true to someone like me, who knew him.

'OK, Mr Grumpy,' I said. 'No train journeys together. I actually wanted to talk to you about a business proposition.'

'You sound like you're going to sell me a pyramid scheme.'

'Pfft! Nothing like that at all. As an adjunct to my day job, I've set up a planning consultancy and I was wondering if, as a property expert, you would like to join us? We all live on Acacia Villas and have some relevant experience in other industries. Mr Bieler, who lives at number 28, used to sit on the council planning committee so he knows that side of things. Kevin Milburn, from number 7, used to be a builder and now runs and oversees-about five construction sites so has a builder's eye view on planning. Hollie Stoltz, from number 29, also used to sit on the planning committee but is now really passionate about getting into politics and so wants to get to know people in the area through helping to get only the best projects approved. Grayson Hinter, from number 24, runs a well-respected local charity and is kind of consulting the consultants, really. He also wants the local area to be nicely done for future generatio—'

'Wasn't he the guy who got completely slammed for throwing the weight of his support behind that new property development which has basically brought a load of misery to the area? Most of the kids at the local school can't hear themselves think, from what I've heard, and the direct neighbours are tearing their hair out. And the road's a mess round there.'

'That wasn't his fault. He supported the development in good faith. After the building work is finished, the local residents and the school will get very favourable rates on using some of their space.'

'Could have sworn it said in Hinter's supporting letter that residents in the direct vicinity, who had been directly affected by the disruption the development caused them, were getting free use of some of the development's services, including the parking. A lot of people – me included – found that dodgy as hell anyway, but they'll be paying to use a space that ruined their lives? Wow, way to get your friends and neighbours done over.'

'You're not being fair. Hinter has joined our business because he's keen on not letting something like that happen again. He said he didn't realise the impact of the— Why am I trying to justify this? I was telling you about my new venture. As I said, we've got all those other people on board, and I'm the one uniting all the areas. So I do the numbers – you know how I love me some numbers – and promoting our consultancy. As well as finding clients, I've been tasked with recruiting someone of a legal persuasion. And guess who I thought of?'

'Who did you think of?'

He was making me work for everything. *Everything.* 'You, of course. I thought you'd welcome doing something on your home turf, helping to keep our environment nice and safe and quiet. Plus, the extra money won't hurt. We get a consultancy fee, which we split equally. That was the fairest way. What do you think?'

'Erm . . . well, I think it sounds perfect for you.'

'No, silly, I mean about you coming on board.'

'Honestly? It's not for me. I don't need a side hustle—'

'It's not a hustle! How dare—'

'It's just an expression. It means not your main job. Like I say, not really interested in a side hustle. When I finish work, I finish work. Rae works erratic hours when she's got a deadline, I need to be able to step into the breach whenever necessary. I don't want anything to come in between that.'

'At least think about it,' I implored.

'I have. When you were talking, I was thinking. And it's not for me, sorry. I'm sure you'll make a huge success of it, though.'

'It'd be better if we could work on it together.'

'You don't need me, Lils, you're more than capable of doing it on your own.'

Wobbling my head, I kind of agreed with him but wanted him to reconsider, too. Going through my mind, though, was the easy way he'd called me Lils. *Lils.* It slipped off his tongue and melted deliciously in my ears, warmed my heart. It was still there, his affection for me. It was just forgotten momentarily, I was now sure of it.

4 June 2021, Brighton

My finger reaches for the flashing green call button, but I plant it fully on the red button and flick it up, cutting the call.

A streak of anger is tearing through my body. I don't know who he thinks he is sometimes. We are in this mess because of him. Because of the choices he made, and he's getting snitty with me? I am not having it. Not having it at all. My eyes could be on fire with how they burn with outrage at his attitude.

'Have you got something to say to me?' I demand, a hard edge running all the way through my words. If he wants to have it out we absolutely can.

'Yes,' he replies, glaring me down. 'But it'll wait. It'll wait.'

'No, tell me now.'

Resting his left elbow then his right one on the table, Clark runs the palms of his hands over his face, over and over and over.

28 March 2021, Brighton

I was still at it, still staying fit, even though I'd had to give up on the gym a while back. Since the first lockdown about a year ago, I went out at least once a day, running down to the outlet street that led into our three-sided oblong road, and on across the main road and down onto the seafront. Then all the way to the Peace Statue. I wanted to go to the Pier but it was too busy out there. So many people who were suddenly exercising or just walking, swarmed along the promenade like marooned pebbles washed up from the sea.

I spotted Clark moments before he spotted me, so I was able to see his face drop, the idea of being in my vicinity a burden too far for him. The rudeness of that look was like a spear into the softest part of my body. Sometimes, I wondered what it was that Clark wanted. For me to go away so he could live the life we should have had – the life we did have – with Rae? For me to debase myself and do anything I could to get him back? For us to just act like strangers? Or for us to become lovers again – I mean, was he trying the old 'treat 'em mean to keep 'em keen' shtick that a surprising number of women my age hadn't grown out of? I wasn't certain *I* had grown out of it because, knife-to-the-heart feelings aside, didn't his behaviour encourage me? Didn't it seem a little too strident and out of proportion for him to be acting like this if he truly felt nothing for me?

'The opposite of love isn't hate it's indifference,' f-wits said all the time. If I'd seen that meme once, I'd seen it a million times. And I always thought how trite it sounded, but maybe there was something in it. Clark really shouldn't be reacting to me at all if he has no feelings for me. He should be indifferent.

'We meet again, Mr Whickman.' Bond was one of his favourites, so I was trying to raise a smile.

'Hey,' was his simple reply.

'Since when have you been running?'

'Years. Started in London and kept it up here.'

'When everything closed I couldn't go to the gym so I started running. I really enjoy it,' I explained.

He nodded, clearly not knowing what to say and at the same time openly terrified I was going to offer to come running with him. As if.

'Why do you always look so nervous around me?' I asked. 'What is it you think I'm going to do?'

'Nothing. It's just awkward. I feel awkward. I don't know why.'

Maybe it's because you're confused about your feelings, I thought. Even though he was older now, as I was, there was something perpetually youthful about Clark. Like life couldn't stand to hit him with the 'ageing experiences' stick with which it beat the rest of us, so it allowed his smooth, brown skin to stay smooth, made sure his laughter lines only gently emphasised those delectable big browns of his, and that when his lips moved, it was usually to smile.

'I need to talk to you,' I said suddenly. I'd been debating whether to do this or not, knowing the devastation it would cause. The plan had been, originally, to work up to it. To spend time together and to see how our feelings developed – or rather, redeveloped. He was making it difficult, though. I understood why. When I first got to Italy, there was a man I was attracted to, who was attracted to me. I had to stop hanging around him because I didn't want to get into a situation where he would kiss me and I would have to turn him down. I loved Clark, I didn't want to cheat on him. And it was almost painful sometimes when I had to turn down invitations for dinner with friends because the guy I liked might be there. I got the impression that was what was happening for Clark right now – he was staying away from me because he couldn't trust himself.

All he needed was a push; the right incentive to stay longer than five minutes with me; a proper, substantial reason to spend time in my company. Then he could remember what it was like being with me. Because I didn't care how many years had passed – there was still a connection, still something that kept us in each other's orbit. I had been upset originally when he and Rae moved down here, but now I could see that it was Fate stepping in, helping me out by giving me the opportunity to be with him again. I'd tried fourteen years ago and he had knocked me back. Life has a way of throwing you lines – lifelines – that you could choose to ignore or you could grab with both hands and do whatever it takes to get you what you want.

'I need to talk to you,' I repeated, much more firmly. It was clear in my mind what I needed to do. Sitting on this for so long was doing no one any good. Confessing, telling him, would kick-start the process needed to get us where we should be – back together. No one had been as good to me, good *for* me, as Clark. I was sure it was the same with him. He had told me constantly that I was the best sex he'd ever had. I don't believe it's truly the same with his wife. How could it be? When Clark said he would lie for me, that he would do something that was against his morals for me, he told me something very clearly: no one would ever compare to me because he would not do that for anyone else.

We were meant to be together. It was as simple as that. 'Can you come back to mine?' I made my voice as non-threatening as possible, tried to sound sensible. I wanted him to think of me as prey, not predator. 'I'd prefer if we spoke in a more private place.'

Almost immediately he was shaking his head, taking a step back. 'No. Not a good idea.'

'Why don't you want to be alone with me?' My despair was like a match – so very easily ignited. 'What are you so afraid of?'

'Nothing. I just don't want to go to your house.'

That anger, the broiling, raging kind took over again. 'All right, if this is what you want, then this is where we'll do it . . .'

'I don't wa—' he began and I had to stop him.

I cut in with: 'You have a child.'

That stopped him. That halted his desperate scrabbling to deny his feelings and get away from me before he had to confront them. He was too shocked to speak. Considering he had two children with another woman, he caught on quick.

'You have a child, with me, in case that wasn't clear. She's fourteen. She lives with my sister, Rose, and her husband in Turin, Italy.'

He was winded; my words were a sucker punch to the centre of his being and he bent forwards, hands on thighs, as though trying to catch his breath.

'There've been so many times I've wanted to tell you. So many times I picked up the phone to call you. When you moved here I thought of telling you. I longed to tell you. That was why I was so desperate to be your train buddy. I thought if we shared that, started to remember what we liked about each other, you might find it easier to hear me out when I told you.'

'Hear you out. Hear you out?' He looked like he was going to vomit, right there in the middle of the pavement of the road that led to Acacia Villas.

'I didn't know how to tell you. Especially because she lives abroad.'

'This is what I don't understand, why isn't she here?'

She wasn't with me because I couldn't cope. I couldn't be a mother and be a marketing executive and be me and stay alive. It was too much for me. My sister came to help with childcare because I was a single mother and had to work or leave the country. And my sister was better at it. I just wasn't cut out for the early years stuff, the bits that required sacrifice and selflessness. I was good at the glory bits – feeding food that was already cooked, reading stories, going to the park, buying stuff – but not the other stuff of getting up several times a night, the eating cold food because you were taking care of her, the never going to the toilet on your own. I couldn't do that. I just couldn't.

When I wanted to come home to England and no one else did, I stayed in Turin. But when I lost my job and couldn't find another one, no one else wanted to come to England then, either. Rose's husband had a brilliant job, they had the best house, they did not want to come here. Not even Opal, who loved me but knew I couldn't be who Rose was to her, and didn't even hate me for it. So that was why she wasn't with me. I couldn't cope and she needed a 'real' mother – not just one in name only, which was exactly what I was. 'It's complicated.'

His body snapped upright, and suddenly he was very big and very angry. 'No. You don't say that to me. You don't say "it's complicated" and then just carry on like that's normal. You've kept this from me for nearly fifteen years. You don't get to "it's complicated" about anything. Does she even know about me? Does she think I've abandoned her, too?'

'I haven't *abandoned* her,' I snarled defensively. 'I'm just a mother who doesn't live with her. And yes she knows about you. And she knows you don't have enough room in your life for her.'

'You *told* her *that*?'

'Yes, well, what else am I going to say? Whenever I've tried to make contact with you, even back then, you didn't want to know. You kept – and you keep – pushing me far, far away. So I stayed away. It's not my fault you couldn't simply talk to me like you do with most people, thereby reminding me that you're a decent human being who I should allow in my daughter's life.'

'Our daughter, Lilly. OUR. Daughter.' He bent over again, the wind seeming to be knocked out of him for a second time. 'She's grown up thinking I don't want her.'

'She has grown up with the best of everything. She's a happy, healthy young woman who wants for nothing, including love.'

'I want to see her,' he said. 'I want to see her as soon as possible. I can't fly there right now, but a video call would work.'

'We'll have to work up to—'

'No, no! You don't get to call the shots now. You've kept my child away from me for all this time. I want to see her.'

'And you will, but there are ground rules we have to establish. One of them is that if you start this, you have to be in for ever. No backing out if you get bored or if you hate me or if there's something better to do. You want to see her, then you see her regularly via video call.'

'I am not skipping out on her. Now I know she exists, I am not leaving her.'

'The other main rule is you can't tell Rae.'

'Not going to happen. I tell Rae everything.'

'We both know that's not true. Have you told her how many times you've seen me in recent years? Including the times when you've pretended you haven't seen me?'

He didn't reply, which meant of course he hadn't.

'Have you told her that – from my calculations – our daughter was conceived *after* you got together with her?'

'That's not how it was.'

'Then how was it?'

'I called her. And then you said you were having doubts about the break-up and I came to see you just in case there was anything to salvage. I hadn't met up with her. We weren't even vaguely together.'

'Have you told Rae that?'

He retreated into silence again.

'Well, there you go. Don't pretend you won't lie to your wife when it suits you.'

He did not like that. He did not like that at all – his face looked as though it was holding in a multitude of thoughts and insults. I didn't want it to be like this. I wanted this to bring us together, for us to share our daughter privately and to enjoy being parents together. If he admitted along the way how he felt about me, if he said he wanted us to be together, then I would not resist at all.

'Listen, I don't want us to be at each other's throats. If we're going to be parents to Opal and you're going to talk to her, then we need to present a united front. I'm not saying we have to pretend to be together or anything, but I need you to act like you don't hate me for a little bit. At least while we talk to her.'

He glared down on me. 'I'll try,' he said.

'And you can't tell Rae. I'm not saying you can never tell her, just in the short term, let's keep this between us.'

'I have no choice, do I? If I want to see my daughter, I have to lie to my wife.'

When he put it like that, it sounded brutal. If I were Rae in that situation, when I found out, that would be the end. Not right away – I was not that much of a drama llama – it would tell me, though, that our relationship was fundamentally damaged and there was no way for us to come back from it. This could be the push he needed, the freedom he needed to admit how he felt about me.

4 June 2021, Brighton

Opal calling . . .

starts to flash on the screen again.

'Are we fixing our faces and speaking to our daughter or are we having this fight now?'

My ex inhales, then exhales in one long rush. By the time he has finished expelling air, he is calm, his face is normal, he is ready to speak to Opal.

I accept the call and both our faces light up as our daughter's image fills the screen. We can argue later.

30 March 2021, Brighton

Opal was angry. In a way I hadn't expected. She was always so laid-back and accepting of her unconventional situation, I didn't expect her to show so much animosity towards the man she now knew to be her father.

Clark was nervous in a way I had never seen him before, too. He was trembling slightly as he sat at the kitchen table in front of the iPad waiting for her call. And when she did call, her face was set, angry, determined. Rose and Ben were sitting off camera, waiting to gather her up if she became too distressed.

'*Hello, Mum. Hello, whoever you claim to be.*' Even in Italian the venom in her voice was apparent.

'English, sweetheart,' I prompted.

'Hello, Mum. Hello, whoever you claim to be.' The venom intensified in English, Clark must have felt it like a hard slap right across the face.

'*Piacere di conoscerti*, Opal. *Mi chiamo* Clark. *Vorrei che ci fossimo incontrati prima. Molto prima. So che parlare in video non è l'ideale, ma è quello che è. Possiamo fare del nostro meglio. E, speriamo, potrò venire a trovarti. Ma non voglio affrettare niente. Parliamo regolarmente e vediamo come andiamo.*'

My jaw dropped that he was speaking Italian. I could understand most of it: *'Really nice to meet you, Opal. My name is Clark. I wish we'd met earlier. So much earlier. I know speaking on the video call isn't ideal, but it is what it is. We can do our best. And sometime, hopefully, I'll be able to come and visit you. But I don't want to rush anything. Let's just talk regularly and see how we go.'* Had he learnt that phrase for her? Or was this something I had no idea about him? It worked a charm on Opal. She dropped the attitude and a small smile danced on her lips.

'How come you speak Italian?' she asked.

'I once thought I'd be living there so I started taking lessons.'

She grinned then. And they continued to chat in English and Italian, smoothly and easily. A warmth radiated outwards from my heart listening to them speak; I felt so full, complete now that the two people I loved most in the world had connected and were connecting. If I'd known it'd be like this, I would have told him earlier.

4 June 2021, Brighton

'I think Rae knows something,' I tell Clark at the front door. After speaking to Opal, no matter how angry or frustrated he is with me or at coming here, Clark is always transformed. He's calmer, happier, less prickly towards me. The fact he clearly loves her when he doesn't even really know her humbles me. And makes me feel guilty for not putting them together earlier. But that's only a small guilt. They're together now, and that's all that counts.

'Yes, I think so,' he replies. 'She said something the other day that made me suspect she knows. Of course, that wouldn't be a problem if we could tell her. It's been months. We're planning a trip to Turin. I have to tell her everything, and soon. Especially with this Priscilla stuff.'

'Can we just keep it between us a bit longer, please?' I have to be soft now, placatory, a gentle place for him to escape to when Rae finds out everything. When I went to see Priscilla on the day she ended up in hospital, I begged her not to say anything. She had completely the wrong end of the stick and I wanted to sort it out with her.

'You're embarrassing yourself,' Priscilla had responded to my pleas that she not tell anyone – least of all Rae – anything.

'I don't care, just don't tell anyone.'

'I don't even know the woman and I know she deserves better,' Priscilla spat. 'Don't forget, Lilly, that I know everything. I know what you've done. I only need a little while longer to finish gathering the evidence and then everything will be exposed.'

'Evidence of what?' I asked, completely confused.

'I know what you've done, Lilly,' she said.

My eyes searched her face for any more clues, any hint that she did actually know what I'd done. Because if she did, and she told anyone – especially Clark – then I was finished. I would never see my child again.

I panicked. When she turned to the door to let me out, I panicked. I didn't even realise what I was doing until my fist landed squarely on the back of her head. It wasn't that much of a blow, I barely felt the connection between skull and hand, but it was enough to make her grab the back of her head and let out a soft howl of 'Ow!' If I thought I'd get the chance to hit her again, I was mistaken. She whipped round, grabbed my wrist, wrenched open the door and quite literally threw me out. She sneered at me before slamming shut the door. My heart was racing, thumping so hard in my chest I expected to see it trying to leap out of my skin.

What was I thinking? I wasn't though, was I? I was not thinking, I *was doing, but without a plan and that is always the point where it goes wrong for me.*

I have a plan involving Clark. This stuff with Priscilla has changed it, made it more pressing to execute, but I have a plan and I need to stick to it. Part of that plan is to keep him onside. I shouldn't have asked about replying to my text. I shouldn't have sent it in the first place. Last night I thought I was being clever, but it backfired when Clark didn't respond, which resulted in me demanding something of him. If I'm not careful, I am going to drive him away.

Without really thinking it through, I cover his hand, which is on the door latch, with my hand, while saying, 'Opal loves you, you know?'

He doesn't immediately snatch his hand away, he instead explores my face, as though trying to work out if what I am saying is true. Success! A little way in.

'You speak to her two or three times a week, but I speak to her every night, and she always brings you up. She talks about you with a lot of affection.' As I speak, I am carefully edging my body – already touching because of our hands both being on the door – closer to him. He isn't moving away – as I suspected, he isn't actually repelled by me. He's just scared about what giving in to his feelings might mean. 'Opal will kill me for telling you this, but she draws you. She's got a real talent, and she captures you so well. I'm not supposed to tell you that. But next time you come over, I'll show you a picture that she emailed me.' With that, I push myself fully against him, and he doesn't move. He stands very still, waiting for me to say more . . . or *do* more.

I allow my hand to slip away from where it covers his and slide my fingers up his outstretched arm. His skin is smooth and warm where it is exposed in his grey T-shirt. He always loved to wear grey and I could never understand why. When we were together I rarely let him wear grey because it drained and aged him. But Rae has no such issues – she just lets him wear what he wants, not caring how it makes him look.

Carefully, as though I might break, he takes my hand away from its journey up his arm and holds it still against his chest. 'Lilly,' he says, quietly and seriously.

'Yes?' I breathe, unable to think properly from how tenderly he is looking at me, how he is letting me feel the strong, even cadence of his heart.

'You know I don't feel like that about you any more, don't you?' he whispers.

Embarrassment blooms first on my cheeks, then my whole body seems to catch fire with it.

I want to snatch away my hand but he holds on to it as he repeats: 'Don't you?'

I can't hide the fact that I don't know that. I don't know that at all. Everything he has done has, in fact, shown me the opposite. By not being indifferent to me, he has constantly and consistently shown me that he still has those feelings for me, even if he doesn't want to admit them.

'Don't you?' he insists.

What if this is part of his denial? What if this is part of distancing me because we've got too close? He's got too near to admitting how he feels and he has to do something to push me away. If he felt nothing, would he really stand there and let me press my body against his? Would he honestly let me run my fingers suggestively up his arm? Don't think so.

This is all just part of his fear.

'Yes, I know that,' I say. 'Of course I know that.'

He lowers my hand then opens the door.

'I'll see you in a couple of days,' he says before he leaves.

Stick to the plan, Lilly, I remind myself. *Stick to the plan.*

Telling myself that allows me to let him go without any drama.

Part 6

Rae

11 Acacia Villas

7 June 2021, Brighton

'Don't suppose you fancy coming for a walk with me?'

'Sometime' to go for a walk with Dunstan the policeman is today apparently – four days after he came over all 'freaked out' and wanting to talk.

'Shouldn't you be at work?' I reply.

I'm a little unnerved by his presence. I mean, why is he here? The police must really think I attacked Priscilla, otherwise why would he be here?

'Maybe I am,' he says, and follows it up with a bad-boy grin that would have had unmarried, thirty-something Rae melted into a puddle. Forty-something Rae isn't completely immune, mind. Just almost totally immune and she raises an eyebrow at him.

'I'm joking,' he adds, putting his hands up in surrender. 'I am not at work, I am not questioning you for the police officers investigating this crime. I am merely . . . interested in you.'

I raise another eyebrow; what is he saying?

'You're an interesting person,' he corrects in the face of the eyebrow, 'and we have shared this thing that we never really got to talk about the other day and I'd like to talk to you about it. On a walk.'

'I really need to work,' I say. 'The last few days haven't exactly been conducive to producing anything useful. I have several deadlines due and I'm supposed to be touting for new editing business. I really need to get my focus back.'

'Come for a walk with me and it'll help clear your head. Get your focus back. You can go back to your desk with renewed energy. We won't be out for long.'

Huh.

Huh.

'I've got to say, Dunstan, this sounds and feels a lot like you trying to get me to go on a date with you.'

'Maybe I am,' he says with the same bad-boy grin. He raises his hands again. 'I'm joking. I'm absolutely joking. I just fancied a walk and a chat and thought you might, too.'

'Right, well, like I say, I'm not so sure that's a good idea. I have work to do.'

'Tomorrow?' he asks.

'Why?'

'Look, I'll be honest: I want to have a chat with someone who I think might understand what it feels like to be deeply unsettled. Reassuring you would really help reassure me. But I don't want to put pressure on you – it's meant to be the opposite of pressure. It was meant to be a show of solidarity but now it's kind of slipped into me being a pest. I'm sorry. I'll go away.'

'No, Dunstan . . . I don't know quite what to make of this. I've had more visitors to my house this past week than I have in years. And it's making me really anxious. Look, let's go for a walk tomorrow. I'm a little better when things are planned. Yes?'

'Yes. Same time tomorrow, then?'

'Yes, tomorrow.'

8 June 2021, Brighton

I'm a bit excited and a bit scared.

I've told Clark, of course. He didn't say much, just kind of nodded and asked where we were going. 'To the park, I think. It's just a walk so he can talk about the Priscilla thing.' To my ears, it sounded like I was justifying going out with another man. I don't think it was the same to his ears, though, because he said, 'Cool' and went to grab some puppy pads to put down for the night.

There should have been more to his reaction, I think. Or do I think that? Am I just looking for things that point to him sleeping with Lilly? Wouldn't he be jealous as anything if he was up to something – projecting his guilt on to me. Or have we reached the point where he doesn't care what I do because he's too far into his other woman?

I push aside all those thoughts when Dunstan knocks on the door. I need to be switched all the way on so I can pick up any clues he might drop about the investigation.

'We have to stop meeting like this,' he says, again with the flashing me his bad-boy grin.

'All right,' I reply and move to shut the door.

'Come on now,' he says with a laugh and steps aside to let me out onto my top step.

We walk in silence down the road, past the spot where it happened, neither of us pausing to have a proper look, then on around the curve of the road, onto the outlet street and on until we reach the main road. Still neither of us speaks as we cross the four lanes of traffic and land at the edge of the small part of the park.

'Honestly, I thought there'd be more talking,' I say, gently ribbing him and myself.

'I have lots of things to ask you, but I'm not sure where to start.'

'Am I assuming you're not asking as a policeman, or am I fooling myself that you can ever stop being a copper?'

'I'm asking as a neighbour who witnessed something truly horrible with you.'

'Do you know how she is?' I ask.

'No different to how she was last week, really – they're pretty sure she's not going to pull through . . . How are you sleeping?'

'Fine, mostly.' When I'm not obsessing over who attacked Priscilla and whether my husband is planning on leaving me for his ex, and forcing myself to read the book – which is deceptively dense with entries – from the beginning and not skip to the part where I find out if I'm getting a divorce or not, I've been sleeping fine, mostly.

'I keep having nightmares about her face. I've seen all sorts of things over the years but the stillness on her face is really haunting me.'

'I'm sorry to hear that, that's awful.'

'Have you always had your "underlying condition"?' he asks, barely registering, it seems, my acknowledgement of how he is feeling. I'm sure he's relieved that he's said it out loud but also embarrassed that it is something he's had to admit to so he's moving swiftly on.

'Yes and no. I mean, growing up, I always had the low-level worry that something was going to go wrong, but nothing terrible. It didn't upset me or make me miserable or miserable to be around. It was just part of how I saw the world. And when I had my children, they had a couple of health issues – again, nothing major, things that most people would consider to be minor like eczema – but it set me off worrying.

'I used to spend hours and hours on the Internet searching for cures or treatments, anything that would make them "better" or keep them in good health. There's a lot of nonsense out there, as well. So much dross and cranks who'll play on every single one of your fears to try to sell you crap that doesn't work.

'But in some of that rubbish, there would be nuggets that led to other things that would help so I had to filter it out. And, you know, sometimes it was a losing battle, there was nothing I could do to stop their health conditions deteriorating and I used to drive myself almost insane trying to find things that would help.

'After a while, I kind of slipped into a place where worrying, being anxious, was normal. Which isn't great, but I got on with it. Clark is good because he balances me out – when I go too far off the rails, he brings me back. He is the "it'll be all right" kind of person that someone like me needs. Things were really hard for a bit when we both suffered bereavements, but we got on with it.

'Then, a few years ago something else happened that was so terrible . . . I couldn't . . . That was when my anxiety went into freefall. Moving down here helped, but it took some time to get on an even keel. It was great for a while, I kind of forgot, got on with things and then . . .' I wave my hand around '. . . then 2020 hits and boom, I'm pretty much back where I started.'

'Sounds tough.'

'Funny, isn't it? It *sounds* tough, but it's nothing out of the ordinary for me now and, like I say, we've always had a good life.'

We're coming up to the part of the park where the path inclines slowly so you don't realise that you're going upwards until you're on a higher level of the greenery. It then loops round and starts to gently go down until you are on the lower level again. This is one of those days where the air is warm, the sun is bright and the world seems to have been touched with a special, joyfully calm glow.

'What was it that happened?' Dunstan asks after allowing my words – a tumble I'm surprised came out considering I barely know the man – to settle before he inserts himself back into the conversation.

'I can't tell you that,' I reply.

'Why not?' He sounds wounded, genuinely hurt that I'm not going to tell him *everything* on our little walk.

'I don't know who you are!' I exclaim. 'I've already told you too much. I'm not telling you anything else unless it's about what I watch on the telly. And even then I don't know if I'll tell you everything in case you go all judgey on me.'

Dunstan laughs. It's a nice laugh, one that would have had thirty-something me doing all sorts of fantasising in her head. 'What about you? Is this really the first time something has got you so worked up?'

'No. But it's the first time I've felt powerless because it's someone I know. I became a cop because—'

'You're a power-hungry wannabe megalomaniac?' I joke.

He laughs again and turns to look at me. We catch each other's eyes at exactly the wrong moment and simultaneously, the laughter dies in our throats and a look that shouldn't be there bolts between us. We stand for a few moments, staring at each other, unsure what to do.

I recover first, look away while clearing my throat. This is not meant to happen. This is not going to happen. 'We'd better get back. I've got work.'

'Yes, yes, of course,' he says quickly, sounding almost as freaked out as I am.

We make it home in virtually no time, both of us walking so quickly it's as if we are training for the Olympics in speed-walking.

'Thanks for the walk and the chat,' I say from the top step. 'I'm not sure if it helped you at all, what with me talking about myself, but thanks anyway.'

'It did help,' Dunstan says from the bottom step. 'Same time tomorrow?'

I shake my head so hard and fast I almost give myself whiplash. 'No, I don't think so.' Like I'm going to embroil myself in *that* nonsense.

'It's just a walk,' he says.

In which reality?! 'If it's just a walk, then you won't mind if I don't join you, will you?'

'All right, I was going to update you on what they've found out about Priscilla.'

'And that's you not working on the case, right?'

'I'm not working on the case. But I did ask them for an update and they gave it to me . . . after a fashion. I was going to tell you what they'd found.'

'Even though I'm a suspect.'

'I told you, you're not a suspect – you're a person of interest. And you're not a person of interest to me – you're the person I go on walks with.'

'I think it'd be wildly unprofessional of you to tell me anything you found out through work. You could get sacked.'

'I know . . . same time tomorrow then?'

Arrggghhh! I almost scream in his face. I do not want to spend any more time with the man I clearly have a huge soft spot for, but I do want to find out what else there is to Priscilla beyond her diary.

'Look, Dunstan—'

'Yes?'

I was about to remind him that I am married so we shouldn't be doing this, when I realise that it is me, the married one, who needs the reminder – not him.

'Same time tomorrow,' I say, turning to go into the house before I see another one of his smiles and have to comprehensively start reminding myself I am married.

Bryony

24 Acacia Villas

8 June 2021, Brighton

As I round the corner of my road after my daily brisk walk, I spot them: a gaggle of people standing on the pavement not far from Priscilla's house, obviously talking but staying apart from each other too. In our street, at least, it seems to have become second nature to keep our distance now; we do it without thinking twice.

My heart skips a little because they are near Priscilla's house, still with remnants of removed police tape on the lampposts and gateposts. Priscilla. The victim. I'd been tempted more than once to call the hospital to find out how she is and/or if she is going to recover, but there is no way for me to do that without the police potentially finding out it was me who called via tracing the call to the hospital. They probably wouldn't do that, but they might. I remember seeing on a television show, or maybe reading in a book, that people who try to find out too much about the condition of someone they're not close to are more likely to be investigated and are often found to be the perpetrator.

And I do not want the police to notice, let alone open, any can of worms when it comes to me. Nor Priscilla and me.

A week ago, I came back from my morning constitutional, as Grayson calls it, and saw Priscilla preparing to ignore me. She may have been right about me being a terrible mother but I hadn't actually *done* anything. It wasn't me who she'd uncovered all that stuff about. And it wasn't nearly as bad as it might have seemed all written down in that book of hers. And let's not forget how she came across that information. How nefarious it was that she even knew that much. I wanted to tell her that. Not the part about her behaving in a nefarious manner – I wasn't going to bring that up unless I had to, but the rest of it. I wanted to let her know that it wasn't all bad. I knew she was concerned for my children but she had no need to be, not really. I had come up with a plan and I was executing it. And also, Grayson just wasn't like that. Honestly. I was trying to appeal to the woman who had spoken so gently to me and who was caring and empathetic. It mattered what she thought of me. I'm not sure why, but it did.

'Can we talk?' I asked over the wall that fenced off her house from the pavement; the lavender reached up and out over the wall to separate us like green and lilac net curtains.

She looked down her nose at me; she was so good at that – making you feel small and insignificant without uttering a word or twisting her face.

'I don't think that would be a good idea,' she stated. She was speaking to me and that was actually more than I expected.

'I would simply like the opportunity to explain,' I implored.

'It's not me that needs explaining to,' she replied. 'In fact, I'm sure I would like nothing to do with you or anyone from your family.'

'You don't understand,' I said.

'No, I don't.' Her gaze flickered away for a moment, focusing on someone coming along the street behind me. She glanced guiltily at me before looking back over my shoulder as the colour rose in her cheeks. What was going on?

I turned to look where she was focused. Dunstan. The policeman who lived on our street.

My entire being felt as though it had been picked up and turned inside out in one move; like the quick removal of a tablecloth under wine glasses. Had she said something to him? Is that why she was looking so guilty?

'Please tell me you haven't said anything to Dunstan?' I said. 'Please?'

She refocused on me properly again, then obviously finding it a disappointment, she trained her gaze on her pink-shoed feet.

'Please tell me you haven't?' I asked again. 'Pri—'

'Come back later,' she said. 'This afternoon sometime.'

That wasn't the sort of thing I could accept – her avoiding the question. 'Just tell me you ha—'

'Bryony, it's later or not at all,' she said sternly.

'Later,' I repeated.

'Any time after two.'

'After two.' I sounded like a parrot.

I went back, of course. A cleverer person would have stayed away and left well enough alone. I'm not prone to thinking of myself as stupid, but the benefit of hindsight makes everyone a fool. I went back before two. I couldn't wait. And things didn't go the way I'd planned. I was a fool. A big, giant fool.

In the spaced out huddle, my neighbours stand. Liesha McNamara lives at number 42, and from the bags in her hands, it looks like she is on her way back from the shops. In her pink string bag is a bottle of very expensive Prosecco, a box of camomile tea, a box of crackers and a cured meat platter. She and I have had more than a few discussions about renovating houses and I'm almost ninety-nine per cent sure she has a kitchen island. Not a skimpy, narrow thing that's a poor consolation prize but a full-on one like Priscilla's. I've never been in her house, oddly enough, and she's never been in mine, but I do feel like I know her.

On her left is Natalie Evans. She lives directly opposite Liesha at number 53. She's in her thirties and works for a charity called Little Green Pig in the centre of Brighton. I had wanted to work for a charity; I knew I could do some good there and I'd gone as far as asking Natalie about it. She'd been ever so kind and had found out lots of information about how I could be a volunteer and how that might help with applying for an office job should one arise . . . and Grayson wouldn't hear of it. Even if it was his sector, he wasn't going to allow me to find something that could turn into a career, something that would take me away from my main role in life – caring for him and the children. And, of course, he came first in that short list. Always. I consider how much I've grown to resent Grayson in these last few weeks and I wonder if I ever really loved him. Because this resentment of him and what he's done to hold me back or put me down feels anything but brand new. It feels like it has always been there in the walls of our marriage and it's now seeping out like poison, tainting everything.

Natalie and Liesha are standing with the new woman. She isn't at all new – having lived here for over six years – but she still *feels* like she is new; like she's only just parked the removals van and carried her belongings in from their place in London. When she first arrived, she was super friendly to everyone and seemed so excited to have escaped the confines of the Big Smoke for the freedom of the sea. From what I've seen of her since, she's still super friendly, still says hello to everyone who speaks to her, but the eager puppy aura has worn off.

'Bryony, have you heard? It was Rae here that found Priscilla's lifeless body,' Natalie says eagerly.

'Well, not qu—' Rae begins.

'She sat with her, bravely holding her hand as the life ebbed out of her body,' Liesha adds. That sounds very dramatic and unlike Liesha who is one of the most level-headed people I know.

'It wasn't quite—' Rae protests.

'And then Dunstan, the policeman, you know, who lives at number 36 came along and heroically threw himself down, gathered her in his arms and started the kiss of life.'

'It was actually—' Rae begins.

'Who wouldn't like getting the kiss of life from him?' My head whips round to look at Liesha. Never in a million years did I think those words would come from her lips.

'Hard agree,' Natalie says, turning to first Rae, then me. 'I absolutely agree with her.'

'Not that I'm not taking this seriously,' Liesha explains.

'Me, either,' Natalie adds. 'I am taking it very seriously. I'm actually heartsick about it. I can't work out who would have done such a thing. What if it's someone she knew who did this to her? What if it's someone who lives on this street? It's just shocking.'

'Really shocking,' Liesha adds. 'It could be anyone, literally anyone who lives around here.'

Rae seems uncomfortable, like she's not sure what she's meant to say to the others, or me, now that I have arrived. I've never really spoken to her for any real length of time before. Although she is ultra-friendly to everyone and people are polite and welcoming in return, I don't think any friendships have been made. I'm not sure that wasn't down to her, actually. She was friendly, but wary. Definitely wary.

'How are you feeling after it all?' I ask her.

She pauses for a moment, not sure what to say. When that pause lengthens, the others stop and look at her, too.

'Oh, I'm sorry, you must be wondering who I am. I'm Bryony Hinter, remember? I live at number 24. Most of the Neighbour–2–Neighbour Watch meetings are held at my house?'

'Oh, yes, I remember. Sorry, my mind is a bit.' She waves her hand near her head to illustrate that she isn't all there; that she is probably feeling how I feel most of the time.

'Completely understandable,' I reply.

'Yes, completely,' Natalie says.

'Thank you,' she says. 'I really should be getting back. If my husband catches me standing on the street again—'

'Men and their need to have dinner on the table or they think you're not doing anything!' I joke.

It was a joke. And yet . . . no one laughs. Natalie looks confused, Liesha seems a little embarrassed and Rae stares at me momentarily before averting her appalled gaze. Yes, appalled. Like she knows something I don't.

'I was joking,' I say to the three of them. And they all do me the disservice of attempting a small, confused giggle (Natalie), an embarrassed grimace (Liesha) and a choked laugh and nod (Rae).

'I was going to say if my husband catches me out on the street again he'll resubmit his argument to leave the dogs with me during the day while he goes to the office. And that can't happen,' Rae says. 'I love those dogs with all of my heart, but if they are here during the day with me alone I will pack up and leave.'

The other two laugh at that, and I can't help but feel slighted. What was amusing about that and not what I said? We had the same intonation and timing, the same ribbing of our other halves, why was hers funny and mine not?

'I'll see you ladies soon,' Rae says and turns away.

And then she does something incredibly odd: she doesn't turn back. Most of us do this, we can't help it, unless there is a reason why you are forcing yourself not to.

When I place my keys in the little dish just inside the kitchen door, I realise what was wrong with Rae. She avoided looking at me. Her face changed when she saw me, I'm sure it did. She didn't forget who I was when I asked her how she was – she couldn't speak because she was *appalled* at having to speak to me.

Which can only lead me to one conclusion: when Priscilla thought she was dying, she gave up her secrets to Rae. And she told the one about Grayson and the children.

My shoulders sag so hard they nearly touch the ground.

This means I'm going to have to talk to Rae and that . . . that I do not want to do. Because I suspect it'll go the same way as it did with Priscilla.

Priscilla

21 Acacia Villas
Diary Excerpt

4 May 2021

Well, didn't Bryony turn out to be something special?

I thought she'd be devastated when I told her what I'd found and instead she dismissed it.

She actually told me I'd got it wrong. That 'Grayson wasn't like that. He wouldn't do that.' In which reality? Whenever one of his associates comes over and they stretch their legs around the close so they can have a cigarette, I've heard the things they say – mainly about females. I've heard Grayson make lewd and quite crude comments about me, Alana and other women. And his 'friend' . . . he has always made comments that turn my stomach. His preferred age-group is much lower and his comments are much coarser.

Even if she hadn't heard those things – possible – why wasn't she absolutely horrified when I showed her what I had on the people who had been in her house?

Why wasn't she desperate to protect her kids from what I showed her?

This makes me want to go and get her children even more. I should have gone to the police first of all. Now she'll probably tell Grayson and they'll come up with stories – plausible ones – to explain everything.

I'm so angry right now.

Why don't people think about others before they act? Why do they try to avoid agony by denying reality?

Well, at least I got the chance to tell her what I think of her before I asked her to leave.

Those poor children, those poor, poor children.

Bryony

24 Acacia Villas

9 June 2021, Brighton

Rae's house is a few doors down from Priscilla's but it is nowhere near as grand. This place is not small, though. It has the stone steps our road is famed for. Some of the people on Acacia Villas have taken the time and expense to have the basements properly converted with the requisite damp-proofing membrane and plastered walls, updated electrics. Most people have done something, even if it's not up to building regulations' standards.

Rae has had something done, but the blinds are securely shut, even though it is the middle of the morning, so I can't see what, and there is an outside entrance to the lower floor, but it is very firmly secured with a lock and a padlock to ensure no one accidentally goes down there.

I hesitate before I ring the bell with 'press' at its centre. This is a monumentally bad idea, but I am struggling to find a better one. If Rae does know, it's better I find out now so that I can go to the police before they come for me. I'm sure I read somewhere that the police are much more likely to release you with a caution – or even release you without charge – if you confess before they come for you.

She answers the door almost straight away and can't hide her shock that it's me on the other side of it.

'Erm . . . hello?' she says, almost as though she is unsure whether she should be speaking to me or not.

'Hello. I was wondering if you had a few moments for a chat?' I ask her. She is avoiding my eye, quite expertly I might add. If I didn't already suspect that she didn't want to talk to me, I'd think she was just busy or waiting for someone, the way she keeps shifting her gaze over my shoulder.

'Oh, erm, what about? I've got a lot to do and I have a video call in about twenty minutes.'

Do people prefer the truth? No twisting, obscuring, bending. Just straight talking. Or do they prefer to dance along with you as you hide your true intentions until you're both so embroiled in the performance it is nigh on impossible to untangle? I'm always fascinated by what people prefer when it comes to the truth, and I know without a doubt that Rae would prefer the truth. I'm never quite sure what it is I prefer. After all, I am standing on this poor woman's doorstep, with half a mind to do her harm in an effort to conceal my secrets because I cannot face up to the uncomfortable truth.

Rae would prefer the truth, I'm sure of it.

'I think Priscilla told you some things about me and I need to find out what so I can set the record straight.'

Rae manages to face me then. Her glossy dark-brown eyes warily find my gaze and, without another word, she steps aside and sweeps her arm in as a gesture of 'come in if you must' rather than 'welcome'.

This is already going infinitely better than my visit to Priscilla.

Rae

11 Acacia Villas

9 June 2021, Brighton

She makes my skin crawl. There's no other way to describe it. If Priscilla was right, and it looks like she was, then this woman . . . *urgh, just urgh*.

After I read what Priscilla had detailed, I was glad that I would never need Grayson Hinter's charity because that man . . . shudder, shudder, shudder.

And now I have to deal with his wife. She's always seemed a pleasant woman, who is nice enough to talk to. Most of the Neighbour–2–Neighbour Watch meetings are held at her house, which is roomy enough to have quite a few people over. Her husband usually chaired the meetings and even though he came off as slightly boorish and buffoonish, he hadn't seemed sinister. Shows how wrong I can be.

Priscilla's diary has shown me how wrong I can be about a *lot* of people, actually. And some things I'd rather not know. There is a lot I would rather not know about this lady but I have to deal with her, even though on an instinctive, visceral level, she makes my skin crawl because her husband makes my skin crawl.

I stand aside to allow her to enter my home. A lot of people have been doing that recently and I'm not sure I like it. Actually, I *am* sure that I *don't* like it. It makes me want to run around with my rubber gloves on and the Milton out, wiping everything down. My health anxiety went through the roof last year and it's not been mitigated this year, really, so I have to control myself when things like this happen. Clark, Bria and Mella don't need me going off the deep end again where I try to deep clean everything over and over, and go into crisis every time one of them coughs or sniffs or says they don't feel well.

'The kitchen is at the end of the corridor,' I state, waving in its general direction. 'You can leave your shoes here, and the toilet is next to the kitchen so you can wash your hands in there.' Yeah, I've chilled the hell out a lot since last year, and I force myself to let things slide by pretending I don't see them, but those are the two things I insist on: no shoes in the house, wash your hands as soon as you get in. To be fair, though, those practices have been with me since childhood.

By the time Bryony has finished washing her hands – I actually heard her singing under her breath – I have sat down at our kitchen table. I'm not going to offer her a drink because after our chat, I suspect I'm going to want to burn anything she touches.

She puts both hands on the sides of the seat of the chair before she primly tucks herself in. I've always had the impression that Bryony was meant to be someone vibrant and 'alive'. She was meant for more than this; in a life that is so overtly endowed with privilege, she has never been given the opportunity to be anything she wants to be. I don't know why I think that, but those are the vibes I get from her.

She frowns at my gloves, which I've pulled on since she arrived.

'I always put these on,' I explain. 'It helps to control the crazy. I got very close to the edge because I have health anxiety, and these gloves make me feel a bit more in control. I'm aware they make me seem a bit odd, but rather that than tying myself in knots while I try to resist getting the cleaning cloth and bleach out.' No amount of bleach will ever erase what I know about her husband, though. 'What is it you think I know?' I ask her plaintively.

'Well, therein lies the rub, Rae. If I tell you something, you may not already be in possession of that information and I will be unintentionally disclosing private family business, thereby violating the privacy of said family.'

I resist the very, *very* strong urge to fire her a 'give me a break' look and instead say: 'Where are you from, Bryony?'

After a brief, slightly confused pause, she replies, 'South London.'

'Whereabouts? I'm from South London.'

She isn't putting on the way she speaks even though, I suspect, she is from the same part of London as I am. She has become posh over the years, those years when she hasn't fulfilled her potential. And the way she speaks now, the way she puts her words together, the aloofness in how she approaches everything, is an affectation. One that is almost first nature now, but not who she truly is.

'South London,' she replies. Exactly. She is from a place as ordinary as me, not the posh area you'd expect from the way she speaks. Anyone from where she *acts* like she is from would have just stated it. The fact she doesn't means that she does not want me to know where she actually comes from because she is ashamed of it. I'm not ashamed of where I come from, I don't care if people know where I'm from, but to someone like Bryony, she needs to push the posh Chelsea over ordinary Erith narrative, even if it is by omission.

I focus on the table, trying to work out my next move.

'Yes, Priscilla did pass on some information about . . . about your husband.' Even now I still struggle to lie, to not reveal that I have Priscilla's dossier and it has told me all these things. 'Not good stuff.'

Bryony sighs, lowers her head and closes her eyes.

'He's not a bad person,' she says when she can raise her head again. Not to look at me – she's not that brave – but she has uncurled enough to sit upright when she makes this declaration. 'My husband isn't a bad person.'

I beg to differ. Hugely. He is a horrific person.

'He . . . he wants . . . he wants to do the best for the people he helps with his charity. And, yes, he wants to be a businessman. That has led him to make some unwise decisions.'

Unwise.

Good euphemism for evil. But there you go. We all have our lines in the sand. Mine stops short of selling my children to get ahead in business, theirs doesn't.

Bryony

24 Acacia Villas

9 June 2021, Brighton

'My husband isn't a bad person. He . . . he wants . . . he wants to do the best for the people he helps with his charity. And, yes, he wants to be a successful businessman. That has led him to make some unwise decisions.'

Rae doesn't believe me. She isn't looking at me with the same disgust that Priscilla did, but it's not far off. I suppose the disgust should be more potent in Rae because she has children, Priscilla doesn't. Rae is probably better at hiding it.

When I sat at Priscilla's table – double the size of the one I sit at now – she was gentle, she was kind. And she was understanding.

4 May 2021, Brighton

'This isn't an easy thing to tell you, Bryony, but I think your husband is involved with some very bad people,' Priscilla said. 'That is actually downplaying the seriousness of it. He is involved with a group of business people who require huge "investments" from their members to show commitment to the group before they are admitted to the inner circle.'

What are you talking about? I wanted to say to her, but I knew. I sort of knew. I knew that the meetings in the Club and the furtive late-night phone calls weren't normal, per se. But I also knew that getting to the next level of power that Grayson was so focused on would mean doing some things that weren't necessarily ethical and sometimes weren't completely legal.

Priscilla continued: 'I know people who have been sucked into this type of thing before. It starts off with them taking you out for lunch and asking your thoughts on things in the community. Maybe asking you to sit in on meetings about various companies' charity work.'

Grayson had been giddy with excitement when he was asked to be a non-exec member of the board of Haduke, Khellen and Craig Enterprises. They wanted him to oversee the administration of funds to various charitable causes. His knowledge of the local community and his position at Westlann Charitable Trust would be key in carrying out this work. He was so proud, so excited. He could do so much for the community in this role and having his name 'out there' could do nothing but good for the reputation of WCT. I had pointed out that Haduke, Khellen and Craig Enterprises were already at odds with the local community because they were behind the twenty-storey block with underground car park that was being thrown up two hundred yards from a local school and residential area. Parents and residents had been up in arms calling for the monstrosity to be rejected by the local planning department.

Everyone had underestimated the 'passion' with which Haduke, Khellen and Craig Enterprises would defend their position. Rumours abounded about payoffs, backroom meetings, anything and everything to ensure that the rubber stamp hit the right papers. The community – including a lot of WCT patrons and trustees – were still sore about that.

'Is it wise to do this?' I asked Grayson about furthering links with them. But my husband was so high on the appointment that he dismissed my concerns, which really should have been his concerns, too. The parents at the local school, the people who lived around us, the wider community hadn't forgotten the open letter of support he'd written. They hadn't forgotten the disruption and noise and traffic. Was it wise to effectively confirm their suspicions about bribery and backroom dealing by taking on this role? Absolutely not. That would have been obvious to anyone. But when did Grayson ever listen to me? Unusually, though, he didn't get angry with me for bringing it up – that's how happy he was.

Priscilla, sitting at her kitchen table, explained: 'And once they've got you on the hook, they start asking for small favours: help with getting planning permission passed, for example. Everyone who lives around here knows that he was paid to write a letter of support for that development. Everyone.'

'He wasn't paid,' I said. 'I promise he wasn't. He thought it would be good for the community, that everyone would be allowed to use the facilities. That it would benefit the area, you know, having access to a state-of-the-art gym and café, extra parking. He thought it was the right thing to do. He got no money for it.'

'Oh, come on, Bryony. Everyone who objected to the planning told anyone who would listen that it would become a drain on the local community. So many of us found evidence of the bad faith in which they were operating and showed it to anyone and everyone. We even wrote that in a letter for the local paper. How could he still support it unless they were paying him off?'

'He just did. He was heartsick when he came back from the meeting where they revealed that the facilities wouldn't be for the people of the

local community, that they wouldn't be building any affordable hous-
ing and that despite all the promises, they were going to cut down all
the beautiful old trees. He was distraught.'

'And yet, when they offered him a role, he jumped at it.'

I had nothing to say to that so said nothing.

'Bryony, once you get involved with these people, you don't leave.
Everything becomes a test of loyalty. Every time you pass, you are
moved a little closer to the heart of the group.'

'But he hasn't moved any closer to the centre of any group, don't be
ridiculous. He has meetings with them to discuss the charity work they
do, that is all.'

'Come on, Bryony. There is not enough charity in the world that
needs that many meetings.' Priscilla pulled the book she had placed on
the table towards her, flipped it open and flicked through its pages.
'See, here . . . here . . .' Flick, flick. 'Here . . . here . . . here . . .' Flick,
flick. 'Here . . . here . . . here . . .' Flick, flick. 'There are so many. It
was not to discuss charity work. There is the company and then there
is the group behind the charity. That is the "business" that he is part of.
That is who obviously paid him to support the development. At these
meetings, they don't just sit around drinking liquor and smoking
cigars. They plan things, they work out how to manoeuvre their people
into key positions. And, in Grayson's case, they discuss what sort of
dowry they would need from him to move on to the next level.'

'Dowry?'

'He has been paying "membership fees" in various ways to move up
in the group.'

She was speaking as though the people Grayson was working with
were a secret cabal of international villains instead of a group of like-
minded businessmen who enjoyed a drink and liked to bestow their

charity on lesser beings. I wouldn't ever think of it in such a way, but I was trying to understand where Priscilla was coming from. How she might see it.

'Everything your husband has done so far is to get him into the inner circle, where the true power resides and where the decisions are made. I'd imagine they have been dangling access to this part of the group in front of him for a while now.'

The way Priscilla talked seemed to suggest this was all a certainty. That she had evidence – actual evidence – of the things she was saying. Although a little voice at the back of my head was telling me that this was all the fantasy of a woman who had too much money and too much time on her hands, part of me wondered if I should take it seriously because she sounded so sure.

'If this is true – and I'm not saying it is – what do you think he would have to do to get into this inner circle, if it does indeed exist?' I asked as I held my breath. Was he going to have to sell the house, or leave us, or something else completely heinous? Those are the sort of things I know he would willingly sacrifice to get on. To be seen as someone important and powerful in the community. If this inner circle existed. He would rationalise it as being in a position to look after everything and everyone in his life.

'You have to understand,' Priscilla implored. 'This group, these *people* require complete and utter loyalty to remain a part of their group. That can only be achieved by sacrifice – something they would call an act of love and loyalty to prove your commitment to the group. Have you had a few dinner parties recently? Where the people Grayson has been working with have come to visit?'

She knew I had because she could see right into my house from her place. She would have seen them coming, seen them going. She probably would have seen them walking around the Villas when Grayson went out for a walk with one of the guests for a cigarette.

I stared out at Priscilla's garden, wondering what I could do with all that space. I would have a large greenhouse that would run along the border wall. I would create a haven of potted plants and climbing delights. Crops and crops of food. I would do all I could to encourage the bees to regularly visit my garden.

'Did your children come to the dinner parties, even though traditionally they have never been invited?'

She knew the answer to that, too. But the way she said 'children' one would think they were unable to speak up if anything untoward had happened to them. They were fourteen and fifteen and perfectly able to voice what troubled them. Unless, of course, their very existence has been shaped around not upsetting their father. In that instance, they may find their voices quietened by the sound of 'business as usual'.

'I'm sorry, I'm so, so sorry, Bryony, but I think your husband is on the path to doing something terrible. I think he's going to allow these people access to your children in return for access to the inner circle of the group.'

'What? No.'

'Yes. That is what happens in these situations. I have found testimony of the children whose parents have been initiated into this group.'

'How? How have you found this out?'

'That isn't important. What is important is what happens to these children and what happens to them when they grow up. They have such privilege that comes from the money their parents – fathers – were given as a result of being in this inner circle. But the children pay the price. They are a walking checklist of post-traumatic stress. Drug and alcohol addictions, unhappy promiscuity, self-harm, mental health problems . . . all from what they went through as children at the hands of this group.

'I've documented a lot of what I've found out. It makes for really awful reading. The abuses are . . . It's so hard to comprehend. I . . . I'm so sorry but I think Grayson is on the way to allowing that to happen to your children. It must be horrible to live with someone like him, but there are people who can help and who will move heaven and Earth to help get your children the help they need.'

This woman sitting next to me was completely hysterical. How could she say such a thing with so much conviction? Of course he wasn't going to do that. That would make him a monster. He would not do that. Not to his children.

It couldn't be true, because no one would do that. Especially not Grayson. He might be despicable in many ways but he would not do this. He might rough up the children, but he never hit them. He might talk down to them, but he wouldn't knowingly put them in danger. No matter what Grayson may be like, he would not do this to his children.

The nausea churning away in my stomach, the rise and fall like a storm out at sea, told me what Priscilla had found and had scrawled on the pad in front of her was true, but Grayson would not go that far. I knew him and I knew he wouldn't.

'I see this is not a surprise to you,' Priscilla eventually stated.

'Why do you say that?' I managed to ask.

'You're not exactly reacting to this in the way most people would,' she replied.

'It's not that simple,' I stated, barely above a murmur. 'You might have seen Grayson with a couple of these people, but I don't believe he would do what you said. You may have seen Grayson behaving badly, you might have evidence of his less than ethical business practices, you might even have proof that he has taken bribes, but he would not do something like this. Not for any reason. He would not prostitute his children. Not for anything.'

'But it's only in recent times your children have been allowed to come to the dinner parties at your house, yes?'

'Yes, but they're older now.'

'Yes, they're older and of that age the people in the group are interested in and can groom to keep silent for the period of time that is necessary to get away with it.'

'Grayson wouldn't. He just wouldn't.'

'Are you sure? I bet he has done so many things over the years that if you were honest with yourself, you would accept this is the next step in his type of behaviour.'

'Grayson wouldn't do this.' Did I sound as convinced of this as I thought I felt?

'You're a terrible mother.' I hadn't expected her to turn so quickly and so viciously, but there it was. She was on her feet. 'I'd like you to leave my house. Immediately.'

I got up, wanting to plead with her to understand that Grayson was not that evil, but 'How dare you say such a thing to me,' came out of my mouth instead.

And then she was in my face, her whole demeanour ready to attack, such was her disgust. '*You're a terrible mother*,' she snarled loudly. 'Now get out of my house.'

9 June 2021, Brighton

In the present I am wary of what Rae is thinking. She isn't ready to throw me out like Priscilla, thankfully. But she must be horrified, too. As was I when I had time to digest what I had learnt.

My hatred of Grayson had begun after that conversation with Priscilla. I didn't believe he would do what she was suggesting, but I had started to really despise him around that time. And since then, hasn't he proved that he is a monster? Hasn't he treated me in such a way that I can't help but believe that he would do what Priscilla suspected him of?

'Bryony, I'm not quite sure why you've come here. I can't absolve you of anything. What I've learnt about your husband isn't going to go any further than me, because who am I going to tell? Who would believe a word I say? Your whole visit is pointless. I have my own worries.'

'Do you have Priscilla's diary?' I blurt out. 'She wrote everything down in it. If you don't care about any of this, then you can give me her diary. Or the part of her diary that references me and my family, and we can just pretend we never had this conversation.'

'I think you'd better leave,' Rae says and stands up.

'Do you have her diary?'

'I'm not sure what your game is, Bryony, but I'd really like you to leave. If you think I have some of Priscilla's property that I shouldn't have, then by all means go to the police. But until then, I'm going to pretend you didn't come here, and I'm going to say hello to you and your husband and your children in the street like normal.'

I'm stuck. Because I can't force Rae to give me Priscilla's diary. She hasn't said she doesn't have it. And she isn't threatening me with anything. In fact, I am the one who has forced this meeting and now I am making demands.

'Please, if you do have Priscilla's diary, then would you please consider giving it to me so I can . . . it could ruin so many lives. Please just consider it.'

'Goodbye, Bryony,' Rae says, leading the way out.

My eyes fly around her kitchen, searching for where she might have hidden it. I can't tell, I can't tell.

'Thank you for the chat,' I say quietly to her at the front door.

'I'll probably see you at the next Neighbour–2–Neighbour Watch meeting,' Rae replies before quickly and decisively shutting the door.

I'm in tears as I walk away. Sobbing and sobbing because I *need* that diary. Now that I have accepted that Priscilla was probably right about him, and that I need to get us all away from him as soon as possible, I need something to have over him. I need evidence that I can threaten him with. I simply can't get rid of Grayson completely and permanently without it. I find myself outside Alana's door without thinking. She opens it, sees my face and takes me in her arms.

Alana leads me into the living room and comforts me as I cry. Through my tears, I tell her a version of the truth that she needs to hear, that I can comfortably voice. I explain that I need that book. I confess that I think that Rae has it. I ask if she will help me?

Without hesitation, my new best friend says yes. Which starts me off again, makes me cry and cry and cry. There is someone out there who is willing to help me.

'Come on, sweets,' she says after a while, 'fire up the old sewing machine. It'll do you good to be earning some money.'

She's right, it will help to know that I'm doing all I can to get away from Grayson.

Lilly

47 Acacia Villas

9 June 2021, Brighton

'Have you told him yet?' Rose's voice is clipped on the phone.

Like me, my sister has never really been one to hide her emotions and she can be so hard on me sometimes.

The power imbalance between us started when she came to Italy to help look after Opal. I wasn't maternal. At all. It felt like there was something wrong with me. The doctors I spoke to said it was normal, probably post-partum depression and things would get better. I didn't dare ask if the medication and recommendation of talk therapy would make me look at the bundle of joy in my arms and feel something. *Anything.* I'd had more emotion from looking at pictures of kittens on the Internet. I just didn't have any genuine response. I knew I had to look after her, pick her up when she cried, shove in a bottle when she was hungry, change her nappy when she was dirty or wet, put her in the cot when she was tired.

I was going through the motions. I could feel other things fine; it was that there was simply nothing there when it came to the baby. It was there for Rose. She didn't need to act as though she cared, it was obvious that she actually did. She loved Opal and did all those things that I had seen mothers do. She spent all her time worrying about

Opal, trying to find the most healthy things to feed her, the best things to nourish her mind, the cutest clothes. Everything was about Opal for Rose. Whereas I would normally rail against any attempts at taking over, I genuinely didn't mind in this instance. It was a relief that someone felt what I didn't and would be willing to make sure she was all right. And Opal loved her back.

I wouldn't dream of splitting them apart – especially when I wouldn't want or be able to do what Rose did. All of this did, however, give Rose a footing above me that little sisters don't usually have. Which ultimately means she talks to me like this whenever she chooses.

'Have you told him yet?' she asks again when I do not reply.

I do not reply because I have not done what she has asked me to. Well, *demanded* I do.

'You can't keep this up, Lils,' she says sternly. I can tell she wants to scream at me but is holding back.

'A woman was attacked on our street last week,' I tell her. 'She lived on her own, like I do. I'm really scared. I can't tell him – he'll hate me and the last thing I need is to be any more isolated than I already am.'

Rose hesitates, not sure what to do now that she understands the danger I'm living with. 'Lils, what you're doing is bordering on evil. I've held my tongue over the years with the things you've done but this is the worst thing of all. The absolute worst.'

'You're exaggerating.'

'Am I? Am I really? All right, I'll tell Opal when she comes home and we'll see if I'm exaggerating.'

'Don't you dare. Don't you dare! She's *my* daughter, you will not do that to her.'

'I'm not doing it to her. You are.'

'Rose, please.'

'At least tell him before you book the trip to come over.'

Too late, I say silently.

'You've booked it already, haven't you?'

'He was pushing me and he's talked to Opal about it loads. There was nothing I could do – he brought his passport over and we booked it.' That had been rather romantic – booking a holiday together to go and see our daughter. I didn't say this to Rose, obviously.

'Nothing except not lie!' she screeches. 'Look, Ben says if you don't tell him, he will. What you're doing is disgusting.'

No, what I'm doing is necessary. Everyone will be happier at the end of it, honestly they will.

'I will tell him, I promise. I just need to get through this bit with the police and this woman being attacked. I knew her and we're all really shaken up. But I will tell him. Honestly I will.'

Rae

11 Acacia Villas

10 June 2021, Brighton

'Mrs Whickman, thank you for taking the time to speak to us today.'

They say this like I have a choice. That this groundhog day of visitations by people who are determined to push themselves into my life is in any way of my own volition.

I'm starting to think that Priscilla not having a real problem with me is a bit of a poisoned chalice – one that I'm having to drink from pretty much every day now.

'We're wondering if you could shed any light on what we have found out so far about Priscilla Calvert.'

'I didn't know her,' I say. 'She is a neighbour and I know very little about my neighbours.' There's the slime of a lie slipping up and down my throat, choking me and making me want to vomit at the same time. Lying is meant to get easier, but it doesn't. Maybe I just haven't had enough practice, maybe I'm not doing it right.

'We're aware that you said that,' the male police officer says. We're straight back into the dance of him pretending he doesn't think I'm guilty of something and me acting like I'm not guilty of something.

'On further investigation of Ms Calvert's life and property, we discovered a very powerful and secure computer set-up,' the other police officer says.

I haven't offered them tea this time, because I can't face it. After they were last here, it was all I could do to not bin everything they'd touched. Priscilla's attack is not good for my nerves. Me being a 'person of interest' is even worse for my nerves. Any more stuff to obsess over is going to mean I have no nerves left because one of the underlying conditions that I have, that Dunstan doesn't realise I was alluding to, is that this kind of stress pretty much always has a physical consequence in that it almost literally 'shreds' my nerves. Constant, sustained anxiety lights up my nerve endings, causing pain – sometimes unbearable agony. There are trigger points all over my body and when I am just that bit too tense, when I haven't slept enough, when the police show up to question me, those points start to throb, then they start to ache and soon I am a walking ball of agony and climbing into a bath of magnesium flakes every night to try to soothe my body.

'I have a lot of laptops – old machines that I keep meaning to transfer data from, but I'm not sure what Priscilla's computers have to do with me.'

'We think she might have been a hacker,' the male officer says.

'Oh,' I say. And my acting is like my lies – it may need work. I know all about Priscilla not just from her diary, but because Dunstan told me during our walk earlier today.

Earlier . . .

We'd got nearly to the incline of the path in the park before Dunstan gave up what he had been hanging on to, the thing that he was obviously in a dilemma about telling me: 'Priscilla is a hacker.'

'A hacker?'

'That's what they found when they went through her house. She's a top-line hacker. Her office was filled with all this powerful computer equipment, all of it with the latest firewalls, VPNs and protections. They haven't even scratched the surface of what she was up to. Apparently she even had a whole set up of false files so if you get into her computer, it looks like you've found what you need so stop looking, when all the while there's a whole lot more hidden behind them or underneath them. Or something like that. Not really my area of expertise.'

'Priscilla? Wow.' Of course that set off an alarm bell – was she keeping information about the neighbours on her computers as well? 'Have they found out what's on her computers?' I asked.

'Nope. Like I said, they're still just scratching the surface.'

'Don't bother – I'll get my daughter Bria on to it, she'll be in like that.' I clicked my fingers.

Dunstan smiled at me quite indulgently for a man who didn't know me.

'Not even kidding. You know, last year, she managed to hack into Clark's credit card and bought a load of bitcoins, then used them to purchase a pile of other cryptocurrency. And then she bought stuff like VPNs and super secure emails, which meant she could buy stuff from abroad because it looked like she lived in various countries. The worst part being Clark and I had no real idea what she'd actually done so untangling that mess was a nightmare. The credit card company wouldn't give us the money back so we had to get her to try to undo what she did. Which meant asking the crim to solve the crime. To be fair to her, I'm not actually sure she knew what she'd done. She's just naturally good with computers and just kept getting sucked into trying the next thing to see if it worked. So yeah, I'll send her over and you'll be into Priscilla's stuff by lunchtime.'

Dunstan laughed. 'Bet it made you feel old,' he said.

'Yes, something like that. But Priscilla's older than me. And you would never look at her and think she's doing the equivalent of sniffing people's underwear online. Was she stealing lots of stuff or breaking into people's bank accounts?'

'Like I say, no idea.'

'Talk about being Half-A-Story Herbert. You have literally given me the headlines and the first part of the intro. What about the rest of the story?'

'I like that you've got a name for me,' he said with that indulgent smile on his face again, but this time it's heavily dosed with something that looks suspiciously like affection.

'It's not a name for you, it was an insult of sorts. I have all sorts of insults like that just waiting to be unleashed.'

'I bet you do . . . Did you know that my first name is actually Herbert?'

'You lie!'

'I do not lie. My name is Herbert, which is why I go by Dunstan.'

'What are the odds?' I wondered, genuinely surprised.

'I don't know . . . when you're in sync with someone, I think the odds of something like that happening are pretty high.' His voice had become silky, smooth and oh so tempting. 'I'm guessing we are very, very much in sync.'

'Can you not, please?' I said as though in pain, wincing so much my eyes partially shut.

'Can I not . . .?'

'Flirt with me. I can't go on walks with you or be your friend if you flirt with me. I know other women can do it and it's fine, but not me. I don't like blurred lines.'

'For you, anything,' Dunstan teased. 'I will not flirt with you. But, just so we're clear, *you* started it.'

Of course I started it. Reading over and over that Clark goes to Lilly's house at least twice a week was another thing that was shredding my nerves.

So of course I started it when it's pretty much certain that my husband has been cheating on me.

'Am I supposed to know something about what she got up to?' I ask the police officers cautiously since neither of them have spoken since I said, 'oh'.

'With the prolific nature of Ms Calvert's activities, we were surprised to find no evidence of what she was working on.'

'Right. What does that mean and again what has it got to do with me?'

'It means, Ms Calvert spent a lot of time researching people. The cyber crime department are working on her computers right now, but we think she was a digital private investigator. And she was involved in some of the public data hacks we've witnessed over the years.'

Dunstan didn't tell me that. Most likely he didn't know because they still have him in their sights as a possible suspect, too.

'Again, what has that got to do with me?'

'We think she was actually one of a group of hackers who unlocked public body accounts and IT systems after they'd been hit by a cyber attack and were being blackmailed to be given access back to their systems. She actually seems to have done a lot of good.'

'Good for her. But, you know, I still don't get what it's got to do with me.'

They exchange looks and I realise I was probably meant to be a bit more impressed by that. 'Most hackers don't keep the information they consider most valuable on computers, clouds or anything digital. Those things are hackable, no matter how many layers of protection you build. Most hackers keep their most valuable information on a USB stick or they even use pen and paper.'

I know what's coming. What they're going to ask me and I am going to have to lie. I hate the lying. So maybe I should just stop doing it. Stopping it would mean, of course, handing over the diary and running the risk of being done for withholding evidence, or tampering with evidence – or whatever it is to do with evidence that I have done wrong.

I brace myself for it. For the question to be asked and my brain to decide at the very last moment what it's going to do.

Booooinnnnggggg! One of the officer's phones suddenly cuts into the tense moment, making me jump slightly. She reaches into her jacket pocket and removes the glowing, noisy rectangle. She answers it straight away and I expect her to get up and walk out. Instead: 'Banford, here,' she says into the handset without moving from her seat. The other officer and I both sit still, awkwardly waiting for her to finish.

She doesn't say much, but she must hear a lot because by the time she hangs up, her cheeks are glowing and her eyes are dancing; she's had some exciting news and she can't wait to share it. Yam does this when she wants a treat, she sits up straight, trembling slightly with excitement while her tail wags and her shiny, eager eyes watch you for any signs of an edible reward coming her way.

'Did you know your husband was arrested for causing an affray, Mrs Whickman?' she asks.

This is not the question I was expecting. At all. I had been gearing myself up for an epic lie; I am now staring at them both with alarm on my face and my heart, which was already racing a little, is galloping.

'What, right now? Who was he fighting with?'

'No, I believe it was back in 2003.'

'You mean when he stopped a man beating up his girlfriend and got arrested for being . . . Bl— the only sensible man in that situation? You mean that?'

'Yes, that. From that we have your husband's fingerprints on record.'

'OK.'

'Where was your husband on the afternoon of Ms Calvert's attack?' she asks me.

OK, I have a suspicion where this is leading but I'm not sure why. 'Erm . . . at work. Unless he had a meeting. Sometimes he has meetings but doesn't remember to tell me until afterwards.' My voice sounds every bit as tearful as I am. I do not like this new track of questioning at all.

'Can anyone verify that?'

'I don't know, I was here. I don't know who he spoke to or saw that day. Why would I?' I look at them both in turn. The one who didn't get the phone call is looking just as smug as the one who did 'Why are you asking me these questions?'

'How well does your husband know Ms Calvert?'

'As well as he knows most of the other neighbours, I'd imagine.'

'Has he had occasion to go into her house at all?'

Has he? There was a time when I would have said no, but that was before he started visiting his ex three times a week. 'Not that I know of,' I reply, the feeling of dread that has been mounting since this line of questioning started reaching a crescendo.

'We found an unidentified set of fingerprints in Ms Calvert's house,' says the phone call one. 'I've just been informed that they have been confirmed as being your husband's. Do you have any idea why?'

Part 7

Priscilla

21 Acacia Villas
Diary Excerpt

7 May 2021

I had an encounter with Lilly Masson today.

I have seen so much over the past few weeks, so much bad behaviour, that I was sick at the thought of her still fucking Clark Whickman. She was in the street near my house and I got angry. How dare she? I mean, I don't know Rae Whickman but she doesn't deserve to have her husband do that to her. I haven't seen him to confront, but when I do, I will give him a piece of my mind.

'Why don't you just leave the Whickmans alone?' I said to Lilly. I may have had a drink and I was a little bit high on what I'd been up to earlier.

'What do you mean?' she asked, all innocence and dimples.

'Stay away from him. He's married.'

'You have no idea what you're talking about.'

'Well, maybe his wife will have an idea,' I shot back. 'Maybe she'd like to hear how he comes to your house three times a week?'

'Please don't; it's not that simple.'

'Yes it is,' I said to her. 'It is that simple. They've been through hell. The amount of fear and anxiety they will have been living with because of what happened. I can't believe you'd go after him. Just leave them alone.'

'What are you talking about?' she asked.

'Stop trying to wreck their home and find a man of your own,' I told her.

'That's not what this is,' she insisted.

'Stay away from him,' I ended up saying, like I was talking about my man. 'Or you will suffer the consequences.'

So many nice people live on this road, in this community, and then there are the Lillys of the world. Not content with being involved with one dodgy scheme, she's doing this as well.

Mella Whickman's joke today:

What do spies wear?
Sneakers!

Part 8

Rae

11 Acacia Villas

11 June 2021, Brighton

It's still raining, although harder now, persistent. I've been looking up at the kitchen skylight all morning, watching the water patter on the glass.

Clark has been wonder dad and husband this morning – getting up early to make breakfast, sort the dogs and then himself before he took the girls to school on his way to work. He's taken the car because of the rain and not having the job of taking the girls to school has left me wandering around the kitchen staring into space and wondering why his fingerprints were in Priscilla's house.

He didn't mention it at all. I was going to ask him, my instinct being to bring it up the moment the girls were in bed, but the part of me that has been reading about his deception and the dishonest behaviour of pretty much all our neighbours told me to leave it. To see if he would tell me because the police were bound to have spoken to him. But nothing. He was pensive and on edge, his features pinched a little tighter, and I could tell he wanted a drink or two to settle his nerves, but he didn't. Probably scared it might loosen his tongue – force him to be honest with his wife.

And this morning, when a night's sleep (there was very little sleep for me) might have inspired him to come clean, has found him sweeping up and sweeping out the inhabitants, leaving for the day before I can have anything approximating a conversation with him.

I'm now standing by the living room window, watching. And waiting. For what, I don't know.

Maybe I'm expecting Priscilla's attacker to come bounding up the stone steps, knock on the door, tell me what they've done and ask me to come with them to turn themselves in to the police.

Out of the window, I spot Trudie from number 22. She's a petite woman who dresses nice in twinsets and court shoes, American tan tights, and carries a vintage-looking handbag. She always goes out of her way to say hello and offers a friendly smile as she bustles along. She also, under the cover of darkness, takes her empty gin bottles down the road to leave in other people's recycling the night before the collectors come. Priscilla said she thought Trudie had a drink problem she's trying to hide from her husband. Priscilla also wrote that when a neighbour politely asked Trudie to stop using their recycling bin, Trudie left a filled doggie poo bag by the front tyre of said person.

Bert from number 16 comes skipping out of his house on his way to the station to get the train up to London. According to Priscilla, he was shamefaced after being chased with a rolling pin by Bette. He gives Bette, who is sitting by her window, a hearty wave and she waves back – like the incident didn't even happen. Both of them are clearly as messed up as anything and both of them are presenting a normal face for the world.

The rain is coming a bit harder now, and the parked cars on either side of the road are like stitches hemming the slick road to the wet pavements.

Walking her dog is Kerry from number 33. She's a bit like Priscilla in that she doesn't really interact with the neighbours and will completely ignore anyone even if they smile at her or if their dogs try to interact with hers. Her dog is a large Newfoundland breed, I think the girls said, and it is a giant bundle of fur. Always immaculately turned out, though. The girls are convinced her dog goes to dog shows, which is why it's always so well groomed, and sometimes has a bow. According to Priscilla, Kerry has a questionable relationship with her dog. At first I was sure Priscilla was just being mean, but now I have extra knowledge that Priscilla was a hacker, I'm wondering where her online 'research' activities took her and what she saw.

At least three different people are having affairs, and each of them has done it with their affair partner in the home they share with their spouse at least once.

And then, of course, there's my messed-up bit of Priscilla's story.

Me, Clark and Lilly.

Tap-tap, tap-tap, tap-tap.

I jump a little, even though I shouldn't because Dunstan comes at this time every day. What would Priscilla write in her book about this thing with Dunstan and me? About how close to the wind I am sailing. Because, let's be honest, this could just be what Clark is doing with Lilly.

'Rain, yay or nay?' Dunstan asks, his usual smile in place. He's wearing a yellow rain mac with the hood up, as well as black wellington boots.

'Don't you ever go to work?' I ask him, delaying the moment our time together will begin.

'All the time,' he replies. 'Rain, yay or nay?'

'Nay,' I say and step aside to let him in.

I don't have to ask him to take off his wellies, he does it like he's on autopilot, before he hooks his damp raincoat over the newel post.

'I was just in the living room,' I say to him.

'Cool. I'll just go and wash my hands.' Again, like he's a regular visitor. He's only come into the house three times, including the original time, but he's obviously taken on board what I've said about my worries and health anxiety. It's odd, I can't really think what we talk about, but we always fill our time together with chat.

'Actually, make that yay. Let's go for a walk. I'll get my rain hat. I do own a rain hat, just for days like this. I don't get to wear it enough.'

Dunstan looks at me as if he knows. He is too comfortable around me and in my house for us to stay here – that would only lead to trouble.

'Have you got something on your mind?' he asks as we cross the road to the park side. The rain is slightly heavier than earlier, meaning there are more cars on the road, more red brake lights and white headlights and schlicks as tyres throw up spray. I'm quite well protected in my burgundy rubbery waterproof coat and matching hat, and my big blue wellington boots.

'I've always got something on my mind, haven't you?' I realise almost immediately how I sound. 'Sorry, that was snippy of me. The police came again yesterday and I completely forgot to tell them I got another vase of flowers for Priscilla,' I say. 'They told me more about Priscilla being this big-time hacker. Makes you wonder if you know anybody at all.'

I think that is what is bothering me the most about all of this. Who are these people that I live amongst? One of the people on our street is likely to have attacked Priscilla, tried to cave her head in. And even if they hadn't . . . the things I know about them are so disturbing! Every time I see someone, I remember what Priscilla wrote about them and I shudder.

'That's what it's like being a police officer – you're never really sure if someone you know is going to commit a crime.'

I sigh silently, wishing again that I could tell him about the diary, about Clark's fingerprints, about my constant fear that someone is going to do to the girls what they did to Priscilla. 'How are your nightmares?' I ask. We're on the incline, our usual place to start a serious conversation.

'Good, actually. Going for our nearly daily walks has made such a difference to pretty much everything.'

'Really? That's good.'

'Stop a minute, Rae,' Dunstan says and stands still. He looks like a bright yellow snowman, built in the middle of a park. When I stop, I'm sure, from a distance, we look like two yellow and burgundy lollipops planted upright. 'I want to say thank you. I didn't realise how much I needed someone to talk to until the nightmares stopped. It really is good to talk.

'Guys like me, people don't expect us to talk or open up. They just kind of expect us to get on with it. Especially with my type of job, you literally have to get on with it. Yes, there is on-the-job support, but you never know who it's going to get back to. Who is going to be using that against you.'

'That's sad you feel like—' My heart stops dead in my chest when he reaches out and touches my hair, then tugs my hat into place. *Don't do that*, I scream inside, *don't do that*.

'Your hat wasn't on properly, your hair was getting wet. And I know what Black women are like with getting their hair wet.'

'That's erm, that's actually a fallacy that water is the enemy of Black women's hair. It's actually—'

I'm babbling to try to downplay what is happening; trying to talk over – and so dismiss – the fact he hasn't moved his hand away but is staring at me in a way he shouldn't.

I should not be doing this. This is the type of behaviour that would get me written up in Priscilla's book. This is the type of behaviour that would end my marriage and mean not seeing my girls every day, not being with the dogs every day. We'd have to sell the house and I'd have to go back to living on my nerves, waiting for the knock on the door.

'You can talk to me, you know?' he says. 'It helps. Unburdening yourself really helps. Tell me what's on your mind, tell me about the thing that happened which set off your anxiety.'

He moves in closer. He is adorable in the rain, water dribbling off his hood, his face nestled slightly out of sight. 'Tell me – you'll feel better if you open up.'

I shake my head. 'I can't do that.'

We stare into each other's eyes for a moment, and in that piece of time, as brief and ethereal as it is, I consider opening my mouth and uttering those words. And at the same time, I think about closing the final gap between us and kissing him. Like he so wants me to do, like I so want to do.

'You can.'

'No, I can't. I can't tell anyone.'

He moves closer still. The next move will have him too close to stop what will happen.

'All right, what if I tell you something about me that no one else knows? Will you tell me then?'

236

'Yes,' I say, to get him to stop moving any closer. If he starts talking he may back off, because the words I need to say to get him to do that aren't rising up to take position in my mouth.

'You promise?'

'Yes.'

He lets me go and steps right back. And I'm grateful. Because I was not sure I would do the right thing in the moment. Again, another element that this whole episode has brought into sharp relief – I *cannot* trust anyone, not even myself.

'All right,' Dunstan murmurs. 'All right.' He pushes his hood off his head so I can see his whole face. He doesn't care that the rain is pelting down, landing on his close-shaved head and then dribbling down his face in a multitude of rivulets. 'I haven't told anyone this. Not anyone. Certainly not the police.'

I can't imagine what he is about to say. Did he do it? Did he try to murder our neighbour?

'For more than three months or so, I've been sleeping with Priscilla.'

Him? All those things. All those things that I read about, the sessions, the acts, the salacious rememberings were about him? *Him?*

On the good side, I don't need to wonder any more what it'd be like to screw Dunstan – from how Priscilla told it, it sounds like it would be out-of-this-world good. On the bad side, I don't need to wonder any more what it'd be like to be with Dunstan because now all I can see are snippets of them together as described so openly by Priscilla.

'Was not expecting that,' I admit. 'I mean, I'm not sure what I was expecting you to say, but not that.' I think on it for a moment, desperately trying to erase one particularly graphic image before I abandon hope and ask: 'Why haven't you told the police, exactly?'

'Because I didn't harm her. If I say I was involved with her, it'll

make me even more of a "person of interest" than I already am, especially since I found her. I just need to hold out until they find who did
it to her and then it won't matter that I was involved with her.'

There's some logic to that, but . . . 'Won't it be a million times
worse if they find out rather than if you tell them? Won't they ask you
why you kept it to yourself?'

'Yes, but at least, hopefully, they'll have the person who did it in
custody by then so they won't try to convict me.'

And this guy is meant to be clever? Even Mella would be able to
see the flaw in that plan. Hell, Yam and Okra would be able to spot it.
'I think that's the craziest, most stupidest plan I have ever heard. When
they catch whoever did it, they won't be super cool about you not telling them. They'll be like, "Mate, why were you withholding evidence?"
or whatever it's called. If I was them, the first thing I would do is go
through all your old files and cases to see where else you've been dishonest. And I'm saying that as someone who doesn't even work for the
police.'

'It's not ideal, but I know how quickly things can change from normal to full-blown suspect and that stain never goes away. Especially
not for a police officer.'

Utter madness! I can't believe someone as intelligent as him thinks
this will work. They will absolutely destroy him when they find out.
And they *will* find out. Especially since I intend to hand over the diary
once we know who did this. This just makes it more complicated. Like
my mind could take any more twists and revelations. And let's not
forget the part where Dunstan has very clearly been putting the moves
on me when the Priscilla thing was recent. And besides . . . 'Won't
they have found your fingerprints in her house?'

'Yes. And that was easily explained – I told them I was always over there doing odd jobs for her. I told them that before my fingerprints were found.'

'It's not just fingerprints though, is it? If you and her were "at it" there'd be a whole load of other "evidence" to explain away.'

'Priscilla was a complete clean freak. Everything like that was cleaned and washed straight away. Which was why I was surprised they found any fingerprints at all. She was a stickler for cleaning. I'm as sure as I can be that they won't find anything.'

'I don't believe I'm hearing this! You lied to your copper buddies, just like that!'

'I omitted things, I didn't lie. It's the absolute truth that I was over there doing odd jobs all the time. That's what it was like – I did work around her house and garden, we hung out together, we went to bed.'

'OK.'

'She was actually really good company. Funny, sweet. But she never wanted anything other than what we had, which was sex and a good laugh.' He steps closer again and I notice that the rain has stopped, that the sun is struggling to shine through the dove-grey clouds hanging low in the sky. 'I've told you mine, now you tell me yours. What is your secret?'

In the shock and aftershock of what he's just said, I'd almost forgotten that I'd promised to reveal all.

'The problem with telling you this is that you get drawn into it as well and I have to know that I can trust you. You can't tell anyone. And because so few people know, I'll know if you do talk. Some people know some of it, but no one – apart from Clark – knows what I'm about to tell you.'

He's not really paying attention. He thinks I'm being dramatic so he is hearing this as the blah, blah uninteresting marshmallowy foam before I give up the chocolaty treat at the centre. He should be paying attention because without the foam, the treat is deadly for me and everyone I love.

'Basically, Dunstan, about six years ago I witnessed someone being murdered and we had to leave everything behind because they tried to shut me up, too.'

Lilly

47 Acacia Villas

11 June 2021, Brighton

There are these little nooks in Brighton, places that most people don't
know about where you can meet up and no one will see you. Technically, it shouldn't be an issue, me meeting up with these people, but
right now, everything is a potential problem, everything could be seen,
pounced upon and dissected in a way that will reveal things that really
do need to be kept hidden.

Along from the Pier, in the opposite direction to Hove and Worthing, there are several of these nook-type places that feel secluded
and safe. One of my business partners, Hollie, has lived in Brighton
and Hove her whole life and it was she who suggested we meet here.
You can only really access this area from the street – you have to walk
along the road from the Pier and the Aquarium, then after a few hundred metres, you take the steep, sheer stone steps to get down onto the
pebbles. Further back, on the other side of the Pier, this area under the
steps has been claimed by shops, playground areas and other community spaces; here that has not happened. Here it is bleak; litter has built
up and seagulls often gather to feast on it. The pebbles are especially
bumpy underfoot and I feel completely ridiculous standing here in my
running gear, waiting for the others to arrive.

I'm still not sure how I got here. My idea had originally been to help people with their planning issues. Property was my obsession. Renovation, decoration, planning. I used to sit and read the plans submitted to the planning register, fascinated by what was approved, what wasn't. And then I noticed a pattern. Which architects seemed to get it right first time, which ones were brought in to take over designs, which planning officers' names were most likely attached to the 'nos' and which were attached to the 'yeses'.

One day, I started to note things down. My interest had moved from piqued to truly fascinated to completely intrigued, to 'I see what's going on here'. Or rather, I *think* I see what's happening here.

Hollie and I went to the same gym, we often ended up on the spin machines together, lifting weights, sitting in the sauna. We'd walk home together and talk about all sorts of things. I knew she worked on the planning committee, so I started asking general questions. It took me months to tease it out of her but she admitted that sometimes applications were passed or rejected based on 'other considerations' and not just on the merits.

No! You don't say! I wanted to reply, but I didn't. Because something was brewing in my mind. I could set up a consultancy where I found the friendly planning committee members and helped people who could pay to make sure their plans were fast-tracked through the system. Hollie's time on the planning committee was coming to an end and she wanted to get into politics for real. Any extra money she could earn would be super helpful. She knew a couple of people who might be interested in setting up this business with us so she said she'd reach out to them. And then there were four. Each with a specialism, each with a way to bring us clients. It was all legitimate. Anything we charged was a consultancy fee. Anything we had to pay after a plan was rejected was also a consultancy fee.

We ran our business in plain sight. We took on cases, we sat in on planning meetings, we found people who would write the right sort of supportive letter – we wrote them ourselves and used other people's details if necessary. But things like that were rarely necessary because more often than not, one of us knew a guy or a gal, and things carried on moving as smoothly as they could.

And then Bieler from number 28 brought Hinter on board.

Hinter knew people. He knew people who had real money and a real interest in investing in development. As well as investing in a property consultancy.

'The development that has just been approved is relatively small fry compared to what my associates are interested in investing in,' explained Grayson Hinter. He gave me the creeps. There was no other way to put it. He wasn't overtly unpleasant, except for his constant need to make you feel small by correcting your grammar or reminding you of how worthy his charity was. It was his manner of speech that bugged me most, though. He would deliberately ... slow ... down ... what ... he ... was   saying so you would be resentfully hanging on every word until he finished. How his wife put up with it, I didn't know, but I did wonder how long a normal conversation took in his house. 'I can bring you the type of clients that a small start-up like yourselves needs.'

That was when it changed for me. On many levels, I craved excitement. But I knew my limits. I knew where to draw the line and walk away. Hollie didn't. Bieler didn't. Milburn didn't either. They all saw pound signs. I saw trouble.

Big money always brings big trouble. Because it turns out that big money doesn't only want help getting their development projects approved, they also want somewhere to 'rest' funds, to scrub funds, to move those newly cleansed funds on to somewhere else. And dealing with these people is like a certain snack food – once you start, you can't stop. Ever.

And I was stuck now. I was in this thing with them, these people I didn't know, and it would be hard to extricate myself. So I stayed. I had a look at my life, and I knew what I had to do. I had to bank the money – overseas. I had to get ready to leave for good. The moment it looked like there was going to be trouble, I would take the money and leave the country. Go back to my daughter. Even if Clark had come out of denial and we were together, I had an escape route.

Rotten luck for me – Grayson Hinter arrives to this meeting first. He's looking rough for a man who usually prides himself on being the quintessential country gentleman with his tweed jackets and light-coloured trousers.

'Miss Masson,' he says, crunching his way over the shingle.

'Grayson,' I reply.

Bieler, small, almost round, comes hurrying across the beach, acting as though he's late to follow the white rabbit down the famous hole in *Alice In Wonderland*.

Hollie arrives and she is dressed like me – for a run – and judging from how flushed red she is, she's run here from home, too. She knows how to make things look normal – she and I are the two who look like we've just bumped into the others while doing something we do every day.

'We shouldn't be meeting like this,' I hiss. 'Doing things like this makes us look guilty.'

'Well, now the police are investigating Priscilla's attack, we can't use any form of communication that leaves a trace,' Hollie hisses in return.

'Do any of you have any idea what Priscilla knew?' Milburn asks. He has a soft voice that belies his tall, solid stature.

'What do you mean?' Hinter asks.

'Like I told you: she said she knew what we'd all done and it was going to blow us all up,' I say.

'She said the same to me,' Hollie stated.

'This is bad, this is bad, this bad,' Bieler says, literally holding on to each side of his almost bald head and rocking back and forth. Watching him reminds me of a Weeble – the funny little toys from my childhood that would wobble but not fall down. 'I shouldn't have got involved in this.' Funny how he wasn't saying that when the cash was rolling in. When we were taking in money hand over fist, everything was hunky dory and I was being pathetic or something – I can't remember the exact word he used – for saying we should be cautious.

'Milburn, with the money you have made you have paid off your mortgage, you have begun the renovation of your house. You even said you'd put money away to complete your children's schooling in the private sector' Hinter has swung into action because he brought these people to us. He changed our league and culpability; basically took us from 'dinner tray on freshly fallen snow' to 'top-of-the-line, all the bells-and-whistles snow patrol buggy'. He must think we blame him. I'm not sure about the others, but I bloody do. I blame him for everything that is happening and could potentially happen.

'And Hollie, your campaign material is top-notch. You have been able to hire the best in designers, social media managers, image consultants. Next stop Parliament for you, I think. Bieler, a similar story with you – your mortgage is paid off twice over, you have been able to holiday in some of the best destinations in the world. All of you have benefitted greatly from the financial boost my associates have provided for you.'

Hinter, whose speaking speed is faster than normal right now, has left me off his litany of riches because he knows very little about me. The others, they talk about what they do with their money, they share. I do not. These people are not my friends and they are not my family – what I do with my cash is my business. I bet none of them have a running-away fund all set up. They haven't used the money to buy a house in another country so they have somewhere to go when everything hits. And I bet none of them got their ex to bring over his passport to use it to add his name to the deeds of a house bought abroad, financially linking him to me.

'I suggest we hold our nerve. The very fact that the police have questioned all of us but as yet have not pursued it further suggests no one outside of us five knows anything more than they need to. And, Lillian . . .' My name is Lilly, but I fail to correct him because I can't be bothered. '. . . you have our Plan B in place, ready to be deployed, do you not?'

'Yes,' I say tiredly.

This is the very thing that Grayson Hinter would love to gloss over: there are other people who are aware of what we do. His associates. And they do not want us talking should we be arrested. Their 'no-squeal insurance', as I think of it, is different for each of us: Milburn – they have proof of him changing safety and other records on sites where workers were seriously injured and one almost killed; Hollie – they have evidence of drug-taking in her youth, which she committed petty crimes to finance and then, as a councillor, used public funds to pay off a blackmailer; Bieler – they have private CCTV footage of him leaving the scene of a hit and run where someone was hurt (not majorly) because he was drunk. They have a copy that can be sent to the police if Bieler decides to step out of line. They obviously couldn't find anything on me because my 'thing' is being keeper of Plan B.

And Grayson Hinter . . . I can't even think about what his 'associates' might have on him.

'I'm not doing this again,' I state, more for myself than anyone else. 'Don't take this the wrong way, but I don't want to see any of you again. We need to think of a way to wind up the business. Maybe tell Hinter's associates that we think we're going to get caught and want to lay low for a couple of years rather than trigger Plan B. Because if Priscilla really did know about this, then someone else is likely to find out. We need to stop while we're this far behind.'

'I agree,' Hollie says. 'I can't be involved in this if I want to get to Parliament.'

'Yes,' Bieler adds.

'Yes,' from Milburn.

We all stare at Grayson Hinter. The earlier rain has gone, but the wind has picked up down here on the beach, and we're buffeted by the salty air as we wait for his response. 'Yes, agreed,' he eventually sighs. 'I'll talk to them.'

I can tell by the deflation of his shoulders, by the worry lines that have multiplied on his forehead, that for him, deciding to walk away is not that simple.

Rae

11 Acacia Villas

May 2016, London

'The things I do for you children,' I was muttering under my breath as I stomped down the dark West London street. Mella and I were on a sleepover at her friend's house and she'd woken up crying for Welly, her pink supersoft bunny that she'd left in the car. It wasn't so much that she needed Welly to sleep through the night, it was more that Welly would be scared out there in the car all on her own. I'd done all I could to persuade her that Welly (read: Mella) would be fine, but she wouldn't hear of it. And, more importantly, she wouldn't go back to bed without her. Which actually meant I wasn't going back to sleep without her.

I'd had to pull on jogging bottoms and a zip-up top, whip off my sleep bonnet and then start the journey to the car. And it was a journey. Iris lived in one of those parts of London that hadn't introduced permit parking yet, even though it was a residential area packed with terraces and semis, which is to say, there hadn't been parking outside her house or on her street or even on the next street. I'd had to park two roads over, so there was no dashing out to the car for me. It was a journey in the pitch black of three in the morning, lit along the way by small pools of orangey street lights.

The night was so still and quiet, I walked as silently as I could in my trainers, fearful of waking up the people whose lights were out and whose heads were probably resting on pillows, dreaming the night away. There was a chill in the air and I wrapped my arms around myself, wishing I'd put on a bra and thrown on an extra layer. I turned the corner at the end of Iris's road and into the next road. Along and then round onto the next road was where I'd managed to squeeze my car into a space between a large people carrier and a smaller family car. My heart had been racing the whole way through that manoeuvre. I'd had to stop and start so many times because I was terrified of scratching someone's car. I probably should have carried on looking but I'd been round five times already, I couldn't bear to do it again.

Wishing I'd tried now—

I saw them before I heard them. They were actually in the middle of the road; about five or six of them surrounding another guy on his knees. Even from where I stood I could tell the man on his knees was beaten up and in trouble; that this was a bad business and I didn't want to get caught up in it. But this man needed help. It didn't take long to realise that the only help I could give him was to call the police – and I couldn't do that without them hearing, and I couldn't run away without them seeing.

Instinctively I pivoted back, flattened myself against the brick wall of the house I'd just passed. I could see them, still standing in the middle of the street, so confident in who they were and their place in the world that anyone driving down here would probably reverse and go the other way. And those drivers would know instinctively not to use their horn or show any irritation, because things would go badly for them. There was a man who was obviously in charge, his curtain of blond hair fell to his shoulders and even from a distance I could see he took care of himself. He stood in front of the man on his knees, talking. I couldn't hear because my heart was hammering out my terror in my ears. I just had to find a way to back off without alerting them that I was there and it would be OK. I could call the police from a safe distance and they would be able to—

Without ceremony or even seeming to care, the blond man casually stuck something into the man on his knees. Just like that. I couldn't believe what I was seeing and reared back, clamping my hands over my mouth to swallow my scream of horror. I had to get out of there. I had to get out of there or I could be next.

More than anything I wanted to close my eyes, escape from the horror of what I was witnessing, but I couldn't. I had to keep them in sight at all times in case one of them spotted me. Thankfully I was wearing black and the street light was out in this area. Again without ceremony, they let the guy on his knees fall to the ground. The blond one talked to the five standing around and two of them picked up the man and moved him to the pavement like he was just a sack of potatoes, while the others went to their cars, strapped themselves in and drove away. They moved him in the opposite direction to where I was standing, which was a relief because they would definitely have seen me if they went the other way. They, too, went to their cars, got in and drove away. I was frozen to the spot for a long time after they had gone, terrified they might come back.

A part of me, the part that is always calm and in control, started speaking soothingly, trying to get the rest of me to gather myself together enough to think about moving. A few seconds later, that part of me was instructing me to move. And then it was ordering me, barking at me, to move, to get back to Iris's and to call an ambulance. He might not be dead.

It was that thought that got me moving. He might not be dead. I was too scared to go to him. He might be dead and I couldn't handle that. He might be alive and someone could come back and catch me. I pushed my hood up and then started back the way I had come. My heart was pounding in my ears, a fast and relentless drumbeat; my blood was rushing like an ocean pouring into a sink, as I ran as quietly and carefully as I could.

In the front garden, shaking, trembling, I called an ambulance. It was likely too late, it'd likely do no good, but I called them anyway. I felt sick with guilt, absolutely sick to my core that I didn't help him. I am ashamed of that. I wish I'd been able to, and that I hadn't been absolutely frozen and terrified.

The police came to our house the next day.

I'd told Clark everything the moment we got home and he was wonderful. Of course he was, that's what he's like. He kept repeating over and over that I'd done the right thing. There's no way I would have stood a chance against six men; I did the best I could to keep myself safe.

'Can you tell us what you saw, Ms Manadacko?'

'Nothing, really,' I said. 'I just saw the guy lying there, and there were some cars driving away. But I didn't really see anything, it was dark and I wasn't sure who was hanging around so I came back to my friend's house to call an ambulance.'

Clark had tight hold of my hand, clinging on to me, anchoring me as I told the police the version of the night before I wished I'd experienced. Every time I closed my eyes I felt the heavy, sickening thud of the blade going in. I saw the look on that man's face – his horror and fear and resignation that it was over. I never wanted to see that look again. I couldn't erase that image – it was scorched into my mind. But I could pretend. I could pretend to the police officers because that was what Clark and I decided.

The casual way that blond man had finished the man on his knees showed me one thing very clearly: he would think nothing of dispatching someone who could identify him. I had no other reason to believe this except I saw how casually he killed that other man – if he found out that I had seen him he wouldn't think twice about doing it to me.

The official story had to be – and had to stay – that I came in right at the end. Right at the very end. The official story had to be – and had to stay – that I hadn't seen a thing.

They didn't believe me – they spent a lot of time trying to get me to tell the truth. And the truth was this: I wanted to live and because I wanted to live, I saw nothing that night. Nothing.

'I wish you would talk to us, Ms Manadacko, Raelynn. We have the suspect who committed this crime in custody and we can protect you. We can keep you safe. We have other eye witnesses. We probably won't need your testimony, but it would be good to have it on record.'

'Yes, I know, thank you, but I didn't see anything.'

July 2016, London

'We're just wanting to check in with you, Ms Manadacko,' the police officer I had never seen before in my life said as he sat in the living room. 'See if anything had come back to you about that night.'

'There's nothing to come back – what I told you is all I remembered then and what I remember now. I didn't see anything.'

He looked relieved for a moment, which made me suspicious. Why was he relieved when I wouldn't help him?

'I've also come to make you aware of the security breach that has occurred on our computers.'

My blood felt as if it was literally running cold. Nothing good could possibly come of what he was about to say. Clark's fingers were suddenly around mine, holding them firm and secure.

'There's no easy way to say this, but some of the files relating to the Risco case have been tampered with.'

'Tampered with?' Clark repeated.

'Some of the files have been tampered with and it looks as though they were downloaded by a third, unauthorised party. Unfortunately, we're as sure as we can be that among the files that were accessed, some of them were witnesses' details. We believe they might have fallen into the wrong hands.'

'But I'm not a witness, am I? I didn't see anything. Tell me my name and address were on the "we spoke to her and she didn't see anything" list and not on your "witness list".' I swallowed. 'You know, seeing as *I didn't see anything.*'

The policeman looked awkward, uncomfortable. Not sick and stricken like he should because he couldn't tell me I wasn't in danger. My name was on the list. My address was on the list. Everything a man who casually killed people would need to get to me was on that list.

At least I didn't have to worry about Iris because the murder around the corner from her house had been the final nail in the coffin for them living in London and they were in the process of moving back to Dublin. No, I just had to worry about me being completely exposed and thrown to the wolves by the police.

'This is a nightmare,' I said, barely above a whisper. Clark pulled me closer, his body a solid and reassuring cushion from this awful news. *This* was why we had decided I would say I hadn't seen anything. *This* was why my need for honesty had been usurped by a paring back of the truth – my safety relied on other people and those other people had fallen, literally, at the first hurdle of keeping my name out of the mouths of criminals.

'I can promise you that we are doing all we can to find out how this happened and to make sure it never happens again.'

'Great, but it'd be better if you could find a way for the criminals to unlearn my name,' I replied. Tears were nudging at my eyes. I was scared. I could be snarky and sarcastic, but I was scared, really, really scared.

'I can reassure you, even though we have had to release the suspect, very rarely does anything dangerous happen to anyone who is involved in a data breach.'

'You would say that, wouldn't you?' I replied before burying my face in Clark's shoulder and giving in to the tears.

Clark pulled me as close as he could, kissed the top of my forehead. 'It'll be all right,' he kept saying over and over as I sobbed. 'It'll be all right. It'll be all right.'

Neither of us believed that, but there was nothing else we could do at that time.

September 2016, London

The large, dark-blue van appeared from nowhere. I was on the way to the big Sainsbury's to do a shop, which was usually Clark's job, but I had a bit of time – I'd delivered the latest copy of the magazine I was working on early, and I thought I'd get this done to take the burden off him.

I pulled out from the side road, which was on a slight hill, to turn into the main road around the park and suddenly the vehicle appeared beside me. The road merged into one about 200 metres further down, so people from the left usually accelerated so they could get down first, and those of us from the turn road would slot in behind them. I had checked before I pulled out and hadn't seen the van.

I waited for him to pull forward, but he didn't, he stayed side by side with me. I left it one second, two seconds for him to pull ahead but he didn't, he kept level with me. I checked the rear-view mirror to slow down, but there was another dark-blue van behind me and it wasn't slowing down. Ahead, the merge was fast approaching, so I put my foot down, surged ahead to get into that space if the man beside me didn't want to go first. My stomach lurched as he matched my acceleration so we were both moving at the same speed towards the merge. My eyes flicked to the rear-view mirror again and the van behind me was right up close, giving me no room to slow down and hang back.

I'm going to die, I realised. *I'm going to die.*

My car wouldn't survive a collision with one of the vans, let alone both, which meant I was about to die.

Something clicked in my head, and I realised what I had to do. I didn't have time to think it through, I just had to do: I put my foot down hard, accelerating forwards and the van beside me surged forwards too, and just as we came to the point of no return, I swerved to the side of the road, avoiding the parked cars and bumping up onto the pavement, while braking hard. Thankfully, no one had come onto the pavement in the moments between me deciding to do this and actually doing it.

My car came to a screeching halt and I was thrown forwards, the seatbelt smacking my chest hard enough to knock all the air out of me. But I was in one piece and the car was, too.

The vans continued on their way, not caring that they'd forced me to do that manoeuvre, putting myself and pedestrians in danger. Not seeming to even notice anything untoward had happened thanks to them.

I couldn't move; my whole body was frozen in horror at how close I came to being run off the road. I *was* run off the road. If I hadn't swerved, I would probably be mangled in this car by now; if I hadn't managed to keep the car under control, it could be embedded in that brick wall.

When I did move, it was to shake; the horror of what had happened finally sinking in.

What happened could have been an accident, it could have been two men behaving recklessly, or it could have been . . .

My hands were quaking and my chest was heaving; my feet and legs were numb. Tsunami after tsunami of nausea crashed over and through me. I tried to pull myself together enough to drive home but it was impossible. That had been so close, too close. As my eyes came into focus, I stared at the opposite lane watching the traffic. Suddenly, I saw them: two dark-blue vans, driving side by side, both within the speed limit. At the exact same time, both drivers turned their heads to look at the woman sitting slumped in the driving seat of her grounded car.

Later that night, after Clark had spent many hours cuddling me up, he said: 'Let's move.'

The relief almost submerged me. I was thinking it, but I didn't want to ruin everyone's lives by suggesting it.

It took us less than two months to sell the house – we took the first offer we got because it was close to the asking price, and that's how we ended up living in Brighton.

Rae

11 Acacia Villas

11 June 2021, Brighton

'And that's how we ended up living around here,' I say to Dunstan.

For the money we sold our house for in London, we were able to almost outright buy a bigger home down here near the sea. That made up for it a little. Obviously, the other downside was having Lilly around the corner. But having the space to breathe, to not look over my shoulder, was something I couldn't put a price on – I would have moved in with her if it meant getting out of London and out of that man – Risco's – mind. I was sure he only cared about me because I was still in London. I was convinced – as Clark was – that once it required a concerted effort to chase us down and intimidate us, he would leave me alone.

Dunstan is silent for more than a few moments, obviously processing what I've told him. 'I . . . I didn't even . . . I had no idea.'

'Why would you?'

'Wow. I mean . . . wow. You poor woman. No wonder you have such anxiety.' He comes towards me then stops, remembers there is meant to be a barrier between us. 'Can I give you a hug? I feel like I need to give you a hug.'

I shake my head; far too dangerous. Even though it was coming

257

from an innocent place, it was very unlikely to stay innocent once we touched each other. 'Not a good idea,' I say.

He looks momentarily frustrated, then he rallies. 'Come back to my place then. Not for long. Just for a little bit. We can talk there.'

I shake my head again, faster this time. That was an even worse idea than the hug.

'Come on, Rae, you know what's going on here – I'm dying to kiss you. You must know that. You must know that I'm desperate to—'

'No, no, no, no,' I cut in before he takes this to a place of no return. 'Dunstan. I've just told you about something really traumatic that happened to me and you're talking about . . .'

'I'm talking about wanting to take care of you.'

'I have a husband for that.'

'I know. But that doesn't stop me wanting to . . . hold you.' He shrugs. 'I can't help it; I want to be with you.'

'That can't happen,' I say. 'None of that can ever happen.' The sun is properly out now, and it makes everything around us glitter like it is brand new, and at the same time it feels like it has been here forever but has recently been washed and put out to dry.

I shouldn't have told him about witnessing that murder. Here I am, squeamish about kissing him or fucking him, when I've done something more intimate. Clark is the only other person on Earth who knows that much of the story. Now that I've breached that boundary and put my whole family in real, mortal danger, sex with Dunstan should be a walk in the park.

I told him, though, because I wanted to see, I suppose, if it's as bad as I've always suspected it is. Was everything I've done since then to protect us – including not being completely honest with the police – justified? I'm none the wiser, really.

'Look, Dunstan, will you keep your promise and not tell anyone?'

'Of course.'

'No, I mean it. I know we've kind of got our wires . . . well, not crossed because it's obvious . . . Look, I've sailed too close to the wind with you. Can you please just . . . later on, if you get a bit ragey that I wouldn't, you know, well, do it with you, can you please not decide to dob me in about this to your mates in the police to get back at me? The last thing I need is for the London stuff to come back to haunt me.'

'I wouldn't do that. Besides, you know something about me that no one else is privy to. If I tell, you tell. We both get in trouble.'

'Thank you,' I say.

'Don't thank me,' he says. 'It makes me feel like . . . I dunno, shit.'

'I'll see you, Dunstan. Not tomorrow or the day after. Let's maybe leave it a few days and see how we both feel.'

'Yeah.'

Every step home makes me feel more guilty, more ashamed, more desperate to find out who attacked Priscilla so I can put this whole sorry mess behind me.

Dunstan

36b Acacia Villas

He always thinks the temperature in these incident rooms and their glass-walled offices is either too hot or too cold – they can never get the balance right. He often wonders if it's done on purpose, to keep everyone uncomfortable, always on edge so they can never be lulled into unwinding while they're at work. No matter the rhythm or the groove they've slipped into with an investigation, the powers that be never want them to be comfortable. Relaxed. Settled.

Their job is about so much more than just investigating a crime, it's about getting to the heart of what people do to each other. And you can never be allowed to slack off when it comes to that.

Or maybe the temperature thing is just because they are in an old building and the system has been tacked on top of what was there, and when you tack something on to something that was already there, it won't work properly, no matter how expert the integration.

Or maybe these incident rooms are too hot or too cold just because they are. Not everything has to have a deep meaning behind it, not everything is part of a conspiracy, Dunstan tells himself.

He's grateful that he's missed the daily briefing about the other cases the team is working on. Grateful because his mind won't settle on much of anything apart from the Priscilla case right now. He is feeling the weight of failure on his shoulders, even though, technically, he hasn't failed. It's more that he hasn't got anywhere, which kind of makes it a failure.

'Where are you with the Whickman woman?' his temporary boss, DI Harry Hallson asks.

Dunstan sits up that bit straighter in the seat on the other side of the desk in Hallson's office. Even though he missed the briefing – to stand in the rain with Rae – he still has to act like the informant he is and update the DI on what he knows.

'Does she know anything or not?'

'I think so. I'm really convinced she does.'

'So you need to keep working on her?'

'Yes.'

'Meaning you get to go for more romantic walks in the rain?'

Dunstan ignores that dig. It still smarts, what happened earlier. It stings in a way it has no right to. 'I've been doing my best to get her to open up to me. That won't happen overnight, guv. She's a really closed person. I've had to tell her a few things I wouldn't normally tell anyone we thought of as a person of interest to try to get her to trust me.'

Hallson looks him over disdainfully. 'Kind of like playing both sides against the middle?'

'Sir?'

'Make no mistake, Dunstan, if I find that you are doing similar to us – withholding information and the like, there will be consequences. You will lose your job. I'll make sure of it.'

'Sir.' Dunstan knows Hallson means it and a moment of fear thrills through him. He can't tell them about Priscilla yet, though. Not yet.

'And what about the London stuff? Is it connected?'

This is it. The moment he reveals that it was just as the detectives in London had noted – she did see something. She *was* a proper witness and she *had* been lying all along. Because this could be connected. The flowers that kept getting delivered to Rae instead of Priscilla, they could be the London lot trying to draw her out or do her harm. Or, like the thing with the temperature in the incident rooms, it might mean nothing at all.

He used to see those elaborate displays and expensive vases in Priscilla's house and feel a pang of jealousy as he wondered who was sending her flowers. He'd wonder if she was sleeping with anyone else and if he should be bothered by that. The one time he'd asked, she'd acted as though *he* should know who sent them, then acted as though she didn't know. It became a bone of contention between them because the casual fucking had turned into something deeper and more involved; the anonymous flowers made him wonder who else she was with.

It was unexpected with Priscilla. She'd dropped her shopping in the street just outside her house when he was passing. She'd looked so defeated and vulnerable that he'd gone straight into rescue mode. His sister regularly told him he had a hero complex – that he was always trying to rescue people. He had to admit that sometimes she had a point but at least his sibling acknowledged it wasn't only the pretty females that had him swooping into action – men were just as likely to get help from him.

'Oh, let me,' he'd said to her, rushing to pick up the escaping avocado and cantaloupe. He knew who she was but she never spoke to him because she wasn't that kind of neighbour. He suspected she had lived on Acacia Villas for longer than most, but she was aloof and stand-offish, preferring to only speak to people on her own terms or if she had no choice, like at the Neighbour–2–Neighbour Watch meetings.

'Why, thank you, kind sir,' she said, smiling genuinely at him as he gathered up the dropped food and broken-handled bag.

She'd ushered him into her house, and he'd noted that her alarm system was top-of-the-range and there were CCTV cameras at various points around the front of the building.

He'd left the shopping in the hallway as she asked him to, and as he was about to leave, she – unexpectedly based on all their previous 'encounters' – asked him if he fancied a tea or a coffee.

They'd chatted and laughed about not very much. He can't recall the substance of that first conversation, he remembers snatches of making her laugh and of her touching his hand, but most of it is lost in the entirety of their time together. He'd been about to leave for a second time when she had smiled at him. It sounds fanciful now to say it was that smile that started it, but it was. He noticed as she smiled, the curve of her neck, the rise of her cheekbones, the glint in her eye that shouldn't be there with someone as reserved as she seemed. She was older than him – at least fifteen years, possibly more, but he liked the way she kept her white, grey and black hair cut short in a stylish bob, the way she wore lipstick to match her shoes, and that she had grinned at him with a bad-girl smile.

Dunstan knew he was good-looking. He'd had women coming on to him from his teen years and he rarely complained about that. He liked it when someone different was interested in him; liked the chance to expand his horizons whenever it arose. Priscilla lived in a big house on her own, and he wondered idly if she got lonely sometimes. If she wished she had someone there to chat to. 'Thank you for the tea,' he said as he got up to leave.

'Thank you for the rescue,' she replied.

At the front door, he said goodbye again and left. He'd got all the way to the bottom of the steps, even began to open the gate before he decided to go back. See what her reaction would be to his return – take it from there.

She opened the door straight away and stepped back to let him in. 'I hoped you'd come back,' she said.

And suddenly they were kissing, their hands exploring each other's bodies over their clothes. Her clothes came off easily, his came off easily. Her body was different from other women he'd been with. She was firmer in lots of places, saggier in others, but she had confidence. It was that which shaped her, allowed her to move with such grace and allure. She kept eye contact the whole time she lay back on her bed, throwing one arm up behind her head in the most seductive gesture he'd ever seen, the other hand she slipped between her legs, beneath the soft, wiry grey and black mound of her pubic hair.

He couldn't help groaning, watching her pleasure herself before he dropped to his knees, moved her hand away. He had to do this. He had to feel her writhing and moaning from what his mouth could do to her. The loud sigh and clinging to his head made him determined to keep her on the edge of pleasure for as long as possible.

The sex had been orgasmic, but what really blew his mind was the lack of embarrassment she felt afterwards. She kept eye contact, she chatted away, she stroked various parts of his body to get him going again without one hint of regret or shame. She had wanted sex, she had had sex, and now she was going to enjoy the afterwards of getting what she wanted.

Dunstan had never slept with anyone like her before. The women he went with were always a little shy afterwards, covering up their bodies, tacitly acting as though they shouldn't have done what they did. By the time Priscilla had stopped teasing him and climbed on top of him, guiding him into her while saying, 'I need to do this again', he was sold. Confidence begat beauty begat the best kind of sex as far as he was concerned.

He liked fucking Priscilla. And she always made it feel like it was *that* – something animalistic and base, yet tender and fun. Which was why the flowers bothered him a little. He wasn't seeing anyone else, he didn't think she was, but the flowers seemed to hint that he and Priscilla weren't going to convert from friends with benefits to a relationship.

'Dunstan!'

'Sir!'

'I was asking you about the Whickman woman and the London incident. Have you found out more about it?'

'Erm . . . yes, guv. She was talking about it this morning, as it happens.'

'And . . . is it connected to this case?'

He shakes his head slowly. 'She said she didn't see anything, that she panicked after the data breach, so they decided to move to Brighton where her husband had spent a large part of his life.'

He's lying for Rae. Withholding, really. But still not coming clean. He promised. That is the bottom line. He promised her and she promised him. Because now he is in another situation. It was meant to be the easiest 'undercover' assignment of all time. He isn't exactly undercover but he is an official informant so has to report everything related to this case that he finds out back to the DI. And it was meant to be easy because he is literally playing himself – living in his yard, wearing his own clothes, being called by his given name. But now it is somehow complex; complicated. He's played the role a bit too well, relaxed a bit too much into being himself. Revealing stuff to Rae in a bid to get her to open up has actually resulted in the straps that bind him, that keep him and his work apart, being loosened. He wasn't lying to Rae: his nightmares *have* gone, he *does* feel unburdened – talking to her *has* really helped. And that's before you get to the part where she is so beddable – many a night he goes to sleep wishing she were there.

Not for sex, even. He'd spent pretty much the whole of 2020 without affectionate human contact; getting it again with Priscilla this year had been like giving an addict the best quality hit after a long period of cold turkey. He'd started to crave that physical contact and quiet affection, and now there is no Priscilla, the nearest person is Rae. But he is doing Rae down. He does genuinely wish Rae is next to him most nights, their limbs holding each other close as they drift off to sleep together. He isn't quite sure what is happening to him, but maybe the last year of being starved of human – female – physical contact has battered him more than he realised, maybe it's tenderised the harder parts of him and made him crave affection and . . . urgh, love?

When his boss suggested he keep in contact with Rae as an inform-ant for the investigation, he'd been fine with it. She was a neighbour just like the others, and it wouldn't hurt to find out if she had been involved in what happened to Priscilla. And he'd somehow found him-self in *this* situation. He wants to take care of her. Now he's heard her story, realises why she is always on edge, why she looks pensive and wears those stupid gloves, he wants more than anything to look after her. To make love to her, too.

'What about her husband's fingerprints being in the victim's house?'

Dunstan shakes his head. How easily he lies – *withholds* – for someone he technically barely knows, but emotionally feels tied to. Not a good situation, especially when you consider the Priscilla factor. Not a good situation at all.

His senior officer's voice once again comes busting into his thoughts: 'The sum total of nothing, then?'

'Sir.'

'Get me something, or I pull you off this informant gig. The only reason you're on this at all is because you know the Whickman woman and you found the victim. Any more delays or dead ends and I'm going to start thinking that maybe you should be a proper suspect.'

'Sir.'

'It's been confirmed today that the second murder weapon – the poison – was on the vase of flowers that was delivered that day to the Whickman woman, who then took it over to the victim.'

Dunstan nods.

'As yet, there's been no trace where they come from. Ordered online via lots of different firewalls and VPNs. Burner mobile, prepaid credit card. Nothing left to chance in tracing back to who sent them. We're talking again to the florist's delivery drivers but it seems more than one florist has been used over the past few months. A lot of those florists have been using lots of different cash in hand drivers since last year. Some are untraceable. If we come up with nothing, we may need to move her from "person of interest" to "suspect", at which point we search the Whickman house.'

'Sir.' The idea of that turns his stomach for a moment. He can't imagine the horror on Rae's face as police officers storm in to tear her place apart.

'There's our version of a Neighbourhood Watch meeting coming up later this week, sir,' he says, hoping to distract the DI from focusing on Rae. 'It'll give me a chance to talk to some of the other neighbours. I'm not convinced it's just Mrs Whickman that we should be focused on.'

'We know that, Dunstan.' His boss gestures to the room outside.

'We all know that, and that's the job we're doing. You have one job in all of this and, I have to say, you're not exactly coming up roses with that, are you?'

'Sir.'

'Who is running the meeting?'

'Not sure, sir.'

'Whoever it is, tell them they'll be replaced by Weaver and Kaplan. One of them will lead the meeting, the other will observe with you.'

'Sir.'

'Time is ticking, Dunstan. If you can't find anything, then fair enough. We'll just haul her in for questioning and search her house.'

'Sir.'

Dunstan has ruined it, though. Rae won't want to come near him now he's shown his hand; shown his heart. The thought of that makes him nauseous. What was he thinking asking her to come back to his place? Saying he wanted to be with her. Rae knew, she's always known, but she had been stoically ignoring it. Once he said it out loud, she'd been forced to retreat. And she'd keep retreating, which means if there was anything she could have told him, she won't now.

Which means poor Priscilla won't get justice.

And he won't get to scratch that Rae-sized itch.

Priscilla

21 Acacia Villas
Diary Excerpt

10 May 2021

I can't believe he came here. Grayson.

Knock on the door during the day and I'm expecting Mr Afternoon Delight. There are some shelves to put up and some Priscilla to bed, so I opened the door with a big smile on my face and the buttons on my shirt opened to practically my navel. No bra. He especially likes when I show off my body to him before we get to it. He gets extra excited, he seems, well, firmer, and his kisses are so much more passionate, it's almost like he wants to consume me. I love to tease him, I have to admit. I love to sit near him while he works, wearing very little, encouraging him to finish as soon as possible so we can fall into each other.

So there I was, no bra, buttons open, 'come hither' smile on my face and on the other side of the door is Grayson Hinter. On a good day that man turns my stomach, but to have him see me like this . . . urgh. His eyes greedily settled on my partially exposed breasts and I swear he licked his lips before he said hello.

I wasn't quick enough at covering up, so I had to deal with him groping me with his eyes. When I let go of the door to hurriedly do up the buttons of my shirt, he used that opportunity to step over the threshold, meaning I had to step back and let him in. He shut the door behind himself and then leaned against it, staring at me while I tried to hide away my body. Usually, I don't care who sees me, but him? That gross specimen of humanity? No. I do not ever want his eyes on me like that.

'Well, that is a welcome that is most welcome.' He smiled lasciviously.

I almost vomited into my mouth. 'What do you want?' I asked sternly.

He stared at my chest, then my legs, which were exposed in a shortish skirt, before his shiny, disgusting tongue moved over his lips as he moistened them in a slow, provocative manner. I wanted to throw up, but instead I demanded again: 'What do you want?' I had an edge to my voice now, my face was showing how disgusted and annoyed I was.

'I have a proposition for you,' he said. 'A mutually beneficial one.'

'I want nothing from you,' I spat. 'You need to leave.'

'I think you should do me the courtesy of hearing me out.'

'I don't owe you anything. Leave or I will call the police.'

'Priscilla! This isn't like you. Is something wrong?'

'Isn't like me? You don't know me! We've barely spoken in over fifteen years. Get out of here! *Now!*'

Before I knew what was happening, he had his hand around the side of my head, his fingers were in my hair, and he was pulling me towards him like he was going to kiss me. 'Priscilla, you may think I don't know you, but I do. And I care about you very much,' he was saying. 'I have long admired your beauty, your grace and your poise. I think, together, we could be a formidable couple. I have powerful friends who would be delighted if I brought you into the fold. We have regular meetings, dinner parties, social gatherings that are always beneficial to attendees. There are a number of investments I can help you to make. Some connections that would prove helpful to you in the business world. And I would be honoured to have you on my arm. What a power couple we would make—'

I shoved him off, almost retching at the fact he'd touched me *and* what he was saying. I mean, what did I ever do to make him think he could approach me like this? That he could touch me?

'*Get out of my house!*' I screamed at him.

He had the audacity to look shocked. Shocked that I wanted him away from me. And then angry. Really angry. Then he started telling me how we were made for each other, each word scorched with his anger that I wasn't responding how he wanted me to. Me and him? NEVER!

Which was when I started to tell him what I knew about him. All of it, in the baldest terms and the loudest voice.

He was puce when I finished, the fury burned in his veins. I could tell he wanted to hit me, to shake me, to get me to see things his way. Despite everything I had said, he was still convinced we were meant to be together.

What did he think? I would forget everything I knew about him and open my legs? I went down the corridor and picked up the house phone. 'I AM CALLING THE POLICE!' I screamed.

That seemed to stop him in his tracks, made him come to his senses. When I started dialling, he turned and fled.

I thought about going through with it and calling the police, telling them what had just happened, but that would lead to a lot of uncomfortable questions about the other things I know.

It took quite a bit of time for me to stop trembling. Not because of Grayson, him I can handle. It's the other people he's involved with. He's probably going to tell them that I know what they do.

I'm probably in danger now. You don't mess with those people and get off lightly. But maybe Grayson will be too embarrassed to tell them.

I hope so. I really hope so.

Bryony

24 Acacia Villas

11 June 2021, Brighton

'I'm not happy about the amount of time you are spending on this "business" of Alana's,' Grayson tells me over dinner.

He resisted for a while, but for the last couple of weeks, he has made it home in time to sit down with us to eat. Because he knows there's nothing he can do if he's not here. We eat and he rages, but the next night is the same again. Alana told me to be careful, but now that I've started to make the point that we exist apart from him, I can't backtrack.

After nearly two weeks of the new way of doing dinner, though, Grayson has obviously decided that it is my sewing that is the cause of the disturbance in his life, not me deciding 'no more'.

'Aren't you, darling?' I say.

The children have bowed heads and they are concentrating very hard on their food.

'No, I am not. The house is looking unkempt. You don't have time to cook proper food – what is this slop?'

'It's vegan lasagne. Tilly fancied trying out vegan eating for a few days, so I'm cooking a few dishes for us all to try.'

'Not in this house you're not,' Grayson says.

'Oh, are you going to start making the meals?' I say innocently.

273

The fire is ignited in his eyes. The same fire that was burning the night he hurt me after the police visit. Alana's words about this being a dangerous time echo in my head and I immediately lower my gaze, make my body a bit smaller.

'Things are spiralling out of control in this house and I do not like it. You are to quit this nonsense with Alana and you are to start cooking proper meals again, and bring the cleaning standards back up to scratch.'

'*And if I don't?*' I want to reply, but instead I keep my gaze lowered and count to ten. This is not the time. 'Don't forget the Neighbour–2–Neighbour Watch meeting in a few days,' I say to him. A reminder that if he hurts me, the neighbours will see. The neighbours will know.

He baulks at the reminder, smarts that he has been thwarted.

'I'll tell Alana about not working with her any more at the meeting, shall I?' I say.

Grayson thinks it over. Realises that bruises or public declarations of resigning from a very part-time job to take care of the family will look like I am being stifled by my husband. And that will be very bad for his public image.

'I do not want you to stop something you enjoy, I would simply like you to put the family first,' he eventually says.

'I will, Grayson, I will,' I reply, sounding grateful. Of course I'm resentful, not grateful. But if he allows me to do this until I get hold of that book, then I will be more than on my way to freedom.

Rae

11 Acacia Villas

11 June 2021, Brighton

Clark has gone to bed early again.

He's avoiding me, probably because if he speaks to me for any length of time, he'll confess something. In all the time I've known him, he's not been able to keep things from me. He's always been straight-down-the-line honest and, like me, he hates lying. We didn't have to discuss making sure that the girls knew that lying is a terrible thing, it was something innate and fundamental to both of us.

Which is why the fact he has been living a double life these past months has shocked me so much.

What has also shocked me is how easily I've been sucked into a 'thing' with my friendly neighbourhood policeman. Who is most likely investigating me for attempted murder. I told him no, earlier in the park, but it took effort. A huge amount of self-restraint that I'm still surprised appeared when I needed it.

I open our bedroom door and Clark looks at me like a husband who was meant to be asleep by the time his wife arrived upstairs. He has his phone in his hand and I can't help but suspect that he was texting *her*. Lilly. I'm trying not to be angry at her. This is on him. This is a

Clark issue because he is the one I am married to. I can't think about that right now, though.

Rather than go to my side of the bed to get undressed and start the process of getting ready for bed, I go to his side. He looks alarmed for a few moments, unsure what I'm up to and if he's going to suffer for it. Staring directly at him, I pull off my T-shirt, unbutton then remove my jeans, unhook my bra, slip down my knickers. Clark stares at me, still confused. Since we've moved here, I haven't done this.

But then, I haven't had my engines revved up so much by another man since I got together with Clark. Yes, I've noticed other men, but I haven't . . . I take Clark's phone off him, put it on the side without looking at it. *His* chest is leaner than Clark's; my husband works out to keep himself firm. *His* body is more slender, *he* doesn't have Clark's height, and *he* doesn't have Clark's thighs. But I don't care. I just need . . . I just need to do this thing to get rid of the feelings that have been burning through my body since I told *him* no.

Clark doesn't complain or resist when I push back the covers and climb on top of him. He looks like he's about to speak, which will spoil it, so I press my fingers onto his lips, stop him talking. In response, he grips my hips and we both groan as I slide myself along the full length of his erection. I shut my eyes and allow tingles of desire to light up my nerve endings.

I slide back and I feel his body buckle underneath me, wanting more and wanting it quickly. Slowly, teasing him, teasing me, I guide him into me and the taste of this explodes inside me.

This is what I want, *need*.

I throw my head back, moving slowly, deeply, carefully, to feel every part of him, every microsecond of pleasure racing through my veins.

I dig my fingers into his hips, moving and grinding, pacing myself, eking out the feelings that are so intense, they're almost painful.

Yes . . . yes . . . *yes* . . . this is what I *need* . . . Thi—

Suddenly, Clark flips me back onto the bed, pulls me towards him, grabs my leg and holds it close to his body as he enters me again, pushing so hard and fast it takes me a few seconds to grasp what is happening. He seems to have caught whatever it is that's making me like this and is giving in to it, too.

His hand closes around my breast, as he pounds into me, pushing and thrusting so hard it takes time to get into the rhythm of it; just as I do, he moves again, flips me over and enters me from behind, moving hard and fast again, his heavy gasping in my ear, his breath against my cheek.

After a few minutes, his strokes become shorter, quicker, he's almost there, he's almost finished. I haven't. I'm nowhere near finished, so I push him off. The moment he is lying on the bed, I climb on top of him again, sink down onto him while digging my jagged nails into his chest – hard. So hard it causes him to wince dramatically and grab at my wrists to stop me. He pulls my hands away from his chest but I keep on moving and he moves with me, allowing me to control the pace, the rhythm, the timing.

He drops my wrists and grabs my hips, hard, so hard it hurts.

This is so utterly different from how sex normally is and it is good, so good, so utterly . . . completely . . . perfectly *good* . . . and . . . and . . . and . . . just how I imagined it would be like with *him*.

I screw up my eyes even tighter as I feel the familiar approach of an orgasm, bite my tongue to hold in my cries and cling to the man beneath me as the ecstasy tsunamis through me.

I flop unceremoniously on the bed and we lie next to each other, our breathing tattered and out of sync, our limbs trying to recalibrate themselves after being pushed and moved into unusual positions. I still have my eyes closed, I'm still in that other place.

'What was that about?' Clark asks as his breathing normalises. He's fitter than me, he goes for runs and lifts weights in the gym, so he's bound to recover faster.

His face flashes up behind my eyes, causing them to fly open as guilt and shame start to rampage through my mind. *I can't believe I did that. I can't believe I just used Clark like that. What has become of me?*

If I told Clark, I'm sure as I can be that he would be fine with it, that he would dismiss it as something that we all do – especially when you've been together a while. I'm as sure as I can be that he would say we all fantasise sometimes. But I would hate it if he did that to me. Especially about someone I know.

What's to say Clark hasn't been doing that with you all these months? A treacherous voice whispers in the deepest recesses of my heart, in the place where I feel his betrayal the most. *What's to say he hasn't actually screwed Lilly, but he's thinking of her every time he's with you?*

Clark turns his head to me. 'Rae, what was that all about?'

'I don't know,' I say. Because truly, I don't. What is going on with me? With Clark? With Lilly? With Dunstan? With Priscilla? I don't know is my answer. I don't know.

Maybe I should just hand the diary over to the police and take my chances because I am hurtling down this path to nowhere. I mean, how am I supposed to work out who hit Priscilla over the head? It's clear that she pissed people off. She liked to find out secrets and then she liked to let people know that she knew them.

Sometimes overtly, like with Bryony, and sometimes subtly, like with Lilly.

I look at my husband. And I have to admit to myself then that I do know what that was all about. Of course I know.

I'm on the verge of having a breakdown. My body is telling me that I am close to falling apart. The morning aches, the pounding head, the tingly fingers and toes, the night sweats, the constant panic, the dips in heartbeat, the raw nerves. I am going to break down soon unless I talk to someone.

And it can't be Clark because he is in Priscilla's book.

'I don't know,' I repeat.

Across his chest are eight deep crescent indents where I dug in my nails. I don't want to look too closely in case I see where I might have punctured the skin and drawn blood. I stroke my fingers over them. 'I'm sorry for this. I don't know what got into me.'

'It was the heat of the moment,' he says, rather generously.

'Can we . . . you know, do it again. But like normal this time.'

Clark leans over and languidly kisses me. 'Yes,' he says. 'I'd like that very, very much.'

Priscilla

21 Acacia Villas
Diary Excerpt

13 May 2021

This was pushed through my door.

> You are in danger.
> Only I can protect you now.
> Say the word and I will be
> by your side to keep you safe.

Must be a little jumpy after the Grayson incident and the note through the door because of how I reacted earlier. Mr Afternoon Delight was over, working on pressure-washing the flagstones out back because they've started to go green. We always 'get together' after he's done some work in the house. I was in the bedroom, folding up my laundry and he came up behind me. He put his arms around me and I nearly went through the roof while trying not to scream. He was horrified and asked me what the matter was.

I couldn't tell him, obviously, so I made up a story about work and how I was a bit stressed so was away with the fairies. Mr Afternoon Delight didn't really believe me but I started to tease him and we ended up falling into bed and having quiet, slow sex. He was a bit confused about why I'd been so keen on taking it slow and sort of loving, but I couldn't tell him that he'd been the palate cleanser I needed after Grayson and the note.

It felt good to be in my body in a way that was mine to control. I don't think it had hit me properly how much Grayson had scared me. It's not him so much as those I know he's involved with.

The note he sent – which of course is from him – sounds like he's set them on me or he will set them on me if I don't agree to become involved with him. The idea! I couldn't bear to have him near me, let alone sit next to him and play nice. And no doubt he'd expect some kind of . . . urgh, the very idea!

It'll be all right. I'm sure it'll be all right.

Rae

11 Acacia Villas

18 June 2021, Brighton

This is like having X-ray vision.

Seeing everyone and knowing their secrets and quirks is like having X-ray vision that allows me to see everyone naked. It is not good. We all gathered in Bryony's house – another not good thing – for the chat with a police officer to talk about community safety.

Bryony's house is beautiful, spacious and can easily accommodate the twenty or so people who have turned up tonight. She fusses around dispensing drinks and passing plates of biscuits around. Her husband, Grayson, moves from person to person, making small talk, smiling and nodding in a paternalistic manner that must go down a storm as the head of a charity. They seem like such a nice couple, you wouldn't think that he makes deals with dodgy business people so he can join their secret society, and she refuses to acknowledge what he might do to get ahead in the business world he has become embroiled in.

I sit in the very corner of the large sofa, staring into my cup of tea so I don't catch anyone's eye and have what I know about them replay in my mind.

Thankfully, Natalie and Liesha arrive together and take their seats next to me on the sofa. They don't really feature in Priscilla's damn book except for when she mentions they spend time talking in the street and why she likes them. They are safe and normal to sit next to. I do wonder why she didn't go to one of their houses to offload her book. I wouldn't be in this mess if she had.

I feel Dunstan's arrival in the room before I see him. It's like I'm tuned into his frequency now that I've told him one of my biggest secrets – and because I am ridiculously attracted to him. I can't help looking round at him as he moves further into the room, and we do an embarrassed stare at each other before he finds his smile and I find mine and I pretend that Priscilla wouldn't be writing this up.

Dunstan and Rae. Saw them walking to the park again. Obviously hurtling towards an affair, blatantly attracted to each other and sharing a different level of intimacy. She's resisting, for now. She's convincing herself she has a marriage worth saving but she's too scared to ask her husband why he's been screwing his ex. Messy. I thought more of her. I thought she was better than that. People disappoint.

I'm embarrassed, too, because of pretending to have sex with him the other night. Clark and I did it again afterwards, eyes open, focused only on each other and it was like sex normally was, but it feels like I came as close as possible to screwing Dunstan the other night and that's shameful.

'If I might call everyone to order,' Grayson says. He sounds authoritative, probably because this is the sort of thing you can see he loves doing – holding court. 'As you know, there was a terrible attack on our beloved and much cherished Priscilla Calvert. In addition to that there have been a number of burglaries in the area and in my capacity as a community leader, I spoke to the local constabulary and asked them to come here this evening to reassure you that these are rare occurrences and to give you all an idea of what we can do to better protect ourselves.'

He doesn't look like someone who would do all the things he does, but who does? Who can you trust? I've recently found out I can't trust my 'good guy' husband, nor can I trust myself to not develop feelings for someone who is most likely trying to put me away for murder.

None of us are who or what we seem.

The police officer leading the meeting stands up and steps forward. Bryony and Grayson have opened up their living room and placed chairs around the room, as well as providing perching space on the bay windowsills and sofa arms. I don't see Lilly, but I know she's not with Clark because he has taken the girls to the drive-in cinema over in Seaford.

The police officer talks very briefly about what happened to Priscilla, says she is still alive despite being gravely ill, and he keeps it so general we probably found out more from the local newspapers and speculation on socials. I notice the other officer with him doesn't do much except sit primly with a box of leaflets on her lap, and in with them are a load of pens that I suspect are for marking property so it can be identified if stolen.

He talks more generally about the burglaries, what you can do to make your property safer. High trellising on the top of walls and fences so it's difficult to get in and doesn't support weight; dummy alarm cases if you can't afford a proper alarm; CCTV.

CCTV. That pops into my head. If Priscilla was such a tech-savvy person, wouldn't she have had CCTV? I can't think now if there are cameras around her house. I suppose there wouldn't be if she set up a separate camera to try to find out who was letting their dog crap by her front gate. But what about inside? She was so high-tech, wouldn't she have set one up inside? Wouldn't it have captured who attacked her? Although obviously not, because the police would have found it. They have her computers, after all. And they would have found out about her and Dunstan in no time.

As his name enters my head, I flash back first to him saying he wanted to kiss me and then to what I did with Clark, and I think my head catches fire because I'm suddenly so hot with shame. What was I thinking? I sneak a look at him and find he's doing the same to me. We both sort of 'eek!' at having been caught then look away. Just utterly embarrassing.

As the meeting goes on, I notice the police officer who doesn't speak has distributed her leaflets and pens to most of us gathered here, and is now watching people quite intently. It wouldn't surprise me if there's another officer here, taking notes on how people react, watching us to see if anyone will give themselves away. How they would, I have no idea, but that's clearly what they're doing.

Buzzz, buzz, buzz. My mobile. It's in my pocket and, I thought, set to silent. I've obviously just turned the ringer off. Everyone can hear and even though I'd love to take it out and check who's calling at eight o'clock on Friday evening, or even turn it to silent properly, I can't. Aware that everyone around me is irritated as hell, I set my face to interested and focus completely on the police officer and what he has to say. I don't need any more attention. I'm already the woman who held Priscilla's hand as she lay in the street and I know people look at me a bit oddly because of it. Unlike Natalie and Liesha who had no qualms about asking me outright what happened, most of them just stare. If they're with someone else, they stare and then, unsubtly, speak out of the corner of their mouths about me.

I don't need any more attention, thank you. My phone will click to answerphone in a moment and I can pretend it never happened.

Priscilla

21 Acacia Villas
Diary Excerpt

14 May 2021

Saw Grayson today. He was talking to Lilly Masson. They both stopped and looked at me. Lilly has hated me ever since I told her to stay away from Clark Whickman. She's involved in the planning consultancy side of what Grayson is into as well. Should I be worried? I'm not sure. I feel less threatened by them together than I do Grayson on his own. Especially after he sent me that threatening note. There's no way he'd tell Lilly about striking out when he tried it on with me, as evidenced by Grayson raising his hand in a short wave.

I gave him my usual nod and tried not to glare at Lilly.

I'm sure it'll be fine.

15 May

'Who are your flowers from?' Mr Afternoon Delight asked today.

'I don't know,' I replied with a grin.

'Why are you smiling like that?' He was confused.

'Because, well, I don't know,' I said. Now I was confused. I'd assumed they were from him, but now I wasn't sure.

'You really don't know?'

'No, I don't. They're from a secret admirer that's so secret, I have no idea who they are.'

'Not even an inkling?'

I looked at him, confused again. That's the sort of thing a person who had given you flowers on the quiet would say, isn't it? 'Not the foggiest.'

'Right.'

'Right.'

We both left it at that. Are they from him or not? He does show his appreciation for me in the best way possible – with sex. And we do enjoy each other's company. Would he really go that extra mile and send me flowers? Would he throw me off the scent by having them sent to someone else's house? Or did he make a typo during the ordering – as Rae and I suspect – so they go to the Whickman house instead of mine? I don't know, but I do like the flowers. They're beautiful and make my hallway smell delightful.

Had an awful thought just then that they could be from Grayson. But that's not his style. To him, *he's* a gold-plated catch – he doesn't need to do any kind of wooing. And these flowers, with their beautiful ceramic vases and elegant displays, are all about seduction.

I've checked, done a lot of checking, and I can't seem to find out who sent them. But, no matter, they are beautiful and I'm going to enjoy them.

Rae

11 Acacia Villas

18 June 2021, Brighton

Dunstan catches me before I've got to the end of the path of Bryony and Grayson's house.

'Rae, can we just pretend none of that stuff the other day ever happened?' he murmurs so the people exiting the Hinter house don't hear.

'Yes, sure,' I mumble back, knowing that I'll be wondering if I should have kissed him in the park and cringing at pretending to have sex with him for a good long while. So yes, we can put it behind us, but it doesn't mean I'll be able to put it out of mind. One sly look at him tells me he's exactly the same – it's still there at the forefront of his mind.

'What did you think of the meeting?' he asks.

'I don't know. It was all a bit odd. I think everyone was expecting them to talk more about Priscilla and to reassure us it wasn't going to happen to us, too. I suppose they can't do that really because it actually could.'

'Don't forget, it's most likely that her attacker was in that room, too,' Dunstan adds helpfully.

'Oh, I haven't forgotten. Especially since I know your mates think it's me. You probably think it's me. And almost everyone in that room thinks it was me because I was with her before she was taken to hospital. Funny how they don't think it's you, though.'

'I guess I haven't got a criminal face.'

I stop and stare at him, outraged! 'How dare you! Take that back, at once!'

'Take what back? The fact I haven't got a criminal face?'

'The implication that I *do* have a criminal face. Take it back!'

'Can you not . . .?' He has a wry smile on his face.

'Can I not what?'

'Flirt with me.'

I return his smile while cutting my eyes at him, and begin walking towards my house again. The car isn't parked outside and I can't see it anywhere along the road, meaning Clark is still out with the girls. I'm starting to wish I'd gone with them but I couldn't have missed the meeting – it would have looked suspicious.

'This is me,' I say to him.

'I know,' he replies.

I start to dig around in my bag for my keys, and my hand brushes up against the diary. I almost snatch it out and hand it over to him – playing amateur detective is getting me absolutely nowhere. My fingers curl around the book and I'm about to pull it out when I see the side gate to our house is damaged, almost as though . . . I peer closer and discover, yes, someone has tried to kick the side gate in.

'Someone's tried to break into my house,' I say calmly to the man beside me. I point to the damaged gate. The lights are on inside, which we always do on those rare occasions we're all out of the house at the same time.

Dunstan immediately transforms into a policeman. It's quite something and I would probably appreciate it more if my heart isn't beating so fast it feels like someone is repeatedly punching me in the chest, and my breathing is so erratic I think I'm going to pass out from lack of oxygen.

'OK, you need to stay here while I go to investigate.'

'I really do not. It looks like they didn't get very far – the gate is still in one piece. The dogs barking probably scared the life out of them.'

'You could be right, but let me have your keys and I'll go and have a look around,' Dunstan replies.

'Narrator's voice: Rae will not be handing over her keys to the policeman,' I say. 'I'm sure it's fine. We have a great alarm system that's serviced every year and it rings our mobiles if it's ever tripped. That light also starts flashing,' I say, pointing to the alarm box on the wall. After the London incident, we were determined to do everything we could to keep ourselves safe.

'I'm sure you're right, but still, I'd like to accompany you into the house to make sure you're safe.'

'Fine,' I say. 'But if the alarm goes when we open the door and the dogs start barking, it's likely that they didn't get past the gate.'

As soon as I put the key in the lock, Yam and Okra start to remonstrate, barking so loud that if you didn't know, you would think they were much bigger dogs. The door opening breaks the circuit and sets the alarm off, causing the dogs to go wild, barking and barking so much, I think most of the street would have heard it. 'I think it's safe to say that no one got in,' I say to Dunstan over the racket. 'We have sensors at the back, which would activate if someone crossed the threshold. And we would have heard that barking over at the Hinters' place.'

'Fine, I'll accept that there is no one in your house. But you need to report this to the police.'

'You can do that for me.'

'I'm serious,' he says sternly. 'You're in most of the time, aren't you?'

'Yes.'

'Well then, it's odd that the first time you're all out at the same time, someone tries to break in.'

What he's saying has already occurred to me. And he doesn't even know about the diary. Since my chat with Bryony about what her husband gets up to, it's occurred to me more than once that other people might figure out that I know their secrets. They might come for me. Or come to see what I have. I am choosing to believe that it is to do with Priscilla and not to do with what happened in London.

'Do you think they knew I'd be at the meeting?'

'Yes. Look, is there any reason why someone would break into your house? Out of a lot of others on the street, I would not have picked yours to break into with the lights on, camera and the alarm box outside.'

'OK, not going to get freaked out – instead I will report it to the police and choose to believe it's just someone really stupid, who didn't think when they tried to break in.'

'Or . . . you could tell me if there's a reason someone would want to break into your house.'

'Yes, there is a reason.'

Dunstan is surprised at my admission. He turns to face me full on. 'What is it?'

'Well, I live in a big house in a nice part of Brighton and with the size of my house, it's likely there is going to be more than one laptop or computer. There's likely to be cash, cards, passports, jewellery . . . everything your average burglar wants and needs. I'm surprised a policeman like you doesn't know that.'

'You are the pain in my behind,' he responds.

'Can you not flirt with me, please?'

Dunstan grins at me, in a much less salacious way than he has been, but it's still there. The spark, the desire that isn't one-way. 'Make sure you do report it,' he says. Then, 'I'll see you, Rae.'

'Goodnight,' I say.

Okra and Yam jump all over me when I open the kitchen door to let them out. They're so affectionate, so pleased that I'm back after a few hours away, that they don't even contemplate running upstairs.

I'm grateful again that the girls and Clark talked me into getting these two dogs because who knows how far the burglars would have got if they hadn't been here? If they were burglars at all.

When I called earlier to report the attempted break-in, the person I eventually spoke to said there had been four other break-ins on the street earlier that night. Essentially, those who were at the Neighbour–2–Neighbour Watch meeting to learn about how to protect their property, returned home to find their efforts might have been too late.

I doubt the irony was lost on anyone. I hung up the phone, convinced that it was someone who was at the meeting, saw who was there, then slipped away to relieve the attendees of their possessions. Or to try to get their hands on the book I have.

As soon as Clark came back, I told him – away from the girls – what happened, and he went out to inspect the damage. Clark climbs into bed explaining the damage is not as bad as it looked. He found a heavy-duty padlock in the shed put it on the gate, then screwed the bolt into place.

'Problem solved!' he says with a smile as he climbs into bed.

I smile too, because we are so far from having our problems solved, they could be in separate universes.

Rae

11 Acacia Villas

I've decided to talk to Clark today.

This can't go on. Depending on how defensive he is, I may or may not tell him about Priscilla's book. But even without it, we can't pretend anything is normal between us right now.

Before breakfast, I ask him if he wouldn't mind taking the girls to school and the dogs for a walk and to plan to work from home today so that we can have a talk. 'What about?' he replies.

'Everything and nothing,' is my response, because even a few words of preview could have him deciding he needs to go into the office today.

My husband observes me for those long seconds when anything could be said or done, then decides it's best he goes along with it. 'Yes, yes, probably a good idea. We haven't had a proper talk in a while.'

I clear the breakfast things away, and wash them up, then I remember that the dishwasher is almost full and I'd avoided running it last night because I was going to put it on after breakfast this morning. Eesh. I can't believe how nervous I am about speaking to Clark. There was a time when I could talk to him about anything. That seems a long time ago – a lifetime ago.

I'm wandering around the kitchen, picking things up, putting them down, deciding to tidy, then deciding not to start something I can't finish. In the end, I give myself a shake, go upstairs and grab my laptop. Usually I work on my big desktop computer when I have to look at full magazine layout pages, but today I'll use my laptop. There are emails that need answering, projects that need updating.

Fifty minutes later and Clark still isn't back.

I've immersed myself in work, every nerve in my body on edge, waiting for his return. Twenty minutes more and I call his mobile. If anything, the dogs will have been out too long – their little knees won't be able to handle walking for over an hour.

'Yeah, this is Clark. Leave me a message.'

Nothing to worry about. Don't immediately panic, I tell myself. *Don't immediately go to a bad place. Maybe he dropped into the office to pick up some stuff to bring home*, I think. *Just try his work number.*

'Hello. This is Clark Whickman, I can't take your call right now, please leave me a message with your name and number and I'll get back to you as soon as possible.'

All right. STILL no need to panic.

Nothing has happened to him. He is fine. He's probably gone to Lilly's. Trying to get their story straight before I confront him with their affair. He's fine. He's honestly fine. In fact, if he's not back soon, I'll take a stroll down there, speak to both of them in a nice, civilised manner.

I continue to stare at my phone. I'm half tempted to call our house phone – even though I know he's not here – just in case he'll answer that. The lock screen on my phone is a picture of me and him. I took it one New Year's Day when we were out for a walk – it was bright and sunny so we're both wearing sunglasses. Our heads are pressed close together and I'm puckering up for a showy kiss for the camera. Clark is side-eyeing my grandstanding with the most affectionate smile tugging at his full lips, and dimpling his cheeks. I'd made it my lock-screen photo because, even though we have lots of other photos of us – some absolutely gorgeous – this one shows who we are. No matter what happens, no matter what life throws at us, this is me and him – two people who absolutely balance each other out.

We had all that. He wouldn't skip out on me just like that, would he? Would he?

Would he?

Why wouldn't he? That vicious voice that's been needling me about him and Lilly snarks. *Why wouldn't he skip out on you? If you start fucking someone else, then leaving is not far behind.*

It's not as if we know each other any more. It's taken not very long for deep cracks to appear in our relationship and I honestly, *honestly* thought we were rock solid. That's what comes from being ever so slightly smug, I suppose. Not too smug, not so as you rub it in anyone's face, but you kind of look at the people around you, the ones who are falling apart and falling out and falling for others, and you know that's not you. That's not what your marriage is about. *Your* marriage is based on respect and love and attraction and shared values. *Your* marriage could never be in this place, this space, this road to destruction. *Your* marriage is strong enough to weather anything life has to throw at you.

Child with a health issue? No problem. Second child with different, slightly more serious health issue? Again, no problem. Stress at work? No problemo. Money concerns. Nope, no problem there. Witnessing a murder? No problem. Moving, new school, new job, new dogs, new stress with dogs, no problem, no problem, no problem, no problem, no problem.

But is it really no problem? Does all of that add up to your ex paying you attention and you spending more and more time with her? Does it all—

BUZZZZZZZZ! Goes my phone, lurching my heart, interrupting my thoughts.

Number withheld flashes up at me.

Nothing good ever comes from a 'number withheld' call. Nothing.

I force myself to answer it, and I hear the fear in my voice as I say, 'Hello.' I clear my throat, try again, this time with more strength and authority. 'Hello?'

'Rae, it's me.' The relief! He's not dead. He's not dead. Oh, thank God. Then I think: if he's not dead, he'd better have a damn good reason why he's not here right now.

'Clark! What are you doing? Where are you?'

'Don't panic.' Does that ever work? Does someone ever say 'don't panic' to a person and they do exactly that and remain calm and panic-free? Because I'm guessing not. Not with me anyway.

My heart – which had been slowing down after the shock of the phone cutting into my thoughts, starts to race so painfully I have to close my eyes for a moment.

'There's no easy way to say this, babe.' Ah, it's *really* bad if 'babe' has been deployed. 'I . . . I need you to find a solicitor and come to Hollingbury Custody Centre, it's just behind Asda. I've been arrested.'

'Arrested? Arrested? For what?'

'For the attempted murder of Priscilla.'

Bryony

24 Acacia Villas

22 June 2021, Brighton

'How did you get on the other night?' Alana asks. She has come over with some scones and her knitting.

The house is calmly empty apart from the two of us, and we are settled in the living room. I am hand-stitching the hems of a couple of dresses that need to be sent out by the end of next week.

The dresses are quite plain denim material in a dungaree style with a pop of fluorescent colour for the edges and the front pocket. It's a very cute design, and I love it, even if I say so myself.

Alana is making a long, chunky-knit cardigan in a rich teal colour. She is expert at wool work, as I call it. Her long, slender fingers with their short, neatly clipped nails are hypnotic; they almost dance as they manipulate the wool around the needles to work it into something delightful. Sometimes I catch Alana watching me when I'm sewing and she's watching my fingers as though they are as fascinating and oddly exciting to her as I find her wool work.

'Not very well,' I admit to her question about how I got on the other night.

'No one saw you, I hope?'

'No, no. As soon as the meeting started, I slipped out. But the side gate was quite difficult to get through. Then the dogs started barking. I've never heard them make a sound let alone that much noise! They're only small dogs but they made the most extraordinary racket! I had to abandon the mission.' Urgh, 'mission' makes me sound like Grayson. But I couldn't think of another word for it.

'That is frustrating!'

'It is. How did you get on?' I ask her.

'I managed to get into four places, but only went properly inside two of them, where I opened a few drawers, threw some stuff around, made it look like someone was looking for something, just as you would have in number II. It's a shame we couldn't get the book this time, but we'll keep trying.'

'I don't know what I'd do without you,' I admit to her. She has been my rock through all of this. My absolute rock. When I confessed to her about Priscilla and Rae and the book, Alana had offered to help me get it back. No judgement, just an immediate offer of help.

'No thanks necessary, my darling. Your friendship is one of the most precious things I have. I think I would do anything to protect it.'

'I am so grateful for you, Alana. Running interference like that so I could search Rae's house was so thoughtful. I'm not one hundred per cent certain that she has the book, but it is the only thing that makes sense. When Priscilla made me aware of it, I think she thought I would need it to back me up when I went to the police.' If Priscilla had known before I sat down with her that I would not be rushing to the police to turn my husband in for whatever crime she thought him guilty of, she probably would not have shown it to me. 'I just need it. It is as simple as that.'

I need the book so I have an insurance policy I can use against Grayson when I ask him to leave. The stuff in the book may not be one hundred per cent true, but if people were to find out about it and his connection to those involved then his reputation would be lost. Mud sticks. And it is this threat that I hope will eventually force him out of the house.

I want Grayson to go. I want him to never see the children on his own and I want him to leave me the house. It is *my* house with *my* beautifully tended garden. I want it. Just like Alana got to keep her house, I want to keep mine.

'When do you think I should try again?' I ask Alana, who is extremely knowledgeable about these things. When I am on the verge of panicking, I just have to channel my inner Alana, remember how she deals with a problem: her dusky-pink lips will come together then curl up in an indulgent smile, her lightly mascaraed eyes will fix me with a cool, calm gaze as she says, 'I know how you can do that.' And she almost always does.

'Sooner rather than later, darling,' she states. 'We'll have to go for daytime this time. I'm not wild about that, but the sooner we get our hands on it the better. You go in the front and distract her, I'll come in the back and look.'

'I suppose needs must.'

'Exactly, darling, exactly.'

I like the way she calls me darling. No, I *adore* the way she calls me darling. The way her lips and tongue wrap themselves around the word feels like she is branding it directly onto my skin.

I wouldn't need for anything ever in the world again, if I could have Alana calling me darling for ever.

Rae

11 Acacia Villas

22 June 2021, Brighton

I am so shocked that they've lifted Clark for the crime, I have to sit back in my chair, all the strength in my body seeming to drain away in one fell swoop.

'I can't talk for long, I just need you to find me a half-way decent solicitor so I can hopefully get out of here,' Clark says to my stunned silence.

'Right, right, of course,' I reply, pulling my scattered, shocked self together. I have to focus. If I'm going to help him, I have to concentrate. 'I'll have to look online. I don't know any solicitors for that sort of thing.'

'Thank you. Thank you.' He doesn't sound like Clark. He sounds subdued. Beaten down. I hope he's all right. I hope no one has done anything to him.

'Are you all right?'

'Yes. Course. Course. I just . . . I just want to get out of here.'

'I'll do my best. I'll see you soon, hopefully.'

'Rae?' he whispers.

'Yes?'

'I love you,' he says, and then cuts the line before I can say I love you back. Would I have said I love you back, though? After all that's gone on between us, I'm not sure it's the first thing that would have come to mind.

'You!' I snarl at Dunstan the moment he opens his door. I must be pretty scary because he rears back, shocked at my temper and fury. 'You're lucky I'm not a violent person. So lucky! If I was, I'd . . . *fear for your safety.*'

'I couldn't—'

'Couldn't bloody what? Tell me that you were investigating my husband as well as me? Tell me that Priscilla isn't minutes away from death like you and your mates made out? Tell me that despite thinking I'd tried to kill your girlfriend, you'd have screwed me given half the chance? What "couldn't" you?'

'You and me had nothing to do with the investigation,' he protests. I think he means that. Coming out of his beautifully full lips and forcing his face into a shape that declares him innocent of my accusation, he doesn't realise what a monumental lie he is telling.

'Of course it did!' I snap back. 'You trying to get me into bed had everything to do with it!' I don't know most of Dunstan's neighbours and I don't think they're mentioned in Priscilla's book, but they are getting a full-on show right now. I can't stop, though. My anger is so fierce and huge that I can't contain it at all. 'I can't believe I fell for all that tortured soul crap! "Oh, I'm having nightmares." "Oh, talking to you has cured me." "I want to look after you". I am *such* a fool! Urgh!'

'All of that was true,' he objects again. 'Every word. Every word. You did help me.'

'Well, isn't that grand? I helped you and you helped to get my husband arrested. That seems a really fair trade! Let me just find the logo to download so we can officially make your nonsense Fair Trade.'

'It wasn't like that, all right? It wasn't that simple. There are other things that put him where he is.'

'Such as?'

'Look, there is a lot of evidence against him. And when he was questioned, he didn't really have any proper answers.'

'Questioned? What do you mean?'

'When they told you about his fingerprints being in her house to try to gauge your reaction and see if you were in on it together, they were questioning him separately. They went back a couple of times and each time he said he didn't know Priscilla, that he hadn't ever been in her house. That was a lie. Why would an innocent person lie? The second time he was questioned, and they said they *knew* he'd been in her house, he changed his story and his answers were . . . flimsy.'

I knew he was hiding something other than the Lilly stuff. The police questioned him more than once and he didn't even mention it. 'Aren't everyone's answers flimsy? I mean, none of us remember where we've been at all times of the day. None of us remember everything. It doesn't make us guilty of murder. Sorry, attempted murder. Because let's not forget, Priscilla, who you've been crying over and who you've been saying is minutes from death, isn't *that* poorly after all.'

'Wasn't like that. I was genuinely upset about— Look, your man, he's got a lot of explaining to do. On top of the Priscilla stuff, there's theft and fraud in the mix.'

The anger and fury stop speeding around my body, and I stand very still before I say, 'What?'

'Rae, he hasn't told you half the stuff he's been up to. I don't know if you'll get the chance to hear it from him, but none of it is straightforward. And that's because he's not straightforward.'

Is anyone straightforward or uncomplicated? Do you have to be complicated and duplicitous to live on Acacia Villas? Because neither Clark nor I were like this before – or maybe we were but just hadn't encountered the right set of circumstances that would cause us to behave in duplicitous or criminal ways. I don't know how many laws I've broken by not turning over the diary. I don't know how many laws I've broken trying to protect my family from the fall-out of witnessing a killing? How many laws has Clark broken or twisted to try to do the same thing? Because theft and fraud? Those are two things I would never think him capable of. And I know our finances. I have seen the bank accounts, I package everything up to send to the accountant. Unless he has a whole life that I am not privy to? I can't contemplate that, though. Not really. Six weeks ago . . . three weeks ago, even, would I have been able to countenance him sneaking off to Lilly's three times a week? Taking the dogs, bunking off work to do so? Priscilla's diary has shown me many, many aspects of human behaviour, why would Clark be exempt from partaking in some of the worst of it?

'Do you want me to take you to the police station?'

'Do— Are you joking?! The best thing you can do is stay well away from me. Well, away.'

'I can probably persuade them to let you see him, even though it's against the rules,' he says quickly.

Those words stop me from storming down the steps. More than anything I want to see Clark, especially since there is more to this than his fingerprints being in Priscilla's house. I need to see him and if Dunstan can get to him . . .

Yam and Okra! I didn't even ask where they were. I was so over-come and shocked that I completely forgot they were with Clark when he was arrested; what's happened to them? Have they put them into kennels? Just left them on the street where they picked him up? Why didn't they arrest him at home? I have to get to the police station as soon as possible.

'Fine. Assuming this isn't just your way of getting me to the police station so your mates can "question" me, too, I will accept a lift. I need to find out what they've done with my dogs first and foremost. If I can also speak to my husband, then all the better.'

'Do you want to come in while I get my keys and turn everything off?'

What the fuck do you think? I silently reply with a look so sour, it has him rushing off to get ready.

Dunstan

36b Acacia Villas

The anger is coming off her like the tide rolls in and retreats. Except her anger doesn't retreat – it just keeps on coming, steamrollering over every molecule in the car.

'I did care for Priscilla,' he states. He feels the need to make that clear to Rae. He wants her to know that he is capable of feeling. 'Everything I told you is true.' *About the other stuff as well*, he wants to add. He wants to explain that there is more to him beyond being a police officer. Priscilla meant something to him. Rae meant something to him, too. *Means* something. Because you don't just switch off those emotions, stunt those passions.

Dunstan also wants to warn her: she needs to brace herself because her husband is not who she thinks he is. He wants to tell her that she deserves better, that when she hears everything he's done, she will be hurt and then she will be fearful and angry, and then she will do what a lot of women in this situation do – try to make it better. She will do everything in her power to bend reality to fit what she wants to be true. She will try to do everything she can to change the inevitable outcome – even lying and making things up. He's seen woman after woman after woman do this to try to save their man. Rae deserves

305

better than the man she married. And, yes, that better could be him somewhere down the line, but those things are not for now. Now, she should be walking into that room knowing she deserves better and not listening to any bullshit.

Anything he says, though, will have to filter through all her shock, hurt and suffering. She won't listen, she won't hear.

How he wishes, wishes, *wishes*, he could protect her from it.

But unfortunately, she's going to have to feel every second of what her husband has done. In the meantime, he can try to convince her that he is a genuine person.

'Being with Priscilla was liberating in so many ways. I felt a lot for her. Probably more than she felt for me, but it was real, what I had with her.'

'I'm glad,' Rae says, staring straight out of the windscreen, as though transfixed by the road ahead. Her demeanour may be robot-like, but her voice is not. It sounds genuine, like she means it. 'I'm glad you both found each other. I'm sorry it was cut short. I hope it works out eventually.'

'Listen, Rae—'

'But I *don't* want to talk to you. I'm absolutely knocked sick by what is happening with Clark and you have a part in that, so I don't want to talk to you.'

Deflated, his head hanging momentarily low, Dunstan nods his understanding and returns to driving them silently through the Brighton streets towards where he knows Rae's pain will truly begin.

Lilly

47 Acacia Villas

22 June 2021, Brighton

'What's the matter, Mama?' Opal asks. She's so concerned that she hasn't even started the conversation in Italian. Our daily video call is earlier in the day because I am working from home and she has something on later tonight.

'Oh, nothing, sweetheart. Just a bit tired.'

'Where's Dad? I thought you said he'd be here today?' Even through the small screen I can see the excitement dancing on her face, twirling in her eyes, shimmying over her lips. 'I think I'm finally ready to show him the picture I've been working on. It's not the best, but I think he'll like it?' She waits like a very young child at Christmas who has just been told that Father Christmas is a few streets away so she'd better get on with going to sleep, even though sleep is impossible.

'Oh, erm, something came up. He's really sorry, but he says he'll see you next time.' God, the way lies are like second nature to me now. I suppose that's what happens, isn't it? You start on one lie and they multiply, they take on a life of their own and they very often just get away from you. 'But you can show me the final thing, if you want?' I add hopefully.

'No, I'll wait to show it to both of you together. I want to see both your reactions. What came up?'

'Erm, he didn't say. Are you sure I can't just get even the sneakiest of sneaky peeks at the picture?'

'No, Mum! I can't wait for you and Dad to visit,' she says. 'It's a shame he can't bring his dogs with him, they are so cute! They'd love it here.' I can hear it in her voice, she has the same hope that I have – that when we arrive we will be together as a couple and we will be staying for some time.

That was the plan.

That was the original plan. The original plan was to have Clark in on the consultancy with me. I thought he would be interested in it and that we would spend time together, build up our friendship, rekindle our relationship and slowly become tied together.

When he turned me down, I knew when we did eventually get back together he'd kick himself for missing out, so I put his name on everything. I had his date of birth, I had his mother's maiden name, I had his bank account details from when we were together, I had his previous addresses – even the one he lived at with Rae. Also, like most people, Clark is a creature of habit, so he wouldn't do things like change his bank account when we split up – he'd just close the joint one he had with me and then get a new one with Rae. He wouldn't change his banking and mobile phone passwords, he'd just carry on until someone or something forced him to change.

I had everything needed to register him with my name in everything I did.

And he wouldn't think twice about bringing his passport and driving licence over to my place so we could book plane tickets to visit our daughter. It wouldn't occur to him that I would photograph these important pieces of ID while he was out of the room and then use them to retrospectively back up everything I did.

The plan was, the plan had always been, to have him with me. If I was investigated for anything, they would have to investigate him, too. And before it went too far, he would have to leave with me. Clark wouldn't survive prison, he'd know that. He would see that leaving the country with me – to live in the house I have waiting for us – would be his best bet. For one thing, he could speak to his children every night via video call – he couldn't do that in prison. In prison, he would have to wait for visiting days and queue up for the phone. I was going to explain that to him when he was scared and pressured and looking for a way out.

Fate brought him back into my life because this was what was meant to have happened – us living abroad together. He would be upset at first, of course he would be, but in time he would see that he didn't have a life with Rae, he had a *lie*. The lie was that they were meant to be together and he and I weren't. This would reset everything and our lives would continue the way they were always meant to be. In time, Opal would come to live with us and we would be truly complete, the family circle finally closed and whole.

It was this plan, my connection to Clark, that was ultimately my undoing because he was my weak spot – the vulnerability that Grayson Hinter's 'associates' exploited. Since the basics of it were already set up, 'Plan B' became Clark taking the fall if we were ever close to being discovered. I tried to stop them triggering Plan B the other day, I wasn't quite ready to leave, especially with the noises Rose was making about telling Clark the truth. Even if the investigation somehow cleared him, the fact there was an investigation would destroy his reputation, particularly in the field of property law. Grayson Hinter's 'associates' didn't really care about that, what they wanted by triggering Plan B was time to clean house – to make sure the deals they couldn't tie off while our company was active were dead-ended and *all* of it led back to Clark.

I felt sick about it, I still feel sick about it, but my original plan wasn't just to drop him in it and run. He was meant to come with me. It was a way for us to legitimately be together. Rae wouldn't want him to be in prison, either, so while she would be upset and angry at first, I believe she would ultimately understand.

'Mama Rose wants to talk to you,' Opal says to me. 'Whatever it is, she and Dad aren't happy, so *buona fortuna* with that. She seems *pissed*.'

'Language,' I say automatically.

'Which would you prefer – Italiano or Engleeshio?' She treats me to one of her wonderfully beautiful laughs that lights up her whole face and creates a song-like sound, and I'm instantly glowing inside. I'll never get over how amazing she is. Not having to do every little thing for her all the time while she was growing up has made me appreciate her so much more. 'OK, bye, Mum, here's Mama Rose.'

She hands over her tablet and skips off to do something else. My sister's unimpressed face fills the screen, anger smearing her features.

'Before you say anything,' I say, 'I haven't told him yet. Mainly because he's been arrested for the attempted murder of that woman on my street I was telling you about.'

That stops Rose and causes her face to contort in a sort of comic-book horror pose. 'What, *he* caved that woman's head in?'

'Wait, how do you know what happened to her?'

'I checked the news story. I wasn't sure if you were telling the truth or not.'

'Oh thanks, that's great to know.'

'That doesn't matter right now. Did Clark really cave that woman's head in?'

'That's what the police have arrested him for.'

'Bloody hell.' She sounds so English at that moment she could be down the road in Kent where she used to live. 'Oh, my God!' She dramatically slams her hand over her mouth as though some new horror has descended in her mind. 'If I'd made you tell him the truth the other day, that could have been you.'

Clark didn't do it. Of course he didn't. Another spear of guilt jams itself into my stomach. *But he might have,* that honest voice inside me whispers. I told him to sort it. I told him that Priscilla had been watching us and that she was threatening to tell Rae everything. I told him that if Priscilla did that, I would stop him seeing or speaking to Opal. That I would cut him off and never let him contact her again. He must have done what I said – he must have gone to see Priscilla and . . . I don't know what happened. I know what Priscilla can be like. If she told him to get lost, which was likely with her, then maybe he . . . no, no, he wouldn't. He just wouldn't. Not even if it was to save his relationship with Opal.

I should tell my sister that Clark wouldn't do that. But I can't, because if he did, then I might have been the catalyst for him doing it. Even if he didn't, this is still a nightmare.

Who knew that Plan B would be triggered not by me or an instruction from Grayson Hinter's associates, but by Clark himself – when he was arrested for something completely different?

Who knew that since it's attempted murder, he's unlikely to be let out so I can't set into motion the resolution to Plan B – us escaping together?

Who knew that the only way to get him out would be to turn myself in and admit to everything? And, obviously, there's no way on Earth that I can do that.

Rae

11 Acacia Villas

22 June 2021, Brighton

They've allowed me five minutes with my husband.

I know this *never* happens and the fact that it took over an hour probably means that Dunstan pulled out all the stops and called in all his markers to make it happen. And it probably means I should be grateful to Dunstan for working so hard to make it happen, but I am finding it hard to feel anything positive towards him right now. I feel completely stupid, totally humiliated. There was I doing all sorts of introspection about being attracted to another man and what it meant for my marriage, and he was playing me all along. I don't care how many times he claims otherwise, he was playing me. More fool me, though, for falling for it.

After much time at the police base around the corner from the Custody Centre where they are holding Clark, Dunstan explained that this thing that never happens and in fact isn't happening, would take place in a little office in this police base. Apparently the detective inspector has to officially sign Clark out for a scene visit. That is the only way this thing that isn't happening could actually take place.

The police officer – detective inspector – who has allowed this to happen is clearly Dunstan's boss. He's shorter than me, so stands tall in his frame, trying to be physically imposing as he patronises and talks down to me. He tells me in condescending tones that this never happens, that it is, in fact, not happening, so if this thing that never happens does in fact happen, it will be solely because the person in question's spouse would be in the best position to get him to cooperate with the police. And it will also go better for the person in question if this thing that is not happening results in that person admitting to the various crimes they have evidence of him doing. This is the only way mitigating circumstances might be taken into consideration – if the police hear these reasons *before* the prosecution process begins.

If I'd been minded to tell Clark to cooperate in any way he could before, this officer's barely concealed sneer and hateful tone of voice would have made sure that was the last thing I'd do. In fact, under most other circumstances, I would be inclined to tell him to get lost. But my current situation demands that I play nice, so I accept the patronising lecture with the sorrowful eyes of a confused, slightly dumb spouse in case I need to persuade them to let me speak to him off the books, as it were, again.

The dogs are fine. They – thankfully – kept them in the CID office, where they've lain down under a desk and gone to sleep. Just like that. Like that would ever happen if they were at home alone with me! (Even Yam, who does not generally like 'people' and usually makes it loudly known, is nicely nestled under a desk.) They didn't see me, so there was no drama about them wanting to come with me before I saw Clark, but my gratitude that they were fine and not in a scary pound was so sweet it was delicious. Another thing I'm meant to be grateful to Dunstan for – he apparently persuaded them to keep the dogs there until I arrived to collect them. That is the official story about why I am there – to collect the dogs, not to speak to my husband.

When I enter the small room they've given us to speak in for Clark's 'scene visit', my husband looks at me like one of the dogs does when she knows she's done wrong and is expecting a telling off. I sit on the chair opposite him and I'm grateful, really grateful, that he doesn't have handcuffs on, even though Dunstan had warned it was likely he would be wearing them given the fact he'd been signed out of the custody block. I want to hug him and smack him all at the same time.

'Bet right now you're regretting not learning to mind-read like I spent years trying to get you to, aren't you?' I say to him.

His handsome, chiselled face creases into a smile, and I remember . . . I remember how he looked at me when we met up for the first time after he was single. His large brown eyes had folded into a smile that took over his broad nose, his full lips and the chicken pox scar on the crest of his cheekbone. I'd been almost winded by how he looked at me. I'd never, *ever* had someone look at me like that before. Not ever. It was like all his dreams had come true and so had mine. And I kind of knew we were going to be together for ever after that. And although I'd thought that before, with men who turned out to be more goon than groom, I'd been right about Clark. Or so I thought. Because right now, it's not Clark Whickman, Rae's husband. It's Clark, the Attempted Murderer. And Clark the Big-Time Crook.

'We've got five minutes and I'm to tell you to confess to the police because it'll go better for you if you do. What the hell is going on?'

'I didn't try to kill Priscilla,' he says. 'I need you to know that.'

'Right.'

He inhales so deeply his broad chest rises and expands to what looks like dangerous levels, and then he exhales deeply to deflate himself. 'But I was in her house. I did have an argument with her, and it did turn violent.'

'Violent?' I say, horrified. *Who is this man?*

'Not me!' he says. 'Her! I was trying to talk to her, I was trying to explain why I was . . . I was trying to explain something and she just got angrier and angrier, calling me a liar and saying I was scum. I told her to stop being so melodramatic and involving herself in things that didn't concern her and that she should get a life instead of spying on people and she just lost it. There was a vase on the side and she just picked it up like it weighed nothing and threw it at me. I was freaked out. Completely freaked out and apologised for what I said.

'I started to pick up the pieces of the vase and nicked myself. Priscilla started to pick up the pieces too, and then she cut herself. Which just made her even more mad. She started screaming at me and then she tried to hit me. I didn't even raise my hand to defend myself. I stepped back and she fell flat on her face. She was so embarrassed. I realised it was a bad business so decided to go. I just left her there with her righteous anger and wounded pride. But none of this happened on the day that she was hurt. They just can't prove when my fingerprints ended up in her house.'

'Why were you even there?' I ask him.

'Lilly.'

Right. Of course. Lilly. He's clearly willing to go to prison for his ex. 'Of course! Yes! Of course you were there for Lilly. Why wouldn't you be there for Lilly? I take it her honour needed defending?'

'No. There's . . . stuff I can't tell you.'

'I completely understand,' I say.

'You do?'

'Yes. I understand that you've already arranged for Lilly to visit you in prison, so you won't need to explain anything to me. I can just leave here, take the dogs home, make dinner for the girls. You know, all the usual—'

'Look, Rae, it's not—'

'No, you look, Whickman! I don't believe for one second you tried to murder Priscilla. And I don't believe you've stolen money and defrauded people. But you're going to get sent down for all of it if you don't stop defending Lilly and start telling me the truth.

'In the two minutes you've got left, tell me who I'm taking my earrings off to fight? And tell me quickly.'

'All right. OK. You're not going to like it,' he says.

'Tell me anyway.'

I leave the police station with my dogs and with my anger burning so brightly all over my body, I'm sure I can be seen from space.

Clark is with his solicitor right now, but it's very likely that he is going to be spending the night locked up, possibly two nights. There is nothing I can do about that. What I can do is get the children and dogs far away from here for the next couple of days.

The police are probably going to come to search our house now that Clark is in custody and the last thing I need is for the girls to be around to see that. I'm guessing they're going to take all of our computers to go through them, which is inconvenient, but necessary, I guess.

Before they arrive, I'm going to have to find a proper hiding place for Priscilla's diary; somewhere they won't find it.

Before I hide it, though, I am going to go through it again, to find out who I am, indeed, taking my earrings off to fight.

Part 9

Priscilla

21 Acacia Villas
Diary Excerpt

16 May 2021

Mr Afternoon Delight was tetchy this afternoon. Work stress or something. Didn't want to fuck, just wanted to talk. I like him, I like his company, but we are strictly 'have a good time' people. It's always when I start to feel something for someone, start to do anything beyond fuck and laugh that I end up marrying them and breaking my heart. Because at this stage, when I know what the outcome is going to be, it is me who is breaking that organ of mine.

When he started telling me something and I didn't reply, he got very snippy and left.

It's bugging me more than it should, but the moment I start to feel is the moment I am lost. He'll be back, I'm sure.

19 May

He came back with a huge box of chocolates. It's been a few days and I was starting to worry, but he's back and I'm happy. The chocolates were my favourites – salted caramel – and I wasn't sure how he knew that. We stayed in bed all afternoon and into the evening. Oh, but I missed him.

Not a good sign for my heart.

I'm going to have to reassess this, aren't I? I can't be missing him like that. It's not fair on either of us.

20 May

Felt bad today. Rae delivered the flowers and was her usual pleasant self. I wish she knew how badly her husband is betraying her. But she obviously has no clue. Poor woman.

I remember how humiliated I was whenever I found out that I'd been cheated on. And I remember how many people overtly and subtly blamed me: you must have known, you must have had some idea, there must be something about you that attracts cheaters.

Yes, there is something about me – I am human. That is pretty much the linking factor between those of us who have been cheated on, especially those of us who have been cheated on more than once.

Everything is coming to a head though, I can feel it fizzing in the air. Something is going to happen that will blow all of this out of the water.

I hope I survive it. I really do.

21 May

I think it's over with Mr Afternoon Delight.

We had a doozy of a row and I don't even know how it came about.

I've been so on edge. Usually he can bring me out of it but the past few times I've seen him, he's just been mopey. He's meant to be the fun factor in my life, not upset and grief. We went to bed and afterwards he asked me about the flowers again. 'You really have no idea who is sending them to you?'

'No, I really don't.'

'Have you tried tracing it? Speaking to the florist? Or Rae Whickman?'

'Yes.' If only he knew what I did for a job, how I had tried everything I knew, hacking wise, to find out who was sending them and had come up with nothing. So unusual for me, especially if it's an honest mistake. 'And didn't we already have this conversation?'

'Not really. You just kind of avoided it last time,' he said.

'I didn't. I've always assumed they were from you.'

'Yeah, I can see why – they do seem the sort of flowers a lover would buy.'

'You think I've got another lover?'

'Have you?'

'I gave you a key to my house, what more do you want?'

'You could have given anyone a key to your house.'

'Get out,' I told him. Disrespecting me like that in my bed. 'Get out of my bed, get out of my house, and get out of my life – *now*.'

'Look, Priscilla, I didn't mean it like that.'

'Yes, you did. Now piss off.'

'I just don't get who is sending you flowers like that.'

'Well, it's not your problem now, is it?' I replied. 'You can get out and not think about it ever again.'

'We have one little disagreement and you're ending it and chucking me out?'

'If that is how you want to see it, fine. But no one calls me a slut and gets away with it, whether I am a slut or not.'

'I'm sorry,' he said.

'I am, too. You have no idea how sorry I am.'

I was so upset, when he left, looking as wretched as I felt, I had a cry. It felt like he was the one good thing in my life.

Now I have all the time in the world to sit here and think about who is going to kill me.

Why does it hurt so much?

24 May

I know who is going to do it.

That is, I know the person most likely to kill me.

I'm not sure how, but I do know *why* and I do know it's going to be soon.

Should I tell someone? Probably. But who will believe me? Until it happens, no one will care. And therein lies my problem: until I'm dead, or as close to dead as I can be, no one will believe my life is in danger. They'll think it's all petty jealousies, problems best talked out over tea and biscuits.

They will not see the bigger picture until it is splattered with my blood and stained with the crocodile tears of those who mean me harm . . . *then* there'll be investigations, *then* there'll be the pulling out all the stops to find out the truth.

Until then, I know that someone is coming to kill me.

I know who.

I know why.

I know soon.

I just don't know how or exactly when.

This is what happens when you know what people have done: danger stalks your every breath.

Would I do it again? Probably. It's not like I can change who I am.

So this is it. My declaration: I know who is going to kill me.

I hope I am wrong. I hope it doesn't happen or I hope that I find a way to outwit them.

That is all I have: hope.

Plain old hope.

Will it be enough?

26 May

Saw Mr Afternoon Delight walking past my house and looking in the window. Wish he'd either come in or not bother. I can't stand the drama.

28 May

He decided to knock this time and asked if it was all right if he came in. He came in, we stood in the corridor asking each other how we were and not really knowing how to be. Then he apologised properly and we went to kiss and I saw him looking at the newest bunch of flowers and that was it! Enough. 'Don't come back,' I told him, and walked away.

Why? Just, why?

Didn't think it was possible to have my heart broken again.

Lovesick.

1 June

It's not even midday and I have had drama! That idiot Lilly has been over begging me to keep quiet about her dodgy activities, and when I wouldn't agree, she had the audacity to hit me. Hit me! She's lucky I just threw her out and didn't go crazy on her ass. Then Bryony rocks up, begging me to let her come in and explain things to me. And while she's blethering on, I see him. Mr Afternoon Delight. And my heart lurched and I wanted nothing more than to push Bryony aside and run down the road to him.

Not sure what to do about him. I so want to be with him.

Maybe I should go and talk to him.

I really am lovesick without him.

I miss him so much. Not just the sex, the way I was when I was with him. I'm going to have to talk to him, aren't I? That won't be so bad. He's lovely. And I want to be with him.

And the look he gave me when I was outside my house earlier – I know he wants to be with me, too.

Part 10

Part 10

The Residents

Acacia Villas

24 June 2021, Brighton

I have Priscilla's diary and it has told me
exactly what you did.
I know everything.
I haven't shown it to the police yet, but I will if you don't do what I say.
You have 24 hours to hand yourself in to the police.
If you don't, I'll come after you.
And then, *everyone* will know what you've done.

Lilly

47 Acacia Villas

25 June 2021, Brighton

I'm too scared to contact the others to ask if they've got this note, too. Pushed through the front door without an envelope, without my name on it, so it might have come to the wrong house; it might be meant for someone else.

But of course it hasn't, it isn't. This is meant for me.

And I have to decide what I'm going to do. I know who sent it, and she'll be aware that I'll know it's from her, that's why she hasn't signed it.

But what do I do?

Do I go to the police and tell them that it wasn't Clark? That's obviously what she wants me to do. Let's be honest, though, and I've been thinking a lot about this since he was arrested – would they even believe me? I was pretty comprehensive and thorough when it came to setting him up. I wanted to be sure that he wouldn't be able to easily shake off accusations from the investigation and decide to ride it out; take his chances in court. But why would they believe me? All the money we paid ourselves came from a parent company set up in Clark's name, paid from a bank account set up in Clark's name. Why would they believe me when I say it was all me?

I can't imagine how awful it is for him sitting there as everything becomes clearer and clearer, as they reveal the details of what he is meant to have done, and realising how comprehensive the evidence against him is. Unable to tell Rae the whole truth because he can't see her. He's bound to panic. And he won't be let out because he's under lock and key for attempted murder.

So what do I do? Turn myself in and possibly not be believed? Or leave it and see if Rae does go to the police? (She could very easily be calling my bluff.) Or, I could run now. I could run to the new life that I've been setting up, then either send evidence that will help to get Clark off, or just pretend it's not happening and get on with my new life.

Obviously the biggest complication in all of this is Opal. She is attached to him now, so this is going to hit her hard. I begged Rose not to say anything to Opal about Clark's arrest until we knew more about what was happening. I obviously didn't mention the fraud stuff to Rose. But Opal is bonded to him and she won't understand why I've ditched her dad, she'll just see it as me bringing him into her life, getting her to love him and then snatching him away again.

She will be heartbroken and she will hate me.

I sit cross-legged on the sofa, wearing black, my hair scraped back under my black beanie, my fingers covered in black gloves.

There is another option. There is the option where I go over to Rae's house and take the diary off her. Where I make sure she doesn't tell anyone anything. Yes, she might have told the police already, but I think I can quite confidently say that if she had, they'd be here already.

My guess is, she actually thinks the threat will work: that I will go to the police and spin my story before she bubbles on me and shows me in a worse light. Like it could be worse, though.

I am going to call her bluff.

I am going to go over there and get that diary.

And if she gets hurt in the process, there is nothing I can do about that.

Bryony

24 Acacia Villas

25 June 2021, Brighton

By the time Grayson walks in, I am a wreck.

That note through the door was like a missive from Hell. I didn't have time to get the book from Rae and now she is trying to blackmail us to go to the police. What I am doing with Alana and our business isn't exactly hurting anyone and Priscilla didn't mention it to me so I'm not sure if she even knew about it. If she did know and she's written it down in the diary, would it really bother Rae enough for her to do this? I wouldn't have thought so.

It must be the Grayson stuff. Or, I realise just as my husband walks through the door, maybe there's even more to what he's been doing than Priscilla told me.

That wouldn't surprise me at all.

All the lights are off except the kitchen at the back. I know Rae can't see us from here, but I don't want to give her the opportunity if she decides to take a stroll past the house.

I imagine, though, that she is sitting at home, waiting for the phone to ring to tell her I've confessed; that I've convinced Grayson to come clean and the police are grateful to her for her part in it. I bet she's got herself a huge glass of wine and she is on her sofa, watching something

331

on television. I bet she feels smug and content that she's thrown this at me and can sit back to wait for justice to be done.

'What on Earth is going on, Bryony? Why is the house in darkness? Where are the children?'

He's talking far too loud for the situation we're in. It feels like our every movement is being watched, monitored, recorded. 'Shhh,' I hush and indicate for him to follow me into the kitchen.

'What on Earth?' he repeats. He stops in the kitchen doorway and looks around, searching for signs that I've started dinner or that I'm interested in starting dinner. 'This is quite intolerable, Bryony,' my husband says, outrage in every word. 'Why haven't you begun dinner? Where are the children? What is going on? Are you having some kind of breakdown?'

That's right, blame it on me when we're in this position because you're a power-mad ogre. That is a thought that was meant to be articulated in my head, only. Not come hurtling out of my mouth at speed and volume, which it just has.

Grayson draws back, stunned and openly appalled by how I have just spoken to him. If more people spoke to him like this, we might not be in this situation, I realise suddenly. If, after the first time he made me leave a job I loved, the first time he spoke poorly to one of the children, the first time he held a dinner party for people he didn't like but wanted to ingratiate himself with, I had told him no, maybe none of this would have happened.

'What on Earth has got into you?' he asks, absolutely disgusted with me. I am being female right now and that is everything he hates in a human being. Grayson is a contradiction that I've seen replicated the world over – he hates women, he despises, derides and dislikes everything that is thought to make women who we are. He thinks, simply because of the bodies we are wrapped up in, that we are inferior. He finds us weak and hysterical and illogical. But he *needs* women. He needs us to spark desire, to stick his penis into, to have as the beings he looks down on. Without women, there is no one to feel superior to and preside over.

'Here!' I almost scream, slapping the note onto his chest. 'This is what has got into me.'

Dropping his briefcase, he takes the piece of paper and, frowning hard at me, he unfolds it. All semblance of colour drains away from Grayson's face as he reads. 'What is this?'

'It was pushed through the door earlier. I have seen this diary. You are all over it.'

'I would appreciate it if you would calm down and explain to me in a logical manner what is going on.'

'AND I WOULD APPRECIATE IT IF YOU STOPPED BEING SUCH A FUCKING DICK, GRAYSON, BUT WE'RE NEITHER OF US GETTING WHAT WE WANT RIGHT NOW!' It feels nothing short of wonderful to shout. I have not shouted in years. If I am angry, I hiss, lower my voice, I force my words out through clenched teeth. I never shout, I never have the freedom of it. My chest is expanded, my throat is uncorked and my mind is unblocked.

The most enjoyable part, though, is seeing Grayson's face. Never in a million years would he expect to be on the receiving end of those words at that volume from me.

'Grayson,' I say, while he is still recovering from the shock, 'before Priscilla was attacked, she asked me over and told me about your "associates". She had articles and excerpts from legal documents. She showed me what happened to the families of the people who were involved with them. The ones in the inner circle are fine, but anyone who wants to join has to make terrible sacrifices to move up the levels.

'She wrote it all down in her book. She showed it to me. And before she ended up in hospital, she gave the book to Rae, the Black woman who lives at number 11. She gave it to her and now she's sent that note saying she's going to tell everyone everything you've done unless you go to the police and confess.'

I move my hands rapidly as I speak. 'I was thinking, you could disappear for a little while. Until all of this goes away. Hopefully she won't go to the police immediately, and if you're not here, then she'll look silly, like she's delusional. I'm sure one of your contacts will be able to get you a year's sabbatical with a charity abroad. Or we can say you've decided to set up a Westlann Charitable Trust overseas. We can say we're planning on joining you at a later date but the new charity is desperate for your leadership.' I was warming to the theme now. It would be the best way out of this for us. 'And then, depending on how the land lies, we can say the sabbatical period has been extended, or we can find you another assignment somewhere else. I can go and start packing now if you want to make some call—'

'You stupid woman,' Grayson finally says. 'You stupid, *stupid* woman! What makes you think you have any say in what I do? What makes you think any of this is anything to do with you?'

'Grayson, she has evidence of what you've done.'

'She has nothing. I could crush that woman without blinking. What evidence do you think she has? She has written something down in a book. People do that every day – they are called novelists.' He jabs his forefinger and middle finger right in the middle of my forehead to shove me away. It's a small blow but it pushes me off balance, causes me to nearly fall over.

'Ow!' I cry, rubbing my forehead. I stare at Grayson, remember the moments when I used to love him. They used to stretch for years, they used to make me feel safe and protected. I had someone who would take control, be in charge, make decisions that would benefit all of us. Except those decisions, over time, not even that long a time, became all about him. Everything was about Grayson, and the rest of us had to go along with it. He put his aspirations to be a top-flight business-man, to be someone who sat on the seat of power, before everyone, including his children. I knew that, and I had tolerated that. I had tolerated, ignored and looked past so much because I thought this life, this house, this stable home for the children was important. Was all there was to life.

I hate myself for that. I am ashamed of myself for that.

My shame *should* be deep and wide and thick as it is because I did not act fast enough after what Priscilla told me. I know I started hating him, I know I had started making plans to get him to leave, but I should have acted earlier. Much earlier. When Tilly retreated and Trent raged. When I saw how the quest for power hardened the lines on his face and made him more physically rough than ever, I should have acted. I told myself I had no money, I had no standing, I wanted more than anything to stay in this house.

My disgrace *should* sit forever on my chest like a millstone as it does, reminding me how I didn't act when my children needed me. I was weak and I was scared and I have allowed this monster to grow out of control.

'I'm trying to help you,' I tell him.

'Who do you think you are to try to help me? Help me with what? That woman has nothing. They are the mad ramblings of a lonely old spinster. What evidence did she have? Photographs of me with these

335

allegedly bad people? Voice notes to these people? Anything physical or concrete at all that connects me to this nonsense she has conjured up?'

He is right. There is nothing tangible in any of what I saw; there was nothing that could one hundred per cent connect Grayson to anyone at all.

'Priscilla tried that nonsense on with me as well. Called me over, showed me her "evidence", threatened me with exposure if I didn't service her and her voracious sexual appetite. I told her what I have told you – show me concrete evidence and I might be interested.'

That causes me to stop. 'You went to Priscilla's house? When?'

'And what's it to you?' He pushes his fingers on my forehead again, shoving me back.

There was no way she tried to get him into bed. It was the other way round. It was the other way around and when she threatened him with her evidence he . . .'It was you, wasn't it? You tried to kill Priscilla.'

'Don't be ridiculous,' he replies, bearing down on me in a threatening manner. 'Why would I?'

'No, there's no evidence, but if Priscilla blabbed, your reputation – your precious reputation – would have been tarnished. No, obliterated. All it would take is for allegations of impropriety to come out and that would be it for you at Westlann.'

'You are even more ridiculous than I thought.'

For someone like Grayson, for someone who *is* Grayson, there is no power without reputation. He would absolutely hurt someone to maintain his reputation. Especially a woman. Especially a woman who has shown no interest in him and is not scared of him.

'Even if I did do it, do you honestly think I would tell you . . . *you pathetic specimen.*'

Grayson is never like this. He is never blatantly vicious; he makes barbed comments, he specialises in unsubtle put-downs, he doesn't threaten in this way. But he has changed. Since the day of Priscilla's attack, Grayson has changed. It was definitely then that he changed. He brutalised me that night, in a way I didn't think he was capable of. Had he attacked Priscilla and then carried on doing such things because he realised he was not only capable of doing it, he may well get away with it.

Looking back, that is certainly how it feels. I'd had small victories, times when I'd pushed him onto the back foot, but the overall balance of power has not shifted. Grayson is still in charge, except now Grayson is openly vicious and quickly violent.

He did! He tried to kill Priscilla!

I have to get out of here. Now. I have to escape.

My eyes dart to the door.

He sees what I am doing, notices I am trying to escape and a slow, sadistic smile meanders across his face. I'm trapped. Trapped in a room with a man who has killed one woman, who thought nothing of forcing himself on me to punish me, who has already been physical with me this evening.

The air, filled with the sound of our breathing, is heavy and ponderous; the atmosphere is thick and syrupy with danger. I have to run. I have to run now.

The smile in place, the look of a ready-to-pounce crocodile in his eyes, Grayson dares me to try to run; goads me to try to escape. His message is clear: he *is* ready, he *will* pounce, he *will* destroy me.

My body jerks towards the back door, and Grayson moves in that direction, and I bluff, darting towards the kitchen door, making a break for it. Grayson recovers quicker than I expect. And as I race through the door, he is right behind me; right on me. A small scream escapes my lips as I barrel as fast as I can down the corridor. I hear him behind me and I feel the weight of him raising his arm, the swoop of the arc as it comes down to hit me on the head. I jerk to the left and the blow glances against my arm, but with all the weight he put behind it, Grayson loses his balance and lands heavily on the floor. Undeterred, his hand snaps out and grabs at my ankle and I scream again, terrified he's going to bring me down.

There's a sudden frantic knocking at the door, as though someone has heard my scream and is now desperate to get in and help. Grayson, who is still flat on the ground, swipes again at my ankle and this time makes contact, grabs hold and pulls me down. I scream again as my body hits the cold, tiled floor. The shock of impact reverberates painfully through my body and all the breath and fight is knocked out of me. The knocking stops and becomes a loud BANG! And another. BANG! And another, BANG! The door bulges with each bang, each bulge bigger and bigger until CRASH! The latch breaks and the door swings open, just as Grayson climbs onto my back, grabs a fistful of hair, intending to snap my head back then drive it forwards onto the tiled floor.

'POLICE! STOP WHAT YOU ARE DOING!' a voice bellows.

I don't really see who it is that comes running into our hallway but without seeming to break stride, they grab Grayson, pushing him backwards off me. I immediately crawl forwards and then force myself upright. I do not want to be down on the ground any more, I want to stand up and face Grayson.

My husband wrestles futilely with the police officer for a second or two, then gives up and flops flaccidly onto the ground. My rescuer is Dunstan, who lives about ten doors down from us in one of the flats. Have they sent him to arrest Grayson, arrest me?

Dunstan, who seems incredibly imposing and solid right now, forces Grayson face down on the ground, holding Grayson's arm twisted behind his back. 'Grayson Hinter, I am arresting you for assault. You do not have to say anything. But it may harm your defence if you do not mention when questioned something which you later rely on in court. Anything you do say may be given in evidence,' Dunstan intones, his voice serious.

When he has finished, he pulls Grayson to his feet and forces him to stay well away from me.

'What the hell is going on?' Dunstan asks me.

'You're not here to arrest us?' I ask. My lip feels big. I think I hit my face when I landed. My right arm feels numb, too.

'Why would I be here to arrest you? I was walking past and noticed that your car lights were still on. I came to let you know, heard screaming.' He looks incredulously at Grayson. 'What's going on?'

'I . . . I think my husband attacked Priscilla Calvert and was just trying to kill me.'

Lilly

47 Acacia Villas

25 June 2021, Brighton

Rae's house is in almost complete darkness when I approach. (To me it'll never be *their* house, it's hers and he has just been living in it until he is mine again.) For some reason, the street light nearest her house is out, too.

Fate is on my side again.

I've been past more than once and I do not see anyone as I near her place this time. No suspect cars with officers waiting to pounce, no coppers lurking in the shadows ready to come when she calls. I have not spotted any sign of life from inside. The upper floors have their blinds closed, and their car is parked outside, so I guess Rae's daughters are asleep. The only light I can see from their property is at the back. I think it's the warm glow thrown out from the kitchen.

Rae is probably sitting in the kitchen right now, poring over Priscilla's diary, trying to see if there are any more secrets she can glean before she takes it to the police. How will Clark feel if I hurt her? It won't be intentional – there'll be no violence if she just hands it over. Will he hate me, though, if I have to put my hands on her? He does care about her; she has been in his life for a while, she had his children, after all. But will he hate me if I have to hurt her to get what I want?

The bolt cutters I have are heavy duty, but they still struggle to cut through the padlock on the side gate. I can feel their padded handles bruising the palms of my hands as I push and push to get them to break the bond, to let me in. I nearly fall over when it finally finds its point and snaps the metal. I manage to catch it before it falls to the ground and I pocket it. I am careful as I ease open the ornate gate, a connection of iron roses, because I'm not sure if it will creak and therefore give me away. It swings on a smooth, noiseless arc and I step onto her property with more than a little trepidation. I'm still carrying the bolt cutters because they can be used to break the glass at the back of the house and as a weapon, but I wish my breathing would calm down. It's so erratic and loud in my head, I can't hear myself think. At least, I suppose, it'll probably drown out Rae's screams if I'm forced to bludgeon her to death. Gallows humour. Yes, someone else's gallows but you can't have it all.

I move towards the end of the side of the house, heading towards the back where the small rectangle of green and the white flagstones that separate the building from the greenery are bathed in a mellow yellowy light. Her garden isn't that big, but she's made good use of it. In the corner is a nice wooden patio where I would love to sit and read. There are hedges and bushes and trees. There's a wooden structure that looks like an upturned rocket and there is a table with four chairs. I reach the end of the path and press myself against the building before I turn the corner so no one can see me once I step into the light. I have to be quick, I have to give her no time at all to call for help. I tighten my grip on the bolt cutters, even though my hands still sting from using them before. Carefully, slowly, I slip around the corner, avoid the drainpipe, return to hugging the wall—

'The worst thing is, you're not the first one who's turned up,' she says conversationally.

I yelp in shock, jumping back and almost dropping the tool in my hands.

Rae is sitting on one of the garden chairs, placed in front of the patio doors, facing me. She has her coat on and a black beanie like mine on her head. She looks somewhat stoic for a woman who obviously knew I'd be coming to see her. I almost said kill her, but that's not what I came for. It's honestly not. I came for the book, not to remove a rival.

'What do you mean, I'm not the first?' I ask, too shocked to affect an attitude of only dropping round in a bit of an unconventional manner.

'You're not the first person to turn up to threaten me/demand the book/try to secretly search for the book/try to do me in – delete as appropriate.'

'You didn't just send the note to me?' I ask, a little outraged that I have been duped, then completely mortified that I have been so stupid. You could not get a more generic message than the one she sent, and I still thought . . . *How fucking stupid am I?*

'Who knew Acacia Villas was such a hotbed of criminality? Not me, that's for certain. Would have thought twice before we moved here, I tell you. I mean, the things you lot get up to. It's a wonder you have time to do your jobs.'

It's funny how you can know someone for years and years and only realise after an incident like this that you actually *hate* them. She's not been a favourite since she got with my man, but honestly, this boiling, broiling mass in my chest is pure hatred. She is smug, superior and utterly hateful. I would love to use these bolt cutters to furnish her head with a couple of well-placed dents. She won't be sitting there, arms crossed, legs crossed at the ankles, head slightly to one side as she waits for my next move if I did that, would she?

'I mean, I'm no angel, I've done things that aren't exactly legal but you lot . . . bloody hell. The thing of it is, though, Clark's not like that. You know that, you were with him first. Clark only became devious when you made him.'

'You have no idea about men and you have no idea about Clark, do you?' I tell her, on the front foot in this conversation for the first time.

'Maybe not. But I know he only started keeping things from me when you dropped a bombshell on him. Son or daughter?'

Yeah, right, like she knows. 'No idea what you're talking about.'

'Have it your way. Daughter. Living with your sister in Italy. Opal. Clark told me.' She smiles at me in such a condescending way the mass in my chest becomes as lava and starts to bubble over. *How dare she use my daughter's name in such an unreverential manner. How dare she!*

'Look, Lilly, my wonderfully naïve husband still thinks you only did this six weeks ago when you got your hands on his passport while you were booking that trip to Turin. He's too trusting. Once I knew the bare basics of what's been going on, it didn't take me long at all to find out that you've been setting him up for months, possibly years. I can't work out why. To be honest, I don't care why. What I do care about is you going to the police and telling them the truth.'

'What truth is that?'

'That he had nothing to do with your scheme. That he is completely innocent and it was you, and Grayson Hinter and Hollie Stoltz and Ralph Bieler and Kevin Milburn. Blame one of them for setting up Clark, if it suits you better, but I'm going to need you to clear Clark's name and get him out of prison.'

'Make me.' The belligerent reply comes out of my mouth before I can stop myself.

'Thing is, Lilly, you should have found yourself some better business partners. There really is no such thing as honour among thieves.'

What is she talking about?

'Although, you're not technically thieves, are you? You're terrible people who "consult" other terrible people further up the planning list, and invest in developments that should never be approved. And you get an inordinate amount of money for it. I mean, who knew that bribing planning committee members on behalf of various "business people" could be so lucrative? Not me. Actually, I still don't believe that bribing planning committee members is so lucrative – I can't help asking myself, you know, if there's another income stream involved?

'I can't lie to you, Lilly, I thought Mr Bieler, all nice and round, was going to go full-on Weeble, the way he was wobbling earlier. And Hollie . . . I've walked to the gym with her more than once, I mean, no I don't go in, but she does. And she seems so nice, who'd have thought she'd be involved in a scheme like yours? But there you go, as I said, you're very persuasive when it comes to making people behave badly. Let's do a quick register on that, shall we? Clark wasn't deceptive until you made him. Mr Bieler was all about living life within his means until you turned him into a criminal. And Hollie . . . well, she said it was all your idea. *Including* the extra income stream, you know, the money laundering.'

What. The. Hell? What. THE. ACTUAL. HELL?

'You look surprised, Lilly. Remember how you set up Clark despite how much you love him? How much do you think it'd take to blame everything on someone you vaguely know? You really think any of them are going down for you?'

No, the answer is no. None of them are going down for me. I have my plan, though; I have my escape plan. But does that work if the others are already leaving me to carry the can? I was meant to escape with Clark. I was meant to get far, far away before the others started confessing to the police. This can't be happening. And maybe it isn't. Maybe, maybe it's just Rae being Rae, trying to bluff me again. Fool me once and all that.

'I take the fact that you're still standing there, weapon in hand, as a sign that you don't believe me. Which is fair enough. But I feel I should tell you that the other two were sensible – they came to my front door, knocked like good neighbours. They came to talk to me, distract me, look for the diary. Sat on my sofa and expected to be offered tea. When I said that no tea was coming but I was giving them a head start to get to the police before I told them, they took it. They both tore off to go tell the police their side of it. And if it was anything like what they told me . . . *girl, you in danger.*'

What do I do? What do I do? Do I run? How far would I get if two people have turned me in? That's the two I – and Rae – know about. What if Kevin Milburn has gone straight to the police? And Grayson Hinter – although he's less likely to have gone since it'll get him into trouble with his 'associates'. If three of them have pointed the finger at me, though, I'll be lucky to get to the airport. *What do I do? What do I do?* I have to lean forward, rest my hands on my thighs, just like Clark did when I told him about Opal. *What do I do? What do I do?*

'As far as I can see, the best thing for you is to go to the police. Tell them everything and blame it all on those other people who hold positions of power far above your own. Say they pressured you. Say they *made* you set up Clark, even though we both know they didn't. If you tell them that, you might be in with a chance.'

Is she bluffing? I can't tell. I can't tell. If she's bluffing and I go to the police, I'm done for. If she isn't bluffing and I don't go to the police,

I'm done for. Best-case scenario is that she is bluffing and the others are sitting terrified in their homes. But she knows that Ralph wobbles like a Weeble when he's stressed, and Hollie would totally blame me.

I hate that she's right: if I tell them Clark is innocent and the others forced me, they may look more favourably on me.

Straightening up, I glare at Rae. I still would love to crack her over the head with my bolt cutters, but that would look even worse for me. And yes, that is the only thing that stops me. The *only* thing.

I back away from her slowly, always keeping her in sight until I reach the corner, and then I turn and run. My feet pound the flagstones that lead to the front, and I shoot through the gate at speed. I need to get home. Put away the bolt cutters, change out of my clothes and race down to the police station. I don't have much time. Every second the other two are there and I am not will count against me. *I've got to move. I've got to move.*

Part 11

Lilly

47 Acacia Villas

28 June 2021, Brighton

They believe me about Clark.

They don't believe me about anything else. The other two did a great job of stitching me up. And when Rae showed them the recording that she'd made of our conversation in the garden – obviously she'd do something so sneaky as videoing us – it was pretty much game over.

No bail for me – I have ties in another country and I have money. Too many means of escape, apparently. I am grounded, my wings clipped, like an exotic bird that no one wants to see migrate; like a woman who had a plan that other people just couldn't help meddling with. All would have been well if other people hadn't got involved.

I am allowed visitors and today's visitor is my old friend Clark Whickman. He doesn't want to see me. It's all about Opal. He didn't even mind not bringing 'the wife'.

'Doesn't it bother you to see me in here?' I ask him the second he sits down. We won't have much time and I know what he's here for but I want to talk about me first.

'If I say no, will you punish me by withholding information about Opal?'

I sit back in my seat, fold my arms across my chest, wait for my

349

anger to disperse. It's not good for me to feel this angry; and so impotent with that anger. It has nowhere to go. Maybe I can wipe that stupid smug smile off his face, maybe that will make me feel better.

I sit upright and make myself soft in that way I always have to with Clark. 'Actually, there's something I need to tell you,' I say seriously.

'If it's that Opal isn't my biological daughter, then no need. I already know.'

How in the hell would he . . . *Rose*. 'Did my sister tell you that?'

'No. Maths told me. She was born eleven months after we were last together, not nine months.'

'You knew?'

'Yes.'

'But if you knew, why did you go along with it?'

'Initially, I was hoping she might be, despite knowing it wasn't possible. I was hoping so hard, but when we first spoke, I knew she wasn't. She's the spitting image of the Swedish economist you were seeing but tried to pretend you weren't.'

'I didn't do it for kicks; I was lonely, I was missing you. We tried so hard to resist, but we couldn't. But if you knew, why keep on coming three times a week?'

'Because she has you for her mother, a wasteman for a father, and two guardians whose judgement I question since they didn't tell me the truth. I wasn't about to abandon her, whatever the DNA of the situation. I want to see her. I'll ask Rose to tell her I'm not her biological father now that I can say we've spoken.'

'What? No! I am not approving that. You don't get to play happy daddies with *my* child. No, not happening.'

'I thought you might say something like that. This was just a courtesy, Lilly. Rae has already found out where they live, she's been in contact with Rose. I'm just letting you know it's going to happen no matter what you say. If she'll have me, I'm going to keep being "dad" to Opal. She doesn't deserve to have another person desert her.'

Stop this! I wail inside. I wish Clark would realise that the reason he wants to stay in touch with Opal is me. I am the woman he loves and she's the next best thing to me. It is his chance to be with me despite where I am. But he can still have me, be with me. I won't be in prison for ever.

'She won't want you without me,' I tell him. 'You're only her "dad" when I'm around.'

'I have to go,' he states.

'No, no, stay a minute. I have to tell you. It wasn't a complete lie. I did get pregnant after our last time together.'

Clark's body sits heavily back in the seat and even though he looks pensive, he is listening. For that, I'm stupidly grateful. I haven't told a soul this. 'I struggled with what to do, whether I should tell you or not. I decided not, because we were over and I'd made such a big deal about us giving each other space. I wasn't going to go through with it, and then I decided I would, I mean, why not? I could do it on my own. And then . . . when I'd finally decided to do it, I lost him or her. Had a miscarriage.' I cover my face with my hands, remember the feeling of loss that I would never be able to recover from. I think that's why I was reckless with Viggo, the Swedish economist that Clark keeps referring to. I'd been so careful with him until then. After that, I just didn't care about being safe, he was all that I wanted because he could help me to replace what was lost. And then I was pregnant again. Except it was the wrong guy's baby. And the right guy wasn't answering my calls. Not after the way I hurt him. Why would he?

'And then I had a baby and a Viggo who didn't want to know. And the right guy telling me he was in love with someone else. And I decided to pretend, all right? Viggo had left and he wasn't coming back. It wouldn't hurt anyone if I just pretended she was yours.' I look down at my interlinked fingers, casually crossed as I tell him my deepest secrets. 'That's what it was, Clark, pretending. It got out of hand but it wasn't vicious.'

'No, I'm sure it wasn't,' he says. 'And I'm truly sorry for our loss, but that doesn't change anything. It can't change anything. Take care of yourself, Lilly.'

'Bye, Clark,' I whisper. 'Bye.'

He might walk away, he might act like he's not going to come back. But he said, 'our loss'. He said something that linked us, bonded us.

And that tells me something clear and loud: Clark will be back for me.

Rae

11 Acacia Villas

28 June 2021, Brighton

Dunstan.

Dunstan is standing at the door four days after Clark has been released from prison without charge. They know he didn't try to kill Priscilla and they know he had nothing to do with the financial Armageddon they are dealing with in relation to Lilly and her merry band of criminals.

I'd suggested Clark leave it a couple more weeks (decades) before he went to see her, but he wanted to get it out of the way so he's there now. I wonder if that's why Dunstan is here.

Clark and I haven't really had time to talk about what happened or what went on in the weeks leading up to it – we've just spent a lot of time cuddling and hugging and playing with the girls and the dogs, and basically acting like a family from a TV ad where we laugh all the time, nothing bad ever happens and conversations are not had.

Dunstan is a bit of an unwelcome reminder that I haven't handed the diary over to the police yet and that there are still some loose ends to tie up.

'Half-A-Story Herbert, what a surprise,' I say.

He ghosts up a smile and then asks: 'Do you fancy going for a walk with me?'

Not really, is what I want to reply. *Not really at all.*

'Last one,' he says to my hesitation. He raises his hands – when he does that, he's almost certainly lying, but I don't say that. 'Promise.'

'Fine.'

Without talking about it, we go along our usual route, neither of us speaking until we get to the incline at the park where he says, 'There are lots of things to update you on, but I'm not sure which to start with. Maybe the good news – Priscilla is getting better. The doctors say she's getting better all the time.'

'That is good news. I'm really pleased for her – and you, of course.'

'Haha, yeah,' he replies mirthlessly. 'Not so sure about that, but we'll see, I guess. But, the other bit of good news is that we caught her attacker.'

'Shut up!' I say, and stop walking. 'Talk about burying the lead! Just in case you didn't know, in the world of journalism burying the main point of the story is a bad thing. Who was it?'

'A career criminal called Dan Ridgewell. In and out of prison, he's well known to us. Didn't think it was him because he doesn't usually attack his victims – if they are in he generally runs away, but apparently he's got "braver" now. He attacked a woman over in Worthing two nights ago. He thought she was alone in the house, turns out her sister was asleep in the spare room. Came out and whacked him a good one upside the head with a rounder's bat. We found some of Priscilla's things – her credit cards and some jewellery – in his place. Confessed when we told him we knew.'

'But your lot never let on that it might be a break and entry? You kind of led everyone to believe it might be someone she knew, or me, basically.'

'The police don't tell people who or what they're investigating. We ask you questions to find out lines of enquiry but we don't tell you what we're thinking. That'd be madness. And to be fair, it didn't look like a break and entry. The back door was open and there was no sign of forced entry. It was a bit of a surprise when the other team found her stuff but there really is no one to identify what was missing from her house.'

'Wow, was that ever a deflating revelation,' I say. 'All the trouble this has stirred up, all those people going to prison, all those relation-ships hanging in the balance and it's some rando, as Bria would say.' I can't help shaking my head in despair. 'It was all for nothing.'

'No, not for nothing. I'm pretty sure those behind bars deserve to be there. I can't speak to the relationships. And, this is something we didn't tell people, either – Priscilla was poisoned.'

'What?'

'Yes, someone tried to poison her and that was what was killing her. And that's why we knew someone did purposefully try to kill her.'

'Oh, yeah, I suppose.'

'And if it wasn't for the attack, we might never have found out about the poison. Someone would have just found her dead. Me, probably, because she gave me a key to her house.'

'Right, didn't think of that. So being attacked kind of saved her life.'

'Exactly.'

'And, just so you know, key isn't casual. Key is quite serious, actually.'

'Yeah, well, like I say, don't know what will happen there.'

I look over at my walking companion and notice again he isn't his usual self. 'What's up, Dunstan? You're acting very odd, guarded and a bit sad. Is it because our walks are nearly done?'

'No, I'll miss our walks but no, that's not it. Rae, the delivery method of the poison was transdermal, which means it was taken into the body through the skin.'

'Yes, I know what transdermal means.'

'It was smeared on one of the flower vases in her house.'

'Which means, what?'

'Which means, since the flowers kept coming to your house for a little while after Priscilla was hospitalised, we suspect whoever was sending the flowers was, in fact . . . well, they obviously don't know about your health anxiety and the fact you're constantly wearing gloves . . . So they choose this delivery method because, we suspect, the flowers were meant for you.'

'What? Why would someone try to—'

I look him over again and he looks upset, worried, concerned.

'You think it's the people from London trying to get me, and Priscilla has just been caught in the crossfire?'

'Basically, it looks that way. All the information that could possibly lead us to tracing the person who sent the flowers has come to a dead end. When they searched your house, they found no trace of the poison, and it looks like a professional did it. We thought, initially, that it was a typo that had the flowers sent to your house in Priscilla's name, but now we think it was done on purpose to get you to handle the flowers while delivering them to their supposed recipient.'

'No, surely not.'

'Yes, unfortunately.'

'But why would they after six years? I mean, I'm always on high alert, but nothing has happened since we moved down here, and we rarely go to London, so why would they?'

'We don't know. Sometimes people hear something, learn a bit of information that makes them think they're going to get caught even after a long time, so they go back and start cleaning up, as it were. I didn't tell my colleagues you'd seen anything, just what was in your original statement. But until we get anything concrete, there's nothing we can do and you need to be careful. I know you are already, but if we're right, then they're going to keep trying.

'So, yeah, you need to be aware. Think twice about who you trust with your story. I know you're not in the habit of sharing what happened, but you never know who can overhear things. If you want to get a panic button installed and have a marker put on your house for a rapid response, you'll have to give them a full statement and tell them everything you saw.'

'Not going to happen.'

'Right, well, then you need to be careful. I'm sorry to be the one telling you this, and probably kicking off all your anxieties again, but I thought it better to say something than not.'

'No, no, I appreciate it. I feel terrible, though, if what happened in London is the cause of what's happened to Priscilla. Has she had many visitors?'

'No. Most of her family live overseas in Australia. They're not close.'

'I see . . . I feel bad for her.'

'It's not your fault,' he says.

'Tell that to my conscience.'

'You'll be all right. As will Priscilla, I'm sure.'

'OK, I'm choosing to believe you. I'll try to go and see her next week.'

'Will you also choose to believe that I didn't get your husband arrested on purpose and that everything I said to you when I opened up was genuine?'

'Yes, Dunstan, I choose to believe that, too. Thank you so much for all your help . . . I'd better head back now, I want to be there for when Clark gets back.'

'I'm going to keep walking.' Dunstan stares at me and stares at me until I raise my gaze to meet his. 'Let me know if you have any problems, yeah?'

I nod. With one last grin and one last unnecessarily flirtatious look between us, we both turn and walk in opposite directions.

Bryony

24 Acacia Villas

28 June 2021, Brighton

'So, darling, Grayson didn't try to kill Priscilla?' Alana asks me.

'No, he didn't. They told me that on the day he tried to kill me.'

'I'm still shocked at that. You never look at a man like Grayson and think he's going to end up banged up for trying to kill his wife.'

'Oh, that's not why he's getting locked up. With regards to me, he's being charged with assault. I couldn't stand to tell them about him forcing himself on me the other week. No, he is being locked up for money laundering, grand larceny, and something else, I can't even remember. But the important thing is he didn't try to kill Priscilla They actually have a video of him sitting in a club in the centre of Brighton over that whole time period.

'Apparently he was really upset because he'd been told that day he hadn't done enough to move deeper into the circle of power. He blamed me and the children for that.'

'Wow, what a prince amongst men.'

'He confessed when I went to see him that he had gone to see Priscilla. He was sweet on her and thought he might be able to persuade her to have an affair with him. He told me that she had propositioned him when I knew it was the other way around.

'Priscilla laughed in his face. Told him to go away, told him she knew what he'd done and threatened to call the police . . . Oh God. I can't believe I told Priscilla that she was wrong. That Grayson wouldn't do that. I was in so much denial. I can't believe I almost let him . . .'

'I can't either, darling. I don't know why you didn't tell me. I would have helped you. Being in denial and telling yourself someone is good when you know for a fact they're not is bad enough when it's you. When it's children involved, that's just unacceptable. You should have left. I know it ain't easy, but, love, you're supposed to protect your children. You've got a lot of work to do to undo that.'

Tears rush to my eyes. To hear that from the mouth of someone I adore, it is horrific. I am ashamed and I am going to be ashamed for a long time.

Alana lays down her knitting and moves to sit beside me.

Tilly is fine. She honestly is. Now that her father isn't in the house, she doesn't spend every spare moment holed up in her room. Now that her father isn't around, she smiles every now and again. Trent is not as fine. I can tell that he misses his father, misses having a man around the house, but he will be fine, too. I know he will.

What Priscilla told me still plays in my head: the children of the men like Grayson are broken and damaged, hurt and wounded. I need to be proactive about their recovery. I have booked therapy for them both and I will make sure they get all the help they need. I will do all I can to undo what I almost let happen and what they lived through as witnesses to our marriage.

The millstone of disgrace takes on the weight of a dwarf star and I fear it is going to crush me.

'Don't be upset, darling,' Alana whispers. She gently tucks a lock of hair behind my ear. 'Don't be upset. We're moving forward, and we're going to do better, aren't we?'

I nod. 'Yes.'

'First thing we have to do is dismantle our business. Go legit,' Alana says.

The first time she told me about it, Alana described her business to me like this: *'You make money by selling the things people want online. We set up a website and have products. And then we tap our friends to buy our products. We tell them that we have this new business selling beautiful hand-made pieces – children's clothes are the best-sellers – and we offer next-day delivery where possible. In the delivery instructions people leave us a note. If they are a known and trusted source, they know how to order with their order.'*

'Order with their order?'

Prescription meds, cannabis, coke. Not so much heroin, I don't like to deal with those guys. People are willing to pay over the odds for hand-made items and we only send small amounts at a time, with the payment already processed. We dispatch the goods with the items from the delivery note included; everyone's happy. We run the site for three months, possibly four, get as many orders as we can, then shut it all down. Our previous customers come with us, legitimate customers find new places to get their apparel. Everybody wins.'

'And you do this?'

'I do this. A lot. It's a sure-fire way to boost the bank balance and we don't ever get our hands dirty. All you have to do is make clothes. I do the rest. Profits split fifty–fifty.'

'But you've put more into it.'

'*And you need the money to get away from your hideous husband.*'

That was our business. And that was what had been helping me to get away from Grayson. 'Do you think we'll be able to make a success of it legitimately?'

'Yes, I think we can. And I know you can do it.' Alana bites down on her lower lip while her eyes stare directly into mine. 'I know you can do anything you put your mind to.'

This is so unexpected, so very unexpected.

'If I kissed you now, what would you do?' Alana whispers.

I lean forwards and press my lips onto hers.

Kiss you back, of course, I say in my head. *Kiss you back.*

Rae

11 Acacia Villas

28 June 2021, Brighton

I've moved a couple of chairs onto the raised wooden patio in the garden and Clark has thrown a heavy cream canvas over the three high sides above it so we can comfortably sit outside without getting wet.

I sit wrapped up in a furry blanket, watching the rain drizzle. Every so often it gathers into large rivulets and drips down from the canvas, creating a line of darker wood that is like a frame along the three edges. Our house always looks different from this angle and I often wonder if I'd be able to pick it out in a line-up viewed like this.

Inside, Bria and Mella play with Okra and Yam, rolling around on the white-tiled floor and giggling while the dogs jump excitedly over them. We're still living the TV ad family life, which is why Clark steps out of the back doors carrying two large wine glasses, looking impossibly handsome in his grey T-shirt and tight black jeans. I've put all my worries to one side – which means I am watching my children play and pretending they are someone else's children rolling on a floor, and letting dogs lick them when I've watched those very same tongues explore unmentionable dog body places. Yes, when I pretend they're on telly and nothing to do with me, I can let all that fun and love and affection go on in the kitchen unchecked.

'So, are we going to talk about it?' I ask Clark after we clink our glasses and take a sip.

'Do you want to talk about it?'

'No, I do not want to talk about it, any of it, which means we *definitely* should talk about it.'

'Yes. But not right now, eh? Can we just sit here and listen to the rain and talk about silly things?'

'Tomorrow. We have to talk about it tomorrow.'

'Yes, tomorrow, for definite.'

I lean over and rest my head on my husband's solid, dependable shoulder.

Tomorrow is for talking, Clark is right about that. Tonight is for drinking wine with my husband and pretending I don't have a care in the world.

Rae

11 Acacia Villas

5 July 2021, Brighton

I've been sitting beside Priscilla's bed for about ten minutes now. There are so many things I want to say, they teeter and dangle on the tip of my tongue and none of them will hit properly if they fall.

Priscilla looks how she looked the last time I saw her when I was holding her hand in the street, except now her hair has been tidied up and her make-up has been taken off.

She is deathly pale and eerily still.

She is hooked up to machines and wires, and there's something soporific about watching another human being's heartbeat move in pulses across a screen. She looks like a fifty-something-year-old woman who is confined to her bed.

'Poor Priscilla,' I've been murmuring since I sat down here. 'Poor Priscilla.'

Thing of it is, Priscilla, I say to her in my head, because that's the safest way to talk to her right now. I do not want anyone to hear, and I'm not sure I want her to hear, either. *The thing of it is, Priscilla, I saw a murder. And nothing has been the same since.*

The thing that no one but Clark knows is that our youngest daughter was there, too. She was out of bed and begging me to get Welly for her from the car. Fine, I'd go, but then she insisted on coming with me because everyone else was asleep and she didn't want to stay in the house on her 'own'.

Why wouldn't I take her with me? It was just around a couple of corners. She was with me and she saw it, too. I covered her eyes as soon as I realised what was happening, I covered her mouth to stop her making a sound, and I nearly shattered my teeth from clenching so hard when a man was killed right before my eyes. I couldn't close my eyes because I had to watch for them seeing us.

I saw a murder and this is the lie we've had to maintain all these years. My daughter was there and no one could know she was also a potential witness. I could never put her life in danger by telling the police about her. And if they spoke to her she would tell them that we had seen. I couldn't let that happen, so I had to lie.

Despite what it seems like, lying doesn't come easily to me. It's not something I do usually or encourage in my life. I just . . . when it came to this, seeing how casually a man took another man's life, how non-chalantly they threw his body to the side of the road, I realised that no one could know she was there.

Of course, the police didn't believe how little I saw. They thought I saw something and tried to pressurise me into telling them what that was.

I stuck to my story, repeating that I'd got there right at the end and had run away to call them. Every visit was the same: them asking and re-asking, them getting the same answer every time. Even the visit about the data breach wasn't apologetic, it was factual; it was telling me what had happened, it was telling me I 'probably' wasn't in any danger.

Until I got a visit that was different: the police, who'd been disdainful of me and irritated by me, and kept saying they just needed me to cross the 't's and dot the 'i's, all of a sudden they were solicitous and respectful; reassuring me that my testimony would go a long way to doing some good.

'What's happened?' I asked eventually, because how they were being was too creepily nice.

The police officer – who was quite similar to the one in charge of investigating what happened to you – avoided my eyes for a couple of seconds and then stared directly at me. 'Nothing,' he lied. 'We just would prefer to have someone else's testimony to help us with this conviction.'

It was one of those moments when I could see right into someone else's head; where you can read their minds like they're a book. 'One of the other witnesses is dead, aren't they?' I replied.

'Hospitalised.'

'Dead.'

'In a serious condition.'

Dead, I thought. Like I will be if they ever find out.

'I didn't see anything,' I repeated. 'And I'd appreciate it if you would stop coming here. It makes the neighbours talk. I didn't see anything. And if you call me to testify, I will say that again and again and again until you and everyone else who needs to hear it gets the message: I. Didn't. See. Anything.'

And then those men tried to crash my car. I didn't tell Dunstan, either, that both girls were in the back. And I'd thought that we were all going to die. They'd both cried after that incident and it took an age to calm them down. How I managed to settle them when I was terrified, I don't know.

That's why Clark said to me that night: 'Let's move.' We knew we had a chance if we could just move on and never bring it up again. Start afresh in a new area. I even changed my surname to Whickman, which hadn't appeared on the files that had been stolen, so we could escape what happened.

Brighton wasn't far – it wasn't the other side of the world, which was where I would have loved to have run, but it was far enough away to let anyone know that I wasn't going to talk. And to protect my daughter. Daughters.

And it's been fine, Priscilla.

Everything was good and we had a new life – a better one, actually. I love living down here, the girls love it, Clark loves it; this was our new life, our new start.

So why . . . Why did you have to go digging into our background, Priscilla? What did I ever do to you? I bet you thought you were being clever saying to me at the Neighbour–2–Neighbour Watch meeting that I must be used to crime coming from South East London. I guess you thought I would dismiss it as you being a bit racist/classist. But I am on high alert. All the time. I am always waiting for someone to catch up with us. For someone to decide our not-so-moonlight flit wasn't enough to show I wasn't going to talk.

And then, when you asked me at that other Neighbour–2–Neighbour Watch meeting something about whether I could ever cope with moving to Dublin after being in West London, I knew. With that seemingly innocuous question, I just knew that you'd done some digging about us. You had found out about my friend Iris fleeing to Ireland, which meant you had found out why we left London.

The thing of it is, Priscilla, normally, I would have ignored it. Let it go. But then 2020 happened. I had thought 2015 was awful, when my father died. I thought 2016 was terrible, when one thing after another went wrong and one celeb that I loved after another died. But 2020 showed me that the world is unpredictable; anything can happen at any time to anyone. And I knew, just knew, that I couldn't take a chance with you knowing this thing about me. You might say something to someone else and the wrong person might overhear; you could make an off-the-cuff remark to someone who knows someone else who knows someone, and it would get back to those people we ran from. I just knew you couldn't keep it to yourself, could you? You wrote it yourself in your book that you told Lilly. Of all people, you told Lilly something had happened to us. Oh, I know you were trying to defend me, but you could have got us killed at the same time. The world is connected in so many ways that you knowing about this and not keeping it to yourself could get my daughter killed.

I would normally never hurt anyone – that's just not who I am. But 2020 showed me that anyone is capable of anything, and I realised the only way to keep you quiet was to properly shut you up.

That's why I did it.

That's why I tried to kill you.

I wouldn't have done it if 2020 hadn't shown me that anything could happen; anyone was capable of anything. I knew I had to do it in a way that wouldn't draw too much attention. I found a form of poison through the upper levels of the dark web that could be delivered transdermally, but dissipates quite quickly.

I started to send flowers to you at my address, again so I could establish a pattern of bringing them to you. I started wearing gloves whenever I could so I could coat the vase in poison and give it to you without implicating myself.

And then someone breaks in and hits you over the head. Makes sure you're found in time, saves your life.

You don't know how happy I was when I found out that you were alive after all. I don't want to kill you. I don't want to be a murderer.

But I don't want to live in fear, which is what will happen when you wake up.

I run my hands over my head, my legs shaking nervously, my body quaking.

What am I supposed to do about you when you wake up, Priscilla? The doctors say that could be quite soon. And your diary tells me you can't leave well enough alone. That you can't be reasoned with. That you'll probably go back to being who you are. Who else are you going to accidentally tell my secret to? Who else am I going to have to fear will be the link that leads back to my daughter? Because even if we move, who will you talk to about us?

So what do I do now?

Hope for memory loss?

Or try to shut you up again?

Because, Priscilla, make no mistake, I will do anything to protect my daughter . . . daughters – even if it means trying to kill you again.

So, tell me, if you were me, in this moment, in this situation, what would you do?

How would you solve this dilemma?

Tell me, please, what do I do?

THE END

Acknowledgements

Thank you to . . .

My wonderful family

My incredible and supportive agents, Ant and James

My excellent publishers (who are fully credited at the back)

Graham Bartlett for the research help

My fabulous friends

My beloved MK2

My adorable Fufu and Jollof

You, the reader. As always, thank you for buying my book.

And, to dazzling G & E . . . always and forever.

Credits

It takes a whole load of people to produce a book – and these are the ones who helped to bring this one to you.

Editing, Support & General Amazingness
Jennifer Doyle

Other Editorial
Katie Sunley

Copy editor
Gillian Holmes

Proof reading
Rachel Malig

Audio
Hannah Cawse

Design
Alice Moore

Production
Tina Paul

Marketing
Jo Liddiard

Publicity
Emma Draude
Annabelle Wright

Sales
Becky Bader
Frances Doyle
Izzy Smith

Agents
Antony Harwood
James MacDonald Lockhart

Read on to find out more about

DOROTHY
KOOMSON

and her inspiration for the book

Author's Note

I like my neighbours.

They all seem like nice, decent people to me. And I've never had so much as a cross word with any of them. I always feel I have to put this disclaimer out when I talk about *I Know What You've Done* because I don't want the people I live amongst to think my tale of dodgy dealings in a Brighton neighbourhood are in any way related to them.

Having said that, I don't think the happenings in Acacia Villas are too far away from the truth of what goes on in other streets around the country, hey, the world. OK, maybe not the attempted murder bit, but everything else. You never really know what goes on behind closed doors.

When I wrote *I Know What You've Done*, most of us were spending the majority of our time at home. And we got to see what our neighbours got up to – sometimes in ways we didn't expect. And it was that enforced, prolonged proximity to the people we pretty much live with that informed the book.

Being honest, as well, I loved being the nosey neighbour. I simply adored creating things that I would be sitting watching with eyes out on stalks if they were to ever happen around me. Like the bins scene. I can picture that happening – something pretty trivial building up and building up until frustrations boil over to comedic effect, and then afterwards everyone pretending it didn't happen. Like I say, that's not happened around here, but from the messages and feedback I've received about the book, what I wrote about isn't too far from what has happened in other people's lives.

I Know What You've Done was written during lockdown(s). And I know lockdown and the Pandemic in general had a lot of authors struggling to know what to do. Should they write about it? Should they pretend it didn't happen? Because, for many of them, they didn't want to write about it and they suspected a lot of book buyers didn't want to read about it. For many authors, the solution was to set their books before 2020 or after 2021.

For me, the solution was to go into the pain, to rip off the plaster now rather than try to edge it off much more agonisingly later. As I've said in the past, my writing is set in reality, it is set in our times and I can't – actually, don't want to – pretend away something that so fundamentally changed our world – physically, mentally and emotionally. So many things have been altered by most of the world being locked down, by the comforting similarities and stark differences between people being so brutally highlighted, and I need to acknowledge that in my work.

I was careful, though. Very careful. If you've read *I Know What You've Done*, you'll know that despite making oblique references and setting my book in a 2021, post-lockdown world, I don't actually mention the Pandemic. At all. You see, I didn't want to shove it in people's faces, I simply wanted to tell a tale that is set firmly in the reality of the world that we've made. I wanted to acknowledge our new reality in the neighbourhood where I spend a lot of time – my writing.

I think I succeeded. I hope you do, too. And I hope you enjoyed it, if you've read it, and if you haven't read it, that you do enjoy when you do.

And, most of all, I hope you're as OK as you can be in your little bit of this planet, YOUR neighbourhood, wherever that may be.

Dorothy x

Dorothy Koomson
September 2021

Reading Group Questions

For *I Know What You've Done*

I decided to do something a little different with these reading group questions so, as well as writing them out for you to read, I'm going to answer them for you. That way you can pretend I'm at your reading group or you can see if my answers match yours.

Just use your phone to hover over the QR code at the end of the written questions and it'll take you to the video interview.

Don't forget – there may be some spoilers in there, so make sure you've read the book before you read the questions or watch the video.

Thanks,
Dorothy x

1. What would you do in Rae's position of having a book with all your neighbours' secrets? Would you read the book or hand it straight in to the police? Why?

2. Which character did you like the most? Why?

3. Which character did you like the least? Why?

4. Despite setting the story during 2021 and making oblique references to it, the author deliberately avoids directly mentioning the Pandemic. Why do you think she chose to do this?

5. At one point, Priscilla tells Bryony that she is a terrible mother. Given Bryony's dire situation and limited means of escape, do you think Priscilla was unnecessarily harsh on her?

6. Lily has an unhealthy obsession with one of her neighbours. Do you think she's genuinely in love, or is she using her infatuation to hide from the larger issues of her life?

7. During the novel, Rae becomes attracted to one of her neighbours. Do you think it is only because of what she thinks her husband, Clark, is doing, or do you think the attraction would have developed anyway?

8. Considering the lies, betrayal and deceit in the novel, which of the characters did you empathise with the most? Why?

9. Which 'reveal' was the biggest and most shocking for you? Why?

Access the videos using the QR code below:

Or visit:

https://smarturl.it/IKWYDReadingGroup

Dog Gone It

An Acacia Villas Story

By Dorothy Koomson

Yam & Okra

11 Acacia Villas

Yam asks: 'So what do you think is going on with the big ones?'

Okra replies: 'Don't know, but something is definitely up.'

Yam: 'Do you reckon it's cos of the stuff the big one has been up to.'

Okra: 'You can't keep calling them "the big ones" and "the big one".
Just call them Mum and Dad.'

Yam: 'Don't think so!'

Okra: 'Well they're totally like Mum and Dad. Dad takes us for walks
and tells us off and Mum feeds us and combs us out.'

Yam: 'And tells us off.'

Okra: 'And tells us off.'

Yam: 'But she doesn't want to.'

Okra: 'Neither does he. Not really. He just gets "upset" when you do
your business inside.'

Yam: 'Like you don't "do your business" inside. At least I do it on the
mat. What about you – freeform Okra? Anywhere and anytime.'

Okra: 'Wouldn't be so quick to cast asper— oh, quick, she's coming
back. Lie down, scratch behind your ear and I'll deploy the "I want

382

cheese" face. She can't resist the "I want cheese" face. We'll be filling up on snacks or that smooth creamy goodness in no time.'

Yam: 'Ooop, false alarm.'

Okra: 'Listen, you really should call them Mum and Dad.'

Yam: 'But they're not. They haven't even got fur.'

Okra: 'Yeah, but you like sitting on their laps, don't you? When you're all snuggled up, it doesn't matter whether they've got fur or not, does it?'

Yam: 'Suppose not.'

Okra: 'And when she's tickling you under the chin, or he's rubbing your tummy because you've got them into the perfect position to do that, or you have to paw paw them to tickle you, the no-fur thing isn't an issue, is it?'

Yam: 'Suppose not. And she does give me mashed potatoes. And cheese. And she did keep buying me harnesses until one fit.'

Okra: 'Do you remember, he was soooo maaaadddd? "Stop buying these thing" he barked, remember?'

Yam (yelping happily): 'His voice went all funny. I couldn't stop laughing.'

Okra: 'Me either!'

Yam: 'They got funny voices anyway, though.'

Okra: 'Yeah, all sort of glooobly, like long strings of sausages.'

Yam: 'Sausages . . . Yum.'

Okra: 'Come away from the thought of sausages, Yam. Come away . . . come away . . .'

Yam: 'Sorry.'

Okra: 'Don't you think it's hilarious when the big one who feeds us – Mum – tries to bark at me sometimes? It always makes me double take. In my head I go, "Do you know that you've just said you've got a lampshade for a head?"'

Yam: 'I know! The other day she said, "My feet are hams" while point-ing at the empty food bowl . . . Oh now I understand why you keep nipping at her toes. You're checking if it's true.'

Okra: 'Yup. And it never is. But maybe one day.'

Yam: 'What do you think is going to happen? I mean, you can feel the atmosphere in the house. It's different. It used to be all happy-happy, now it's *blah*. That's why I keep barking at anyone who comes near. I don't want them interfering with them.'

Okra: 'You keep barking at them cos you're aggro.'

Yam: 'I am not aggro, you're the aggro one! You're the one who can be fast asleep, have a dream, wake up and go running down the kitchen calling me because the giant pigeons are invading or something.'

Okra: 'Yeah, well, they usually are.'

Yam: 'And then you toddle off and make me look like the bad one.'

Okra: 'Can I help it if I thought the giant pigeons were circling overhead?'

Yam: 'But what do you think is going to happen? I'm worried. Bertie said—'

Okra: 'Who's Bertie?'

Yam: 'Bertie's the whippet from over the back. And you said I don't make friends! Bertie said this is how it started with his big ones. One of them taking them somewhere he shouldn't. Atmosphere. Next thing she's crying, and he's gone.'

Okra: 'Gone? Not walkies. Gone, gone?'

Yam: 'Yes, gone, gone.'

Okra: 'I don't want Dad to be gone, gone.'

Yam: 'And I don't want Mum to cry.'

Okra: 'We have to do something.'

Yam: 'I have been doing something! Why do you think I bark at every-one? I'm trying to keep them away.'

Okra: 'OK, I'm going to bark at them all, too. Even the nice lady with the nice house and the meaty treats that he takes us to.'

Yam: 'Especially her! We shouldn't be going to her house.'

Okra: 'But those treats are really good.'

Yam: 'And that other girl is really nice.'

Okra: 'The one who lives in the box? Yeah, she is. And those treats are nice.'

Yam: 'But not as nice as Mum.'

Okra: 'No, not as nice as Mum.'

Yam: 'So we're agreed – we're going to keep Mum and Dad together at all costs?'

Okra: 'Yes we are. And I like it when you call them Mum and Dad.'

Yam: 'Yeah, so do I.'

Okra: 'Quick, I can hear Mum coming. You give her the cheese face and I'll see if her feet have turned into hams yet.'

Yam: 'Right. Here we go   '

Read your heart out...

Have you read them all?

THE CUPID EFFECT

Ceri D'Altroy has an extraordinary talent for making people follow their heart, with occasionally outrageous consequences! But will it ever be Ceri's turn to find love?

'Colourful characters and witty writing' *Heat*

THE CHOCOLATE RUN

When Amber Salpone has a one-night stand with her friend Greg Walterson, neither of them are prepared for the trouble it will cause in both their lives.

'A fantastic blend of love, friendship and laughs' *Company*

MY BEST FRIEND'S GIRL

Best friends Kamryn and Adele thought nothing could come between them – until Adele did the unthinkable. Years later Adele needs Kamryn's help. Will Kamryn be able to forgive her before it's too late?

'Both funny and moving, this will have you reaching for the tissues . . . A heart-breaking tale' *Closer*

MARSHMALLOWS FOR BREAKFAST

Kendra Tamale has a painful secret, one she swore she had put behind her. But can she build a future without confessing the mistakes of her past?

'So darn good that we had to read it all in one evening – *****' *Heat*

GOODNIGHT, BEAUTIFUL

Eight years ago, when Nova agreed to be a surrogate for her best friend and his wife, she had no idea things would go so drastically wrong. Now, faced with tragedy, can they reconnect before it's too late?

'Irresistibly complicated' *Red*

THE
ICE CREAM GIRLS

As teenagers Poppy and Serena were known as the Ice
Cream Girls and thought to have committed murder.
After twenty years leading separate lives, they are about to be
forced together once again. Will they both survive?

'Incredibly gripping' *Now*

THE WOMAN
HE LOVED BEFORE

How Jack's first wife died has always been a mystery to Libby,
but when she almost dies in an 'accident', Libby starts to
worry that she will end up like the first woman Jack loved ...

'It had us all gripped from start to finish' *Woman*

THE
ROSE PETAL BEACH

When Tamia's husband is accused of something terrible, she
doesn't think things can get any worse – until she finds
out who has accused him. Someone is lying – but who?

**'Pacy and compelling, the twists and turns
come thick and fast'** *Heat*

THAT DAY
YOU LEFT

The murder of her husband leaves Saffron grieving
and alone. But no one knows what she did to protect her
family. Now, as secrets threaten to reveal themselves, is she
prepared to do it again?

**'Combines romance with dark themes, and has a
surprising twist'** *Sunday Mirror*

TELL ME YOUR SECRET

Ten years ago, Pieta was kidnapped by a man calling himself
The Blindfolder and she was too afraid to tell anyone. But when
he starts hunting down his past victims, Pieta realises she
may be forced to tell her deepest secrets to stay alive.

**'A totally addictive, can't put down, rollercoaster
ride of a story'** Araminta Hall

ALL MY LIES ARE TRUE

Verity is telling lies. Serena has been lying for years. Poppy's
lies have come back to haunt her. Everybody lies. But whose
lies are going to end in tragedy?

'One of the best books I've read this year' *Sun*

The brand new novel from
Queen of the Big Reveal

DOROTHY
KOOMSON

MY OTHER
HUSBAND

Coming July 2022

REVIEW

All About

DOROTHY
KOOMSON

Dorothy Koomson is still trying to come up with something interesting for this bit of the book. In case you didn't know: she wrote her first, unpublished novel when she was thirteen and she's been making up stories ever since. Her third novel, *My Best Friend's Girl*, was chosen for the Richard & Judy Book Club Summer Reads of 2006, and reached number two on the *Sunday Times* Bestseller List.

Her books *The Ice Cream Girls* and *The Rose Petal Beach* were shortlisted for the National Book Awards and a TV adaptation loosely based on *The Ice Cream Girls* appeared on ITV in 2013.

Dorothy has won awards, had most of her books on the *Sunday Times* Bestseller List and is currently working on her eighteenth book.

Dorothy has lived and worked in Leeds, London and Sydney, Australia, and is currently residing in Brighton on the South Coast.

Get in Touch

To find out more about me and my books,
as well as writing tips and more,
take a look at my website here:

www.dorothykoomson.co.uk

You can also sign up to my newsletter to
make sure you're the first to hear about what
I'm up to next.

You can also keep in touch by following me on:

🐦 **@DorothyKoomson**

📘 **@DorothyKoomsonWriter**

and

📷 **@dorothykoomson_author**

I'd love to hear from you!